THE SHADOW SAGA

THE SHADOW BEYOND

DANIEL REINER

VULPINE
PRESS

Published by Vulpine Press in the United Kingdom in 2019

Cover by Claire Wood

ISBN: 978-1-83919-279-1

www.vulpine-press.com

For Mom and Dad

FORWARD

I am not dead; nor am I fully alive. The intangibles of thought and memory are nearly all I have in common with the man I once was. Half consumed, I sit upon the floor, a biblical leper. I have neither mirror nor light, but I imagine my appearance—formerly somewhat pleasing—must now be repulsive. I would not want any living thing to gaze upon my ravaged visage.

I am grateful that I still own my senses. Though there is precious little stimulation here, I can still feel the unyielding stone of the floor upon which I sit; hear the dripping water; smell the dankness of my tomb. On sight and taste I cannot comment. The darkness is total; and it has been years since I have eaten or drank.

The passage of time and my apparent existence outside of it are the most remarkable aspects of my current condition. I cannot sense it as I once did, but I have noticed that the dripping of the water stops for a while—perhaps in winter—then resumes again some time later—in spring, presumably. In this manner I have counted eight years. In all that time, I have known no physical pain or discomfort—not thirst, hunger, heat nor cold. From time to time I have felt the occasional insect or rodent crawl over me, but they have shown no more interest in me than they might a rock or a stick. I once feared spiders and rats. After all that has happened, those reactions seem absurd and irrational now.

Since entombing myself here, I have spent much of my time dwelling on the sins of my past. In this unique state, my memory has sharpened a thousand-fold. The smallest detail remembered, the largest anguish relived. All sounds, all smells, from even the remotest corners of my youth, are with me still. The opportunity of living in the fantasy world of my past has allowed the years to pass quickly.

1

Several times I have gotten lost, caring just enough to will myself back to the present.

No more. The procrastination has gone on long enough. I must not allow myself to wallow. The story of how I came to be here must be set to paper before the temptation to enter my memories and not return becomes too great.

Before I continue, I must ask you please excuse my handwriting. I shall try my best to keep my script uniform and neat, but as I have said, it is very dark here—completely, in fact. The most insignificant bit of light would only serve to worsen my peculiar plight and cause excruciating pain. Too much would mean my utter annihilation. My aforementioned physical deformities are another obstacle to legibility. My right hand and wrist, at least, have not been affected; however, I have no control of the arm from elbow to shoulder. I believe that the flesh is yet intact, but the joints have been fused. My left arm moves freely at both the shoulder and elbow, but the hand and forearm are simply gone. Given these restrictions, my story will take some time to record. Fortunately, I have a large supply of paper and ink. And of time I have plenty, unless enough light would be allowed to penetrate the underground sanctum I now inhabit. At this point, that is all that I fear—that my effort here may be for naught. I do not regret the final action of my human life. But due to my rashness at the last, I cannot guarantee I will be able to stay here. Of all the human failings that led me to this point, that may prove to be the worst.

Raised as I was, I never suspected the existence of that unnamable evil which I discovered. I was raised to trust. In my idyllic youth, evil was something only heard about on Sundays; or something that happened far away, in barbarous Eastern countries. In retrospect I see how foolish those beliefs were. I was the one who naïvely made the choices. I was the one too ignorant to question the decisions being made for me. My presence here is my atonement. If you are reading this story, I can only beg for your forgiveness.

It is my supreme hope, however, that this manuscript is never read. If it is, then I have failed in my attempt to rectify my mistake. If these words are ever glimpsed by human eyes, then the horror I currently hold is once again loosed, free to roam across time and space, inflicting its terror.

If these words *are* read, please heed them. Let those who have ears hear. Take up my work. Most of the knowledge to which I had access is here with me. Use this manuscript and the other accursed volumes here to undo what I have done.

But be careful. Knowledge is dangerous! Let this be the first lesson I impart: If you know of Them, you can be sure that They know of you. You can make no mistakes.

ONE

My name is Robert Thomas Adderly. I was born in the spring of 1901 and raised in the town of Mount Haverton, Massachusetts. My mother, Theresa Anne Adderly—née Pershing—was a frail woman, not in the best of health, and was told that the stresses of another pregnancy could kill her. For that reason, I remained an only child. That is all that I was ever told, for my parents never wished to discuss things of that nature with me.

At the time of my birth, my father, William Wescott Adderly, worked in a bank owned by the Pershings, who were themselves relatively wealthy. But the fact that my mother was a Pershing did not guarantee my father a job. The Pershings were a pragmatic people. They were certainly affluent, but not enough to afford bad business decisions. Father was a very dedicated worker, and good with numbers: an ability I inherited. In time, he proved his worth, working his way up through the ranks to become the assistant manager.

When I was five years of age, he moved his small family into the only home I can remember. The neighborhood was pleasant, filled with two- and three-story Victorian houses with large yards, and many magnificent trees. The only drawback was that a great portion of the inhabitants was quite old. There were few children in the vicinity to begin with, and most of them—save one—were much older than myself.

As a result of this dearth of youth in my immediate neighborhood, for the first several years that we lived in the house on Maple Street, my sole childhood companion was Vincent Marsh. Being the same age, we attended the same classes at school. He was very pale and odd, and not much liked by the other children, but we got along well, sharing an interest in outdoor activities. We were always in agreement about what to do, each of us seemingly able to read the other's mind.

"Visit the beaver dam?" I might suggest.

"Yes," would be the answer.

"Hike up Tristam Hill?"

"Of course."

Wandering through a wooded area one summer day, we found a tree that was perfect for climbing. The branches grew out from the trunk at intervals we could manage with our small arms. The lowest branch was out of reach from the ground, but it was situated right next to a large boulder that we could scramble onto: from ground to rock to tree. It was great fun, challenging ourselves to go ever higher. And we did, to the point where the thin trunk swayed with our combined weight.

There never seemed to be a need to speak when engaged like that, the silence only punctuated by an occasional laugh of exhilaration or grunt of exertion. When we did talk, it was I who did most of it. Vincent was quiet by nature, almost sullen. He viewed the world through some sort of sinister filter. To me, a random rustling of leaves was simply a squirrel or robin; for him, it was a hidden snake—not that he was afraid of such a thing. At times, he would eagerly root around, trying to locate it, and hoping for a big one.

Once, I remember seeing a jumble of connected clouds that loosely resembled a man, or perhaps a bear standing on its hind legs.

"No, not even a bear," he told me firmly. "The teeth are certainly sharp enough, but look at the scaly flesh."

Even after a prodigious amount of squinting and goggling, I was just not able to see what he did. It was hard enough for me to imagine a snout on the white puff that was supposed to be the head of the bear, let alone clothe it in fur, or scales. My mind was constrained by science and numbers. His worked differently.

I think he received his imagination from his mother. She had an artistic side, displayed in her intricate embroideries. Some of her work was on pillows scattered around their home. Flowers, small animals, and even some scenes from around the town, such as the old grist mill at the end of Hallow Road, or the covered bridge that crossed Jenner's Creek. Despite her legs having been partially crippled by childhood polio, there was not even an ounce of darkness in that woman. She was the ray of sunshine in a household that sorely needed it.

Vincent's father, on the other hand, was known for his drunken fits, during which he would severely thrash both his wife and son. My own father had been mystified as to how two so very different people could have even met, let alone married. The theory that made the most sense was that it had been an arranged marriage, he of course coming from the dwindling remains of the infamous Marsh wealth of Innsmouth. Her family was from Boston, and they did what they could to protect her from her husband's unpredictable moods—mainly in the form of vacations to the big city for her and her son, many of which seemed to be unplanned. Vincent often returned from them with healing bruises, and once with his arm in a cast. From the rumors that drifted around town, supplemented with the evidence of my own eyes, I found it amazing that Vincent survived his childhood. Some suggested that two of his unborn siblings had not.

The other residential area of Mount Haverton was separated from ours by the Miskatonic River. As it passed through town, the river was only fifty feet wide, but the geology of the area had forced the water to cut a deep channel. My parents preferred that we boys not cross either of the bridges that spanned it unattended, but didn't prevent us from doing so. Initially, I thought their apprehension was simply due to the swift current, but eventually I learned of another reason: several unsolved disappearances from years gone by, disappearances whispered to be the doings of the Fensters.

Decades before I was born, the Fensters had emigrated from Germany and moved into an ancient manse across the river, already decrepit at the time of their arrival. According to the little information I was able to glean from my father, the foreigners were universally despised by the rest of the town. They dwelt there for several years until one blackly evil Halloween night, when all of the inhabitants of the house died in a particularly horrible manner. My father did not go into detail about that, merely stating that their savage deaths were atonement for the sins they had visited upon themselves. The house, being in a state of severe disrepair at the time of their death, was soon after declared uninhabitable and torn down before it could fall. Because the house abutted a hillside, however, the entire south wall and some other bits of foundation were left intact to shore up the hill. Though there was practically nothing left of the house itself, and the terrible rumors associated with it were years in the past, the property was still shunned at the time of my youth.

Due to the reputation of the place, it was a small thrill to go onto those grounds from time to time. One day near the end of summer, while poking into a hole in the ground with sticks, we discovered that it was possible to dig rapidly through the loose debris under the thin layer of compacted soil. Naturally, we started pulling bricks out of the ground, some heavy enough to test the limits of our strength. Before long, we'd made a pit about a yard across and at least as deep. What were our plans? There were none that I knew. I just wanted to explore, curious as to what secrets might be concealed beneath that unholy ground. I wondered if we would come across a body, or at least bones, but said nothing about that. It would be years before I became familiar with the word *macabre*, but by that age, I had learned that there were some subjects that should not be voiced.

We never got the chance to find anything, however; my father showed up unexpectedly and put an end to it. He stood and waited for us to fill it back in, chastising us repeatedly, *That could easily have collapsed on you.* We walked Vincent home first. His mother answered the door, but after only a few words from my father, she was joined by the man of the house. He grabbed Vincent and pulled him inside. The door slammed shut, and the shouting began.

Father looked down at me, lips thin. We left without a word.

My punishment was light on that occasion, but I was promised that there would be no further warnings. I must never again set foot there. And I obeyed that command—at least, for a while. It was easy to avoid it at first; the Fenster property was really the only reason we had to cross the river. In the weeks following, when we did venture to the other side, we only looked at the grounds and hillside from a distance.

Vincent was absent the day after our excavation, but on the one after that, I found him. He was sitting on a large stone at the border of a lot with scattered trees and overgrown with weeds. It was our usual place for watching squirrels, though that year, a rabbit had moved in, and we had been able to spot it now and again. It was tremendously skittish. We were never able to get any closer than twenty feet or so, but we would sometimes expend the energy chasing it anyway. The thing always found a hole to dive into; there was never a chance of success.

When I first saw Vincent, he seemed to be sitting oddly, tilted to one side. As I got closer, the bruise on the side of his face stood out. Upon reaching the rock where he sat, I could see that he was gripping something brown and fuzzy.

"What do you have?" I said.

Without looking up, he relaxed his arms to reveal a rabbit. *The* rabbit, I assumed.

"It's dead," he said, the words spat out in a higher pitch, tinged with grief, or fear. It sounded as if he was on the verge of tears, but a moment later he repeated, "Dead," and that tinge of emotion was gone.

I knelt down and stroked the fur.

"Still warm," I said.

He suddenly tensed up and jerked the rabbit away. But just as quickly, he tilted his head and relaxed again.

"I've been holding it," he explained. "For a while. I must have warmed it."

"I guess we should bury it."

"I guess." He shook his head, looked around, focused on me for the first time. "I can't get dirty though."

"Me neither."

We agreed that the best thing to do at that point was to place it back in its burrow; it would at least be under the ground. After locating a rabbit entrance far back in the field, he placed the limp body into the hole. We covered it up with a few heavy rocks. I said a short prayer, and we left.

A weekend in late August of 1911 stands out singularly in my memory. On that Friday, a particularly horrifying storm lashed our neighborhood, the likes of which, I am sure, occur only once per century. The winds arrived first, just ahead of the darkness, shrieking with an inhuman frenzy. We could see the awful line of clouds coming from the west; they turned the evening sky prematurely black. My father set me to the task of closing the shutters on the lower windows, while he attempted to latch the upper. We finished just as the first large drops fell. He ushered Mother and myself into the cellar, a place I dreaded to go alone. Our only source of illumination was a few small candles, for the cellar was never wired for electric lighting. A grimy window set into the north wall, high above the floor, afforded minimal view of the outside world. At the height of the storm, the clouds snuffed out any light cast by the setting sun. We sat for almost an hour in the near darkness, listening to the roar of the wind and the crashing of the waves of rain. I remember being frightened more of the dark cellar itself than of the power of nature unleashed. And I remember the lightning providing brief glimpses of the world. Here, now, I long for an opportunity like that again—just a glimpse.

The dawn revealed shocking devastation. The trees that were young and supple had yielded to the maelstrom, losing only leaves and small branches. The older, nobler timber had no choice but to topple in the face of the onslaught. Our house did indeed withstand the fury, but there were others nearby not as blessed. As I cleaned the branches and leaves from the yard, Vincent came by earlier than usual. He was more agitated than I had ever seen him, stuttering with excitement.

"A se-se-secret room! Th- there's a secret room i-in th-the hillside!" he insisted, tugging at my arm. When I didn't understand what he was getting at, he silently mouthed only one word.

Fenster.

Despite the warnings from our parents, this event was too extraordinary to ignore. I dropped my rake. He led the way and I followed, filled with the anticipation of exploring a heretofore-unknown room.

As we approached the ruins, I could see that the deluge of the evening had eroded the hillside where it met the remaining wall. With the soil swept away, the wall had toppled, revealing a man-made space that would have been accessible from a room on the second floor.

We stared in wonder for a moment, looked at each other, checked about to see if anyone was near, then looked for a way to climb up. The particular pattern of the rubble afforded us an easy, stair-like route from the ground up to a narrow ledge, which constituted the current top of the south wall of the Fenster estate. The debris was still saturated with water and could have easily shifted under our weight. An adult with an ounce of sense would not have scaled that slippery mass of rock and mud. But we were children,

11

and the sun was shining brightly on a Saturday morning. It was an adventure.

After making our way onto the ledge, we could see that the room had been hewn from the solid rock that made up the living heart of the hill. The walls and floor had been smoothed over with mortar, leaving a clean finish. It was a small space, but the sparse furnishings made it look larger. Only a delicate writing desk and matching chair were set against the back wall. Above, perched on the wall, were two shelves lined with dampened books. The find was overall disappointing, but we decided to explore what little there was.

I jumped up on the desk to examine the tomes on the shelves while Vincent searched the drawers. Of all the books, there was only one whose title I saw clearly: *De Vermis Mysteriis*. At the time I was just learning Latin in school, and was only barely able to translate. *The Mysteries of the Worm*. As I moved down the line of ancient volumes, I heard Vincent move away, toward the entrance of the room. Only after finishing with the contents of the shelf did I turn to look at him. What I saw made my heart skip.

He stood with his back to me on the slippery ledge—but he was not alone. Behind, towering over him, stood an improbably tall, dark-skinned man, looking over his shoulder. If Vincent was aware of his presence, his posture did not let on. The man's size and appearance were as foreign and exotic as his clothing, which consisted of a plain, dark robe and sandals. He *was* there, looming over Vincent, his presence both menacing and eerily quiet. And then he *wasn't*.

I blinked and rubbed my eyes. The man was gone. Fear clutched me as my parents' warnings, and the stories that were told of that place, became very relevant. Vincent still faced away from me, looking down at his hands. He was holding something. Then, just as I climbed off the desk, the phantom man suddenly reappeared in the same spot. He looked at me and smiled. Even as I screamed, he vanished again.

Vincent jumped at the sound. Already dangerously close to the edge, his balance faltered and he began to slip. With both hands I grabbed him by the collar of his jacket. His weight pulled me forward and I went down onto my knees. But I held on. He landed squarely on his bottom on the filthy ledge, but managed to maintain his purchase. I quickly glanced over my left shoulder, afraid of who—or what—I might see standing there. But there was nothing.

"Why did you scream like that?" He was nearly in tears. "I almost fell."

"Ghost," I gasped. "I saw...a ghost."

His eyes widened. I neglected to mention that the apparition had appeared directly behind him—and seemed to be watching him.

"We should go," he said. "I'm going to get in trouble for even coming here. And these trousers are rather new." As he stood up, I thought I saw him slip something into the pocket of his jacket, though at the time I couldn't be sure.

We made our way back down the pile of debris the same way we had come up. Once at the bottom, we tried to wipe the muck from our clothes. It was useless. Proof of our wrongdoing clung to us despite our best attempts. We went our separate ways, each knowing a reprimand with the belt or the switch was in our future— in Vincent's for sure. I cringed at the thought of the beating he would likely endure.

That was the last I saw of Vincent Marsh for over a decade.

Upon returning home I received the only thrashing from my father I can remember. I knew that he didn't want to sink to the same level as Vincent's father, but he felt the need for emphasis, and there was no excuse for my blatant disobedience. On Sunday, I was forbidden to leave the house except to go to church and ask God for forgiveness.

Then, on Monday, the town was shocked to learn the news of the gruesome deaths of Vincent's parents: slaughtered in the dark of the night by an unknown assailant. Vincent, luckily, had been passed over, unharmed. The authorities labeled the crime as a robbery/murder, but according to my parents' hushed discussion, nothing was vandalized or missing. Apparently, nobody was willing to classify the ghastly deed as a crime of passion because the Marshes had no real enemies, despite the poor reputation of Vincent's father. Robbery simply had to be the motive. The young boy was promptly shipped out to relatives in Boston in order to spare him the horror of the situation.

After he left, unanswered questions still nagged at my mind. I had to go back.

Just a week after our previous excursion, I again found myself in front of the pile of debris. The area had been roped off, the town planning to haul away the rubble and possibly remove some of the hill so as to avoid any mudslides in the future. From street level, there was no way to see what I needed. To get caught this time would ensure another painful disciplining from my father, but I *had* to get a closer look.

When I was sure that no one was watching me, I scampered up the same path over the rocks as before. It hadn't rained during the intervening days, and with the August sun working to dry the ubiquitous mud, I made it to the top of the ledge unsullied and with little effort. I could see right away that the shelves above the desk were empty. On the floor, our overlapping footprints were almost nonexistent. The mud along the path we'd walked had been too thin to hold a print from our small feet.

But, off to the right, what I saw nearly froze my innards.

For better or worse, I at least was able to confirm the theory for which I'd risked my father's ire: The ghost had left footprints. The tall man, when visible, had stood off to the side of our path through the small room and hadn't moved. The prints of his sandals weren't deep, but the outlines were very obviously there, and of a size befitting a man seven feet tall.

Mesmerized by the strangeness, I reached out to touch the imprint, but stopped myself. It seemed wrong to do so. My fingertips hovered an inch above the ground as repeated warnings of evil from Sunday sermons flashed through my mind. But even if Satan had stood there momentarily, would the very earth in that spot have been cursed? I thought it possible.

The call of a bird carried over the trees and roused me. There was nothing left to see. I scurried back down the path and took off for home, not once stopping to look back.

Nothing there, I told myself. *The Fensters are all dead.*

If only I had known.

Two

My marks in later years were high enough to allow acceptance into Miskatonic University in Arkham, and I moved on to college with enthusiasm. I had grown into an average-sized, if somewhat thin, young man. I had never had much interest in physical pastimes, but I did have a gift for theoretical mathematics, and in time came under the tutelage of Professor Samuel Josephson, one of the more respected professors at the university. Josephson was an incredibly intelligent and fastidious man who tolerated few mistakes. He was by nature very quiet, but when he spoke, his deep voice carried a commanding quality one would not expect to emerge from such a tall, lanky frame. His memory was immense, and his ability to recall details almost legendary.

I believe that he sincerely expected everyone else to be equally as gifted, or at least those people with whom he chose to associate. He helped me rise to the top of my class, and encouraged me to pursue my doctorate in mathematics. Those years were somewhat difficult. My parents were of course proud of my scholastic achievements, but the tuition weighed upon their finances. I helped pay the expenses as best I could with some part-time jobs, but really only contributed enough to cover my rent at the boarding house where I stayed in Arkham.

To that end, it was during this period that I began my short career as a tutor. I had taken on several students already, and had just enough time available for one more. It was the professor who helped fill that gap.

I was standing in his office, giving him an update on my thesis, but it turned into a protracted discussion over a point I knew we had covered two weeks before. As we spoke, I became more and more flustered over his uncharacteristic inability—or unwillingness—to remember my proof. He seemed to be trying to drag the discussion out unnecessarily. Seeing no alternative, I cleared his largest slate, took up the chalk, and began to retrace the path through my thought processes. I knew it would take at least thirty minutes, a seeming waste of time, but he settled in and patiently observed.

Just as I was writing the last of the formulae, there was a knock at the door. When I glanced at the professor, there was an odd look on his face—a brightness in his eyes I had learned to associate with his seldom-exposed sense of humor.

"Very good, Robert," he commented. "I shouldn't have doubted you. Come in."

Through the door walked one of the loveliest young ladies I had ever seen: a slender wick of a woman, average height, with shoulder-length auburn hair and delicate features.

"Professor, I'm sorry to intrude."

I was entranced as she glided over to us.

"Doctor Gardiner asked me to deliver this to you." She handed over an envelope. "He was interrupted with an urgent matter, and your office was on my way."

"Thank you. I believe I know what this is." He turned to me. "Robert, this is Elizabeth Wentworth. Elizabeth, Robert Adderly."

We shook hands.

"Pleased to meet you," I managed to croak out.

"Likewise."

She turned to go, but Professor Josephson spoke up before she reached the door.

"Elizabeth, how are your studies coming?"

She struggled to find the right words.

17

"Fine, Professor," she said, not convincing even me. "I'm getting back on track."

"Robert can help you with mathematics. If you'd like. Can't you, Robert?"

"Oh, yes," I said with a genuine grin, those simple syllables dripping with desperate eagerness.

She considered the offer, looked at me, and nodded with a smile.

I'll always remember that first smile.

Elizabeth was in her junior year, and not of the type to typically require tutoring. Her intellect was on its own captivating. However, her parents had recently died very tragically while traveling in Europe and the shock had caused her to drop behind in her studies. That little bit I learned from Professor Josephson; she offered nothing in the way of an explanation.

During our first session, I could only stare at her as she worked, enthralled by her beauty. She rarely needed guidance, and I believe the questions she did ask were purely to make me feel as if I was actually doing some tutoring. She needed so little help in fact, that almost right from the start, I suspected Professor Josephson of playing the matchmaker. He presented a mathematically precise exterior, but there must have been a bit of a romantic deep within him.

Our sessions grew to twice, then thrice weekly. I stopped taking her money, and we started seeing each other as often as possible. We talked unendingly, and I learned much about nearly every aspect of her: She had interests in archaeology and poetry, loved seafood in all forms, rarely ate sweets except for apple pie, enjoyed crunching through fallen autumn leaves, and on and on. I learned about everything, in fact, except for her family. She always sidestepped any questions about her relatives, I assumed, because she was still mourning. I respected her wishes and did not pry. I was content to think that I would eventually know all that there was to know about her. It would just take time.

At the conclusion of her junior year, all exams successfully passed, we relaxed together into a truly memorable summer. She also enjoyed riding horses, so we spent some time every week at the university stable. I knew the man in charge, and he allowed us to help exercise the horses and brush them down. He was grateful for the help, and Elizabeth so enjoyed the activity. Her joy brought warmth to my heart. We also frequently found ourselves in a rowboat on the lake. While I rowed us around, she would take off her shoes and trail her feet in the cool water, occasionally splashing me when I least expected it. In the evenings we would take to the park, to sit on our bench and read in the dimming light. There we would be together—she with her Dickinson, I with my Poe—until the sun went down. That summer was unique in all of my life: a zenith.

With autumn came classes and studying once again. I helped Elizabeth when needed, but without the tragedy of the year before, it was easy for her to keep up with her studies. It was also about that time when I found myself working more often *with* Professor Josephson than *for* him. He found my work to be 'satisfactory,' which from him was high praise indeed. Between my work with the professor and our busy class schedules, it was difficult to find the time to see each other, but we managed. We grew very close and our love blossomed. To me, it seemed inevitable that we would spend our lives together.

As that autumn turned to winter, I learned that she also *wrote* poetry aside from reading it. One cold, wet day we met in the common room of her dormitory, and sat in front of the fire. She held a notebook in her hand. She was very pleased with her most recent effort, and wanted me to read it. It was honestly very good; I told her so. She showed me another, and another. Everything that I read that day had a bittersweet thread—sorrow for the past intertwined with hope for the future. I remember making that comment to her about one poem in particular. In that one, a repeated line stood out to me.

> *Afraid to be recalled, afraid to be*
> *forgotten*

"Yes, it refers to my—" She stopped for several heartbeats before finishing. "My brother."

"You have a brother?"

"Had."

"He died? I'm sorry to hear that."

"The War." She sighed and whispered, "We're cursed."

Accidental or not, I felt bad about broaching a sensitive subject, and tried to continue on past it. It was a poor attempt.

"You speak so little of your family...your father...I'd actually hoped to meet him in particular, one day."

Despite knowing that he had died, I smiled, trying to imply that I'd like to ask him for permission to marry her.

Her face fell. She closed her eyes.

My stomach did flips. Minutes before, things had been going so well. Right then, I thought I may never see her again. Unable to trust myself with the simple task of speaking, further apologies didn't seem to be prudent, so I excused myself and left her alone.

The following day I had flowers delivered. I gave her time away from me, but sent carefully-worded notes. After spending a week apart, we met again. I don't know which one of us was more uncomfortable at first. But after catching each other up on the news, we relaxed, had a laugh. In a few more days, everything was very much back to normal. I've wondered from time to time if I should have been more forceful, or sly, or used some other method to learn more about her family. Had I known certain details, could subsequent events have been avoided? Possibly, but after that misstep I vowed to myself never again to ask her another question on the subject. Ironically, the fear of losing her was too great.

After knowing Elizabeth just over a year, I was certain she was the one with whom I wished to spend the rest of my life. With the help of my parents, I secured an engagement ring. Admittedly, it was not as spectacular as I would have liked, but given the circumstances, it would have to be enough. In the middle of May 1925, the day of her last exam before graduation, I ironed my finest suit, put the ring in my pocket, and set out for the building where she was sitting for her exam.

On my way there, I noticed Professor Josephson walking toward me, deep in thought. On occasions such as that, I had learned that it was usually best to let him be, but as he drew nearer, his deeply furrowed brow alarmed me slightly.

He spoke up as our paths crossed, as if he had intended to meet me there all along.

"Robert, I may need your help."

"Certainly, Professor. What is it?"

"Over the last decade I have been loosely involved with a group of…intellectuals. They have asked me for help from time to time when their research has required my abilities as a mathematician."

He paused, searching for words. I had the distinct feeling that he did not wish to reveal many details.

"Recently, I was asked to render in three-dimensions a non-Euclidian curve intersecting a set of points representing certain stars in the heavens."

He stopped again. The furrows in his brow deepened.

"Robert, as odd as it may sound, I would like you to check over my work. The stars are aligning. If I am correct, heaven help us if…"

He looked away from me and gazed off into the distance.

"Professor? Is everything alright?"

"Yes, yes." His usual, stern expression reappeared. "I'm sorry, my boy. For being an alarmist. It has become difficult, knowing what I do. No need for any worry, though. Can you please just come by my home tomorrow afternoon? I need to spend some time verifying my information for accuracy."

"Yes. I can do that," I reassured him despite being confused by the request. "Also, Professor, I thought you might like to know. To you this might seem…I'm proposing to Elizabeth today. When she's finished with her examinations."

It took him a moment to digest the information.

"Yes, of course. I had the feeling that that would come to pass eventually." His rare, brief smile was tantamount to a confession of his involvement in our relationship.

"Until tomorrow then," he said as he walked away. "Good day, Robert."

In the years I had known him, he had never asked for help from anyone. When the subject at hand was mathematics, Professor Samuel Josephson was the undisputed authority. Putting aside my bewilderment, I continued on to meet Elizabeth.

I had timed it well. She emerged from the building just as I arrived, the relief on her face turning into a large, welcoming smile when she saw me.

"I didn't expect you here," she said as she rushed down the steps and embraced me. We were an island in the current of students, flowing by.

"I have a surprise for you," I said, unable to contain a large grin. I took her by the hand and guided her out of the crush to a place that would give us some privacy. Around a corner of the building, partially concealed by a row of hedges, I got down on one knee, pulled the box out of my coat pocket, and opened it. The ring glistened in the sunlight, and I moved it ever so slightly to emphasize the effect.

"Will you marry me?" I asked nervously.

To that point, I thought we were alone. The path between campus buildings was yards away, and no one on it was paying us any attention. The problem, I realized too late, was that we were situated directly in front of a window—on the other side of which was a classroom full of students. They, too, were taking their final exams. Every previous time I'd been by this spot, the room had been empty. I had assumed, wrongly, that it was unused. Even with the room occupied as it was, all eyes inside *had* been focused on their papers—until I exposed the distracting diamond to the light. Now, all eyes were on us. Even the professor in the front of the room watched.

Her lovely smile grew even larger, and she nodded.

"Yes."

She had been looking at me and the ring the whole time, so I wasn't sure if she had noticed our audience. An eruption of cheering from inside called her attention to it, however. Regardless, we hugged and kissed, triggering another round of cheers. Embarrassment set in at that point—at least for me. We waved and ran off while the professor tried to get his students to calm down and refocus.

When my heart rate slowed, I informed her of my plans for the evening. She had previously told me of her intention to leave the following day to visit her Aunt Marie and Uncle Thomas in Boston for a few days. Knowing that, I wanted to prepare a dinner for her and spend time with her before she departed.

Never knowing me to cook, she agreed with delight. I walked her to her sorority house, then went straight home to make preparations.

My landlady, Mrs. Bettings, greeted me at the door when I

arrived.

"What did she say, Robert?" she asked me eagerly.

I smiled broadly, unable to conceal my glee.

"She said yes!"

Mrs. Bettings squealed with delight. She reached out with both arms to hug me, and I had to bend over to accommodate her, for I was nearly a foot taller than she. I was by far the youngest tenant in the building, the other men being in their fifties and sixties, or even older. On top of that, Mrs. Bettings was childless, and I came to sense that she favored me as a son. She had been running the boarding house by herself since the War, her husband one of its many casualties. I had a great respect for her, as did all of the men who lived there.

It was half past six when Elizabeth came to call. With the aid of Mrs. Bettings and the cooperation of the other tenants in the building, everyone had retired to their rooms in order to give us our privacy. We had the kitchen and dining room to ourselves. I served a meager meal of onion soup, fish, potatoes, and some deliciously fresh bread—baked, of course, by my landlady. We filled ourselves. The evening air was a bit cool, so I started a fire in the dining room hearth. We sat on the floor in front of the fire, snuggled close, and drank apple cider from ornate wine glasses, which Mrs. Bettings had removed from storage for the occasion.

"It will be a large wedding, Robert."

"As large as we can afford, Elizabeth."

"We can afford quite a lot," she said with a knowing smile, then paused. "I've never spoken to you of my family, and I am grateful that you never pressed the issue."

She looked at me, as if wanting me to guess what she might say next, but I simply waited for her to speak.

"My family is…quite wealthy, Robert. I had to be sure that you were not pursuing me because of my money."

"No, I—I had no idea."

"I know," she said, smiling. "I know."

The initial shock took a moment to wear off.

"But I do know that I love you."

I held up my glass.

"To us," I toasted.

"To us."

We continued to enjoy the cider and spoke of all manner of things—our hopes and dreams, our future. The wedding would be in a year, we decided, following the defense of my doctoral thesis. After emptying the bottle, I kissed her on the forehead, stood up, and stretched. The fire was waning, so I added one small log, then took the glasses and the bottle to the kitchen. As I cleaned up some of the dishes, the clock struck eight. The last of the notes was fading when I heard her voice drift in from the dining room, the words forever etched into my memory.

"That's odd. The fire is changing my shadow."

And then she screamed.

I was back in the dining room in an instant—but it was already too late. She was standing, screaming, flailing her hands at the flames that covered her entire body. I got her back down onto the floor and tried to smother the fire first with my bare hands, then with the upturned end of the rug. But it was no use. The inferno seemed to originate from within her, flames emanating from every pore.

Her agony did not last long.

As I watched, not believing, I saw her melt before my eyes. Flesh and muscles and bones shifting with a morbid liquidity, then disappearing from sight. She was fully consumed in a minute, her shrieks still echoing in my ears. Nothing remained but ashes. It didn't seem possible. Only moments before, we were talking and laughing about our future together, and now there was nothing—no future, no present. Even the past was just a dream.

She was gone.

THREE

Mrs. Bettings was first to arrive on the scene, opening the door of the dining room more forcefully than I would have thought possible. She asked where Elizabeth was. Nearly in a trance, I described the flames that I could not extinguish. The look of concern on the poor woman's face turned to horror. She only stared at the bits of ash on the floor, mute with disbelief. It was only the arrival of Mr. Dunderhill, a boarder from the second floor, that brought her back to reality. With the commanding presence I had grown to respect, she escorted him from the room and told him to find a policeman. He knew her as well as I, and yielded to her request. After he had left, she closed and locked the door. We sat then, and waited, Mrs. Bettings trying her best to comfort me.

And all the time I watched the fire. I wanted to ask it how. Why. I needed to know. I hoped that it would whisper to me its secrets. But except for the occasional hiss or crack, the flames were silent.

A stout knock upon the dining room door announced the officer's arrival. Mrs. Bettings showed him in, careful to keep out the rest of the small crowd that had gathered outside. His gaze moved around the room, settled in front of the fireplace: the ashes, the displaced rug. After a while, he removed a notebook and pencil from a coat pocket and looked at me.

"Your name, sir?"

"Robert Adderly."

My answer went into the notebook.

"What happened, Mr. Adderly?"

"My fiancée and I had just finished dinner," I began. "I left the room. I heard her scream. When I rushed in she was already covered in flames. I couldn't put them out no matter how hard I tried."

"And her name?"

"Elizabeth Wentworth."

A pop from the fire, and a spark spiraled outward.

"A spark," I added. "I left her sitting by the fire. A spark must have…"

Even as I spoke the words I couldn't even bring myself to believe them. His expression indicated to me that he shared my opinion.

"No one else saw this? It was just the two of you?"

"Just us, yes."

His eyes narrowed and he frowned.

"Thank you, sir. That's all for now."

Careful with the placement of his feet, he turned from me and moved closer to the fire. I watched him make a sketch of the rug, fireplace, and ashes. When he was through, he crossed the room and opened the door.

"Mrs. Bettings, please come in. And the man who—yes, you."

As a distraught Mrs. Bettings entered, the officer directed her toward me. She sat back down next to me again and held my hand. As soon as Mr. Dunderhill entered the room, the officer closed the door and pulled him to the side. They had a short conversation on the spot, with the policeman facing away from us and speaking very softly. Mr. Dunderhill tried to keep his voice down, but his answers were loud enough for me to make out most of what he said.

"No…screams and…"

"…both been living here…"

"No, no, no…I can't believe…"

Mr. Dunderhill was then gently ushered out the door, looking more confused than when he came in. Questions were set to Mrs. Bettings in the same manner. She, I could tell, made a point of raising her voice to the point where I could hear her answers, but still low enough that the policeman couldn't object to the volume.

"No, I didn't see anything. We all agreed to give them their privacy."

"Yes, she was most definitely here."

"Robert has lived here for years, and I trust him completely."

"I'd met Elizabeth several times in the past year or so. She was so pretty. Frail-looking, but still very strong."

"I had all the fireplaces and chimneys cleaned a month ago. Krüger's Chimney Service, on Elm."

The officer put away his notebook.

"I'm done here for now," he stated. "There's no body"—that comment being directed pointedly at me—"so there's no need to disturb anyone further tonight. Don't touch the area in front of the fireplace at all. Someone will be by first thing in the morning to take a closer look."

Again he looked directly at me.

"And do stick around, Mr. Adderly. I have no doubt there'll be more questions for you."

With that, he let himself out. Mrs. Bettings hurriedly closed the door behind him

"Stay here and catch your breath for a while, Robert," she whispered to me. "I'll clear the hall for you."

I heard her quietly dismiss the small crowd in the hall, and when that failed, not so quietly. I sat for a time, alternately watching the fireplace and the floor, still waiting for an answer, a revelation. The fire dwindled to candle flames, then glowing embers, and still I couldn't trust it.

In all the time I sat there, filled with both fear and anticipation, nothing happened.

When even the orange of the embers faded, I let out a breath. The fire had merely been a fire then. But the fact that my irrational fear of the flames proved to be exactly that did nothing to help matters, explained nothing. Elizabeth was still dead. It was then that the reality of the situation struck me. How could this have happened? Could the Devil himself have reached up from Hell and grabbed her? But why? She was innocent. Was it something to do with her mysterious family? Any mention of them had always been colored with sorrow. Were the sins of the parents being visited upon the children? Without her to ask, there was no way to know. A few hours previous, I'd been ecstatic, the happiest man alive. And now…

A tremendous wave of despair overwhelmed me, and I succumbed to it. The tears poured out of me. I grieved for my lost love.

I couldn't spend the night in that building. I had to get out, go somewhere—anywhere. I began to walk, no singular destination in mind. The streets were mostly clear of passersby, and for that I was grateful. The puzzle of Elizabeth's demise filled my mind. But something nagged at me. Some detail of the bizarre event raised a flag in my subconscious, but I couldn't lock onto it.

I walked for at least an hour. As I ambled numbly through those decadent streets, I experienced the world with only one sense— smell. There were no sounds to be heard but my own footfalls; all else was deathly still. There was precious little to see, for illumination from artificial sources was almost entirely lacking, and light from the moon was minimal that night. But the odors…the smell of decay hung over the world as a fog, in some places devastating in its intensity. The stench of refuse and sewage—in all of their myriad forms— constituted the bulk, while traces of mold and mildew seemed to be threaded throughout, binding everything together so as to prevent it from dispersing. But in the midst of that, an unnaturally pleasant scent grabbed my attention. From where it wafted I shall never know—an open window, perhaps—but for a fleeting instant, I experienced the heavenly aroma of lilac. Elizabeth had used just such a perfume occasionally.

Elizabeth.

I relived that final scene once again. Her arrival at the boarding house, our dinner together, our conversation afterward. Her hideous death. Her wails, the unquenchable flames, burning, consuming every bit of her.

I had it!

There had been no smell of *anything!* That was the bit of information for which I had been sifting my memory. I was dumbstruck. There hadn't been the least amount of the horrid smell of burning flesh or hair. I stopped dead on the sidewalk and looked down at my hands. They should have been covered with gruesome burns. A fire intense enough to incinerate a human being should have caused me serious injuries. But they were undamaged.

All at once, I realized where I was. My meandering walk had led me to a crumbling neighborhood on the outskirts of Arkham, a place inhabited by the outcasts of society. Aside from drunks and thieves, the area had a reputation for inexplicably savage murders. During times of lucidity, it was a place that I avoided even in broad daylight. What had led me there that night? I reversed direction and got my bearings, but in my haste to make my way out of that noxious district, I turned a corner and nearly collided with a very tall gentleman. I did not sense him until I was upon him. I stopped and nervously excused myself, but received no response. Assuming that he did not hear me, I was about to speak again when a strange iciness gripped my heart and stole my breath. The effect lasted only a moment before my heartbeat tripled, spurring me forward, and I continued on around him. After going some distance, I looked back to find him, but he had already been swallowed by the darkness.

Upon arriving home, I crept into the dining room and inhaled deeply through my nose. I smelled the smoky remains of the fire and the omnipresent rosy scent of Mrs. Bettings' perfume, but there was nothing untoward; nothing that might suggest the awful scene that had occurred only hours before. I tried again, filling my lungs, and received the same results.

Instead of turning on the overhead lamp, I reached up for the candleholder on the shelf beside the door. Even lighting that small flame inspired some trepidation in me. But I couldn't allow it to continue; that ridiculous new fear needed to be conquered. Holding the candle in my right hand, I put my left over it, hovering just above the flame. The pain grew as I moved it closer, and before I lifted it away entirely I lowered it into the flame for a full second. The results were simply what any sane person would expect—it hurt, but I did not catch fire. Next, I singed the hairs on my wrist that extended beyond the sleeve of my coat. As they hissed and shriveled, the odor of burning hair was obvious and unforgettable.

The room seemed to be the same as I had left it. Next to the hearth, I knelt down and closely examined the floor. It was un-marred—and nearly clean of the ash, of which there had been re-markably little to begin with. I put the candle down and lowered my head to the floor, concentrating on a tiny bit of the grey, ghostly matter, careful not to disturb it in any way. The pile seemed to be smaller than I remembered. And indeed, over the span of the next several minutes, it shrank in size. It was astounding but true: The ash was evaporating. It would surely be gone by morning. The rug, too, was undamaged. In that room, there was no physical evidence whatsoever of any flame beyond the edge of the fireplace.

I had not even the start of an explanation for any of it. How could a linen rug emerge from a raging inferno without being singed? How could a human body be so completely consumed by fire? And what physical process could cause the remaining ashes to evaporate into nothingness?

FOUR

In the morning, Mrs. Bettings knocked on my door to wake me up. When I went downstairs, the officers were waiting for me, faces stern. The table had been pulled away from the hearth as far as possible, with Mr. Dunderhill, Mr. Hunt, and Mr. Harrison attempting to enjoy their breakfasts. Mrs. Bettings bustled around, serving food, refilling coffee cups—and listening in as best as she could.

"Mr. Adderly, my name is Lieutenant Ryan. The officer who was here last night wrote in his report that there were ashes on the floor in the vague outline of a body. He drew a picture of the placement."

I only nodded, waiting for a question.

"And yet there are no ashes here this morning," he said. "We asked your landlady about this and she insists she knows nothing. In fact, as it stands now, there is no evidence at all that Elizabeth Wentworth died here last night."

"Sir, I told the other officer exactly what happened and he wrote—"

"Interfering with a crime scene is a serious offense, Mr. Adderly."

"I assure you, no one has interfered with—"

"Unless there was no crime as described. We have witnesses to the fact that she arrived here. She presumably ate dinner, based on the dishes in the kitchen. But that's all. After that, she simply disappeared."

"Yes!" I hissed, not caring if my voice carried to the table. "She disappeared! Burned alive! The flames were so fierce, I was unable to put them out!"

I stopped and lifted my left hand to show him. The lie came easily.

"My hand was burned in the attempt. I didn't realize it at the time. Everything was so confused."

He examined my hand and wrist, not showing any sign that he believed me.

"That burn is trivial," he said. "It could have been faked. This whole story is nothing but an elaborate hoax, isn't it, Mr. Adderly? A college prank?"

I had no response for that. The suggestion was outrageous, and yet from his perspective, the reasoning was logical.

"That's absurd," I declared flatly.

The other officer approached from behind and tapped him on the shoulder. They walked to the far corner of the room and conferred quietly for a short time, then approached Mrs. Bettings.

"Thank you for your help, ma'am," the lieutenant said. "You can put your dining room back in order."

She smiled nervously and nodded.

"Mr. Adderly," he said, leaning in to me. "You are not being charged with anything. *Yet.*"

With that, they left.

Mrs. Bettings was beside me the moment they were gone.

"I can't believe what they were saying," she said, trembling slightly. "I didn't tell them, but I *know* you did nothing wrong."

She paused, tried to continue, paused again. Then it poured out.

"I hope you'll forgive me, but I have to admit, I spied on the two of you last night. It's not as if I didn't trust you. Well, I wasn't watching, just listening. Not the whole time. Just here and there.

35

The two of you were talking about your wedding plans—just before she…"

She wiped away tears as they dampened her cheeks.

"Oh please forgive me. This is so terrible."

I hugged her.

"Of course I forgive you," I said. "Though I hope if I'm arrested, I can count on you to clear my name."

She nodded vigorously.

Two of the men finished their breakfast and left, leaving Mr. Hunt from the second floor to eat alone. Though we had never spoken before, I had seen the man frequently around the halls of the boarding house. In fact, from what I had gathered, he rarely spoke to anyone at all. But he had never been unkind to me, always just ignoring me. Mrs. Bettings dried her eyes and poured me a cup of coffee.

"I'll be right out with a plate full of eggs and potatoes," she said, and hustled off into the kitchen.

I sat down and nodded to Mr. Hunt. This time he did not ignore me. Just the opposite, his response was to stare at me. I picked up a section of the morning newspaper and tried to distract myself with it, hoping to not find any mention of the events of last night. One article I did scan through was a report on the annual contributions to the university, with a Mr. Jebediah Higgins of Boston at the top of the list, outranking even the DuPonts. When I turned the page, I noticed that Mr. Hunt continued to stare at me.

It was more than a little unnerving.

At that point, I began to just look at headlines, but a mention of Doctor Gardiner caught my attention and I stopped to read it.

LOCAL ARCHAEOLOGIST TO
LECTURE IN EUROPE

ARKHAM—Yesterday, Doctor Quentin Gardiner of Miskatonic University announced plans to lecture across Europe this summer. He will be spending the month of July crisscrossing the continent, with stops planned for London, Paris, Bern, Rome and Heidelberg. The focus of his talks will be on the comparative architecture of tomb structures, taking into account the materials available, as well as the subsurface geology of the surroundings.

More recently, Doctor Gardiner may be better known for his work with charitable organizations than in the archaeological field. His last expedition, an excavation in the Egyptian desert three years ago, met with some measure of difficulty. The mummified remains discovered by Gardiner and his team were unfortunately destroyed by a rapid decomposition of unknown cause, after being shipped all of the way back to Miskatonic University. The Doctor was quick to accept the blame for the incident, although rumors at the time suggested otherwise. Nevertheless, his forthrightness only served to reinforce his reputation and integrity in the community that loves him so dearly.

The lecture trip is being initiated and sponsored by Doctor Rainer Donau of the University of Heidelberg. Doctor Donau is world-renowned for his decades of work in the Middle East, and it can safely be stated that he was influential in shaping the field of archaeology into the form it has taken today.

Another turn of the page, and Mr. Hunt's eyes were still boring through me.

"Is there something I can do for you, Mr. Hunt?"

I did not expect a reply. The fact that I got one was almost as shocking as what he said.

"You can *die*, Mr. Adderly," he said sharply. "Although it is probably too late for that to remedy the situation, it is nevertheless still my sentiment. The mark of the Accursed is strong upon you."

He finally dropped his gaze, then gathered his things and stood up shakily.

"I'll be dead inside of a week. I know it. In the time I have remaining upon this Earth, I do not wish to see you again."

And with that he walked off.

I was astonished. I had never sensed any animosity from the man, just indifference. And this was not just animosity. The mark of the Accursed? And what did he mean when he said that he would be dead inside a week? I was still reeling when Mrs. Bettings emerged from the kitchen a few minutes later with my breakfast.

"Do you know anything at all about Mr. Hunt?" I asked her.

"Not really. He keeps to himself. He's the ideal boarder, actually," she said with a little laugh. "He's quiet, he's clean, and he eats very little. He owned a small shop in town for many years—a bookstore. After his wife died two years ago, he sold his home, gave the business to his son, I think, and moved in here. Every morning at breakfast he reads the newspaper from front to back—*every single word*. That's all that I know. He's been here for two years, and that's all I know about him."

"Well, I spoke with him briefly just now, and he treated me as if I were the vilest person on the face of the earth. He said he wished to never see me again. Do you know if he's ill?"

"Well, I suppose I can't say for sure," she said, setting the plate down in front of me. "Don't be offended by his words, Robert. He's old and very lonely, I imagine. It's been eight years since I lost my dear Edward, and I still have days when I feel bitter because of it."

As she returned to the kitchen, I became aware of my ravenous hunger, and attacked the food she had prepared. I would have to send telegrams to my parents and to Elizabeth's relatives, informing them all of the tragedy. First, however, I had to locate her Uncle Thomas and Aunt Marie. They would be expecting her to arrive on a train that afternoon.

The events of that day were a blur. After changing my clothes, I raced out of the building and off to the telegraph station. The clerk helped me compose a telegram to be delivered to Elizabeth's aunt and uncle. Because of the uncertainty of the surname, he recruited the aid of a telephone operator in Boston who informed us that there were two men with the name Thomas Wentworth. He recorded the addresses for both. I offered to pay for two telegrams, but after hearing my situation, he would have nothing of it.

Word of Elizabeth's demise had spread swiftly around the campus, and upon returning to the boarding house, I was met with a flood of friends and acquaintances offering condolences. Mrs. Bettings provided refreshments, and even a light dinner as day dragged on into evening. It was late when the last of the visitors departed. Weary of playing host, I desired an escape from the confines of the house. Upon stepping outside, my eyes turned to the night sky, exceptionally clear that night and full of stars. Professor Josephson's rambling speech from the day before came to mind. *The stars are aligning,* I remembered him saying. And he had asked me to stop by and help him with some calculations. With no particular goal in mind for my walk, I decided to try to visit with him, despite the lateness of the hour.

His home was only a few blocks away on the east side of campus, and I covered the distance quickly. When I arrived, the library was still brightly lit, and I could see the shadow of a figure moving about through the curtains. After hesitating for a moment, I knocked on his front door loud enough to ensure that he would hear me. Within a minute it opened—just a crack at first, until he could see that it was me.

"Robert? Good heavens, it's late. Is everything alright?"

"Professor, forgive me for disturbing you, but I wanted to be sure you had heard the news. Last evening there was an…accident."

My voice caught in my throat.

"What is it, Robert?"

"Elizabeth is dead. She…burned to death. I felt that I needed to inform you, and you had asked me yesterday to visit you today, but I was unavoidably detained during the course of the afternoon."

"Elizabeth Wentworth is dead?"

I closed my eyes and nodded grimly. He continued to stand in the doorway without speaking, obviously shocked by the news.

"Professor, what did you mean yesterday when you said that the stars were aligning?"

At that, he swung the door open fully, and pulled me inside. After stealthily looking around outside, he slammed the door closed.

"Robert, you must believe me when I say that I never expected any of this to affect you." His voice shook as he spoke. "But I was wrong. The stars are not aligning; they are aligned. I discovered it last night after triple-checking myself."

He stopped, and silence hung between us. I could not comprehend what I was hearing.

"The stars are indeed aligned, and something has come through. And your Elizabeth is dead because of it."

"Because of it?" I said. "Because of *what*? Elizabeth died in the dining room, not out under the stars. How could the stars have anything to do with the fact that I watched her burn to ashes right in front of me?"

"Perhaps the two of you should come in here."

I looked behind the professor. Standing outside the open doors of the library was Doctor Gardiner.

"Both of you. Let us sit down and discuss the matter."

Professor Josephson nodded and led the way into his lavish library, and Doctor Gardiner closed the huge double doors in the east wall. The room was much as I remembered it from my rare visits, the north and south walls being filled floor to ceiling with hundreds of volumes. A large fire burned fiercely in the hearth in the west wall—I found myself partially hypnotized by its awful splendor, so much so that when I finally looked away, I was surprised to find there was another gentleman standing beside the large mahogany table in the center of the room. I didn't recognize him.

"Robert," Professor Josephson said, "I believe you are familiar with Doctor Gardiner."

"Sir," I acknowledged. He was of medium height and build. Though he was more than fifty years old, he still sported a full head of brown hair. We had never officially met, but among the archaeology students I had become acquainted with—Elizabeth being one of them—his eyesight had a legendary reputation. With the retirement of the previous head of the department a few years previously, Doctor Gardiner had been appointed to the position at the unusually young age of forty-eight.

"And this gentleman is—"

"You may call me Mr. Carter," interjected the fourth man. "Howard Carter."

I had seen a picture of Howard Carter recently, and this was not he. This man was very handsome and much younger than the other two, though still older than me. I guessed he was near forty, and he had a muscular build. Dressed as a businessman, he really seemed to be the kind of man more comfortable on safari in deepest Africa than sitting in an office. For some reason, he wanted to remain

41

anonymous. At that point, I just wanted answers to my own questions. His identity was of no concern to me.

"Gentlemen, this is Robert Adderly," said the professor. "He's a graduate student at Miskatonic University with whom I have worked for several years now. I trust his work and I trust his word. It seems he has endured a great tragedy, which I believe is directly related to our current predicament. Robert, if you please."

I did my best to recount my tale—from my proposal the previous afternoon, to my arrival before them that evening. They listened without interrupting. It was only after my testimony that the questions began—inane queries about fishy smells, sounds of whippoorwills, or wild, rushing winds. I repeatedly tried to emphasize to them that the fire had not so much as singed a single object—myself included—while Elizabeth was completely consumed.

At last the questions ended. My throat was very dry, and I asked the professor for a drink of water. He walked to a shelf on the west wall of the room, removed some books, and extracted an exquisite decanter from a hidden compartment. A generous amount of the liquid was poured into four brandy snifters, which he also pulled from the hideaway. After the glasses were distributed, we sat and wordlessly sipped at our drinks.

As I sat there, their persistent and nonsensical line of questioning forced me to doubt myself. Had I overlooked some other detail of the event? I searched my memory, but nothing came to mind. Nothing else stood out. I could feel my anger returning.

As if on cue, Doctor Gardiner spoke up.

"I think I speak for all of us, Robert, when I say that I am sorry for what has happened to you. You have our condolences on the death of your fiancée. I spoke to her several times. She was a bright and wonderful young woman."

He paused there, and I sensed I wouldn't like what he was about to tell me. I was right.

"However, you must believe me when I say that there is nothing we could have done to prevent it. This phenomenon you describe has been documented throughout history. Though the science behind it is not fully understood, it falls into the category of mundane physical processes. No connection has ever been established between spontaneous human combustion and the...phenomena we concern ourselves with. In other words, your fiancée was no more than an unfortunate victim of circumstance. There is nothing we can do to help you."

"But how can you be sure?" I asked. "What do you mean the phenomena you're concerned with? Professor Josephson seems to think there's a connection. Can't you at least tell me what it is that you do?"

Mr. Carter answered me bluntly.

"We cannot. And as I'm sure Professor Josephson can tell you, it is information the likes of which you do not want to know."

He paused, and I looked over at the professor, who only nodded and closed his eyes.

"The human race, in general, cannot hope to comprehend the knife-edge upon which our reality is perched. There are a fortunate few in all the world who can experience the horror—"

"What about my hands?" I shouted in frustration. "Not a mark on them!"

"Who can experience the horror," he reiterated slowly, emphasizing each word, "that is so inextricably intertwined with the history of this planet and *not* go insane."

I looked him in the eyes, still angry. He matched my gaze. He continued only when I looked away, the professional chill returning to his voice.

"We must apologize for misleading you, but Professor Josephson spoke rashly when he suggested a connection between your experience and our field of expertise. He was wrong to mention anything *at all* to you."

This last comment was directed at the professor, who did not look at him.

"Once again, we offer our heartfelt condolences. Please try to accept that your fiancée had a fatal, if extremely uncommon accident, and leave it at that. Good night, Mr. Adderly."

I looked over at the professor. He rose from his chair and waited for me to do the same. I finished my brandy, then stood and left the table without a word. The professor walked beside me to the library doors, opened them, then escorted me to the front door.

"I'm very sorry, Robert," he said as I stepped outside, his voice sounding as dejected as I felt. "But please, try to forget all that you have heard here tonight. Please. Forget it all."

There was much I wished to say to him. What nonsense! Sounds of whippoorwills? Smells of fish? My temper boiled up and I fought to control it. The clock in the hall struck midnight as I pulled on my coat and walked out into the cool air, ominous stars filling the night sky.

With the bitter aftertaste of the previous night's encounter still in my mouth, I arrived on campus at eleven o'clock the next morning, knowing the professor would be in his office at that time. As I turned the corner past the library, I noticed a familiar figure about fifty feet in front of me. Doctor Gardiner was heading in the same direction as I—exactly the same, as it happened.

I slowed my pace a bit to be certain that he would not detect my presence. Sure enough, he made his way directly to the professor's office on the second floor of Beaumont Hall. I followed him as closely as I was able, always staying out of his sight. As we reached our common goal, I hid around a corner about twenty feet away. The door to the classroom neighboring the professor's office was cracked open. It was clearly empty, the lights switched off. I crept in silently and locked the door behind me. Beside the lectern stood a connecting door that led into the professor's office. I put my ear to the keyhole and listened.

"—any more! That abominable Higgins can perform his own calculations! He *questioned* my work. For nearly an hour he questioned my work. I would not have notified you if I was not one hundred percent sure."

"Sam, please. You are not the first to be insulted by his abrupt manner. But he is right. He's one of the few who have seen beyond the veil and retained his mind enough to tell it. As have Dunlevy. And MacNulty. And I...at least, I'd like to *think* I've retained my mind."

He chuckled briefly before his tone turned serious again.

"We must stay together—we *must*—despite petty personality differences. We have a duty to fight as well and as long as we are able. We need you, Sam."

There was a long pause.

"Quentin, I must know. Why question the boy's experience?"

"It was a ghastly, fantastic coincidence. The event that the stars foreshadowed could not possibly have occurred in our own backyard! We could not *possibly* be so lucky. The Earth is yet intact, and while it seems that the event was not blatantly catastrophic, it may take us weeks, or even months to discover what transpired that night. We shall pay attention to the news reports from every corner of the globe. And when we do find it, we'll let you know."

I heard Professor Josephson sigh tiredly.

"This time, I don't think that I want to know. I have learned far too much these last ten years. I'm frightened, Quentin. I'm old. I've lived a full life, as full as could be expected. I...I know this line of work can be dangerous. You warned me right at the start. But at this point, it's not my life I'm afraid of losing. It's my *soul*."

There was a long pause before Doctor Gardener next spoke; it was so long in fact, that I worried he had slipped out of the professor's office without my noticing. When he finally did, he too sounded tired.

"I'll respect your wishes," he said. "But if we require similar services in the future, we'll need you to recommend someone to take your place."

"Yes, of course. But whoever it is, ensure they never have to deal with Higgins. His presence only makes the task at hand—any task—more difficult."

"I agree that Jebediah Higgins does not make the best ambassador for our cause. When you think of someone, please let me know; I shall make an effort to insulate him. Before I leave, though, I do have one more request."

"Yes?"

"With the 'alignment' of these stars—the terminus being Earth—the path presumably ends in a specific spot on the earth's surface. If you can give us any help at all in that respect, we can narrow our search."

"I've tried to solve that problem already. *Repeatedly*. The ancient sources you supplied are not explicit enough. Using the information at hand, the path traced through the heavens does not touch the Earth at a single point—it's nothing but a chaotic tangle. Like a length of string with horrendously complicated knots at both ends. Those equations simply do not yield precise values at the endpoints."

With that answer, I heard Doctor Gardiner ready himself to leave.

"I'm off to lunch. Care to join me?"

"Thank you, but I still have quite a bit of work that I need to attend to. Tomorrow, perhaps? Half past noon?"

"Excellent. I'll drop by here then. Until tomorrow."

"Good day, Quentin."

The door opened, then closed. I heard Doctor Gardiner's footsteps retreat down the hall. The professor would surely continue working for a while. I decided to wait in the empty classroom so as to not appear too soon after the doctor's departure. From time to time, I heard the professor move about or shuffle papers. But even as I waited there, gathering my courage, Gardiner's words bounced around in my head. *A ghastly coincidence. Fantastic. We could not possibly be so lucky.* Somehow, in that moment, I felt myself anything but lucky.

FIVE

I considered a dozen opening lines, discarded them all. There was no need for justification or explanation. I crept out of the classroom. A knock on the door of Professor Josephson's office resulted in the familiar, *Come in.*

His face initially displayed irritation at being interrupted, but it was quickly replaced with a mixture of relief, sorrow, and possibly embarrassment, when he saw me.

"Hello, Robert."

"Professor."

I'd been in that room dozens of times, but this time, there was a stillness that chilled me. The grandfather clock in the corner ticked loudly. I'd never noticed the sound of it before.

"Please," he said, gesturing at the chair in front of his desk.

As I sat down, he put his work aside and eyed me. My hands twisted in my lap.

"What brings you here today?"

"Elizabeth's death," I began. "I mean to discover what happened to her, and I need to know all that you can tell me."

He sighed deeply, almost painfully so.

"Robert, that path is the wrong one to follow. Once begun, there is no turning back. The knowledge is a constant burden. And it is dangerous. Blackly dangerous."

"Professor, please! Two evenings ago, I watched helplessly as my fiancée was consumed by flames," I said, my voice rising with the memory. "And they were not ordinary, earthly flames. The floor, the rug, my hands—*none* were burnt. Only Elizabeth was reduced to ashes, which evaporated as I watched. I need to find out what happened. And why. If you won't help me, I will find someone who will!"

He was silent for a long time. I had never before raised my voice to him, and was afraid that my outburst had offended him. When he next spoke, his voice was barely audible.

"I have always trusted the diagnoses of Doctor Gardiner and his associates," he began slowly. "But this time they appear to be wrong."

He looked down at his desk.

I waited.

And waited.

I shifted in my seat, ready to prod him, but just my stirring was enough. He waved at the papers on his desk.

"Numbers," he blurted out, still looking down. "Despite their abstract nature, numbers are concrete to me. They are *real*. Other people may not share the same opinion, but I have come to accept that. Everyone in this large world is different. Other people may take comfort in the concreteness of other objects or concepts. Different people, different backgrounds, different ways of thinking and dealing with the world. But despite differing opinions, we can all of us share numbers as a science."

At last he looked up at me.

"Science," he repeated, but stopped after the one word.

I sensed him starting to lose steam.

"Please go on, Professor."

He sighed once more and seemed to reach a decision.

"Science, Robert, has many more facets than those traditionally taught at this university—at any university. In mathematics, we take for granted that a certain sequence of numbers and formulae, calculated correctly, will consistently produce the same result. Yes?"

I nodded.

"Mathematics, chemistry, physics are all hard sciences. Experiments are repeatable. Results are consistent."

A note of nervousness had crept into his deep voice, giving it a higher pitch. I nodded, and keep eye contact with him as he spoke, both to reassure him that I was following along, and to keep him going.

"Words, I've come to learn, are as much of a science as numbers."

He spoke the sentence with finality, as if it had been the goal he had been trying to reach. Unfortunately, it made no sense to me.

"Words," I said. "As in giving a speech?"

"No." He cleared his throat. "I misspoke. It's more than just words. Words and actions, combined in a specific manner, and perhaps with other components, can consistently produce the same result. And for those who know the correct words, the correct actions—a great many things become possible. Things any sane man would question."

Had it not been for the shaking tone in his voice and the events of the last twenty-four hours, the thought would never have entered my mind, the word would never have left my mouth.

"Magic."

"Yes," he said, almost sadly. "I was raised as you were. The Church was always there for me. In my youth I strongly considered entering the priesthood. Magic? For most of my life, it was impossible for me to lend any credence at all to such a concept, though superstition was always there. Spill some salt, throw a pinch over your shoulder. Hmm? But people can change, given enough time and an open mind. And given proof. I had an experience which I consider to be proof."

He rose from his chair and poured two glasses of water from a pitcher by the window, handed one to me. I thanked him and took a sip. He resumed his seat and drank deeply. When he spoke again, his voice was strained, haunted. I could see fear in his eyes.

"About three years ago, Doctor Gardiner received a shipment from Egypt: a sarcophagus. He had removed it from the shipping crate and invited me to the unveiling. I was puzzled at first, as I had no interest in the field of archaeology. He insisted, however, that the mummy within was special, and pertained to something with which I had helped them. When I arrived as instructed—at sunset—at his office in Clemmons Hall, he unexpectedly guided me upstairs to the roof. As we finished our climb I noticed three other men there. I'd met none of them previously, but now I know them to be friends of Doctor Gardiner. They surrounded a large stone sarcophagus. Gardiner asked me to examine it. On the lid was a drawing I interpreted as a horizon with stars. One star in particular was drawn with more emphasis than the others. Above the drawing were two symbols that made no sense to me. However, below the drawing were some hieroglyphics I recognized. It was then that the reason for my presence that evening became clear.

"After finding the artifact, they had managed to translate the symbols on their own, but had been stymied as to their meaning. It was the very problem Doctor Gardener had handed to me some weeks prior, albeit without any context. I'd applied certain cryptographic methods, and discovered that the symbols described specific days of the year. Now, with the situation presented to me fully, the drawing with the symbols seemed to imply some sort of causality: When certain stars were above the horizon at certain times of the year, some event might occur. But what? I relayed this thought to the group. Gardiner smiled grimly, and told me that the sarcophagus was discovered buried under tons of debris. He had surmised that the underground chamber in which it had been placed had collapsed due to an earthquake. He went on to say that chambers of that type were usually created with narrow passageways linking the chamber to the hillside under which they were hidden, so that the dead could have an unimpeded view of the stars.

"But according to Gardiner, that particular sarcophagus had not seen the light of the stars for over four thousand years. He pointed to the symbols above the drawing. The first, he said, was the man's name: Keraph Thet. But it was the second that had alerted them to attend to this particular mummy. It was the symbol for a being known as Hastur. And as he spoke that name, the sarcophagus lid *moved.*

"I almost shrieked aloud. Or maybe I did shriek. We both jumped back, and the other three men produced weapons—an axe and rifles. The man with the axe introduced himself to you last night, Robert, as Howard Carter; his real name is Jebediah Higgins."

I frowned at the memory of Higgins.

"He moved into position on the right while the men with the rifles stood on the left. The lid slid noisily towards us. As the opening grew, the overpowering stench of abyss engulfed us. Gardiner and myself, directly downwind from the opening, covered our noses and mouths to protect ourselves from the fetid odor.

"The lid moved a full six inches, then stopped. What I saw then I don't think I will ever forget. The skeletal remains of two hands emerged from the inside, clamped onto the edge of the lid and begin pushing it towards us. My heart was close to bursting. Whatever was entombed inside of that crypt was shifting the heavy stone with ease. It appeared, however, that I was the only one close to panic. Higgins was readying himself, apparently planning on taking a swipe at the creature. Doctor Gardiner calmly removed an object from his pocket, something flat and star shaped. At last, the sound of grinding stone ceased. To this day, I thank God that the light from the surrounding buildings and street lamps did not reveal even more to me than what I did see when the creature within *sat up.*

"Imagine a man dead of starvation, naked, with the skin and muscles contracted tightly around the bones, dried and decayed by the passage of four thousand arid years. To my horror, I noticed traces of hair still left on the desiccated skull, and the teeth were completely exposed with no trace of lips to conceal them. The eyes, though, were the most memorable detail: the only aspect of the creature that betrayed the least sign of life. They glowed a dim orange-red. That is all that I had a chance to see. Gardiner presented the object in his hand, holding it boldly out towards the undead corpse. Its effect was immediate. The creature froze, and in that instant, Higgins pulled the axe back and landed a deadly blow on the neck, severing the head cleanly from the body. The torso collapsed backwards into the sarcophagus as the head flew off, landing a few yards away."

He paused here as if attempting to read my reaction, but whether he was satisfied or disappointed in the expression I wore, I couldn't tell. I hardly knew how I felt, myself.

"The three men then put down their weapons, and with much effort, managed to twist and shove the lid completely off of the crypt. Using a spade, Higgins retrieved the head, and lifted it into the sarcophagus, placing it at the feet of the corpse. The other two men swiftly produced several large beakers of liquid, and poured the contents into the open sarcophagus. It quickly became evident that the liquid was a very powerful acid. Only when the last bit of corpse bubbled and dissolved did Gardiner lower his hand, and return the star shaped object to his pocket."

As he finished the water in his glass, I noticed his hand trembling. He seemed to be satisfied to stop there, but there were still too many unknowns. I waited a respectful few seconds, then gave him a gentle prompt.

"What was it, Professor?" I asked. "The object that Doctor Gardiner held. What was it?"

"An Elder Sign. It's a potent symbol of protection from the Ancient Ones. Doctor Gardiner informed me later that this particular one was found in a cave along the southern shore of the Mediterranean by Higgins himself."

"Ancient Ones? Professor—" But he cut me off.

"As for the inhabitant of the sarcophagus, it was what's known as a lich—at least, that was the term that Gardiner used. It had been a man at one point, apparently a high priest of...that being I mentioned. But through the use of powerful invocations, involving a good deal of human sacrifice, the priest was able to continue to live, as it were, after his death. But you see, my boy, this is precisely why you must stay away from this. All of it. Yes, these magicks are a science—and like a science, can lead men to enlightenment. But they can also lead to terrible darkness."

"For by thy sorceries were all nations deceived." I spoke the verse to myself.

"Indeed."

In the silence that followed, I half expected him to burst with laughter and explain that it had all been a horrible joke. But his face remained serious.

"I know this is a terrific amount to digest all at once. Doctor Gardiner was kind enough to introduce the concepts to me over a period of months—perhaps even a year. After that event on the roof, he'd slowly gotten me thinking differently about the world. He had tested me with debates over hypothetical, nonsensical situations. At first, I was secure in my logic. But over time, my view changed, as uncertainty seeped in. That experience with the lich shook me to my core, but I was able to handle it. Gardiner had prepared me." After a pause he added, "Of course, I have no proof of any of what I just told you."

Magic. Lich. By the laws of God and Nature, how could I possibly accept such inanities? My own religious convictions aside, it seemed insane to believe such abominations existed. I was a man of science! But then again, so was Professor Josephson. As well as Doctor Gardiner. They were both brilliant, respected men. Each had decades more experience than I. Were there simply things out there in the world that I was not aware of? Or things that were purposely hidden?

"Magic," I muttered. It was an alien word with evil undertones.

"Try thinking of it as a science that is poorly understood."

I mulled that over.

"That does help," I reluctantly agreed. "But where in—Where would one go to learn about such things?"

The professor frowned at the question.

"A few hideous tomes have managed to survive the centuries. It's not common knowledge, but some are housed here at this very university. I've not seen them. The ones that Doctor Gardiner mentioned to me are the *Necronomicon* of Abdul Alhazred, *De Vermis Mysteriis*, the—"

"Wait, Professor," I nearly shouted. "Did you say *De Vermis Mysteriis*?"

"Yes. You know of it?" he asked, leaning forward in his chair.

Right then, I very nearly told him of the time I'd seen that volume, of my encounter as a child with a ghost that left footprints. And I very nearly voiced a theory, newly formed in my mind, that the ghost could have been a man using 'magic' to blink in and out of existence. But I didn't. His look of concern stopped me. His warnings made me think that I may never get another chance to learn anything from him, and right then, I needed to learn as much as possible.

So, I lied to the professor for the first time that I could recall.

"No." I shook my head. "No, I must be mixing it up with something else."

He nodded, visibly relaxing—but too much. His concern, fear, nervousness were all gone. I felt he might dismiss me at any time. But I had one avenue left to exploit.

"Professor…the other day, you mentioned that you wanted me to check over your work."

"Yes. At the time, I was in a state of severe agitation. I doubted myself, allowing my imagination to run wild. There's no need for you to bother yourself. I just wish that…"

His voice trailed off again, and his fingers tapped the desktop as I had seen him do a few times in the past when confronted with a devilishly difficult problem.

"Yes?"

"Those blasted endpoints!" he said, raising his voice uncharacteristically. "This problem has confounded me completely."

I smiled inwardly with a grim satisfaction. I knew him just well enough, knew that academic curiosity could at times drive him relentlessly.

"Let me start at the beginning," he said, leaning forward. "Gardiner and his associates found a pattern of star names hidden among the pages of the *Necronomicon*. They did not reveal the exact nature of the pattern to me, but let it suffice to say it was not easily discovered. One would be required to be intimately familiar with most of the text of that godforsaken tome. The book spans a thousand pages, written in Latin. Nearly all of it symbolic, requiring a detailed knowledge of both magic and the myths of the Ancient Ones to comprehend it."

That was twice he had mentioned the Ancient Ones, I realized.

"They handed to me two things: The pattern obtained from the *Necronomicon*." And here he stood and walked over to a small safe, which sat on the floor behind the desk. It was unlocked. He swung it open, and extracted a framed document, about eight inches by twelve inches. Secured beneath the sheet of glass was a piece of old, yellowed paper.

"And this," he said, handing me the frame, "recently surfaced in Baghdad. It is nearly four hundred years old, written in Portuguese. I have the translation here."

He handed me a paper from a corner of his desk, written in his own, scrawling hand.

I have trafficked with the devils of the deep, and they have revealed unto me the formulae of old. He shall rise once again. Even the eldest among them cannot say whence this knowledge came.

But there is more within these formulae than even they know. All of the Ancient Ones are attuned. It is but necessary to know for each the correct star. To that end I work.

Below the verse on the page was a set of equations written in a notation with which I was not familiar. At the very bottom of the sheet were two more lines:

For each that I am certain, here are listed the stars:

Hastur ~ Aldebaran

"Unfortunately, this sheet was found alone," said the professor. "The author may have compiled an extensive list, but we shall never know. The equations that you see there are composed of both astrological and magical symbols. Doctor Gardiner provided me with just enough information to translate them."

He handed me another sheet that was much more legible. The equations on it seemed to describe an arc through the heavens, but there was something odd about them. As I looked them over I became more confused.

"As you can see," he said, "this system of equations is utter nonsense."

I nodded in agreement, my brow furrowed.

"As is typical of documents of this type, the information is incomplete. The author deemed the knowledge important enough to be recorded, but was clever enough to excise the information necessary for total comprehension. Anyone else reading his notes would be perplexed unless the missing pieces were applied. That's where the pattern from the *Necronomicon* fits in."

He handed me yet another page with a list of star names along with their spatial coordinates, and presumably, their equivalent magical symbols. The first star on the list had a name that I did not know. The coordinates for it were crossed out, and different numbers were recorded to the right of the originals.

"These stars are the missing factors. The first one was the cause of my miscalculation. I had to consult several sources before I could determine which coordinates were correct. But the number of stars matches the number of equations. I'm sure you can see where the data should be inserted."

Surprisingly, I did see. With a one-to-one correspondence between the list and the equations on the two sheets, I was able to solve the first equation easily, and apply the answer to the second. It became more complicated after that, and I stopped; but I acknowledged that the pattern definitely existed.

"Finally," said the professor with some degree of satisfaction evident in his voice, "we arrive at this."

I received another page, this one with just a few greatly simplified equations.

"After merging the data from those two pages, and performing a non-Euclidian transformation to clean up the calculations, these equations are the result. They describe a path from some point in the heavens to here. To Earth."

His voice sank nearly to a whisper.

"Given an origin star, such as might be found on the bottom of that page by our unknown Portuguese author, the date and time of the next spatially compatible alignment for the corresponding entity can be calculated."

I remained silent, for I did not know what to say.

"Yes. It's amazing, isn't it? As chaotic as those infernal beings are, they too are subjected to definable, predictable physical laws."

"But if you don't know what happened the other night…"

"We don't know what happened because we don't know the origin star," he said. "We don't know for which entity the stars were aligned."

"But how…"

"I was dissatisfied that there was only one name recorded on that Portuguese document. I decided to try solving the equations backwards."

And here his eyes took on the haunted look they had while relating his encounter with the thing from the sarcophagus.

"It was the morning of the day Elizabeth died. I tried using the current date to solve for the spatial coordinates of a star. It was the most shocking thing I have ever experienced as a mathematician."

He picked up three more sheets of paper and handed them to me.

"I discovered a nearly perfect alignment. Thinking that I'd done something wrong, I tried several other days randomly chosen in the past and future. Each time, nothing. I recalculated for Thursday's date and received the same result. But at the time, the exact coordinates for that one star—the last link in the chain—were uncertain, and I realized that I needed to adjust them. It was then that I left here and ran into you."

I looked over the latest set of papers.

"I see what the issue is," I said.

"Do you understand what has baffled me?"

I did. Solving backwards from a known time, the spatial coordinates were unknown. The path through the stars, as represented by known, fixed quantities in the equations, was straight. At the two endpoints of the path, though, the equations had several non-linear variables. We both stared at the papers for a while. I understood what the professor was trying to do, but could offer no hints. He was obviously stumped. If I could study the situation further, I thought that I might find something that he missed.

"Professor, may I take your notes with me? I could return them tomorrow."

He seemed to remember himself.

"Just take them. I have no interest in this mystery any longer." He collected all of the relevant papers and handed them to me, but when I reached out for them, he did not let go. "But you must *promise* me you will be careful."

"I promise."

As I turned to go, he spoke up once more.

"I realize that you are probably depending on me to be a source of knowledge, someone to whom you can turn for help. Don't."

"But—"

"What I know is very shallow indeed. I would be of no help to you, and I must say, I do not wish to be complicit in you possibly harming yourself. I tried to warn you before; I shall try one last time. You will not like what you discover. At best, you will find yourself being tormented by the knowledge; at worst, you will find yourself dead."

"I *must* get to the bottom of this. I must know."

He glowered briefly at my stubbornness.

"Elizabeth," I reminded him. Just the one word was enough.

"Then you will have to rely on Doctor Gardiner. He can grant you access to the volumes locked away in the Library. Failing that, there is a bookstore—Hunt's Fine Books. Well, not the store itself so much as the owner. Up until a few years ago, Mr. Bertram Hunt owned it, but I believe his son is in charge now. Perhaps you could inquire into his whereabouts?"

Just hearing the name gave me a start; I wondered if his son would be as hostile.

"I know of the store," I said, keeping my voice even.

He gave a brief smile, but it was half-hearted, and his voice became somber as he ushered me out the door.

"And once more, I must say that I am very sorry about Elizabeth. She was a fine young woman."

Once the door had closed behind me, I leaned against the wall and thought. I looked over the professor's notes one more time. Still uncertain as to where the information would lead me, I was glad that I at least had a starting point for my investigation. I felt certain that I was on the right path.

SIX

No sooner had I emerged into the sun from the dark offices of Beaumont Hall, than did the professor's encounter seem to be little more than fiction—a ghost story from a frightened, old man. No, that was disrespectful, and I reprimanded myself for even allowing the thought. But fact or fiction, what I held in my hands was real enough. Could the information somehow prove the reality of what he had said? I didn't care. I was only fixated on the promise of an insight into Elizabeth's death.

Back at the boarding house, I recalled the professor mentioning Mr. Hunt. For years I had walked by his door on every ascent and descent of the steps, and had never even thought of him once. Perhaps Mrs. Bettings was right, and the man was just lonely. If I made a genuine attempt to befriend him, perhaps he would warm up to me. On the secondfloor landing I paused and looked at his door, considered knocking.

No, too soon, I thought.

And it *was* too soon, but to be truthful, I was also lacking the courage. It was easier to convince myself to leave him alone for a few days and then approach him, so I continued on up to my room on the third floor.

That afternoon disappeared as I immersed myself in the equations on those sheets of paper, and struggled to unravel them. It did occur to me that I was attempting the impossible—trying to find an answer to a problem so difficult that it had defeated one of the greatest mathematical minds alive. But I imagined myself as having an advantage over the professor: grief. But this was a different kind, having none of the typical despondency. My grief didn't slow me. On the contrary, it drove me. I was determined to attack the problem from all angles, even using techniques that made no sense. I pored through my old textbooks, searching for new and different ideas to try. But despite my determination, my eyes eventually grew weary, and I succumbed to a nap.

It was early evening when I was awakened by a gentle knocking at my bedroom door. Mrs. Bettings entered, bearing a hearty dinner and two telegrams: the first from my parents, getting into town that evening; the second from Elizabeth's aunt and uncle, who were due to arrive the following day. The Wentworths generously offered to pay for a small ceremony to be held for her friends at the university, with the formal burial a few days later in Boston.

When Mother and Father arrived, I escorted them to a local hotel where I knew they would be comfortable. I hadn't seen them in almost a year. I tried to speak of Elizabeth's death in the broadest possible terms, but Father insisted on hearing all of the details. Mother could only cry.

Elizabeth's Aunt Marie and Uncle Thomas were, by all indications, exceedingly wealthy. Thomas was tall, and vigorous for a man nearing sixty. His wife exuded an aura of elegance. Both were dressed in finery, he in a well-tailored dark suit, she in a stunning blue dress, which matched the color of her eyes. So far removed were they from the picture of my dearest Elizabeth: humble, demure. It was clear she had taken great pains to hide her family's status from me.

The Wentworths had a room reserved at the magnificent Hotel Dunbar. After delivering the luggage and ensuring that Aunt Marie would be comfortable, Uncle Thomas and I first visited a minister with whom I had spoken in the past. The sympathetic man eagerly volunteered to help. That was the easy part. The meeting at the funeral parlor was more difficult. I tried to explain the situation to the director, but questions regarding the body—or lack thereof—caused me to stumble. Thomas Wentworth took over at that point, billfold open.

"No further questions," he said flatly. "There will be neither body nor coffin. We require a small room tomorrow morning. You need do nothing else. This should cover it."

The man's eyes widened as he accepted the offering.

Outside the shop, Thomas Wentworth apologized to me.

"I'm sorry for having interrupted you, Robert. I'm just tired of dealing with vultures. I've had plenty enough of it. Lately...there's been enough."

There was no mistaking the anger in his final declaration.

He then returned to the hotel, and I ran over to the university, where I did my best to find and inform key people of the service. I successfully located three friends of Elizabeth and myself, and asked them to spread the word around the campus. It was short notice, and I hoped that it would be enough time.

When I returned home, Mrs. Bettings met me at the front door with a note that had been delivered just minutes before my arrival. It was an invitation to dinner from the Wentworths for my parents and me. I was grateful for their continued generosity, and hoped that my parents would enjoy their company. They did. The conversation was a bit forced at first, but a need to talk and perhaps feel 'normal' kept the words flowing. The evening was as enjoyable as it could be, and with thankfully few tears given the inevitable topic to which the conversation turned again and again.

The following morning, I was pleasantly surprised to find the rented room packed full of people ready to pay their last respects to my beloved. The minister conducted a simple, yet appropriate, ceremony. Several in the audience were called upon to share their thoughts. The love that poured forth from her friends touched me. I believe that it also affected the Wentworths, who although respectfully silent, obviously did not relish the company of such a youthful, bourgeois crowd.

Professor Josephson must have arrived late, for I only saw him after the ceremony ended. I told him that I had been invited to Boston for the formal burial, and asked him for a few days off. He told me to take a week, and to meet with him when I returned in order to review plans for my final year. I thanked him for his understanding. After the crowd dispersed, I saw my parents off to the train back home. They had also been invited to Boston, but declined; my father could not be away from business for that length of time on such short notice.

The train ride to Boston the next day was quiet. At dinner the previous evening, we had covered a number of topics, and there seemed to be nothing left to say. Of course, the service the day before, combined with the promise of another yet to come, had left us in a somber mood anyway. The Wentworths played a dispirited game of gin rummy for a while, but abandoned it midway through. Aunt Marie occupied herself with solitaire at that point while Uncle Thomas sat, eyes closed, not asleep, but lost in thought. A few times, I noticed a scowl form on his face, then slowly dissipate.

As the New England countryside moved by outside the window, my mind was abuzz. The mathematical puzzle had been left behind in my room; I knew full well that I would be lacking the concentration necessary to tackle it. Instead, I pondered Professor Josephson's rooftop encounter. On the one hand, it was pure insanity. Anything that is dead simply cannot be reanimated—save for when the Lord intervenes, and His presence could clearly have not been there that night. On the other hand, I had entrusted my future to the professor, looked to him for guidance. It did not seem possible that he had concocted that story. If he had, from whence could such an intricate tale have come? His imagination was powerful, but confined to number theory. There was no fiction in him. Somehow, I had to reconcile the two opposing views.

I began with confidence that he had been on the rooftop with Doctor Gardiner, and had seen *something* that night. Unfortunately, when science and logic were invoked, it ended there as well, as the bulk of the details were too fantastic. I wracked my brain for an explanation and came up with only one, and a shaky one at that: an elaborate hoax, but one that required the participation of Doctor Gardiner. The minds and motivations of men are impossible to know, and a combination of intersecting circumstances *can* cause any man to act against his natural character—but I could imagine no scenario where Doctor Gardiner would deliberately deceive the professor in such a manner. Their friendship was genuine. No, it could not have been a hoax.

But perhaps the scene could have been…misremembered. Professor Josephson was growing older each day. He had said as much to Doctor Gardiner. Recently, I had observed him forgetting where he had placed his hat or chalk. Still assuming that a normal, dusty mummy had been unveiled that night, was it possible that the events had been twisted in his memory? It was *possible*, I had to admit. However, his mind was still so sharp. I was routinely a witness to it, and at irregular intervals a victim, as he would point out errors in my thesis. Calculations I had thrice checked, he had to scan but once. But it was certainly a staggering leap from forgetting a hat to having a mind so faulty that a memory of a mummified priest is distorted so dramatically.

But what sort of physical process, or science, would allow a dead man to return to life after being exposed to the light of a star? Plain and simply: None. But just thinking of stars brought me back around to the equations. I could not deny the reality of a thing that had perplexed the professor. Was the story true? Was the missing science actually magic? Could any of it be linked to Elizabeth's death? I wanted answers.

Have faith, I told myself repeatedly. *Have faith.*

At the Wentworth's expansive mansion west of Boston, I stayed in a guest room—one of many. The grounds extended for acres and acres, gently rolling hills sometimes covered with trees, but more often open, grassy fields. It was much larger than I had time to explore, though I intended to try. There was enough time before dinner to stretch my legs, and so I set off on a ramble, even though a misty drizzle had begun.

As I returned, Aunt Marie met me. She seemed to have been waiting for me. We walked over to the stables, and led me straight to a particular horse. The mare was on the smaller side, chestnut brown with a circular white patch on either side of the neck.

"This is Emily," she said, feeding the horse a carrot. "Elizabeth always favored this one when she visited here."

She seemed to want to say more, but stopped there. I recalled Elizabeth's joy around horses, and imagined her riding through the surrounding fields. With both of us perhaps taking comfort with memories, we stroked the horse for a few minutes, then returned to the main house.

Dinner that evening was very good, but silent—in fact, uncomfortably so. The tension eased up when dessert was served: Thomas Wentworth did not eat any sweets, and so excused himself. With his absence, the two of us enjoyed the treat, and made some small talk about puddings and pies. Aunt Marie retired soon after.

I thought it good form to bid my host a good night, and searched for him with a stroll through the rooms downstairs. He was easy to locate. I found him in the library with cigar and brandy. He had heard me approach, and looked up as I entered.

"I don't mean to disturb you, sir," I began. "I just wanted—"

"Robert, please join me."

I sat down in a leather chair across from him.

"Would you like a nightcap?"

"Thank you, but no."

He collected his thoughts, and I gave him time to do so.

"I must apologize for my foul mood. I had to bury my brother and his wife not long ago. I still feel the sting of that."

"I can sympathize. Three deaths…"

"Three!" He spat the word out bitterly.

"Oh…Elizabeth did mention her brother once, also."

"Michael. Yes, he died in France. But the total is up to six now. Twin sisters, Mary and Catherine, succumbed to influenza. They were the first."

"My Lord. Is anyone left?"

His jaw clenched visibly then relaxed only enough for a curt, "No."

He took a drink of his brandy. It seemed as if he had still more to say, so I waited.

"I was going to speak tomorrow," he finally said. "I can say a few words, but I would prefer if you handled the bulk of it. Can you please?"

"Yes, of course."

He nodded thanks, apparently done speaking. The 'foul mood' he had mentioned swooping in to engulf him again.

The funeral service was exceedingly formal, held in a well-respected parlor in downtown Boston. A large, painted portrait of Elizabeth in an ornate golden frame stood atop an empty coffin in the front of the room. Of almost two hundred friends and relatives who attended, I recognized none except for my host and hostess. The three of us received everyone who came in. I did my best to accept handshakes and sympathy, but it became wearisome to manufacture meaningless small talk, especially when it was so forced. I was obviously a stranger, an outsider. All of the visitors tried to disguise it, but I felt it from everyone. Even the Wentworths, as nice as they'd been, seemed to hold me at arm's length with the family around.

When the flow stopped, I took the opportunity to step away for a drink of water. It was an odd feeling, maneuvering through that crowd. Only a scant few made eye contact with me, seemingly wanting to speak with me, but not doing so. Even the children seemed to have been taught to steer clear. Was association with me some kind of social taboo? Or was I being blamed for Elizabeth's death? Or perhaps I had a stigma associated with me: The bizarre death curse of her family had transferred over, and I would be next to die. Or maybe it was simply the fact that my best suit was nothing that any of the men there would want to be caught dead in.

One nameless woman who did acknowledge my existence seemed braver than the rest. About as old as my mother, she wore a subtle smirk as she moved in my direction and began talking to another woman not far to my left. She spoke more loudly than needed, confirming my first impression of her: She enjoyed flaunting the rules.

"Oh, this is terrible, so soon after the parents," I heard her say. "Did you know the girl?"

"No, not well at all," came the reply from the other woman.

"Neither did I. But it seems that most everyone is here today. Only a few absentees."

"Yes. My son Edward and his new wife are still on their honeymoon. Mr. Rafferty begged off, with the excuse of a business meeting that could not be missed. He never comes to any of these anyway. He won't even go to his own funeral, I'll wager. And Jonathan Donaldson is doing so poorly these days that he can't be moved. I fully expected him to be the next to go, not this poor girl."

"And there's that cousin."

"Oh. Yes. He's still overseas."

"What was his name? I can't quite—"

At that moment the crowd was asked to quiet down and take

seats.

The minister led a wonderful service. When it came time, Thomas Wentworth said only a very few words before introducing me. To me, it seemed as if he was tactfully biting his tongue, successfully holding in…something. The crowd was silent and distant when I stood and went to the front, but I accepted the challenge of winning them over. I praised Elizabeth from the very core of my being, trying my best to evoke emotion from those gathered. It took some doing, but one woman, then another began to sob. In turn, my grief surfaced, and washed over me during that speech, causing more tears. Round and round it went. I got through to them, and—I think—managed to connect with some, though the few names I learned weren't retained, and I never saw any of them again.

The rest of that day was lost in sorrow, but in retrospect, I found the experience to be very cathartic. The bulk of my grief had been purged from me, and afterward, I found myself much more focused and able to concentrate.

The following day, I spent a good deal of time with Emily, riding her around the entire estate. I thought of nothing for those hours except grass, trees, and the horse. That small amount of relaxation was just what I needed to restore my energies, and I found myself growing eager to return home and begin looking for answers. When I informed the Wentworths that I was ready to leave, they invited me to stay longer, but I declined. The return trip by train for the next day was arranged, and I found myself back in Arkham four days after having left.

Seven

The first words I heard upon walking through the door of my boarding house were spoken by the shaking voice of Mrs. Bettings. Mr. Hunt, it seemed, was dead. He had died in his sleep the day I'd left. His funeral had been just hours before, while I'd been traveling back.

"Threes," she told me nervously. "Death always comes in threes."

Less than a week, he had said to me. Less than a week. He was right.

Since Professor Josephson's suggestion to speak with Mr. Hunt was no longer an option, I had but one avenue left to me. I would have to visit the bookstore and talk to his son, whom I hoped would be less hostile. The store was located at the edge of the small commercial district downtown, where the familiar gambrel-roofed houses of the surrounding residential areas met the islet of business. I arrived early the next morning, just in time to see a young man, who appeared to be approximately my age, unlocking the door from the inside.

"Good morning, sir," he welcomed me with a deep voice, holding the door open. He was clean-shaven with dark brown hair, a bit taller than me, and somewhat sturdier.

"Good morning," I replied, stepping in.

"You are my first customer," he said almost jovially, closing the door. "How may I help you?"

"The previous owner, Mr. Bertram Hunt, had occasion to do business with my mentor, Professor Samuel Josephson of Miskatonic

University. I am aware that Mr. Hunt—God rest his soul—has recently died. He actually lived in the same boarding house as I, though I admit I barely knew him. But I was wondering if I might talk to the current owner of this store, who I understand to be his son."

"Sir, you are mostly correct. Mr. Hunt was my grandfather. His son-in-law—my father—and I *had* been jointly operating this store for the past few years, but with my grandfather's death, ownership has been relinquished to me. This is my first day at the helm. You see, you really are my first customer. As such, I shall do my best to help you."

The last was spoken very sincerely, filled with pride. He extended his hand.

"Andrew Cooke."

"Robert Adderly. Very nice to meet you," I said, shaking his hand, and trying to hide my disappointment.

"How may I be of service?"

I paused to collect my thoughts. Presumably, Professor Josephson had referred me to Mr. Hunt because his decades of experience had resulted in a large store of knowledge upon which to draw. His grandson could hardly be expected to have the knowledge I needed to further my quest. Complicating matters, I wasn't sure of what to ask for, or how to phrase it.

"I'm looking for some more...uncommon information, and I was told that this might be the right place to find it."

He waited patiently for me to continue, grinning slightly.

"I'm working on my thesis, you see—mathematics. And I've come up against a problem that requires some more specialized volumes. Related to astronomy. The alignment of stars. A particular set of stars, actually." I swallowed. "Known as Ancient Ones?"

His grin faltered briefly. When restored, it had a forced appearance, as if taking every ounce of his strength to maintain.

"The field is rather obscure. It's perfectly fine if you cannot offer any help. I may have to search quite a long time before I find what I need."

It was my turn to wait. In the silence that followed, I saw his eyes dart around the store, as if following a bird in flight. When he finally did speak, his tone was very business-like.

"This place is usually slow for the first hour. How about we sit down and you can explain a bit more about what you're looking for. Coffee?"

I didn't expect the offer, but welcomed a cup. He walked into a back room, giving me a moment alone. The exchange had been awkward for the both of us. I found myself wishing for the first time to not go any further down the rabbit hole of this unfathomable nightmare. I considered leaving quickly, before he returned, but made the mistake of looking around. That sealed my fate. The store was filled with beautiful, solidly bound volumes of all shapes and sizes. The subject matter ranged wildly—fiction, reference, history, biology, religion. There were several first editions of Poe displayed nearby over which I stopped to marvel.

A minute later he returned, carrying a tray with milk, sugar and two filled cups. He set it on the counter and we sat down on a pair of stools.

"Now," he said. "This problem of yours."

I spoke carefully, determined not to trip on my words.

"It is not so much a problem, as it is…an academic curiosity. During the course of my research, a number of questions have come across my desk whose answers require knowledge that neither I, nor my advisers in the department possess. Purely theoretical, of course. Nothing practical. But my thesis depends on such answers."

He nodded and sipped his coffee, lowering the mug slowly to the tabletop before speaking.

"No."

"I'm sorry?"

"I can assure you," he said, "your problem is more practical than you know."

The hair on the back of my neck bristled.

"I think maybe you're confused. I only meant—"

"I learned a lot from my grandfather over the years. He was an extremely aloof man, forming only the barest of relationships with anyone. I can't mourn him, but I can say that I'll miss being able to rely on his knowledge."

He leaned forward and lowered his voice slightly.

"Though the Ancient Ones may seem only theoretical, they are in fact quite real. And whatever it is that they are—they are not stars."

Despite the ominous implications, his words cut through my skeptical defense. This man knew something. I was sure of it. Just how much, I would find out soon enough.

"So then," he said. "Your real problem, if you please."

As I conquered my embarrassment, he grabbed his mug and took another sip.

"A few days ago, I proposed marriage to the love of my life," I began. "Her name was Elizabeth Wentworth. She accepted my proposal. Then, only hours later, I watched helplessly as she burned to death in front of a hearth in the boarding house in which I live."

A mist had begun to form in my eyes and I blinked it back, the mention of Elizabeth still too much for me to handle. My host nodded his head, concern written into his features.

"I tried to extinguish the flames, but in the space of a minute, she was *completely* consumed."

With that statement Mr. Cooke put down his coffee.

"Only a small pile of ash remained. But even that eventually disappeared—evaporated. I, however, was completely unharmed by the fire. My mentor suggested that it may not have been mere happenstance. He made mention of things heretofore unknown to me which may be connected to her death, but in lieu of providing further help, he directed me here."

"I am truly sorry for your loss."

"Thank you. This week has been beyond difficult."

He stood then, and checked the contents of a few shelves.

"I've heard of the phenomenon you describe," he said as he sat back down. "It is known as spontaneous human combustion. Unfortunately, I currently have no books here that even mention the topic. It might take some time, but I could search around. My grandfather constructed quite a large network of contacts over the years to which I have access."

"Thank you," I said. "Whatever you can find would be greatly appreciated."

"But," he said, then stopped himself. "I'm sorry, I probably should not ask. But I am curious—too curious for my own good, perhaps. It will be the death of me."

"I'm beginning to understand the feeling."

He smiled briefly at this, as did I. It felt good, after all that had happened, to smile. Especially in the presence of another.

"What is it that made your mentor connect your fiancée's...unfortunate demise with the Ancient Ones?"

"I don't really know how much I can tell you. Much of the information that he related to me was in confidence."

"Just tell me as much as you're comfortable with."

I managed to summarize it into something coherent.

"The professor was asked by a colleague to mathematically analyze some information from a few ancient sources," I began. "After doing so, he came to the conclusion that the data predicted that a certain occurrence was coming to pass. An event. An alignment of stars, somehow associated with these Ancient Ones. The timing of Elizabeth's death coincided eerily with that event."

We sipped at our coffee. For several minutes, he appeared to be lost in thought.

"Mr. Adderly."

"Please, call me Robert."

"Robert," he said. "As I mentioned, finding information on spontaneous human combustion will be difficult, but not impossible. The Ancient Ones, however, are a different story. Books of that nature are sprinkled sparingly around the globe. Were we anywhere else in the world, I would suggest you give up your search before it drives you mad. Are you aware, however, that your very own Miskatonic University is home to an extensive collection of such volumes?"

"I recently learned that."

"You should plan on taking advantage of it. During the course of his life, my grandfather had access to some of them. He took copious notes when he could, sometimes transcribing several consecutive pages. But the sum of it all is nothing compared to an entire text. You may examine those pages if you wish. I keep them in the back. I haven't had much time to look deeply into them yet. But between the two of us, we may be able to learn something."

It was the first piece of heartening news I had received since the loss of my Elizabeth, and I momentarily allowed myself to feel relief. But it was short lived, as Andrew abruptly stood and walked to the front door, turning the lock on the knob and securing the chain. When he turned back toward me, his face was furtive. I honestly could not imagine the reason for locking the door, and I grew a little concerned. He returned to his seat at the table, leaning close and gesturing for me to do the same.

"I do not intend for this to be made public knowledge," he said. "But my grandfather, Bertram Hunt, was for all intents and purposes…a magician. As am I."

He seemed to need my reaction before continuing. But after the things that Professor Josephson had revealed to me, his admission didn't have the effect he seemed to expect.

"You needn't be concerned," I said. "Recently my eyes have been opened to…the possibility of…a great many things. I am still trying to come to terms with it all, though."

He seemed to relax.

"Of course," he said. "I must say I was a trifle reticent to admit what I just did. There are few people willing to think beyond the teachings of traditional science—or those of the Bible, for that matter."

"But what is science if not the search for answers?"

"Precisely," he said. "Now, I hope you will continue in your open-mindedness when I say that the other thing that I can offer you is the chance to communicate with your dead fiancée."

Mentally, mine was a reflexive reaction, the years of teachings putting me on the defensive: *Do not turn to mediums or seek out spiritists, for you will be defiled by them.* I must have started as well though, betraying my thoughts, as he swiftly tried to reassure me.

"I have done it before," he said. "In fact, the more recent the death, the easier the ceremony is to perform. All you need is an item that belonged to her. Ideally, it would contain some sweat or blood, but that is not absolutely necessary. Might you have a letter from her? It would have to be burned, I'm afraid. And of course, it would have to be after business hours, some evening."

"You can't be serious."

"I am quite serious."

I felt myself starting to get upset.

"I sincerely appreciate you allowing me to examine your private notes," I said, then cleared my throat. "But please, Mr. Cooke, do not insult my intelligence."

He was genuinely surprised.

"What do you mean?" he said. "You just admitted to accepting the existence of magic. Why—?"

"She is dead," I said, my voice lowering to a near whisper. "She is dead, and I wish it were not so, but it is. It is."

He sighed, lowering his own voice to match mine.

"Mr. Adderly, I am sorry," he said. "Obviously I have offended you. I did not mean to."

"Perhaps I should be going," I said, standing up. "I shall be in touch if I have need of your services."

My abrupt pronouncement seemed to have caught him off guard. But he regained his composure, and also stood.

"Of course," he said. "I shall be right here if you need...if you would like to speak about this further."

He then escorted me to the door.

I walked home in a daze. A hundred thoughts raced through my mind. Was what he proposed possible? If I believed the professor's story of a man cheating death and transforming into a gruesome, not-dead thing, could not a soul be reached from beyond? Did not the Lord God gather the souls of the saved in heaven? Could He not allow for such communication? Supposing it was even possible, there remained the question of Andrew Cooke. It was perfectly conceivable he was a fake, who would demand payment up front before staging some sort of charlatan act. Alternately—and more likely, based upon my initial impressions of him—he could just be deceiving himself into believing that he is a powerful wizard of the highest order, able to conjure fantastic spells, when in fact he would be completely impotent. The very idea of being able to speak with Elizabeth filled me with an incredible anticipation. And yet even then, I also felt myself gnawed by a subtle fear.

During lunch that afternoon, I was finally approached by one of the other boarders. Throughout the past week, I had formed the distinct impression that the other men in the building were avoiding me purposely. That feeling was confirmed and clarified when Mr. Dunderhill first sat down beside me. The glare Mrs. Bettings gave him transformed into a smile the second she saw that I was watching her. I knew then that she, God bless her soul, must have ordered the other tenants to not pester me about Elizabeth's death. In that building, her word was law. After a tentative start, Mr. Dunderhill and I ended up having a normal conversation about the weather, the neighborhood, the death of Mr. Hunt, and yes, Elizabeth. Though it was still difficult for me to speak of, it was a relief to have at least this small aspect of my life returning to normal, to once again feel part of society.

With Mr. Dunderhill having risked the wrath of our landlady and broken the ice, dinner that evening was a pleasant affair. When we were all sated, random bits of small talk turned into a debate on baseball. Most of the men were enthusiastic about it, and guessed at how long it would take the Red Sox to win another championship. As per usual, Mr. Dunderhill took the opportunity to complain about the Babe Ruth trade, and bitterly suggested, "A hundred years!"

Everyone laughed. Even I found the notion ludicrous.

"Mark my words," he insisted. "It'll be the next century before they win it again."

At that, the conversation turned to batting, pitching, fielding. I knew statistics, of course, but not as applied to that game. There were too many names being discussed, and I recognized only a scant few. Losing interest, I turned to Mr. Pfenniger, a German immigrant who had lost his family in the War.

"I understand that game not," he confided to me. "It is…"

He waved his hands, trying, and failing, to convey a concept to me.

"Langweilig," he said finally, unable to find the English word.

I nodded sympathetically, pretending to know what he was getting at.

As we sat and listened to the others, he took out a cigar and a match. Even before he struck it, my gaze was focused on that tiny match, my heart pound with an unknown trepidation. Days before, I had proven to myself that a small flame can cause a burn if stupid, stubborn persistence is applied—but that burn would be nothing more than a red mark and some lingering pain. My fear of fire had been overcome.

What, then, was the problem?

The moment it flared, I knew. I tried to not appear alarmed, but excused myself and went into the kitchen for a glass of water. I drank deeply, then allowed myself to consider the horrifying insight. It was simply this: I was terrified that, upon speaking with Elizabeth, she would accuse me of letting her burn to death.

I was afraid of discovering that she might hate me.

That night in bed, sleep did not come. Sick with worry, I turned on the light and pulled out the box of her letters stored beneath my bed. I picked out and re-read a few at random. Slowly, her words comforted me. It was plain that she had loved me. There could never be room for any hatred in her heart.

On and on I went, stopping when I found the one that she had written after our first night together. There was no postage on it. She had hand-delivered it to me, unable to trust the postman, or Mrs. Bettings, or anyone else who might come into contact with it. She seemed to be afraid that our new secret might be revealed just by touching the paper. I read it again and again, until the words were burned into my brain.

I fell asleep with it still in my hand.

EIGHT

Despite all that had happened, my world continued to spin—though not smoothly, to be sure. I lazed around the following morning, conflicting priorities pulling me in opposite directions: one being the burning curiosity regarding the bizarre mysteries confronting me, the other, the reality of a thesis that needed to be finished. For the latter, the aid of Professor Josephson was needed. It was time to meet with him as he had asked. Knowing that his usual schedule would keep him busy until about noon, I had some free time.

Still trying to decide upon the validity of Andrew Cooke, his recommendation, at least, seemed to be worth exploring. Late morning, I made my way to the university library. In a back corner of the first floor, hidden behind a maze of bookcases, were the history and archaeology sections. I had never had a need to visit this area of the building, and did not recognize the desk clerk; I hoped he would not know me either. He stood sorting books in a cart beside the counter. The subject matter and questionable reputation of the tomes made me wonder: If I were to simply ask, would I be told that I was mistaken, that no such books existed? I decided to bluff.

"Good morning, sir," he said as I approached. "Can I help you with something?"

"You may be able to, yes," I said quickly. "I am aware that the university has several ancient volumes stored here. I require access to one of them: The *Necronomicon* of Abdul Alhazred."

Arms folded, I stood there, awaiting an answer.

"That one…" He consulted a sheet of paper on the desk. "Yes, that one is on the list. Do you have written permission?"

"Permission? Why do I need anyone's permission? This is a library."

"It's a relatively new policy. That particular volume can only be viewed with written permission from either the Director of the Library, Doctor Trautmann, or Doctor Gardiner of the Archaeology Department."

I tried my best to not let my façade falter.

"I spoke with Doctor Gardiner only a week ago or so. I work with a collaborator of his. He has given me permission. For research purposes."

"Be that as it may, I need to see it in writing."

I allowed irritation to creep into my voice.

"At that point, nothing was actually written down. But I can go back to his office right now and bring that back for you."

"Doctor Gardener was called away within the past few days and is traveling abroad at the moment," he said.

That statement took the wind out of my sails. We stood in silence.

"Doctor Trautmann's office is on the third floor of this building," he offered, returning to his sorting. "You may schedule an appointment with his secretary."

"Very well," I replied, trying not to sound annoyed. "Thank you for your help."

I walked away as casually as possible, stopping to grab a copy of the small university newspaper from a stack near the stairwell. There was a strong smell of ink; they had been newly printed. My eyes passed over the headlines, but nothing registered while I paused to think. Lying had never been my strong suit. I had heard of Doctor Trautmann, but could not recall what he looked like; we had certainly never been introduced. Was access to the books worth the effort?

I tucked the newspaper beneath my arm and climbed the two flights. Viewed from the outside, the topmost story of the building was significantly smaller than the other two, as if it had been added on as an afterthought. Inside, from the third-floor landing, the entire layout of this much smaller level was revealed. More than half of the available floor space was simply a large, open area with several desks, most of them unoccupied. The few people present were busy writing, typing, or filling out paperwork. Set into the far wall were two pairs of ornate double doors. The ones on the left were open, revealing a large, empty conference room. The ones on the right were closed.

I assumed that the woman seated at the largest desk in the open area was the secretary of Doctor Trautmann. She looked to be in her fifties, and her appearance—hair, nails, and clothing—was immaculate. I approached her, continuing to play the same character, but taking care to be more polite.

"Good morning," I greeted her.

"Good morning," she replied coolly. "Can I help you?"

"Yes. I am aware that the university has a copy of an ancient volume—the *Necronomicon* of Abdul Alhazred—in this building. I was directed to obtain written permission from Doctor Trautmann in order to view it. I have already spoken with Doctor Gardiner and he has given me verbal permission, but as he is currently abroad, he cannot provide it in writing. So, if Doctor Trautmann has a few minutes—"

"Doctor Trautmann is a very busy man."

"Of course," I said, trying to sound patient. "This is not an urgent request."

She looked back at me, obviously irritated, then began paging through an appointment book spread before her.

"Next Wednesday at eleven o'clock is available."

"Next Wednesday?"

"Eleven o'clock."

I sighed.

"Be here promptly," she said.

Professor Josephson was in his office when I arrived. The door was wide open.

"Good afternoon, Professor," I said as I entered and seated myself. I placed my briefcase on the floor beside my chair, and set the folded newspaper on the professor's desk.

"Hello, Robert," he replied. "All went well in Boston, I hope?"

"As well as could be expected."

"Good. I realize that you're likely still reeling, and will be for some time, but I wanted to meet with you to ensure that you would have something upon which to focus." He cleared his throat. "I know that I was able to distract myself and take some comfort in my work after my wife died some years ago."

He handed me a sheet of paper.

"I drew up a list of classes you will be required to complete for your degree. As you can see, there are not many. I feel that your comprehension of the basic theoretical principles is superb. These final ones will fill in the few gaps in your knowledge."

"Thank you," I said, smiling at his praise.

"The reason why I am requiring the lesser course load is so that you have plenty of time to correctly *apply* those concepts in your thesis. After reviewing and evaluating your progress this past semester, I must also recommend that you dig deeper. Your current work, as it stands, is too broad. You must both narrow your scope, and create something that is uniquely your own."

"I understand, Professor. I did think of a few approaches I can take. We can discuss the merits of each after I take some time to evaluate them better."

"Good. Did you have any questions for me?"

The way he asked that—with an odd emphasis on the word *questions*—made me wonder if he meant my thesis, or my new extracurricular interest. With the subject at hand being my thesis, I saw no need to muddy the waters by bringing up anything else.

"Not right now, no."

When I stood up to leave, he moved around to meet me. I grabbed at the newspaper I had left on the desk, but instead knocked it onto the floor. It opened up to display a headline that was impossible for either of us to ignore.

ARCHAEOLOGIST MISSING

Our very own Doctor Quentin Gardiner, head of the Department of Archaeology, has been officially declared missing. Doctor Gardiner traveled to Guyana last week to study a site that had just recently been uncovered due to a landslide induced by heavy rains. Those same rains also threatened to destroy the site, and so, with time of the essence, he departed posthaste. Unfortunately, the worst occurred shortly after his arrival there, the unstable area being struck by a second slide. The search for Doctor Gardiner's group has begun.

The university would like to remind the entire Arkham community that *missing* is not the same as *dead*. As long as the search continues, please keep all involved in your thoughts and prayers.

In the silence that followed, the professor kept a hand on the desk as he slowly backed to his chair. We both sat down heavily. When he spoke, voice hollow, his mind was far away.

"He…We had a lunch appointment. He broke it on short notice. He tried to explain where and why, but I didn't let him. It was his affair, and I sensed some…reticence from him. He said South America, and we left it at that."

"Professor," I said. "This can't be a coincidence. Can it?"

"I'm sorry, I'm…I'm not following."

"Do you think it possible this has something to do with the stars? The alignment?"

He was still in the grip of shock, face blank.

In a whisper, but with emphasis, I said, "The Ancient Ones."

At those words, he blinked. The stupor was gone. I could see his mind whirling, considering the data, working through probabilities.

"It's possible," he said. "But you must realize that Quentin Gardiner was, first and foremost, a committed archaeologist. Any significant find would have demanded his presence."

The professor sat silently. Able to offer nothing else, I was ready to leave him alone, when he spoke up once again.

"However, there are few true coincidences," he said. "Things happen for a reason, whether caused by the hand of man, God, the Devil…or the Ancient Ones."

I don't know if he meant it so, but I took his words as a prompt.

"Professor, regarding your suggestion to me that I contact Bertram Hunt…"

"Yes?"

"That's no longer possible. He died last week. While I was in Boston."

He was clearly stunned by the news.

"This is a disturbing set of events."

For me, it was disturbing in more ways than one, as I

remembered Mr. Hunt's final words to me.

"However, I did manage to contact his *grandson* who has inherited the bookstore. He is willing to provide some help, as you said Mr. Hunt might have."

"That is…reassuring. I had hoped to rid myself of involvement in things of this nature, but I may have to contact Higgins." He frowned. "Did you…Did you make any progress on those equations?"

"Nothing so far, no."

"Of course. The past week has been awful for you. I think it would be unwise to spend too much time on them. But—" He paused. "But consider the time I first showed them to you. Those matrix transformations I employed to reduce the complexity?"

I nodded.

"That is an example of the *application* of principles I would like to see in your thesis. Yes. That is an excellent example."

Surprised by his change of attitude, I readily agreed.

"I see. So…I should use them as a…mental exercise. To get me to think differently, and be creative. Then apply that creativity to my thesis."

"Exactly."

There was an unspoken finality in that word. I think he was embarrassed. He had just given me permission to do something contrary to his previous position—though, to be clear, by no means was it an enthusiastic endorsement to do so.

Our business concluded, I rose to leave.

"Professor, is next Wednesday a good day to have our review?"

"Yes, that should be fine," he said distractedly. "At about this time. Good afternoon, Robert."

NINE

I arrived at the front door of Hunt's Fine Books that evening shortly after six o'clock, and knocked three times. The store was dark, and I could detect no movement. I had the opportunity to turn around, go back to the boarding house and forget all about this. I could review my thesis. I could do anything else. But I stayed. Then I saw a shadow approach the door from the far corner of the room. When Andrew Cooke opened the door, he wore a satisfied grin.

"Good evening, Robert," he said "Please come in."

He led me through the darkened store, pointing out obstructions over which I might stumble. We went through a doorway at the rear of the room, then up a flight of stairs to his living quarters on the second floor. From the stairs, we emerged into a sitting room, or den, or dining room—it had elements of all three. A very comfortable-looking, but well-worn leather couch was straight ahead. Against the wall on the right, a desk was positioned between two windows. In the center of the floor was a small round table of a dark red wood, just large enough to seat four people, and hold their plates of food for dinner—*though not if Mrs. Bettings hosted it*, I thought bemusedly. To the left were two doorways, the near one leading into a bedroom, the farther one into the kitchen.

And books. Did I mention the books? Every wall was filled with shelves, every shelf packed with books, standing vertically from one end to the other. Between the tops of the texts and the shelf above them, others had been inserted horizontally into every free space. I was flabbergasted by the amount. It seemed possible there were more books in that room than were for sale in the store below.

Andrew closed the door behind us, took my coat, and hung it on a hook on the door.

"What brings you here at this hour?"

As if he didn't already know.

"As you saw from my reaction, your offer…shocked me. I think that *shocked* is the right word. It was both repulsive and tempting at the same time, but the temptation was itself repugnant."

"Repugnant? That's a strong term. In what way?"

"I have accepted the tenets of Christianity. My parents placed my feet on that path, and I walked it. When I came of age and was able to make a choice, I stayed on that path, and I remain on it to this day. I take comfort in it. But speaking with the dead…that flies in the face of all that I have learned. I also thought…"

I choked up, hesitant to actually speak the words. Andrew waited patiently. When I did speak, the syllables were vomited from my mouth.

"Given the opportunity to speak with Elizabeth, I was afraid I would learn that she hated me for not saving her."

"I see. And despite all that, you've changed your mind."

"I was able to rid myself of the fear. She was just not capable of hatred such as that. And as far as a possible conflict with scripture goes: *And you will know the truth, and the truth will set you free.*"

"How utterly appropriate."

"Science is an invitation to know the truth. Physics, mathematics…as scientists we learn more and more of the truth of the universe every day. All data can be used for good or evil purposes. Professor Josephson related a fantastic story to me about a dead man returning to life, which I'm still trying to come to terms with. But in that case, the evil was obvious and prevalent. Our case also involves death, but after examining it forwards and backwards, I cannot see any aspect of evil in this. I cannot see the harm. We are seeking truth through the use of no tool of the Devil. Magic is just another science provided by God."

When I had finished speaking, his head was nodding slowly up and down, as if to affirm my words. Then, without warning, he stood from the table and walked into the kitchen. He returned with a clear glass vase, a box of matches, and a stick of chalk. He put the vase and the matches down on the table in front of me, then got down on hands and knees, and began to draw something on the wooden floor, moving in a slow circle around the table and chairs, until he popped back up where he'd begun. He then took a seat at the table, and invited me to do the same.

"Please notice the circle I have just drawn on the floor," he said. Not only did it encompass both the table and us, but its edges sported an intricate, curlicue design, reminiscent of spring shoots off a young tree. "Under no circumstances will you place any part of your body outside of that boundary during the ceremony. This is very important. I will inform you when it is safe to do so."

The edge of the circle was fully two feet behind the back of my chair, so I did not feel the least bit nervous about coming anywhere near it. I nodded my understanding.

"What we are about to do is open a gate between this world and the spirit world," he said. "We will be specifically requesting the presence of the spirit of Elizabeth, but it is possible that something else will notice the gateway and attempt to pass through. Please do not worry. You will be safe. The other entities cannot come through unless we invite them, or provide a bridge from our world to theirs by compromising the integrity of the circle. For the duration of the ceremony, everything within the circle, ourselves included, will no longer reside entirely in this realm. We will be transported to a nether-region, an in-between place where both material and spirit worlds can co-exist. You have something of hers?"

I removed the letter from my shirt pocket and handed it to him. He unfolded it, then rolled it up, and twisted it tightly. When he

90

placed it in the vase on the table, I noticed that it actually held some small amount of fluid. He tapped the vase with a finger.

"This is a special oil. At the moment it is odorless and color-less—nearly invisible. Your letter will be lit and will act as a wick. While the wick is burning, the fluid will change properties. It will become multi-colored, many-scented."

He closed his eyes and took several deep breaths.

"I am nearly ready," he said solemnly. "First, I shall invoke the power of the circle to protect us, then I shall open the gate. The wick will be lit, and soon afterward you'll feel a cold wind. This will be Elizabeth's spirit, and will concentrate over the flame. You will know when she is here. You may speak your questions, but need not, as the spirits communicate with us through our thoughts. This amount of paper will probably last for ten minutes. At that point she will depart, and I shall conclude the ceremony. Do you have any questions?"

I hadn't expected things to proceed so quickly. But there was no turning back now.

"Please begin," I said.

He chanted for perhaps a minute in what I thought was Latin. When he stopped, I felt my skin begin to tingle. The room became unnaturally quiet. Not long before, sounds from the surrounding neighborhood had drifted through the relative silence of the room—children playing, a dog barking. Now there were none. All I could hear was the echo of my heart hammering away in my chest, the blood rushing through my veins.

After a short pause, Andrew once again started chanting. I listened more closely this time, and positively identified the language as Latin, but with the addition of a great many proper names that were unknown to me. The room outside of the circle took on a distant quality, as if a water glass had been upended over us, trapping us beneath it. Everything appeared somewhat transparent, ghostly.

A painting that hung on the wall behind Andrew became blurred, and I could see the wall behind the painting.

There was another short pause, and then he picked up a match, and struck it. I held my breath as the flame touched the paper. A large flame erupted from the vase, and the oil became a vibrant, prismatic mixture of colors, constantly flowing and shifting. The aromas that assailed my nostrils were just as varied as the colors: orange, jasmine, rose, vanilla. Uncountable others. Even as I inhaled and tried to analyze the scent, it would shift, transforming smoothly from subtle mocha, to pungent garlic, to the salty smell of sea air.

I tried to ignore the overwhelming sensory input by closing my eyes and breathing through my mouth. With my heart threatening to burst from my chest in anticipation, I concentrated on clearing my mind. Calming myself. Several minutes went by as I awaited the cool wind that would announce Elizabeth's presence. When nothing noticeable happened, I opened my eyes. Andrew was clearly confused. He motioned for me to be still, and we sat there looking at each other, watching the flame slowly consume the letter. From time to time I looked around, or listened, or tried to otherwise detect the presence of Elizabeth. She was not there. At last, with the paper gone, the flame extinguished itself.

Before I could make a sound, Andrew motioned for me to remain silent. He chanted in Latin again, and the odd sensation of being visually separated from the rest of the room disappeared. Another short, Latin phrase, and the sounds of the outside world once again intruded upon us.

"I'm sorry," he sighed.

"What happened? I don't understand."

"I don't either. I performed the rite correctly. Her spirit should have come to us the moment the letter was lit. But nothing happened."

His voice faded out and he stared off into space.

Frowning, I rubbed my eyes and leaned back in my chair. After all of this, all the fear and anxiety and painful excitement—it looked as if I had been right all along. Thankfully, no money had changed hands. I had only wasted time, but I was still upset at my gullibility. I had allowed wishful thinking to influence my logic and my faith. Magic, as he believed in it, was not possible.

His self-confidence, though…He clearly had convinced himself he was capable of communicating with the dead. So there was no dishonesty here. It was just disillusionment. His parlor tricks had certainly been impressive, but they did not help me in the least. There was no reason to stay there any longer. I needed to step back and re-evaluate the events of the past week.

"I should be going," I said, standing up. "If you—"

"No!" he shouted, leaping to his feet so rapidly that his chair nearly tipped over backwards. His movement was so jarring I nearly raised my fists in defense.

"Wait!" he said. "I've performed this ceremony before. In every case the outcome is *always* the same. There is no reason for it to have failed like that! None!"

I froze at his outburst, aware of the delicate balance of tension in the room. Might he become violent if I were to voice any disbelief? I looked at the door, measuring the relative distances. His head now hung in shame, turned away from me. Right then, I could have escaped. Or simply left; he may not even have chased me. But just as had occurred earlier outside the front door, I didn't move. The sincerity of his reaction gave me pause.

"What can be done?" I asked hesitantly.

We stood in stalemate, each waiting for the other to react, until suddenly, his head snapped to attention, as if a light bulb had gone on somewhere in his mind.

"I know! I'll prove it to you. We must determine why Elizabeth did not answer her summons. We will call upon the spirit of my grandfather."

"Bertram Hunt?" I was cowed by the thought.

"He was a voracious reader, and knew a great deal more than I. For whatever reason, spirits called in this manner are compelled to be truthful. If he knows, he'll tell us."

When he went into his bedroom, I looked at the door again, feeling that there was more than enough time to race out of the building and not look back. I paused, though. There was still within me the desire to see this through. Still tottering with indecision, I wondered what to believe. I needed answers: proof, disproof, something. And for some reason, I had not yet fully lost faith in this strange, excitable man. Another few minutes, then. I would give him one more chance.

He returned holding a clear glass beaker with a tight-fitting glass stopper. The container seemed to be empty until he removed the stopper, and poured more of the near-invisible fluid into the vase on the table. After placing the beaker on the desk, he located a notebook, and began paging through it.

Though I was still not fully convinced I would be faced that evening with the spirit of my fellow boarder Mr. Hunt, something had been weighing on me since my first meeting with Andrew. I needed to tell him.

"Andrew," I said slowly, "before you begin, there is something you should know."

The heaviness of my voice caught his full attention. He stopped what he was doing and looked at me.

"I am hesitant to admit this," I said, "but your grandfather and I had a brief conversation within a week of his death. It was not pleasant."

"What happened?"

"I have no idea what may have triggered it," I said honestly. "But he stated, in no uncertain terms, that he wished to see me dead.

Also, he did not wish to speak to me again before his own death, which he predicted to be forthcoming shortly. It was only days later that he died."

"That is very strange, indeed," he said softly, returning his attention to the notebook. "Although, based on his background, I can believe quite easily that he knew the time of his death beforehand."

Andrew turned a page, another, then stopped and looked up at me.

"It's odd you should mention that. He would make the strangest comments sometimes, or look pityingly at people. I remember being on the receiving end of that more than once."

He looked down at the page he had turned to, and tore it out with a snap of his wrist.

"It was not an endearing habit, as you might imagine."

He rolled it up and twisted it in the same manner as before, then placed it in the vase. He took his seat, prepared himself, and began the rites once again. Just as before, my skin tingled as silence enveloped us. He spoke again, and again we seemed to become disconnected from the room, which became phantasmal.

Once again, the match, the flame, the onslaught of colors and scents. I hardly had time to notice them however, because this time something very different occurred. A frigid wind appeared from nowhere, blowing from every direction. Yet the flame was undisturbed. After ten or fifteen seconds the wind died down, but the coolness remained.

Andrew cleared his throat.

"Grandfather, it is I, Andrew," he said, his voice taking on a more booming quality than I had heard before. "I have with me Robert Adderly."

The outpouring of hatred that I received then was so strong and shocking that my heart skipped a beat. I gasped and recoiled, nearly losing my balance as the chair tipped backward. Luckily, I caught the edge of the table, and pulled myself flat again. If Andrew had noticed my plight, he seemed unaffected.

"Not long ago, we tried to contact the spirit of his dead fiancée, Elizabeth Wentworth. But the attempt did not work. Can you tell us why?"

A pressure in my head, and a boiling sensation behind my eyes, formed into three short, animosity-filled words, directed at me:

SHE IS NOT!

I put my hands to my ears, but to no avail, for the words were not sounds. The flame, which had been burning steadily, abruptly increased in intensity tenfold. The paper was consumed in no time. The winds lasted only seconds; the ensuing silence was breathtaking.

I was left shaking. Andrew also had to compose himself before speaking the words to end the ceremony. In a minute, the sights and sounds of reality were restored.

"Robert, I'm sorry," he said, a note of sadness in his voice, "that you had to be on the receiving end of my grandfather's wrath."

I laid my head upon the table, and tried to calm myself.

"What of his answer?" I asked into the table's surface. "She is not what? What sort of an answer is that?"

"Unfortunately," he said sadly, "it is the only one that makes sense. I should have known, even before I asked. She is not: She does not exist."

"Of course she does not exist. She is dead."

"No," he said, shaking his head. "That's not what he meant. There's a difference between the two. She does not exist, living *or* dead. Somehow her spirit has been…erased. The reason we received no response from her, is because there is no bit of her anywhere to respond."

I lifted my head and looked at him, dumbfounded.

"I'm sorry," he said. "But she is truly gone."

TEN

On the scale of devastation, or morale, once the limit is reached, how does one go past it? Is there a point lower than the lowest? An even-more-impossibly difficult? There must be. Somehow, I had breached that barrier, and sunk to a point far below where any sunlight could go. Enveloped in the darkness of the night, it felt so, anyway.

But in the morning, the rays did stream in through the window and touch my face. That warmth was a reassuring thing to feel, but only served to remind me how alone I was. The past hours spent in fitful sleep, there had been only numbness; now, my thoughts were coherent once again, but not the least bit pleasant.

It is admittedly a poor thing for one yet living—and as young as I had been at the time—to consider, but my own death was foremost in my mind. After Elizabeth's death, I had taken some small consolation in the belief that she and I would be reunited in Heaven. We had pledged ourselves to each other; a ceremony is a necessity for human society, but spiritually, it had been done. Now, though...that was no longer possible. She was forever gone, and I was alone.

But how is it possible for a soul to be wiped from existence? Once again, I was confronted with a concept that contradicted my system of beliefs. It was maddening, even somewhat infuriating. Again, it seemed as if I was being *forced* to make a choice. For one, I could accept the fact of her surreal death, ignore all of the mysteries associated with it, take comfort in my faith, and move on with my life. Or, I could dig. I could dig down deeply and unearth the hidden truth behind some or all of it: definitely the hows, perhaps also the whys. At the end of it, having employed science to get answers, I might still have my faith as an anchor. I *might.* I also might not. That was a frightening unknown.

Round and round in a circle I went all that morning, thinking, thinking, and unable to muster desire for any sort of activity. And where exactly does a circle like that end? In that house, it ends when a concerned Mrs. Bettings knocks on the door. Because I did not go downstairs for breakfast, she visited at lunchtime, and inquired as to my health. I told her that I felt under the weather. When she offered to bring a sandwich up to my room, I declined, stating that I would be downstairs before much longer.

I needed to make a decision. But before facing the world, I also needed to wash up and shave. I began there, hoping that those simple, physical actions would help me concentrate. My thoughts gelled while I looked at myself in the mirror. The fact of the matter was that I was still alive, and even if I had communicated with Elizabeth the previous evening, the inescapable reality of her death would yet remain. We would still be separated, and to one of the living, was there truly a difference between death and total obliteration? The events of the previous evening had changed nothing: She was still gone; I still lived. It was difficult to absorb, but that acknowledgement allowed me to conquer the despair. With the negativity gone, the choice of whether to bury my head in the sand or dig into the mysteries was easier.

I would dig. As well as I could, I would dig—but on my own. Andrew had access to information that I needed, but actively involving him further did not seem like a good thing to do. It would be selfish of me to use him in this venture. I decided to reimburse him for his efforts and remain on friendly terms.

Mrs. Bettings' lunch had an oddly energizing effect on me. Different problems demanded my attention, but there were priorities, and so my thesis came first. I found and reworked a flawed section, then made a few notes about how to zero in on something uniquely my own. But they were only notes, and none of them inspiring. I ran out of ideas, and my notes became meaningless scratch marks and scribbles. I needed to be creative, and thought that perhaps the professor's equations would provide a spark.

The matrix transformations he had applied were clearly correct. It was not a trivial task to work through them, but I arrived again and again at the same answer as he. As far as creativity goes, there was no inspiration to be found there: He had done the logical thing, and correctly, and I could think of no other methods to apply.

To the endpoints, then, the source of his frustration. The equations clearly described an asymptotic behavior, such as when a tangent approaches closer and closer to infinity without ever reaching it. But instead of a simple two-dimensional line drawn on sheet of paper, a path through five dimensions was described! Because of the complexity, the curve *seemed* to be non-linear, varying unpredictably—but no. It was simply the fact that the human mind was incapable of picturing the path it traced through those multiple dimensions.

Multiple dimensions! That was the angle I needed! New ideas sprouted. Working past midnight with a drive long absent, I made prodigious notes for Professor Josephson's review. I sketched out four options, with pros and cons for each. At least three seemed to be promising. The following morning, I reviewed my work and fleshed it out further. When finished, I felt very satisfied, having accomplished several days' work in the space of about one. I was now ready for the next meeting with the professor and could spend the next few days however I pleased.

When I entered the bookshop that afternoon, Andrew was busy in the reference section, speaking with a pair of older women. I waited for him to finish in the small section on mathematics, browsing through a text on algebra. I found it amusing. Having displayed my talent with numbers at an early age, my father had tutored me in the subject before I had even taken it in school: *Solve for x.* What a simple concept. But something about that tickled my mind. I could sense an answer for some unasked question forming.

"Hello," said Andrew as he approached me from behind.

At the sound of his voice, whatever had been forming dissipated. I put the book down and turned to greet him. He wore a large, toothy grin.

"Hello," I said. "You seem to be in good spirits."

"Those two women were commissioned to buy a set of encyclopedias for a very wealthy family. Naturally I sold them the finest volumes that someone else's money could buy."

He winked at me and chuckled.

"Now," he said, clapping his hands together. "To business. I realize that the events of the other night were shocking, to say the least, but I anticipated that you would want to continue in your search for answers. I've arranged some materials in the back for you to begin your search. I warn you, it's quite dense—"

"Andrew, thank you for your offer, really, but I hadn't planned—"

"—finished with what's back there, there's plenty more—"

I cut him off by holding out to him the roll of bills I held in my hand. When I had counted it out that morning, it equaled almost twenty dollars, though his assistance had likely been worth more.

"What's this?" he said.

"Payment. For all of your help."

He looked down at the bills as one would a rat, then the bell over the door chimed, and a woman entered the store. Andrew walked over to her, and after a short discussion, directed her to some shelves on the left wall. She examined only two or three books before selecting one. After the transaction was complete, he helped her through the door.

"Put that away," he said, returning to where I stood. "If you so desire, you can pay me when we've finished."

"Andrew. This is my personal quest. I understand that I'm getting involved with forces beyond my comprehension, and that there's a certain amount of risk involved. If I make a mistake, I don't want to see anyone else harmed."

He shook his head.

"It will take you years of study and practice to reach the level of mastery I have—and I myself have only scratched the surface. You would need to learn all of the base knowledge—languages, symbology, mythology—that I know by rote. Have you the background? Or the time?"

He looked at me expectantly. I could only shake my head: He was right. My Latin was passable, but for the last several years, my education had been concentrated in mathematics. With him as an ally, I could make much faster progress than if I worked alone.

"I know of the risk involved," he said. "Believe me, I've known it for years. I thank you for your concern, but I've made my own decision. I would like to help you get to the bottom of this mystery."

I sighed in resignation.

"Promise me," I implored him, "that we will both be careful."

"Of course!" He sounded excited. "I have some—"

The front door opened again, and a smartly dressed gentleman entered. With a nod to me, Andrew walked over to his latest customer. Apparently, the man had only a single question, for which he received a negative answer. After the man departed, Andrew motioned for me to follow as he made his way to the rear of the store, and through the door in the back wall. An overhead light was switched on, but its feeble rays did little to dispel the darkness. Boxes were piled everywhere, quite often six or seven feet high. A small table just inside the doorway had a single wooden chair next to it.

On the table was a small stack of notebooks.

"My grandfather was generally very good about keeping notes," he said. "These ones will help provide a base to build on. I thought it might be good for you to first become familiar with the concepts, if not the details, of both magic and the forces with which we are dealing."

I pulled out the chair and sat down at the table, looking at the books laid out before me. I hardly knew where to begin.

"Think of them as reference material," he said. "But please, do not try to memorize them. It would be a waste of time. I will be—"

The front door opened again and a small group of women's voices floated back to us.

"I will be available to answer any questions you may have between customers."

He smiled and left me alone.

The rather heavy door closed with a solid thud, effectively muffling the noises of the store. The dim lighting and the silence of the room conspired to remind me of a tomb.

I listened for anything to help dispel the illusion, and found only the unsettling sounds of scurrying rats somewhere within the towering piles of boxes. With some trepidation, I looked at the notebooks sitting upon the table, notebooks penned by a man who even in death wished me ill, and I froze with indecision. After an anxious, still minute, a faint noise stirred me. Andrew and his latest customers must have made their way toward the rear of the store, for I could hear—just barely—their dull and lifeless voices penetrating the intervening wall and door. I removed the top notebook from the pile, and creaked its binding open.

That afternoon, I learned a great number of things, many of which would have made the average man pale with fear. But if any good had come from this whole ordeal, it was this: I was now much less susceptible to shock. The first of the notebooks was very old, indicated both by its raggedness, and the dates recorded within. The whole of it was filled with tables of all sorts: astrological, alchemical, astronomical, and more. There were lists of mythological deities, and their associated odors and colors. The entire thing was just as Andrew had described: A reference volume.

The second, however, was far different. In plainest terms, it was a diary. A young and extremely thorough Mr. Hunt had recorded in that book the results of his first experiments into the science of magic. Each set of initial conditions was recorded, down to the meteorological details, and even what he had eaten that day. Each outcome was described in terms of physical, mental and emotional effects. The experiments ranged from simple meditation at the start of the volume, to speaking with the dead—as we had with Mr. Hunt— at its end. I spent an untold amount of time pouring over its pages. The third notebook picked up where the second left off. As I delved deeper, it became apparent that Mr. Hunt had been working toward a goal. The detailed notes became more and more complicated, and I found myself referring back to the first notebook as a dictionary, though not always successfully. About three quarters of the way through, the entries ended abruptly, the remaining sheets being completely blank. After closer examination, it appeared that two pages following the final written page had been cleanly removed. The only clue to their content was a mysterious comment on that last page:

I have learned all that is necessary from J.F. I
know what I must next attempt.

Those initials had occurred sporadically in the second and third notebooks, but I could find no reference to a matching name. And even with all of the pages I had read, I could not determine the unspecified goal of Bertram Hunt.

The last notebook was an awful revelation: some sort of

macabre scrapbook filled with articles clipped from newspapers around the world. Interspersed among the newspaper items were handwritten sentences, paragraphs, and sometimes pages, of notes and ideas related to the information in the accompanying article. Each clipping detailed a sinister or mysterious event, but it was the added notes that chilled me.

There was a recurring set of stories in the scrapbook that spoke of incidents at sea, where frightened people encountered strange beings described as a weird amalgam of human, and either frog or fish. Others talked of people missing from seaworthy vessels in calm waters, which Mr. Hunt confidently linked to those same creatures. I saw that the stories of these encounters weren't confined to any one area, but were spread throughout the Atlantic, the Pacific, even the Indian Ocean.

The rest of the articles had no specific pattern. They spoke of gruesome, unsolved murders; strange, recurring noises in haunted forests; mysterious livestock deaths; and other bizarre occurrences too numerous to list. One in particular described the death of a man in India who was found with his skin, hair, nails, teeth and bones found whole and intact. The remainder of him—all organs, muscle, and sinew—was gone, apparently dissolved or eaten from within. The handwritten note alongside this account was simply:

Could be the work of the things I saw.

I was nearing the end of the scrapbook when I was startled by a knock at the door.

"Have you been asleep?" Andrew asked he asked as he entered the room.

"Why?" I asked. "Did I miss something? I've been reading."

"All of this time?"

"Yes."

"Good heavens, man!" he said. "It's after five o'clock! I just ushered my last customer out the door and locked up for the night."

"Five o'clock?" I asked incredulously. The day had flown.

"You must be starving."

In all that time, I hadn't felt hungry, but as soon as he mentioned food, I realized I was famished.

"Come on," he said, slapping a hand down on my shoulder. "This has been a very good day for me. Let's go out for a good meal. I know a fine restaurant just a few blocks from here. My treat."

Living as frugally as I did, I depended heavily upon Mrs. Bettings' daily meals to sustain me. But dinner was served promptly every night at five. By now, my fellow boarders would already be tucking their napkins into their shirt collars. In the time it would take me to get home, the food would be gone.

"An excellent idea," I said, standing up and stretching my bones. My eyes burned from hours of struggling to read in the dim light. As I slid the chair under the table, I happened to glance down at the open scrapbook. Andrew's entrance had interrupted my reading just as I had turned a page. The headline at the top was stunning.

"Wait!" I shouted, snatching the scrapbook from the table. Andrew followed me as I walked toward the center of the room, until I stood directly beneath the light. The words were almost too fantastic to believe, but their presence soothed my tired eyes: *Man Burnt To Nothing.*

Together, we read, horrified. Nearly forty years previously, a man in rural Britain had been completely consumed while sitting in front of a fireplace to warm himself after coming in from the cold. Three witnesses had seen him convulse, and then burst into flames. They tried, but were unable to extinguish the blaze. There was no mention of ashes, but not even one small bit of bone remained. Apparently, Mr. Hunt was unacquainted with this particular type of occurrence, and his accompanying notation read simply:

Being of flame. Salamander?

A clue at last! I laughed with joy—then nearly fainted,

lightheaded from hunger. A hand reached out to steady me.

"Andrew, do you have any more of these scrapbooks?"

"Yes," he said. "There are at least another dozen upstairs."

"A dozen? We must—"

"We must eat," he insisted firmly. "They'll be here when we get back."

He held out his hand, and reluctantly, I gave him the notebook. He closed, it and placed it on the table, then put a hand on my back and pushed me gently through the door. On the way out, he grabbed an apple from the counter, and handed it to me.

"Here," he said. "I don't want to have to carry you into the restaurant."

Before he even had the front door locked, I had the apple reduced to its core.

ELEVEN

"Robert, are you familiar with the relatively recent work of the physicist Albert Einstein?"

For a moment, I wondered if Andrew had heard my question. We were sitting in the back room at Le Bistro Paris, bent over one of the finest meals I could ever remember eating. As the waiter had moved around us, taking our orders and pouring our drinks, the conversation had been restricted to mundane matters. It was only after the man had disappeared once again into the kitchen that I posed the question that had been preying on my mind: *What was your grandfather's final experiment?*

And now he was asking me about Einstein.

"I know the name," I replied.

"He postulates that the structure of the universe consists of three spatial dimensions and one temporal dimension."

His voice dropped to a barely audible mumble, and I had to stop chewing just to hear him.

"But he is wrong," said Andrew with some authority. "There are more than three spatial dimensions. We cannot perceive the ones beyond the third, but they do exist. And our universe is embedded in those higher dimensions."

"Speak up, man," I said. "I can barely hear you over the growling of my stomach."

He glanced around the restaurant, which was mostly empty, save for a few other diners scattered on the far side of the room.

"You can never be certain of who is listening," he said quietly. "Never."

"You can't be serious," I objected. But seeing his glare, I lowered my voice to match his. "This is Arkham, not New York or Paris."

"With regard to sensitive matters such as we are investigating," he said, "always be aware of what you are saying in public. Always."

Even at a whisper, his tone was serious.

"As you may have surmised," he continued, "my grandfather discovered something that frightened him so badly he stopped his magical research."

"The notebook's missing pages," I said.

He nodded.

"He learned the magical formulae for traveling beyond our sphere and going Outside."

"Outside where?"

"Outside."

I waited for further explanation, but none came. Instead, he continued, as if what'd just said made some kind of logical sense.

"He saw something terrible while he was there. Upon returning to this sphere, he destroyed those pages. He never went into any details, and warned me not to try. I must admit that the concept of entering a higher dimension makes me a bit nervous. But at the same time…"

He trailed off.

"Have you any idea of what he saw?" I said.

"I can only guess."

"Please do. I have no idea."

He took another cautious look around the room before continuing.

"Picture the most gruesome and alien creatures that exist in nature: jellyfish, sea urchins, squid, octopi. Of the land creatures, insects and spiders can appear unearthly. Yet as gruesome as they are, these organisms are constrained by the physical laws of our universe, laws that we are coming closer and closer to fully comprehending every day. But consider how creatures may evolve and grow in a four-dimensional reality, a place we cannot even begin to conceive of, much less understand the physical laws which apply."

"Well, thank you," I said, "for providing plenty of new material for my nightmares."

"You're quite welcome." He laughed.

But his dread had begun to transfer itself to me. Alien beings that were unholy combinations of incompatible creatures filled my imagination. Though in retrospect, the things that my mind could conjure were no match for that which I would soon encounter.

The next few days proceeded much the same, in the backroom of the bookstore, skimming through Bertram Hunt's collections of newspaper clippings. My enthusiasm, high at the start of each morning, waned as the day progressed. Twice more, I came across stories pertaining to the topic of spontaneous human combustion, neither of which provided any new information. The first, concerning the death of an elderly woman from Pennsylvania, had written underneath it as a comment only a single question mark. The second described the fiery death of a young woman in Germany. Despite an incomplete knowledge of the German language, I was able to get the gist of it. The comment below it, however, was penned in English.

> *Not a salamander, demon or elemental. Still unknown.*

That, at least, was promising. It seemed as if Mr. Hunt had been just as confused by these events as I was myself. I could only hope he had eventually found the answer. If so, he may still have written it somewhere in the volumes that I had yet to search.

As time wore on, I began to notice a change in my thinking. Page after page, the articles detailed the most brutal deaths imaginable, and yet, before long, I found myself anesthetized to the horrors laid out before me. Subject matter that would have repulsed me days before became routine. There was an eerie rhythm of violence. In fact, it began to seem odd if too many pages passed between, for example, instances of corpses found missing their viscera. Mr. Hunt believed that the events described in the articles indicated the influence of the entities known as the Ancient Ones. I was skeptical at first, but by the time I reached just the midpoint of the collection, I had to admit that I was convinced. Even more importantly, the commentaries were so detailed and consistent that I was unable to refute this nearly unthinkable new fact: As far as intelligent beings go, Homo sapiens is not alone.

Once again, my belief system was shaken. Man is not the jewel of creation, the crowning achievement of God. There are fantastic, immensely powerful beings that exist, hidden in the far corners of the universe, and of our globe. There are also other alien races— mortal races—that serve and worship those Ancient Ones. They are evil—or, they are so alien that their motivations appear to humanity to be evil. Regardless, they were here on this world before us and wish to reclaim it from us.

One example of these, for example, was the amphibious race of creatures I'd read about earlier, reported to live in seas around the globe. Mr. Hunt indicated that they could breed with human beings, and produce viable offspring who can pass as human beings unless examined very closely. He said they worshipped a being known as Cthulhu, asleep in his city of R'lyeh somewhere in the deep oceans. The thing would sleep until the stars are right—thus bringing me back around to the enigmatic equations. The 'facts' all continued to reinforce each other in a consistent framework.

I found other names, such as Tsathoggua, Shub Niggurath, Hastur, Yog Sothoth, Azathoth. Of these, there were no details beyond the conjecture that these Ancient Ones were at the root of a depraved cult of worship, thereby explaining the mutilated animals and people. These god-like beings seemed to be content to accept sacrifices, and from time to time, respond to requests, but never truly interact with humanity—save for one. Nyarlathotep, though described as having a thousand-and-one forms, was reputed to be able to walk as a man among us.

Near the end of the penultimate notebook, my head aching from the dim lighting, I could not believe my good fortune when I finally found the answer for which I had been searching. The headline stated simply: *Man Burns To Death*. The story itself was almost a repeat of the first that I had found days before. My heart nearly stopped, however, when I read the two paragraphs of Mr. Hunt's notes associated with the article:

> *Found obscure Egyptian reference to "suit nebtet" or "shadow of fire." Upon entering through the eyes, victim bursts into flame. No worshipers, from what I can find. Also reasonably sure that this reference from p. 115 of the Necronomicon (Misk Univ.) describes the same thing:*

> *Of Yog-Sothoth, the Gate, for whom time and space are all and nothing, it is said that the infinite light of the demon-sultan Azathoth had cast a shadow to create Sothoth Pnath. The Shadow echoed the Gate, being part of it, yet different. Dwelling in shadow, it lived, it lives, it will live. Here and there, then and forever.*

My whoop must have been loud enough to penetrate the walls and carry out into the store, for Andrew burst into the room a few seconds later.

"You found something!"

"Mr. Hunt found it"—I looked at the date on the article—"eight years ago. Here!"

He read it over, and then looked at me with evident glee.

"My grandfather had others," he said. "Other notebooks with more detailed information. Aside from his diaries and scrapbooks, he took copious notes. We can still search through them and—"

But he was interrupted by the sound of another customer entering. I watched him through the open door as he hurried back to the middle of the store to greet a pretty young woman with long, blond hair. She stood beside the psychology section, twisting her hair around her finger. Andrew appeared nervous, motioning with his hands, and sporting an excessively wide grin. He directed her toward the front of the store, and just before following her, glanced back at me, smiling comically. I returned the look, silently wished him luck, then closed the door and leaned back against it.

For the past few days, I had been concentrating on these disturbing collections of events, and trying to come to terms with the theories of Mr. Hunt. Any thoughts of women were fleeting, nebulous. But watching Andrew interacting with his latest customer called to mind memories of my dearest, especially the dimples in her cheeks when she smiled broadly, just like the young woman beyond the door. I remember seeing them often.

I finished with the last of the scrapbooks shortly before dinnertime. When I emerged from the back room, Andrew was exchanging money with a gentleman at the front counter. I waited until the customer left to announce myself.

"I've finished with the scrapbooks," I said. "I didn't find anything else."

"That you found anything relevant is astounding."

"What I found was nothing, compared with your discovery." I

winked at him.

"My discovery?"

He was perplexed for only a moment, until he realized that I was speaking of the young woman.

"No," he sighed. "I'm sorry to say that she was in here searching for a gift for her *husband*."

"Oh, that's too bad."

"She was beautiful," he agreed. "So beautiful, in fact, I didn't think to look down at her hand."

He forced a smile.

"There will undoubtedly be others," I said, but my own words unsettled me. I knew that, for myself, it was doubtful. Could there be anyone after Elizabeth?

"May I start examining the other notebooks that you mentioned?" I asked. "On Monday, perhaps? I need to rest my eyes."

"Of course," he said. "But it's going to be much tougher from here. The remaining notebooks are written in the language of magic, filled with very specialized terms and symbols. Much is written in Latin, with a smattering of Greek, German, and French. I have a few volumes that you can use as reference, along with the initial notebook that you perused two days ago. But it will likely be very slow going."

I nodded. It was discouraging, but there was nothing to be done. I walked back into the backroom to gather my things, Andrew following closely behind me.

"Tell me," he said slowly. "Do you have any vengeance in mind?"

"Vengeance?"

He cleared his throat.

"I hadn't seriously contemplated this option until you located that information an hour ago, but consider this: The Ancient Ones, generally, are scattered across interstellar space. Typically, they do not visit our planet unless summoned. Yog Sothoth falls into that category, so it is reasonably safe to assume that its shadow, Sothoth Pnath, does also." He paused to make sure that he had my attention. "Whatever can be summoned can also be banished. Not killed, mind you, but sent away. Would you be interested in pursuing this goal?"

"You can't be serious," I said. "Banish this Sothoth Pnath from the Earth?"

"Yes, so that the fate that befell Elizabeth, as well as those others you came across, could never happen to anyone else again."

"Don't you think that goal is a bit lofty? Not to mention dangerous?" I tried to sound more logical than afraid, but I could not edit the fear out. "Learning about the Ancient Ones is one thing, but this…"

"I understand your trepidation, believe me, I do," said Andrew quite seriously. "This isn't something to attempt tomorrow, or next week, or even six months from now. I'm still learning. It's a lifelong process. But isn't it better to have a goal to work toward? Would it not feel good to thwart the devils?"

The look on his face as he spoke those words was odd, but I interpreted it as equal parts confidence and righteousness. For whatever reason, the net result was simply that I felt I could trust him. Any particle of doubt concerning his abilities or intentions that I may have continued to harbor disappeared.

"Of course, we still have no proof that this entity is the culprit."

"You're right," he said. "First we must learn. We confirm that it is, or is not, the source of the spontaneous combustion phenomenon."

"And if we have proof that it is indeed the source of my misery…"

"Then you will seriously consider the option?"

And despite an unease in my soul, I found myself nodding.

114

It was still early enough to make it home in time for Mrs. Bettings' dinner. When I arrived at the boarding house, Mr. Dunderhill was sitting at the dining table with several of the other boarders and a deck of cards. Mrs. Bettings served a modest dinner of corned beef and cabbage, and yet after my days spent in the back room of Hunt's Fine Books, it tasted as if it had come straight from the kitchens of Le Bistro Paris. When we were finished eating, we wiled away the hours playing canasta—with Mrs. Bettings soundly trouncing us all. Later that evening, the weather turned foul, and the thunderclaps accompanying the downpour kept me awake long after I lay down to sleep. But I was at least content, because for the first time since I'd lost my Elizabeth, it seemed that maybe there was something worthwhile to be done. It is said that the journey is more worthwhile than the destination, but still, for a journey to occur, a destination is necessary. Now, I had one.

In the morning I awoke to a grey, rainy day. For perhaps the first time in my life, I had no desire to go to church. I did go, but the words passed right over my ears without being heard. Faced with the existence of such aberrations of nature as I had come to learn about, there were certain things that no longer added up. I created an artificial dividing line in my mind, and tried to sort them to one side or the other. The creed of *Do unto others?* Yes, that one was kept. The concept of man having been given dominion over every living thing? That one was discarded. Some were completely set aside, with me unable to make decisions about them. In the end, I came to wonder on what day God created Cthulhu. The Bible had made no mention of *that.*

I spent the afternoon on the more practical matter of Professor Josephson's equations, bent over a pad of paper, trying every mathematical trick and transformation at my disposal, wearing my pencil closer and closer to the nub. But I made no progress of any kind—

until I realized why I was making no progress. It was very simple: Something was missing—more than one something, actually.

I found two problems. The first was that, although the transformations applied by the professor were a perfectly valid thing to do in order to reduce complexity, it gave the illusion that the line was truly straight: as he had described it, a line with knots at both ends. Far from it. The line had been forced—or approximated—to be straight via his process. In reality, the line was only *nearly* straight—very, very nearly—but not. Imagine adding two values: the number one, and one-billionth of one. For all practical, earthly intents and purposes, the fractional part can be discarded and the sum considered to be one. In the vast distances between stars, that extra one-billionth has an effect and needs to be considered. The original line is most straight at the midway point, but fluctuations do occur, and get worse nearest the ends. Lacking that extra one-billionth, the knots seem to be fantastic and unpredictable, when in fact they are not. That extra factor, if considered properly, provides a starting point for the slope of the curve, or knot, at the end.

Which brings me to the second problem: Information was missing, perhaps accidentally, perhaps not. Considering the sequence of stars making up the line, even the closest one to Earth was far, far away. The equations did not include the sun, our nearest star. Had they, the precision would increase, perhaps tremendously. Would that additional factor be enough to make a calculation accurate enough to untangle the knot? It was impossible to say. The endpoint would always appear knot-like due to it being threaded through the extra dimensions. With some small amount of hope, I tried to join the endpoints to create a circular path, by projecting the line into a higher dimension. A uniform construct, such as a circle, or anything with a predictable path, would allow for a fantastic precision. My nugget of hope grew as I labored. I was sure that was the solution!

But it failed for the same reason—the lack of a data point for our sun.

My frustration had grown to the point where I could no longer think, so I abandoned the papers, and went downstairs to sit on the back porch. The air was warm, and the rain was falling gently. I took a seat in a deceptively comfortable rocking chair, the sounds of raindrops relaxing me. I fell asleep. And dreamed.

I was walking along a beach with Elizabeth, holding her hand in mine. She wore a white wedding dress. It was night, but the full moon, low and large in the sky, provided plenty of light. We did not speak. The only sound—for a time—was of waves crashing on the shoreline. Eventually, I began to hear another sound, a roaring which grew, but she paid no attention to it. I located the source: a singularly massive wave approaching the beach. It towered above us, and I knew that the force of its impact alone might be enough to kill us, never mind drown us. I tore my eyes from the wall of water to look at Elizabeth, but she was gone. In her place stood a large stone, glossy black and polished to a mirror finish. I saw with horror that a very sturdy chain was set into the stone and that the other end of it terminated in a manacle locked to my wrist. The wave grew closer, but struggle as I might, I could not free my wrist. The crest of the wave reared up high enough to blot out the moon, and the night sky came alive, full of stars. The more I stared, the larger they grew, as if they were moving nearer. Some also jogged left or right, then back again; some undulated, their light blinking off and on; and still others swelled beyond their bounds, changing shape, some seeming even to grow limbs with claws, mouths with teeth. They took on unimaginable, sinister forms, their heavenly fire burning hot and bright. The stars! I opened my mouth to scream for Elizabeth, and the wave broke down upon me.

Suddenly, I was awake, and soaked to the skin. The drizzle had become a downpour, the winds steadily blowing the rain sideways, far enough to catch me. The rain, though—it did not wash the terrible residue of the dream from my mind. And one especially dreadful thought remained.

I bounded up the stairs. The papers were still sitting on the bed.

I shuffled through them until I found it. There, at the bottom of the translated page, that too-short list of Ancient Ones with their corresponding stars:

Hastur ~ Aldebaran

What we needed was a complete list, with each entity matched to their star, though I was truly only concerned with the one. With those starting points, we could eliminate the confounding variable—we could know immediately what it was that had caused the event, where it had struck, whether it was the thing that had killed Elizabeth. But the only one who could possibly provide that data was the author of the ancient parchment himself. All we had to do was ask him. He being dead, this was normally an impossible task.

But this was the loathsome inspiration that had occurred to me: We could! The original parchment, likely still in the office safe of Professor Josephson, could be burned, and the spirit summoned. Of course, that was out of the question. Destroying a valuable archaeological artifact was lunacy. I had to stop this. I put away the papers and tried my best to distract myself with other thoughts for the remainder of the day. After supper, I talked with the other boarders for a while, then tried reading my favorite, dog-eared volume of Poe. Still, as I lay down to sleep, the idea clung in my mind, polluting it like excrement.

The following morning, the rain had stopped, but a dense fog hung over the town of Arkham. The thick mist and cool temperature combined to produce a most unwelcome atmosphere. My journey to the bookstore, ordinarily a mindless and simple venture, became confusing and frightening. The fact that I could not see through the mist more than fifteen feet in any direction was unnerving. Familiar landmarks dissolved into formless blobs, and the fog seemed to magnify and blur common noises into unwholesome, alien resonances. Twice I stopped, sure that I was being followed, but each time was unable to either confirm or deny my suspicions. My imagination amplified the smallest mouse steps into monstrous stomps. I quickened my pace to a trot, then a run. Andrew must have opened up a few minutes early, for the door was unlocked when I arrived. I darted in, and slammed the door shut behind me. Through the store's windowed front door, I studied the thick fog as it rolled past the store. But nothing emerged—no people, no animals, no creature of any sort.

"I assume that's you, Robert," called Andrew's voice from somewhere I couldn't see.

"Yes," I shouted back. The store was seemingly empty.

"Good," he called. As I walked towards the middle of the store, I could see that the door to the back room was open. "I have something to show you."

I took off my coat, and sat down at the front table. In a few moments, he emerged from the back room carrying a notebook, presumably one of his grandfather's.

"I did some research last night and discovered this passage," he said, placing the open notebook on the table in front of me. He pointed out a specific paragraph, his finger repeatedly tapping the page. It was written in German, in a scrawl that was by now familiar to me.

"My knowledge of German is adequate, but rudimentary," I said. "You'll have to translate it for me."

Taking a seat opposite me, he cleared his throat and read aloud:

> *This is one method for dealing with those who have sinned against us. The enemy will have his eyelids cut off or sewn open. He shall sit in a chair and be restrained such that his head shall not be free to move, neither side to side, nor up and down. A fire shall burn behind him always, casting his shadow before him. The fire shall heat water to create steam enough to prevent*

119

blindness. He shall be fed and watered and cared
for, for his life is not ours. He shall sit there, for
days and weeks and months, contemplating his
shadow, until the darkness of Sothoth Pnath
emerges to consume his soul.

"My grandfather was fluent in German and French, so he usually did not take the time to translate anything that he copied in those languages. He was also very good with Latin and Greek as well, but there are some translations of those passages."

I nodded mindlessly, my head reeling with the graphic description of such awful torture. That, combined with my experiences in the fog, left me speechless.

"This one is from another of those volumes that may also be in the university's library," he said. "*Unaussprechlichen Kulten*, by Von Juntzt."

When I didn't respond, he looked almost disappointed.

"Robert, snap out of it," he said sharply. "Don't lose your nerve already. We've hardly just begun."

"No, not that," I said. "Not just that, anyway. On my way over here, I…I imagined I was being followed. I just scared myself."

"Followed?" asked Andrew, alarmed. He gazed through the front windows into the impenetrable whiteness beyond. "Did you see anyone?"

"No. There was nobody there."

He still looked concerned, so I tried to downplay the whole affair.

"The fog is unusually thick," I said. "Sounds echoed very oddly, got distorted. It just played with my imagination."

He looked through the front windows once more. With a harrumph, he stood up, and motioned for me to follow. We went into the backroom, now much brighter than it had been. On the wall above the table was mounted a new light fixture.

"I took some time yesterday to rig this up for you," he said. "It will be much easier on your eyes."

There were four books lined up on the table. I recognized one as the first notebook I had examined the week before.

"These are just a few of the general reference volumes I have on magic; you should probably start there. This one's a Latin to English dictionary. I have German and French upstairs; I'll get them for you shortly."

He pointed at a notebook sitting unopened, directly in front of the chair.

"And here is your first assignment," he said with a smirk. "There will be a test at the end of the week."

"Yes, sir," I replied, flashing him a mock salute.

"I'll get those dictionaries."

"Andrew?" I stopped him before he could leave. "What about the notebook that mentions Sothoth Pnath? Shouldn't I start there?"

"Your primary goal is to learn," he explained. "You need to start at the beginning. No more random browsing—for either of us. We both need to proceed in order."

He exited the room, then returned soon after, dictionaries in hand.

"As usual," he said, "if you need help, just ask."

The hours drifted by as I tried to fill my head with new information. My goal was simply to read and comprehend Mr. Hunt's notebook. More often than not, though, I would find myself paging through the reference to find a symbol in a table; or reading an entire chapter from one of the books on magic that Andrew provided. He was right; it was slow going. When at last my hunger persuaded me to break for lunch, I emerged from my study room to find a gorgeous spring day awaiting me. The sun had burned off every trace of fog. I walked the four blocks to the marketplace, purchased some fresh fruit, and enjoyed my simple meal on a park bench under the clear blue sky. After relaxing in the sun for a few moments, my energy restored, I returned to the bookstore and shut myself in the back room again.

By late afternoon, I began to feel I was actually learning something. I still needed to search the reference books to translate nine-tenths of the information that I was attempting to read, but the one-tenth that I retained was an encouraging sign. By the end of the afternoon, I still had not learned anything truly practical, but my understanding of the material had begun to clear up some questions.

Nearing dinnertime, my hunger pangs overwhelmed my thirst for knowledge. As I readied myself to leave, Andrew cracked open the door and stuck his head in.

"Do you realize what time it is?" he asked.

"Yes, yes," I said, turning off the light. "I'm finished for the day. I'm starving."

"See you first thing in the morning again, then?" he asked as we made our way to the front door.

"Actually," I said, "I won't be in until a bit later tomorrow. I have a meeting. With the director of the Library."

"Doctor Trautmann?"

"Do you know him?"

Andrew placed his hand on the doorknob, barring my exit.

"We've never been introduced," he said. "But as one of the only men in the world with unlimited access to these volumes…"

"What is it?" I pressed.

"As you have undoubtedly learned, knowledge of the true nature of the universe—it can do strange things to people. Warp their minds."

"Are you saying that—"

"Just be mindful answering *any* questions. Granted, the probability is small, but there is always a chance he could be the enemy."

"Enemy?"

"A worshiper of the Ancient Ones," he said quietly. "If not a member of the cult, then possibly an ally."

"The thought had never occurred to me. Can you not be more trusting?"

Andrew ignored my question.

"You will need to be very careful with what you say," he continued. "If you are too vague, he may assume that you are intending to read the entire volume. Too specific, and you may frighten him with your knowledge. You just need to impress upon him that we—that *you*—have the definite goal of simply being able to confirm some important theories, and that the entire process will not take all that long."

He paused again and shook his head.

"Never mind. I probably needn't have told you that. I trust you'll be up to the task."

I walked the blocks back to the boarding house in silent contemplation. The appointment with the director of the library had seemed like just a formality, but Andrew's concern had inflated it into something much more. Because of his paranoia, I was suddenly worried that speaking with the man might put my life in danger. My dreams that night were of the forthcoming encounter with the ominous Doctor Trautmann, a hulking monster of a man who dripped slime and reeked of blood. Reality turned out to be far different.

TWELVE

At eleven o'clock the next morning, I arrived at the desk of Doctor Trautmann's secretary. Beyond her, same as last time, the doors to the conference room on the left were wide open; the doors on the right were closed. I stood there while she continued her work. She finally looked up.

"Can I help you?"

Although her tone of voice was pleasant enough, I could tell that she clearly did not wish to help me.

"Yes," I replied, trying to be my most polite. "I have an appointment with Doctor Trautmann. My name is Robert Adderly."

She consulted a notebook on her left.

"Yes, Mr. Adderly. Doctor Trautmann's current meeting is taking longer than expected. Please, have a seat."

She pointed to a line of chairs on my right, then returned to her work. I sat down and waited. And waited. Twenty minutes passed while I sat there patiently, trying to not fidget. The thought occurred to me that Doctor Trautmann may not even be in. Or, that he may be, but had no intention of seeing me. Just as I started to despair, the doors on the right opened and a well-dressed man emerged—and not just any man, either: Jebediah Higgins. The chair in which I was seated was out in the open, and he spotted me right away.

"Mr. Adderly, isn't it?"

I stood as he approached. He held onto his hat with both hands behind his back, and though he smiled in greeting, he did not offer a handshake. I was not offended. Frankly, I did not wish to shake his hand.

"Yes, hello, Mr. Carter," I said, feigning geniality as well as I could. "Does this day find you well?"

"It does. And yourself?"

The secretary caught my attention and pointed to the open doors. I nodded to her.

"I would love to stay and talk, Mr. Carter, but I have a meeting right now with Doctor Trautmann."

"Yes, I'm sure that you do," he said in a manner that puzzled me slightly. As he turned to leave, I thought I heard him chuckle.

Despite Higgins' rude nature, he was fighting *against* the Ancient Ones, therefore Doctor Trautmann could not possibly be a member of the cult, or even allied with them. My monstrous dream-image of Doctor Trautmann was shrinking fast as I walked toward the door of his office. It vanished completely when I entered the room, and laid eyes upon the Director of the Library.

He was only a few inches more than five feet tall, and sported a completely bald pate. Large, thick glasses obscured much of his clean-shaven face. His small, thin frame produced an appropriately mousy voice.

"Good morning, Mr. Adderly. Please close the doors and have a seat."

He indicated the single, undersized chair in front of his expansive, but mostly empty, desk.

"Good morning, Doctor Trautmann."

I started to extend my hand, but he was already seating himself, paying no attention to me.

"What can I do for you today?" he asked without looking up.

I took a seat while he made some notations in ledger before him.

"Doctor Trautmann," I began. "You are undoubtedly a very

busy man, and I do not wish to take up too much of your time today. I was told that I would need permission from either Doctor Gardiner or yourself in order to access a very ancient volume in the library: The *Necronomicon* of Abdul Alhazred. I am aware that Doctor Gardiner is currently away in South America, and so—"

"Mr. Adderly, please forgive me for interrupting you," he said, holding up one hand, and finally making eye contact with me. "But it would be best if neither of us wasted our time."

I could feel my heart starting to sink.

"You are aware of the status of Doctor Gardiner, are you not?"

"I believe I saw something in the paper, yes."

"Then you are aware," he said, "that he is not 'away' in South America, as you have said. He is missing."

"Well, I try not to put too much stock in everything I read in the papers."

I could feel the conversation slipping from my control.

"It is precisely because of that situation," he said, "that we have decided to restrict access to the *Necronomicon*, as well as the other volumes of similar ilk stored here at the Library. For the time being, no one will be granted access to study them—for any reason. If you return again in six months or so, I will be glad to meet with you again, and listen to your petition."

By the time he finished, I was crestfallen, but tried my best to conceal it.

"This will set my research back months," I said, trying to sound as if I was on the verge of discovering something Earth shattering. "Is it possible that you can make an exception?"

"I'm sorry, but no," he said flatly. "Please be patient. Come back in a few months."

The pleasantness in his voice that I detected upon my arrival was gone.

"Please," he said as I rose, "close the doors on your way out."

Upon emerging from the Library into the afternoon sun, disappointed and upset, I was only mildly surprised to once again see Jebediah Higgins. He was standing beside a statue in the courtyard at the front of the library, waiting for me. There was no way to avoid him.

"How did your meeting go, Mr. Adderly?" he asked with a smirk.

"You should know," I replied venomously.

"Indeed," he said. "How fortuitous that I managed to convince Doctor Trautmann to see my point of view only minutes before your arrival. Don't you agree?"

When I remained silent, he became upset. He kept the tone of his voice low, but the irritation was evident.

"Listen, boy," he hissed. "You don't know what you're getting into. You should be grateful I stood in your way. I've probably saved *your life.*"

On each of the last two words, his finger thudded against my chest for emphasis. He reached into his coat, took out his billfold, and removed a twenty-dollar bill.

"Here," he said with a smile, his voice returning to normal. He held the money out to me. "Go buy yourself a bottle of whiskey and a clean whore. Forget your problems for a while."

I was furious. Never in my life was I challenged to such a degree to control my temper. I took the bill in one hand, crumpled it into a ball, and dropped it to the ground. All the while, my eyes never left his. The smile that he wore disappeared, as his nostrils flared, and his teeth clenched. For a moment, I thought it would come to blows, and I readied myself.

His reaction surprised me. He bit his lip, dropped his gaze, and took a deep breath.

"Foolish child," he said. "Never forget that I tried to help you."

And with that, he turned and walked away.

The anger had dissipated by the time I made it to Professor Josephson's office, but it had not been replaced with anything positive. My
attitude still sour, I wanted to get this meeting out of the way as
quickly as possible. A knock on the door and call of his name received no answer. That crumpled twenty may still be on the ground,
I thought, and the idea of drinking myself into a stupor was appealing...but no. I needed to see this through.

Since he was typically in his office at that time each day, I assumed he had just stepped away for a short time. I tried the doorknob. It was unlocked, so I entered, and took a seat in my familiar
spot in front of the desk. The clock in the corner indicated that I
was a little early, despite having wasted the time waiting to see Doctor Trautmann.

I revisited the series of framed certificates on his wall. Soon,
with patience and perseverance, another one of those would be
added to my own collection. *But a lot of patience*, I remember
thinking. And what would happen after receiving that piece of paper? Would I get an office in this building? Work with the professor?
Those thoughts gave me comfort while Elizabeth was still alive;
now, they were bland, unexciting. I sighed, pondering my options.

As if in answer, Fate intervened, as I focused upon the safe behind his desk. My thoughts—may God forgive me—turned to the
ancient parchment within. As before, the door to the safe was ajar.
Access to those ancient volumes had been thwarted by Higgins, but
that single sheet of paper in the safe represented the potential to discover what was needed.

The temptation was too great. Only seconds later, I found myself kneeling in front of the safe, briefcase in hand. I swung the door
open. There it sat, squarely atop the pile of objects within. I grabbed
my prize, shoved it into my briefcase, and closed the safe to the same
degree to which it had been open when I arrived. Heart pounding

in my ears, I knew there would be no way to conceal my guilt. I had to flee the scene—if only I could.

I opened the door a crack, and listened. Silence. Pressing my eye to the opening, I peeked out. There was no one there to be seen. Stepping out as nonchalantly as I could, I closed the office door behind me, and walked quietly down the hall. With the semester having ended a few weeks prior, the campus was only sparsely occupied. My odds of running into anyone were slim. But it wasn't *anyone* that I feared. I had no idea what I would do if the professor were to suddenly emerge from behind one of the many closed doors that I passed. Muted sounds of typewriters and conversations leaked into the hallway, increasing my nervousness. When at last I made it through my gauntlet to the top of the stairs, I stopped to gather my composure. With some measure of calm achieved, I started down the stairs, the last few taken in a bounding leap. Then out the door. Success. I had done it. I actually made it out of the building without passing a single person.

Once outside, I did my best to act normally. But my sin, weighing heavily upon me, made me feel very conspicuous. I took a long route from the campus to the bookstore, one that would avoid the most congested areas. I had crossed a boundary; there was no disputing that. But could it still be justified by my attempt to fight for the greater good? There are degrees of evil. My petty theft would be put to good use; we would prevail. By the time I arrived at Andrew's store, having made the trip while only passing random strangers, my mind was more at ease. More at ease, but not entirely comfortable.

Given a choice, I would have preferred to not steal from the professor. The man had guided my education, trusted me, acted as an authority figure for the past few years. Before the theft, I had been musing about the possibility of working with him. With enough effort, I might have even elevated myself to a point where I could have taken over his position when he eventually retires. All of those years of trust were gone now, as well as that potential future, erased by my bold act. There was regret on my part, and it could convincingly be argued that I did have a choice. I could have chosen to force my eyes past the safe, cultivated patience, and let my future unfold in a more Christian way.

But as I saw it, there had been no choice. By my calculations, events had conspired to present me with an answer. The answer was to steal. Despite that transgression, I was still doing good; it was just that a slightly different perspective was needed to fully appreciate it. It could take some time, but I determined to realign my moral compass moving forward.

Andrew was assisting an older gentleman when I entered the shop, so I browsed through some books in the back of the store while I waited for him to finish up. I skipped past the section on mathematics, and moved on to mythology and anthropology. A full set of the third edition of Frazer's *The Golden Bough* was displayed prominently at eye level on one shelf. Both Andrew and Mr. Hunt had made random mentions of it, and I wondered how much enthusiasm was needed to plow through all twelve of the thick volumes.

"I didn't expect to see you here so early," said Andrew from behind me. "Is that good or bad?"

"Both," I replied. "My meeting with Doctor Trautmann did not go well. A gentleman with whom I have had the displeasure of meeting in the past—apparently, he convinced Doctor Trautmann to deny all access to those hidden books for the next six months."

His face fell visibly.

"Six months," he muttered.

"There is some good news, however," I said with a nervous smile.

I unbuckled the straps on my briefcase, opened it, and removed the ancient parchment mounted in its frame. Andrew gasped as I handed it to him. He studied it for a moment.

"What is this—Spanish?"

"Portuguese."

He gave me an odd look, and handed the artifact back to me.

"What exactly are we going to do with that?"

"That is going to require some explanation," I said, returning it to my briefcase. "Do you have time now?"

He poked his head up over the bookshelves, and looked around. Except for us, the store was empty.

"There's usually a lull this time of day," he said. "We can talk between customers."

We walked back to the table at the front of the store and sat down. Andrew looked at me with curious concern.

"When we first talked," I said, "I neglected to tell you certain details of my recent past. I apologize for that. I was afraid that doing so might violate a confidence. However, my hesitance with respect to that is gone. We are on a different path now, and I feel that the end *does* justify the means."

Andrew's brow wrinkled at that statement, but he did not interrupt me.

"A few weeks ago, my mentor, Professor Josephson, was asked by a colleague to decipher some equations. This colleague is a member of a small coalition—an unpleasantly smug lot—to combat the forces of the Ancient Ones. It was one of these men who interfered this morning."

"Who are these men? Are they affiliated with any sort of organization?"

"I'm not sure," I said. "I don't think so. But that's not the point. The professor did an excellent job with the task he was given. In these equations, he discovered a relationship between the Ancient Ones and certain stars. According to his analysis, the calculations can be used to predict when and where one of their kind might next appear. All you would need to know is what *source* star corresponds to what entity, and the next astral alignment can be calculated."

His eyes lit up instantly.

"That is unbelievable!" he said.

"This piece of parchment," I said, patting the briefcase, "was one of the reference materials that Professor Josephson was given. It indicates that the author knew about this relationship between the stars and the Ancient Ones. It was his intention to discover the source star that corresponds to each of them. But this list is far from complete. It contains only one entry, for an entity named Hastur."

I stopped myself there. Even though I had committed the act and made up my mind, something inside me still objected to what I was about to say. But it seemed Andrew could see where I was headed.

"And this man wrote that piece of parchment," he said slowly. "With his own hand?"

That question nearly threw me. I tottered. We had no possible way of knowing if the nameless experimenter had penned his own notes or dictated them to an underling. But if that were the case, the equally nameless helper would surely remember such important details. In the blink of any eye I convinced myself. With lying now easier for me that it had previously been, I nodded in answer to his question.

"So, all we would have to do to learn the rest of what he learned," I began.

"And destroy a priceless archaeological artifact," he finished bitterly.

"Andrew," I said, "if he knows which star belongs to Sothoth Pnath, we can easily find out once and for all if that thing is responsible for the death of Elizabeth."

Even before I had finished speaking, he was shaking his head.

"I understand the temptation," he said. "But will you please listen to yourself? This is—"

"What, foolish? Criminal?" I sighed. "You have already asked me to suspend my beliefs, and have faith in your plans. Now it's my turn to ask something of you. Certain sacrifices *must* be made. Think of the knowledge that can be gained. I certainly would have preferred to do the research myself, wading through those ancient tomes, page-by-page and line-by-line. But that is no longer an option. We must resort to whatever means possible."

I held out my briefcase in one hand towards him.

"This." I pointed to the case. "*This* is our key. Right now, it's only a piece of paper. It contains a certain amount of information. But by sacrificing it, we double, triple, quadruple our knowledge—knowledge that can be shared. We would be serving more than ourselves. We would be serving the *greater good.*"

I had nothing left to say. He sat with his eyes closed, elbows propped up on the table, massaging his forehead. Frowning heavily, his head shook slowly from time to time. It appeared his mind was made up. But before he could speak, our conversation was cut short by the sound of the front door opening.

I first noticed Andrew's unblinking gaze. I had been seated with my back to the door, but upon turning around, I was met with the sight of a beautiful young woman, perhaps only eighteen or nineteen, with long brown hair, and dressed in white. She was extremely wan, and as she entered the store, her movements were stiff. In her left hand, she held a red rose; her right was concealed from my view.

"Good morning," Andrew said, standing from the table. His voice was much more pleasant than it had been with me. "Can I help you with anything today?"

She seemed to have not heard him at first, looking distractedly around. When she did speak, her voice was a haunted, despondent whisper.

"I am searching for knowledge," she said. "Knowledge attained through the pain of sacrifice."

Andrew looked at me, his brow furrowed. I stayed where I was as she continued to speak.

"A pound of flesh? If I could muster the courage. But I am weak from the struggle."

"Miss," Andrew said, walking toward her. She also took a few more halting steps, then stopped directly in front of him.

"Shadows from the past stalk me," she said. "Pursue me. A moment's rest and they engulf me. I am tired. The shadows…they are everywhere!"

With that final exclamation the object in her right hand flashed into view: A knife! She raised it high above her head, but awkwardly. She lunged at Andrew. I could only watch in horror as the glinting metal slunk toward him, but slowly as if through water. He had more than enough time to react. Stepping to the side, he grabbed her right wrist with his left hand, and with the other, slapped her firmly across the face. Her legs collapsed from beneath her, but he caught her before she fell. The knife and flower fell to the floor from limp hands.

"Bring her over here," I said, clearing space on the table. Andrew carried her over, and laid her carefully on top. He felt her neck for a pulse, and paid careful attention to her respiration. Curious about the items that she had dropped, I walked over and picked up the rose. Almost at once I noticed a peculiar odor.

"Don't smell it," Andrew said. "I know that spell. It's been poisoned. Just throw it away. It'll be harmless before long."

He pointed at the waste can near the checkout counter. After disposing of the flower, I carefully picked up the knife. It looked more like a surgical blade than anything else, with a long wooden handle and a thin blade, only about two inches long. The grip was intricately carved, and colored the same glossy black along its entire length. The blade had the same Egyptian-looking symbol engraved into both sides. I handed it to Andrew. He examined it for some time, turning it over repeatedly.

"Interesting," he said, indicating the design on the blade. "This symbol, *Aptu*, means *Messenger*. I've come across it once before."

"Where? What does it mean?"

"It was in reference to Nyarlathotep," he said. "Servant of the Ancient Ones."

He looked from the knife to the motionless woman to the wastebasket with the poisoned flower.

"It would seem that we are being watched."

I felt the hair on the back of my neck stir.

"Watched by whom?"

Just then, the young woman spasmed so violently on the table that I thought she might fall off. Andrew and I both reacted, but before we could touch her, her eyes flew open. Having two strange men reaching out to grab her must have been a fearful sight, for she let out a shout of pure terror. When we both jumped back and held up our hands, she silenced herself and sat up on the table.

"How did I get here?" she asked. "Who are you?"

"What is the last thing you remember?" Andrew asked her calmly, trying to sound non-threatening. Realizing that the knife was still in his hand, he turned and placed it out of view on a display stand. He turned back to her and smiled. She seemed to relax a little.

"I bought a rose," she said slowly. "From a street vendor. He was crippled. I felt sorry for him. It smelled…"

She trailed off and felt her left cheek, undoubtedly still stinging from Andrew's blow.

"Miss…" prompted Andrew.

"Manning," she replied. "Elizabeth Manning."

"Miss Manning, my name is Andrew Cooke. I own this store. This is Robert Adderly."

I nodded at her.

"You came in just minutes ago. Do you remember?"

She shook her head.

"This may sound like an odd question," Andrew began, "but—"

Just then, the door of the shop flew open, and a middle-aged woman hurried into the store.

"Mother!" Elizabeth cried, jumping from the table and rushing to the door.

"Elizabeth, are you alright?" She handed the young woman a small, white handbag. "You just dropped your purse and wandered off."

She looked at her daughter's left cheek—still red—and eyed us suspiciously.

"Yes, mother," she said quietly. "I'm fine."

"Your cheek—"

"Is fine." Her mother did not seem to be convinced, so she repeated, "It's *fine*. Really."

Mrs. Manning frowned.

"Very well. Let us be going. We shall be late to meet your father."

As her mother pulled her by the arm toward the door, the young woman turned back to us as if to say *Good-bye*, but no words came out. She simply lowered her eyes. The older woman, on the other hand, made no attempt at civility, as she ushered her daughter out of the store, glaring at us all the while.

When they were far enough away, I turned to Andrew.

"What just happened here? Who is watching us? Was that some kind of warning?"

He looked at me very somberly.

"Someone has taken notice of our actions," he said. "That young woman was sent to deliver a message. Did you hear that rambling soliloquy?"

Considering that the message had come with a knife, it seemed to have been more than a warning—though he had easily avoided her half-hearted attack.

"Knowledge attained through the pain of sacrifice…" I mused.

"The words she spoke were not her own," he said. "She mentioned shadows. Sothoth Pnath is a shadow. Granted, I'm just conjecturing, but that is precisely what we were discussing before her arrival—the knowledge that would be attained by sacrificing the parchment. More significant to me, however, was the method of the warning."

Andrew sounded as if he was about to explain further, but he stopped and turned away from me. I waited a few seconds, but he said nothing else.

"The young woman?" I finally asked. He still did not speak. "Because her name was Elizabeth? That is an interesting coincidence, but…"

"There are no coincidences."

"Someone else told me that recently." It was an attempt at humor, but the delivery was deflated by my own disbelief in what I said.

"But no, not her name." He sighed deeply. "I made a shameful mistake a few years ago. Using that very same hypnosis spell."

He began to pace.

"A mistake," he repeated. "It seems someone knows quite a few things about us. This is no warning. It's a challenge. I believe that we are being challenged, Robert."

I had not known Andrew long, but the tone of his voice, the set of his features, implied to me he did not intend to back down from this provocation.

"Are we on the right trail then?" I asked. "If we're being told to not speak with the author of the parchment."

"Yes."

He stared out the front windows to the street beyond, down which Elizabeth Manning and her mother had disappeared, just as quickly as they'd come.

"Are you afraid?" I asked hesitantly.

"Yes."

"But we're doing this?"

Andrew grabbed my briefcase from the floor and pulled it back up to the table. He rested his hand on top.

"Yes," said Andrew. "Yes, we are."

THIRTEEN

In late afternoon, I returned home to change out of my good clothes and eat dinner, while Andrew prepared for the ceremony. Before returning to the bookstore, I gathered up all of the papers from Professor Josephson related to the Portuguese parchment. The journey back was one of paranoia and fear. Everyone I saw was a potential enemy, a servant of the Ancient Ones. I neither made eye contact nor spoke with anyone. I repeatedly crossed and re-crossed streets to avoid any encounters at all. Before long, I began to feel I was being followed, and reversed direction, walking three blocks out of my way. When finally I arrived at the darkened store, it truly was not a long time before Andrew appeared and let me in, but they were long moments spent searching the shadows, finding nothing but the shadows themselves.

"Make yourself comfortable," Andrew said when we reached the room upstairs. "I just need a few minutes to clean up. Unless you would like something to eat? I have plenty of chicken soup left."

It was a wonderful aroma, but I had filled myself with Mrs. Bettings' dinner not long before.

"Thank you, but no," I replied.

"In that case," his voice floated in from beyond the kitchen doorway, "see what you can do about removing the parchment from the frame. I have some tools in the stand near the door."

I set the papers I had brought from home down on the couch, and found the tools near the door. The parchment, however, was a different matter. After a thorough scan of the room, the frame with the ancient document within was nowhere to be seen.

"You do still have it," I called into the kitchen. "Don't you?"

"Of course," came the response. "It's on the table."

I looked at the table at which we sat the previous week, the table where we spoke with Andrew's dead grandfather, where we had failed to speak with Elizabeth. It was clearly empty. Was it possible that, in my absence, a saboteur had broken in and taken it? Had this next attempt to thwart us been a success? But before I could sound the alarm, he emerged from the kitchen, drying his hands on a towel. He looked at me calmly, as I stared at him, at the empty table, and back at him.

"Touch it," he said. "Go on."

Hesitantly, I walked over to the table and laid my hand upon it. But I did not feel a wooden tabletop. Instead, my fingers encountered what felt like a silky, diaphanous cloth, which, sure enough, sprang into view as soon as I touched it. There was no pain at all associated with the sensation, but still I withdrew my hand as if shocked. Through the cloth, I could see the parchment, still mounted in its frame, sitting on the table.

"It's a very simple spell," said Andrew. "*Hide in plain sight.* As long as the illusion is not touched, it will persist forever. It's amazing what can be done with it."

When he returned to the kitchen, I reached out again and placed my hand on the cloth. It moved like the surface of water. It certainly was not the most incredible magic I had seen thus far. Communing with the dead was a power I had previously thought reserved for the Lord alone. But there was something about this spell—something about such practical, tactile magic—that constituted a new shift in my mind. It seemed a miracle, though Andrew had treated it like a mere child's toy. Was this how Moses had felt, watching his rod transform into a snake?

I carefully lifted the cloth, and set it aside to examine the frame. It seemed it would be simple to remove the document. Taking the pliers I had found, I was able to bend the clips away, and easily lift off the various layers of board and backing paper. In order to handle it as little as possible, I carefully slid the thick, brittle paper out of the frame, and directly onto the table. Looking at it, laying bare on the wooden tabletop, I felt some small regret over what we were about to do. *The greater good*, I reminded myself. *We have no choice.*

"Very good," said Andrew as he returned from the kitchen. "You didn't damage it."

He moved the sheet so that the lower right corner hung over the edge of the table, then grabbed the corner with thumb and fore-finger and tried to crease the thick paper. The small piece he had in his fingers snapped off sharply. He grimaced and shook his head.

"This material is far too brittle," he said. "I should have realized this. We will not be able to twist it into a wick."

"Is that a problem?"

"It will burn very fast."

"How much time will we have?"

He looked at the paper closely.

"A minute. No, not even."

"Will that be enough?"

"Perhaps."

"That is," I said, "if he even knows the information we seek."

"*Someone* believes that we're on the right track," Andrew said. "Otherwise, what happened today would not have happened."

I nodded, the young woman's strange words still ringing in my ears.

"Very well," he said. "Let me find a dish wide enough to hold this thing."

He went back into the kitchen, and I heard some clattering, as pots and pans were shifted around. He returned with a clear glass bowl and set it in the center of the table, along with matches. He then retrieved the container of that unique, near-invisible liquid from his bedroom, and started pouring some carefully into the glass bowl. He upended the container, waiting for the final drips.

"I hope this experiment pays off," he said, and set the empty container on a nearby shelf.

At last, the stage was set for our drama. We took our seats at the table, and as silence descended over the room, Andrew began to meditate. After a few still minutes, he began the incantations. Once again, I felt myself a spider trapped beneath a glass. When both introductory spells were complete, he struck a match, and held it to the corner of the parchment. To my horror, it caught fire immediately, and almost half of it was consumed in the space of two or three seconds. I nearly cried aloud, but regained my composure when I saw that the wicking effect had at last taken hold. The burning slowed. Andrew and I exchanged glances of relief, and waited for the cold wind to blow.

Unlike the experience with the spirit of Mr. Hunt, it was a relatively long time before the air stirred. But slowly, the draft became a gale, and then a hurricane, as I watched the parchment burn steadily, completely undisturbed by the fury whirling around us. I was astonished that those mystifying forces—much stronger this time than last—did no harm to the room or us. When the winds ceased, and the cold presence of the spirit concentrated above the flame, I noticed with some alarm that only a third of the parchment remained.

"Unknown spirit," said Andrew, "we are seeking information we believe you discovered while alive. Did you determine the astral correspondences to the beings known as the Ancient Ones?"

Trying to relax, but unable to forget my previous experience with Mr. Hunt, I grabbed a hold of the table, and emptied my mind. There was a long pause of icy silence, then a voice from nowhere spoke.

Yes.

The word was clear and strong in my mind—and in English, or

my mind interpreted it as such. For some reason, I had expected Portuguese.

"We would like to know which star in the heavens corresponds to the entity known as Sothoth Pnath, the shadow of Yog Sothoth."

There was another pause before the reply came. I got the impression, for some reason, that there was an enormous gulf between ourselves and the spirit with whom we were speaking, despite the fact that it was theoretically hovering above the flame only inches from us.

The star is known as Regulus.

The answer! We had the answer! And none too soon—only a sliver of the parchment remained.

"Spirit, we have one final question," said Andrew hurriedly. "Which star corresponds to Great Cthulhu?"

The flame began to sputter during the silence after Andrew finished speaking. I clearly heard the voice say, *The star*, then the flame died and the winds began. I could imagine that I also heard *known as*, as the noise of the winds picked up. But try as I might, I could not discern any other words above the rushing and whistling that ensued.

When stillness returned, Andrew concluded the ceremony by uttering the two separate sets of magical phrases. When he had finished, I could no longer contain my excitement, and jumped up out of my chair.

"Regulus!" I said. "We did it!"

"Yes! One answer, anyway. And so close to a second one." He sighed. "So close."

But despite his tone, a smile covered his face. Bounding over to the couch, I retrieved my papers and spread them out on the table. But even with this new revelation, I was still missing one vitally important datum.

"The coordinates for Regulus," I said. "I need the sky

coordinates."

Andrew hesitated only briefly.

"I can get that."

He ran downstairs and returned holding an expensive-looking volume. I quickly located the information I needed, and inserted the numbers into the equation. My fingers trembled as I performed the calculations. To be sure, I performed them twice more, before looking up at Andrew and nodding.

"Confirmed," I said. "There is no doubt."

"So that's it."

We paused there, looking at each other. I was unsure what to do next. That is, until Andrew spoke up.

"We must make a decision, then," he said. "Or rather, you must."

"Decision?"

He leaned on the table with both hands and looked squarely at me.

"If you recall," he said, "I asked if you were interested in vengeance—if we could determine that Sothoth Pnath was the cause. Now that we are sure: Do you accept the task before us? That of banishing this monster from the Earth?"

"At the risk of my life, yes."

Hearing my solemn tone surprised even me. Was I truly that committed?

Andrew, too, was taken aback.

"Well, that's…it's good to hear your dedication, Robert. But I don't plan on risking either of our lives. We just need to proceed cautiously."

He picked up the dish from the table, and headed for the kitchen.

"And be paranoid," he added as he disappeared through the

doorway. "Very paranoid."

There was a clatter, as if he had dropped the dish onto the counter instead of setting it down cleanly. He was moving much more slowly when he emerged from the kitchen.

"The demands of the ceremony seem to have caught up with me," he said haggardly, grabbing onto the table. "The longer the spirit has been dead, the more energy is used by the magician. But I didn't expect it to be this taxing."

He attempted to sit down, but began to fall. Having seen his unsteadiness, I was already partially out of my seat, and managed to grab him before he hit the floor. As I maneuvered him into the chair, his stomach growled audibly. He tried to focus on me, but his eyes fluttered.

"You need food in your stomach right now," I said. "You mentioned chicken soup?"

"Yes, it's still warm. Warm enough, anyway. On the stovetop."

The pot held enough for two people to fill themselves, but in my estimation, it was just enough for Andrew to replenish his strength. I found a towel, and a spoon as well, and returned to the table. In the small amount of time I had been gone, he had already started to list to one side. I placed the towel before him as a placemat, the pot on top of it.

"Do I feed you, or hold you up?" I asked, grinning.

He laughed, straightened up, and held his hand out.

"Spoon, please," he said. "Neither, but it wouldn't hurt to be ready to catch me again."

He practically *inhaled* the soup, only pausing when two-thirds of it was gone. There was an enormous belch, followed by a giggle.

"Pardon," he apologized. "I feel as if I've had three bottles of Merlot to myself."

"Please, do share some of that wine next time," I said, trying to keep the mood light-hearted.

"If I get any more, certainly."

He chuckled occasionally as he polished off the soup. When finished, he sat back in the chair. His smile faded.

"No, I shouldn't laugh," he said, looking at me. "This is serious. Someone is watching us closely. Too closely."

He was at least able to focus on me, though the weakness, or dizziness, was still evident in his slumping posture. As he began speaking, some of the words were slurred.

"That business earlier today...the girl..." Wincing, he shook his head. "It touched on a very embarrassing event. I never mentioned a word about it to anyone. And I won't go into the details with you, but you should know this much. Years ago, when I had just started exploring magic, I used that very same hypnosis spell. I enchanted an apple, and gave it to a young woman. She was a willing participant, mind you. But some foolishness on my part nearly resulted in both of our deaths. These days she walks with a barely noticeable limp. I sustained a wound here."

He tapped a spot low on his neck.

"Another half-inch, and my carotid artery would probably have been punctured," he said. "I learned a great deal that day—about my limits, about consequences, about fear."

"If you never told that to anyone, how could such a thing have been discovered?"

"I can imagine a few ways, most involving magic, of course. Some not."

He closed his eyes, took a deep breath, held it, then exhaled. When he opened them again, I could tell that a certain light had returned, perhaps the soup lending him some strength.

"You look better," I said. "Do you feel better? Back to normal?"

"Still tired, but yes," he answered confidently. "Do you feel safe walking home?"

I had to admit that recent experiences had taken a toll on my nerves. I could still remember the feeling of invisible eyes on me, soundless footsteps, shadows of shadows.

"I do. Just…you wouldn't happen to have a weapon that I could borrow, do you?"

Andrew bit at his lip, thinking.

"Hmm. Not really, but…"

He stood up and started to move, then sat down again.

"Can you go get it, please? I'm still feeling dizzy."

"Yes. What—?"

"On the dresser." He pointed. "You'll see."

I walked into the bedroom, and recognized the knife on top of the dresser right away: the one wielded by the young Miss Manning only hours before.

"Just keep it. Be careful, though. It looks very sharp."

I turned it over in my hands, then slashed and poked at an imaginary attacker. The smooth, glossy black handle felt slick in my hand. In an actual melee, I thought I might have to grip it very tightly in order to keep it from slipping from my grasp.

"It's better than nothing."

I slipped the small knife into my coat pocket and gathered my papers together. As I was turning to leave, Andrew handed me a key.

"I don't want to navigate those stairs twice more in this condition," he said wearily. "Please lock the door as you leave. Can I assume that you will return in the morning?"

I nodded.

"Good night, then."

"Good night."

I went down the steps, and through the empty, darkened store alone. Even before stepping foot outside of the building, my imagination was set afire by the sounds of rodents scurrying and gnawing within the walls. *Courage*, I reminded myself. After a few deep, calming breaths, I walked out the door and locked it behind me.

Fourteen

Having been given the key to the bookstore, the next morning I was able to let myself in and begin reading earlier than usual. The walk was much less scary in the daylight, but I still made it needlessly stressful by searching every shadow for hidden foes. I had been bent to my studies in the backroom for about an hour, when familiar footsteps descended the stairs. Andrew knocked and entered, smiling. After the fatigue of the night before, he seemed to be back to normal, after a sleep he described as coma-like. He brought down coffee and muffins—I had one to his three—and I took the opportunity to ask him some questions about the material I had read before his arrival. Breakfast finished, he got ready to open the store, leaving me to my studies once again.

Late morning, there was a knock at the door before it opened, and he flew in holding a few pieces of paper.

"Robert. Look at this!"

He shoved the papers into my hand. It was a letter. I skimmed over the first sheet as he explained.

"This is from one of my grandfather's contacts. He had been travelling through Eastern Europe for almost a year, and has just recently returned to Boston."

"I can tell you nothing about spontaneous human combustion," I read aloud, "but the following pages detail two spells which may help you with your research."

"Yes. The mail arrived a while ago. Business has been slow this morning, but I'm not complaining. It's given me the time to study the first spell."

I looked at the next sheet, and got more excited as I read. That first set of instructions was very simple, and involved animating a flame and directing it with one's will.

"I may actually be able to handle this one," I muttered, looking it over again.

"No," he declared. "There's no *may*. You *can*, even today. But I'd prefer you wait a day or two. I want to make sure you fully understand the basics."

He paused, then added with a grin, "And I want you to watch me."

"Watch you? Now?"

He nodded.

"I already locked the door, and put up the 'Be Back Shortly' sign," he said.

An open flame was required. I looked at the wooden floor, then at the stacks of boxes around us.

"My bedroom has a fireplace," said Andrew, pointing at the ceiling.

I nodded and we went upstairs. In the bedroom, he opened the flue, and got a fire going with a single small log. While the flames spread, he closed his eyes, and concentrated silently. He then opened them, and uttered a short phrase in Latin. That was all there was to it.

I was mesmerized as he made the flames dance around the log. First, all of the tongues gathered into a single, tall one on the far left side. That one then moved all the way to the right, then began wandering all over, all the while under Andrew's control. At first, he pointed with his index finger to direct the movements, but soon discovered there was no need for that. His final act was to shape the fire to his initials: AC. To end the spell, he uttered a single word in Latin. Aside from relinquishing control, it had the added effect of extinguishing the flames completely.

We both laughed with joy.

"And look at this," he said, prodding the log.

It seemed to have been the gentlest of touches, but the structure dissolved instantly, collapsing into a pile of ash in the general form of a log.

"This is another reason why I want you to start with this spell," said Andrew. "Instead of the magician providing the necessary energy, it comes from the material being burned by the fire."

I dabbed my finger into the ashes, then stared at my fingertip. They did not disappear.

"These are normal ashes," I said.

"Yes. I still cannot come up with an explanation for the behavior you observed."

He closed the flue. I glanced at the second incantation before handing the papers back to Andrew. That one was much more complex. It allowed the magician to summon, control and banish a salamander, a supposedly mythical creature with the ability to endure fire without harm.

"And this other one," he said enthusiastically, waving the paper. "We'll do this one on Saturday."

After witnessing the results of the first experiment, I became excited by the potential that lay before me—before both of us. The rest of that day and all the next, I pushed myself, but adopted a new approach. Instead of studying non-stop, I took frequent rest breaks to ensure that my concentration would stay sharp.

The new strategy worked. It felt as if I was making larger strides. I began to practice simple mental exercises and meditations, with successful outcomes. My confidence grew with every hour spent in study, and consequently my fears—fears of strangers and shadows—diminished. The trips back and forth to the bookstore were no longer the ordeals that they had become.

Nothing mattered except for my new obsession. No thought was given to my thesis, the professor, my other friends, my parents, the world. Mathematics was boring when compared to the study of magic, but as I read, I tried to determine how I might combine the two sciences. Were there any points where they overlapped? How many magicians were also mathematicians? The potential intrigued me.

Saturday finally arrived. Early in the day, Andrew had asked me to run out and purchase a few items we would need for the ceremony. It took some legwork, but I was able to locate and buy them all. At seven o'clock, I knocked on the door of the shop. It was not long before he appeared and yanked me inside, closing the door swiftly behind me.

"Were you able to buy everything?"

"Good evening to you too," I said. "Yes, I was."

He locked the door and looked out the windows suspiciously.

"How was your walk over here? Did you hear anything odd? Any feelings of being followed?"

"No. Should I have?"

"No, no. Just trying to be extra cautious, given what we're next attempting."

I followed him to the room at the back of the store, which by now felt to me like a second home.

"We'll be conducting the ceremony in here," he said, grabbing a hold of the doorknob. "Cross your fingers."

Then he opened the door and turned on the light.

The room was vastly different than it had been the day before. Andrew had cleared out a large area in the center, and the boxes that had previously been stacked everywhere were now lined up against the walls. My study table was nearly completely hidden behind the stacks. And at the back of the room, sitting on the floor near the edge of the clearing, was a small, metal cage, and inside: a medium-sized, brown rat. It was clearly in distress.

"It worked!" cried Andrew, rushing to the cage. The rodent squealed and ran in circles, failing to find a way out.

"I assume…we need the rat?"

"Well, it's either the rat or we lop off your hand."

I took it as a joke, but there was no humor in his voice.

"Everything is coming together," he continued. "Now, the items I asked you to purchase?"

I opened my briefcase and extracted what he asked for: a bottle of cooking sherry; a small vial of chloroform; and two long, thin tapers, one red and one white.

"We'll use the candles to construct a prison for the creature," he explained, setting the items down beside the cage and its small prisoner. "The chloroform is for the rat."

"And the sherry?" I asked.

He uncorked the bottle and took a long swig. Smiling, he held it out to me. I accepted, and took a large mouthful. When I returned it to him, he took another drink. He seemed to consider a third, staring at the bottle in his hands.

"The sherry will be needed for the summoning," he said. "It's one of the most fascinating aspects of magic. Most spells require specific components in order to work correctly. However, substitutions are allowed—encouraged, in fact! Ninety percent of magic occurs here."

He tapped himself on the side of the head.

"Never forget that. This sherry could be nearly anything as long as I—the magician—am *one hundred percent* convinced that the component I substitute will work as well as what has been specified. In this case, the specified component is a fluid known as Oil of Y'trass, a very versatile concoction. For our purposes, however, the only important characteristic is an extreme flammability. Any liquid with a high enough alcohol content will do the same. Therefore, we use the relatively inexpensive sherry, instead of a rare and expensive mixture made from crushed pearls and fermented vampire bat blood."

"Vampire bat blood?"

He nodded.

"No," I said. "I don't suppose I would have been able to find that very easily this afternoon. The sherry and the chloroform were difficult enough."

He retrieved a few other things from atop one of the nearby stacks of boxes: A small rag, a long, thin piece of wood, some matches, and a shallow copper bowl about a foot in diameter. After placing the bowl on the floor in the center of the room, he poured a small amount of the sherry into it.

"Now," he continued. "A salamander is a dangerous creature with potentially awesome power. Don't be fooled by its diminutive appearance. It is effectively a demon, in every sense of the word. Its physical size on this plane is only restricted by the size of the flame used to summon it."

With that, he walked over to the cage and upended the scrambling rat into the bars on the far side.

"Get that stick," he said. "Try to pin it down."

I did as I was asked. Looking back, I believe that this was the moment when things truly changed. Though seemingly innocuous, pinning a rat in a cage was in fact my first real act in the realm of magic. Up to that point, I had been but an observer, a student of theory. But as I poked the stick through the bars and struggled to trap it in the corner, I moved from mere student to practitioner. However insignificantly, a small step had been taken.

While I held it as still as I could, Andrew poured some of the chloroform onto the rag, and held it to the rat's snout. It stopped struggling and was soon asleep. Then, he carried the cage to the center of the room, and emptied the rodent onto the floor near the copper bowl. Leaving the candles and matches nearby, we cleared everything else away. I stood near the door, and watched.

Andrew knelt down beside the copper bowl, and meditated for a minute. When he was ready, he struck a match, and lit both candles. After intoning some phrases in Latin, he held the candles out in front of him, close to the floor, white in the left, and red in the right. He tilted them so that the melting wax dripped off of them, then slowly traced an arc with each arm. When finished, he had drawn a semicircle around the bowl. Then, he stood up and turned one hundred eighty degrees, repeating the process. The completed circle alternated red and white quadrants around its circumference. Next, he dripped wax from the white candle on the ground to the left of the bowl, where the red and white arcs met. There he stuck the still-burning candle in the melted wax, and held it in place until he was sure that it would not fall over. He did the same with the red candle to the right of the bowl. After stepping backward out of the circle, Andrew knelt down with arms held high, and spoke at length in Latin. When finished, he struck a match, and threw it into the bowl.

What happened next would have been impossible to believe had I not seen it myself. The sherry, of course, burst into flame. There was a large puff of white smoke, and the flame immediately went out. Even before the smoke had dissipated, I could see that he had been successful. A red, lizard-like creature had materialized inside the bowl. Only as big as a rat itself, it leaped out of the bowl, ignoring the sedated rodent, and ran on its hind legs straight for Andrew. But suddenly, it stopped—as if shocked—when it reached the wax circle. As it paused, I examined the thing. It looked very much like its namesake, except for a few differences. The skin was rough and dry instead of smooth and moist, with needle-like teeth that were disproportionately large, occupying a great portion of the head. Most disconcerting of all, however: It had no eyes.

Despite this, it seemed to somehow detect my presence. It moved towards me, but once again, its progress was limited by the wax border. Andrew, still kneeling in front of the circle, had been quiet for some time now. Slowly, the creature began to walk around inside of the circle, studying the invisible barrier. It had explored nearly the entire circumference when I noticed the rat twitch. So did the salamander. It watched, eyelessly, as the rat slowly righted itself, and started to hobble away. But the salamander was faster. The creature was a blur as it crossed the distance and hungrily attacked. The rat squealed as the razor-sharp teeth tore into its fur, and flesh, and bone. Most remarkable of all, where the salamander bit into the rat, the wound was cauterized, and the fur smoked. In no time at all, its squeals fell silent. Except perhaps a drop of blood on the floor, there was no evidence that the rat had ever existed.

When it was completely consumed, Andrew spoke a single phrase in Latin, whereupon the creature turned around to face him, becoming immobile as a statue. Andrew breathed a deep sigh, and stood up.

"That's it," he said with evident satisfaction. "The sacrifice has been accepted. As long as those candles burn, the creature is under my control."

I looked at the candles. They would burn for hours.

"You have a task in mind for it?" I asked.

"Yes—I'm going to tell it to eat all the rats in this house."

"But to do that, it would have to leave the circle."

"The circle is only needed to contain it until it is under my control. Right now, it is."

I looked at him with obvious doubt, fear rising in my throat.

"Please trust me," said Andrew. "The most difficult part is over."

He retrieved the stick with which I had restrained the rat, and began scraping away a bit of the wax circle. I watched the creature closely as he did so, but it never stirred. The gap ended up being only a half-inch, but that was apparently enough. When Andrew uttered another phrase in Latin, the salamander left the circle and started searching the room with an unnatural speed. It rapidly examined the perimeter of the room, then somehow squeezed its body between the boxes and the wall. Minutes later, we heard muffled cries from somewhere within the wall.

"And now," said Andrew, "we wait."

Almost two hours went by. We tracked the progress of the creature through the building by ear, upstairs and down. At times, we might catch a glimpse of a red blur as it emerged from a crack that was plainly too small, run along the floor, then disappear into another tiny crevice. Eventually, we lost track of it. And try as we might, we could no longer hear it. I began to worry that the candles had burned much more quickly than planned, and that there was now a demon on the loose. The thought would have been more terrifying had my brain not found it so ridiculous: *demon!* But Andrew wasn't worried. He suggested we return to the storeroom, and to my surprise, there was the salamander, sitting in the same spot from which it had departed on its mission. Despite the fact that we had heard it kill and presumably devour several nests of rats, its own size had not changed at all.

With its assignment completed, Andrew entered the broken circle and knelt down at its center, positioning himself once again over the bowl. He wet the fingertips of both hands with saliva, and reached out so that each hand hovered above a candle. The salamander continued to sit where it had eaten the sacrificial rat, on the left side of the circle near the white candle. With his hand positioned as it was, Andrew's left wrist was alarmingly close to the creature. One bite from that diminutive monstrosity would sever arteries, veins, tendons. I held my breath as he spoke a short phrase in Latin, then lowered his hands even closer to the flames. But he simply extinguished both candles, simultaneously, and the salamander vanished.

"As you can see," he said, sitting down on the floor with a heavy sigh, "the conclusion of the ceremony is one excellent reason why *not* to summon a large salamander. If you don't get both candles at precisely the same instant...well, you can imagine. There is rarely a margin for error."

I shuddered at the thought of a man-sized salamander free of the bonds of the spell, with a helpless magician kneeling before it.

"How did you like our little friend?" he asked, with a familiar note to his voice that had been missing. He must have been under a terrific amount of stress for his personality to change so much prior to the ceremony.

"There's one thing that I do not understand," I said. "There was no bloating in its midsection, no indication that it had eaten anything at all."

"Did you see how it squeezed itself into those cracks?"

"Yes."

"As with any demon, it's true size is unknowable," he said, as though it were a concept with which I should already be familiar. "It was merely clothed in a form constrained by me. Demons have certain inherent abilities, one of which is the power to change shape. It performed its task very well, don't you think? In fact..."

As he stared off into space, a look of supreme satisfaction blossomed on his face.

"Both of those spells were magnificent!" he announced. "I must mail Mr. Fenster and compliment him. Perhaps he'll be able to send another."

Mention of the name jarred me. It had been buried in my memories, only brought to the surface recently when speaking with Professor Josephson. To hear it actually spoken was strange.

"Fenster?" I asked.

"Yes. Sound familiar?"

"Not really. Just something from my childhood."

Andrew's enthusiasm was contagious. I helped him up from the floor, and we went upstairs to open an old bottle of champagne that he had hidden away for celebratory purposes. For the next hour, he gleefully walked me through the subtleties of every step of the ceremony. Despite the length at which he described it, I was excited to see that, even though there were some intricate concepts involved, I grasped all but a few of the details.

On Sunday, I awoke with a slight headache from the champagne. As I lay in bed, the bells of the church rang out soulfully, calling to me. I ignored them. Faith had been a comfortable concept while Elizabeth was still alive, and likely would have remained so had she lived. But faith is passive. The sculptor cannot simply believe that the statue exists within the stone. Action must be taken to remove the excess material and reveal it. I could no longer be passive. I needed to act.

Although the bookstore was normally closed on Sundays, and we had made no plans for me to be there, I walked over anyway. The morning was pleasant, and so I sat down on a bench in a nearby park and watched the shop for signs of life. As I sat there, other church bells rang out. People walked by me, singly and in families. Smiles were exchanged. Greetings. Their faith was their own personal affair, but how strong was it within them? I wondered how many of them would question it if confronted with a crisis similar to my own, or the truth I had subsequently discovered.

Before long, the curtains in the windows above the store were opened, signaling that Andrew was at least awake. I gave him a few more minutes before going over. A few stout knocks on the door got his attention. He stuck his head out of the window over the door.

"I'm sorry, but the shop—oh."

"Andrew, may I come in?" I asked.

"I'll be right down."

The door opened shortly.

"Good morning," he greeted me.

"Is it too early? I can come back later, or tomorrow."

"No. If you want to study, please do."

He waved me in and closed the door.

"I want to do more than study," I said. "I want to act."

"The flame spell?" he asked, smiling.

I nodded.

"After last night's success, I was wondering how long you could restrain yourself. I do need to run some errands today, but have some time to spare. You can prepare yourself while I get ready."

We went upstairs. He handed me the page with the instructions on it and went into the bedroom. I looked over the paper, but only to verify that what I had previously committed to memory was correct. Even so, I still held onto the sheet as a talisman while I sat at the table, and made an effort to calm myself with some meditation. Mentally, it worked; I could tell that I was focused. Physically, my heart rate barely slowed.

The bedroom door opened.

"Ready?" asked Andrew.

I stood up and went in.

"Please proceed," he said. "First, get the fire going. Always remember that the magician needs to handle as many details as possible. I could have built the fire for you, but not performing that act yourself could have introduced the smallest amount of doubt in your mind. When the flames are strong, stop and ensure that you have the right frame of mind. I'll be able to tell if you're ready."

"How?"

"It takes time to develop the sense, but a certain *tension* can be felt. Sometimes, it manifests as an odor."

I opened the flue, picked out a nice, dry log, and soon had it burning. Right away, I found another reason to start my life as a magician with this spell: The flames provided a very convenient focal point. Time seemed to slow slightly, as I knelt in front of the hearth, and gazed into them. I looked over at Andrew. He nodded once. I took a deep breath, released it, and uttered the words to begin.

The flow of energy was an unmistakable and unique feeling. Some sort of force ran *through* me, from the unburned wood, into me, then out into the fire. Initially, I performed the same actions as Andrew had: grouping the flames at either end, then moving them around randomly. After that, I moved on to simple geometric figures, all the while pointing with my finger. When I tried to manipulate the flames with just my mind, there was a sputter in the flow. Feeling that hiccup, I tensed up. That choked it off even more. Just in time, I managed to relax. The energy was restored and I began to control the fire with only thoughts. Seeing that the wood was nearly gone, I got inspired to try something creative, though I must admit somewhat childish. Within a flaming heart, I put my initials along with Elizabeth's:

R A

+

E W

That configuration was only visible for an eyeblink as the flow of energy dwindled to nothing. The log crumbled to ash the moment I ended the spell by uttering the final word. When I looked at Andrew, he seemed to be shocked.

"I…" he began, then paused. "That was impressive."

I beamed.

"I fully expected you to rely on finger movements for control," he explained.

"Well, I watched you do it without pointing. It did falter. I felt the control slipping away."

"Yes, but you regained it. That was an advanced technique to master so early on. You may have a knack for this. But that's enough for today. I know it doesn't seem like much, but you need to step back and let the experience sink in."

It was a little deflating to hear that, but I reluctantly conceded that he was right. I closed the flue, and stood up. My heart bursting with triumph, I needed something to do.

"You mentioned errands before," I prompted him. "Do you need help?

"If you want to help me retrieve and sort books, you're welcome to come along."

"That sounds fine. It will at least count towards *beginning* to repay you for your time."

"Nonsense," he said with a smile. "We're both helping each other. You've given me a goal to work towards. That's something I never had before."

For a few days after that, I foolishly reveled in the power I imagined I controlled. But mid-week, guilt, in the form of a man, paid an unexpected visit to the bookstore.

I was sitting in my well-worn chair in the back room when I heard a knock at the door. Growing tired, I was due for a break, and welcomed a short distraction. But it was not Andrew who had come to find me.

It was Professor Josephson.

"Good afternoon, Robert," he said calmly, closing the door behind him. "I hope that I am not disturbing you."

I was aghast. At that point, I would have preferred to contend with the enraged spirit of Mr. Hunt, or a ravenously hungry salamander.

"H-h-he-lloo, Professor," I managed to stutter out. I stood up slowly, trying to regain my composure. "What brings you down here?"

"Robert, as I recall, we had an appointment this past Wednesday for the purpose of reviewing the work on your doctoral thesis. Now, I must admit that I am a doddering fool, growing older every day, so please correct me if I'm wrong."

"No, Professor, you are correct," I said meekly. "We had an appointment."

"And as I recall, you were not there, correct?"

"No, Professor."

"Good, good," he said. His expression was difficult to read, and he kept his eyes down as he spoke. "I was beginning to worry that you had been there, and I simply could not remember. Much the same as I had forgotten where I placed the artifact I once showed to you."

I looked at him, caught completely off guard, but he still didn't look at me. Despite the relative coolness of the storeroom, I began to sweat.

"I remember placing it in my safe," he said. "But poof!" He threw his hands up in the air. "It's gone."

I felt my eyes grow huge at that point. I was trapped. He clearly knew my guilt.

"Your friend out front," he said. "Mister Cooke, was it? He was very helpful when I arrived."

"Don't place the blame on Andrew," I said. "I was the one who took the parchment from your safe. It was my idea. I convinced him to go along with me."

Now I was the one who would not look up. But when I finally did, I saw him shaking his head at me.

"I would never have thought you capable of theft," he said. "Especially theft from me. At first, I thought indeed that I had misplaced it, but as the days went by with your presence blatantly lacking..."

He sighed mournfully.

"I stopped by your boarding house this morning, but your Mrs. Bettings told me I might find you here."

If I had never seen Professor Josephson again, had I simply immersed myself in the study of the esoteric arts and never looked back, perhaps I could have forgotten what I had done to him. But with him standing before me, it was impossible to suppress the immorality of my recent actions. Stealing is always wrong, and always shameful. I tried to form words, but none would come.

"I am not here to berate you, Robert," he said sincerely. "I'm only here to help you."

Hearing that, I began to imagine what it might be like to return to my old life: finish my thesis, graduate with a Doctorate, and live a normal life in a world in which magic is the realm of stage entertainers, and monsters only hide under the beds of children.

"Robert, I beg you," he continued. "Forget this destructive pursuit. Take a few weeks to refocus your energies. You'll have plenty of time in the summer to catch up on any work you might need to do on your thesis. Just return the parchment to me…"

The parchment. Those words jarred me out of my melancholy reverie.

"Professor, I can't."

"…and finish your work as we planned. After you graduate, if you still see fit…"

"I can't."

"…you may continue this line of research, with a more complete knowledge of the ramifications, and I may even…"

"I can't!"

I looked at the man I had for so many years considered as more than a mentor. I had treated him like a father, and he, in turn, had looked after me like a son. Truth be told, he had done more than most fathers would have. His act of introducing me to Elizabeth had been a defining moment in my life. Elizabeth! Could I ever have a *normal* life without her? I tried to compare my old life, my old values, against my new *purpose*. True, I had stolen the parchment, and had been complicit in destroying it, but oh! What we had learned!

"I cannot return the parchment to you," I said, trying to keep my voice level. "Because it has been burned."

I waited for his response—something, anything—but none came.

"We sacrificed it to summon the spirit of its dead author."

"Robert," he said, his voice melancholy. "My boy, why on Earth would you—"

"We know! Professor, we discovered the source star. Magic has done what pure mathematics could not. Regulus! I checked it against the equations! The star corresponds to an entity known as Sothoth Pnath, a thing that *incinerates its victims and destroys their soul.*"

"And you think somehow," he began slowly, "that perhaps this entity—"

"Not perhaps!" I said, stepping closer to him. "There is no doubt. This Sothoth Pnath obliterated the soul of Elizabeth, and I mean to have my revenge upon it!"

The professor stood before me, stoic and silent. In the years that we had known each other, I had never spoken to him before with such passion about anything. It was something our mutual study of mathematics had never brought out in me.

"I fear for you, Robert," he finally said, his voice trembling.

After staring at me for a few seconds, he turned to leave. He stopped at the door, his hand gripping the knob. But he did not open it. He did not leave.

"Mr. Bertram Hunt," he said, his back still to me, "the previous owner of this shop. He was a very odd man. Odd habits, odd mannerisms. One time, I accompanied Doctor Gardiner on a visit here. It was my first time in the store, despite having been at the university for a number of years by that point. Quentin gave no explanation as for why I should go along, except to say that he wanted me to observe Mr. Hunt. He was very emphatic on the point. 'No matter what happens, keep your eyes on Bertram Hunt,' he told me."

Up to that point I had been trying my best to not listen. I had no desire for what I assumed would be a lecture in morality. But with those words, the professor gained my attention.

"When Mr. Hunt looked at me for the first time," continued Professor Josephson, "he squinted and nodded before greeting me. Gardiner had only been in the shop twice before, but he received a vigorous handshake and a large smile from the man. Those two talked near the front of the store, while I moved away and did as I had been instructed. Aside from our relatively strange meeting, I didn't see anything out of the ordinary about him. But then something happened. A shout from outside called our attention to two men who converged directly in front of the shop from opposite directions. There was a short argument about money. One man apparently did not like the answer he received, because he pulled out a small handgun and shot the other point blank through the heart."

The professor released the knob and turned to face me.

"As might be expected, the victim collapsed to the ground, chest already bloody, and the other man ran off. What was unexpected was Bertram Hunt's reaction, or rather, the lack of it. He did not act as if he had just witnessed a cold-blooded killing—that is, until he realized that both Doctor Gardiner and I were watching him. Only then did he display any shock or fear, and to me it seemed artificial. The gunshot rapidly attracted a crowd, and the police arrived. At that point the 'dead' man got up from the ground."

Professor Josephson looked at me, as if guessing what might be going through my mind.

"No, this was not another man rising from the dead," he said. "It was faked. This was all Higgins' idea, of course. He was the shooter, but he used a blank cartridge. An expertly rigged bag of blood and some convincing acting made it all look very real—to me, at least. I learned afterward that Gardiner and Higgins had suspected that Hunt had some insight into the future, or at the very least some experience in…this area. Magic. That bit of trickery was their last attempt to get him to expose himself and learn the truth. Quentin was satisfied by the outcome of the experiment, convinced that the man knew more than he was letting on. But they were never successful in getting any kind of an admission from him."

He paused.

"I was, however."

He looked at the floor and nodded to himself.

"Months later, I came back to this store to buy a present. For my wife Anne, actually. I had hoped that Mr. Hunt would not remember me, but he did. We both pretended that that embarrassing incident had not occurred, and it worked for a while. But I was the only customer in the store. There eventually came a time when the question just popped out of my mouth. 'What is it that you see?' I asked. It was such an ambiguous question that he could have feigned ignorance and laughed it off, but instead he smiled grimly, and began to talk about the days of his youth, when he was about your age, Robert. He admitted to being driven by foolish curiosity. He wanted to learn secrets, and he did. Somehow, he learned how to venture out beyond our three-dimensional realm. He used the term *Outside*, and described it as being more *real* than all this."

He swept his arm around at the room.

"Bertram Hunt maintained that our universe was but a ghostly shadow compared to that place, and yet the two of them somehow fit together, relied upon each other. While there, he had seen horrid things that had chilled him to his marrow. There were bizarre creatures that feasted on dreams. He described them as shapeless and having shape, both angular and curved at the same time, and insisted that they were around us continually, invisible and immaterial in that extra-dimensional space."

The professor stopped and looked at me. As much as I knew that he was telling this in hopes it would horrify me, deter me from my path, I couldn't help but find it fascinating. Extra-dimensional creatures? Subsisting on dreams? I waited eagerly for more information, not unlike a starving man begging for bread.

"Almost every other person on the face of the Earth would dismiss what I have just said as utter nonsense," he said. "But you believe me, don't you, Robert?"

I nodded.

"Yes, Bertram Hunt discovered secret knowledge," he said. The tone of his voice changed, becoming at once both sad and angry. "Much like you're attempting. Yes, he visited that other dimension. And yes, he returned safely. But he was there too long, and it exacted a price from him. What he witnessed nearly drove him mad. He experienced things no man was ever meant to. Only after his return did he appreciate that fact, when he discovered he had been changed—cursed. From that moment on, when looking at someone, he would know how that person would die."

I disguised my shock by feigning a cough and clearing my throat. But my insides had frozen.

"At the time," said the professor, "I didn't know how to react. Doctor Gardiner had begun to open my mind to such possibilities, but it was all too much for me to digest at once. Still, I did not disbelieve him either. Confusing me further was the fact that he had been hiding that information from Gardiner and Higgins. I asked Hunt why he had confided in me. He thought for the longest time. In the end, all he said was that he saw that he could trust me to keep it a secret. Over the subsequent years, we crossed paths from time to time. He would always look at me knowingly, never explaining why. And I must say that, if he actually saw *my* death, I think I prefer it that way. But he's gone now, as is my Anne and your Elizabeth. And Quentin."

The professor dropped his eyes, then looked up at me again.

"I do not have cause to pray much anymore," he said. "But I shall pray for you."

With that, he turned and left, shutting the door behind him. From beyond the wall, I heard a mumble, presumably a word of farewell to Andrew, then the muted jingle of the bell above the outer door once, then twice. Then there was silence.

The professor's visit was more than just a slap; it felt as if I had been pummeled mercilessly. While proof of Bertram Hunt discovering the means to go Outside was equal parts frightening and captivating, this was not the information that caused my throat to tighten. Mr. Hunt had told me that he knew he would soon die. The way he had looked at me that day at the boarding house, what he said…it sounded as if he knew my death as well, and some aspect of it had caused him to despise me. *How bad could it be to provoke such a reaction?*

I was still sullen when Andrew knocked at the door and entered. He said that he was surprised when the professor introduced himself and inquired after me, and that he innocently directed him to the backroom. When I asked Andrew how much he had overheard, he admitted that although he had heard little clearly, some of the more animated segments had come through. I was embarrassed by it all. Thinking back, I realized that I had never revealed to him that I had stolen the parchment directly from the professor. Not wishing to bring that up, I repeated what little I had learned about the Outside realm, stressing how dangerous it sounded. He was especially captivated by the description of the dream-eating creatures. Too captivated.

"I want to go there," he declared.

"Did you hear nothing I said? And I do remember you saying that your grandfather had warned you not to try. He was permanently changed by the experience."

"Yes, and that goes a long way toward explaining his aloofness. Seeing death constantly would affect anyone. But that change was a result of him staying there too long."

"But how long is too long? An hour? A minute?"

"We can't know that, but we have one advantage he didn't. We are forewarned of the side effects."

The tone of his voice indicated that his mind had been made up. That part of Andrew that could not back down from a challenge had returned. It was then that I considered telling him the full story of the interaction with his grandfather shortly before his death, as well as my suspicions. I really wanted to, but something held my tongue: selfishness. I wanted to continue down this path of magical exploration, and I needed his help. Burdening him with my theories could threaten our relationship in two ways. First, he could see me as afraid, possibly weak, while I needed to project a strong and dependable image. Alternately, and worse, he might see the truth, come to his senses and refuse to continue.

Even then, I recognized the danger for both of us. In retrospect, I should never have ignored that moment of clarity. But pride intervened. I convinced myself that we could continue the work, and that I could keep us both safe from harm by constraining Andrew from rash, impulsive behavior. The most important detail in my favor was that neither of us knew the method for traveling Outside. Mr. Hunt had learned, of course, but I had the feeling it would be a point of pride for Andrew to discover the answer for himself. He would likely not call upon his grandfather's spirit for the information. Not right away, anyway.

After Andrew returned to mind the store, I spent the remainder of the day in a war with myself. The drive to learn all that I could, and as quickly as I could, conflicted with the need to be as safe as possible. That thought of safety also called to mind the encounter with the young Elizabeth Manning. Despite the fact that that event had implied our actions were being monitored somehow, we had noticed no other warning signs. And, adding to the complexity, another issue completely at odds with the study of magic was the very real requirement for me to be able to support myself. By severing my connection with the professor, and consequently the university, I was depriving myself of income in the short-term, and a future in the long-term. I needed a job, and so needed the professor. But each time I focused on the mundane requirements of reality, the very real fact of Elizabeth's death—and a growing obsession with revenge—was right there as well.

My thoughts looping endlessly with no answer in sight, I accomplished nothing the rest of the day.

Despite Professor Josephson's stressful visit, a full night's sleep and the light of a new day brought a fresh perspective. There was no reason why I had to choose between my magical studies and the admittedly less stimulating topic of mathematics. It would be difficult to commit time to both, but in theory, I should be able to. Andrew would understand my need to address both aspects of my life. The professor would clearly have a harder time accepting the dual path, so I simply would not tell him. All that was necessary was for him to think I was back on track. Though he may suspect otherwise, I only needed to ensure that I provided him no proof. And I would have to ask for his forgiveness—but not yet. I wasn't close enough yet. I decided on one week—one week before I would begin to split my energies and recommit myself to mathematics. In that time, I intended to learn as much magic as I possibly could.

I was midway through the fifth of Mr. Hunt's notebooks when the subject matter changed abruptly. They had previously been filled with spells and notations from various sources, with the entries grouped logically together. All of a sudden, however, I found passages copied seemingly haphazardly from different ancient tomes, mainly the *Necronomicon* and *Unaussprechlichen Kulten*. Never were these passages the texts of spells; rather, they revealed—in bits and pieces—the cryptic, forbidden knowledge of the Ancients. It was as if, at the time of the writing, he had begun to research at random, perhaps only satisfying his curiosity on certain topics and recording his most interesting findings in the notebooks. And while all of the information was interesting to some degree, I found one fragment to be particularly memorable.

171

It is said:

The Lord Azathoth fears the nothingness that came before and will come once again.

Yog Sothoth, the Gate, fears those few shards of the Crystal which survived the Struggle, aeons ago.

The messenger Nyarlathotep and the shadow Sothoth Pnath both embrace the darkness and fear the light.

That one which dwells below, Tsathoggua, fears the cleansing flame.

The Great Cthulhu does not fear.

According to the notation above it, this fragment was reputed to have originally come from the *Pnakotic Manuscripts*, a fact that Mr. Hunt apparently found difficult to believe. Although doubting its source, he indicated that he trusted the content as being consistent with other research he had done. Despite the fact that I had once again come across an incomplete list, I was fascinated by the concept that beings such as these could possibly fear anything.

With this transition of the notebook's contents from detailed magical data to miscellaneous odds and ends, I knew that my time of self-instruction would soon end—and my time of personal tutoring by Andrew would begin. The thought was more than a bit exciting. I fantasized about which spells I would next attempt, and tried to set deadlines for my own personal goals. The requirement of finishing my thesis, though—that wet blanket kept me grounded.

Two days later, another letter arrived for Andrew from his contact in Boston, Mr. Fenster. This one detailed only one spell. At first glance, it appeared to be similar to the ceremony used to summon and control the salamander. But as we sat together at the table in the backroom, our heads nearly touching as we bent over the paper, the gravity of what we read slowly became more apparent. By the time I had finished the whole thing, my stomach had knotted.

It was indeed another summoning spell, but the potential for danger was far greater. It purportedly allowed the magician to call and control a creature from the Outside known as a Servitor of Q'yoth. The ceremony consisted of only a few simple steps, but in each case, safety was sacrificed. To begin, the magician would essentially hypnotize himself, so at the proper time, his unconscious self would speak aloud a magical phrase. Then—and at first this seemed absurd to me—he would cast a spell to force himself to fall asleep. After a few minutes of deep sleep, the first spell would take hold, forcing the dreamer to speak the words *while still sleeping*. The dream conjured forth by those words would act as the incapacitated rat, to be consumed as a sacrifice—and by what, we presumably already knew. After the magician awoke, the Servitor could be commanded in R'lyehian, a blasphemous language from beyond the stars. When the thing had finished performing its duties, the magician need only utter a single word in order to dismiss it.

Now, there was nothing in the letter which explicitly stated, 'This is how to go Outside,' but considering what we had recently learned about that realm, it now all made sense. It made even more sense when we looked at the final page of the letter. There was a list of simple commands written in English. The first two commands listed were 'Pick me up' and 'Put me down.' Below the list was an additional note:

> *You will not see the Servitor, but you shall know its presence as a dull thrumming, a slow vibration. It is not a sound that one hears with the ears, but rather feels. It is unmistakable. If you proceed with this spell, you shall readily know what I mean.*

In all, I found the explanatory notes in the letter to be quite informative, but they did nothing to reassure me that the safety of the spellcaster would not be at risk.

"You intend to try this," I said. It seemed to be pointless to phrase it as a question.

"I do," replied Andrew.

"You do see how dangerous this is, though? Through hypnosis and sleep, you render yourself helpless. The creature cannot be seen. The commands are strings of nearly unpronounceable consonants, clearly not intended for a human throat. The potential for error is immense. And your grandfather warned you—"

"But my grandfather succeeded. He just stayed too long."

"Yes, but—"

"Look. I share your concern, but this spell is a necessary step along the path to greater command of my magical abilities," he insisted. "From this point forward, very little will be easy. I must— *We* must—continually attempt more and more difficult spells until we reach the level of expertise necessary to banish Sothoth Pnath. Sooner or later, I shall need to attempt something like this anyway. Why not now, if I'm confident that I can succeed? And I am confident."

He had harped on the theme of confidence since the start. It seemed not the best idea to introduce doubt into his mind, but his safety—our safety—was paramount.

"What about this contact in Boston?" I asked. "Can you trust him?"

"I have no reason to distrust him. My grandfather began to exchange letters with him just before he handed off the shop to my uncle Charles and me."

"But Mr. Hunt never met him?"

"Not that I'm aware."

Andrew was calm about my line of questioning. I think he could see what I was attempting, but his confidence was unshakeable. I had one tactic left.

"Okay," I began. "Let us assume that his moral character is honorable, as there is no evidence to the contrary. However…what if, though his intentions are good, he accidentally made an error in writing down the instructions? Or miscopied one of the commands in that preposterous language? It seems easy enough to get one of those words wrong. Can we trust him not to have made a mistake?"

That got a reaction, but not the one I was expecting. Andrew grinned.

"I was wondering when you would realize that," he said. "That issue is a constant with everything we attempt. There is *always* a chance of an error creeping in. Just because the information has been handed down through the ages does not guarantee that it is correct."

For me, that revelation was terrifying.

"But how…"

"How is anything ever accomplished?" he finished my question.

I nodded.

"You should know," he said. "Faith."

The word echoed in my ears. Yes, I was well acquainted with the concept. Or had been.

"Faith, not in God, but in the good will of other men," I said.

"At times, I am sure that good will plays a part. But it's not necessary to stretch your faith that far. Greed is likely often a driving factor. And pride. It doesn't matter. Ignore the motivation that drives anyone to record the information we need. The only thing we are concerned with is its accuracy."

"An accuracy which is a complete mystery," I insisted, brimming with doubt.

"No," countered Andrew. "Not necessarily. Consider the case of the magician who works alone. Let's assume that he comes across errant information. If he survives the mistake, he either destroys the data or corrects it. In either case, that error is not passed along. If he dies, it is also not passed on, unless his notes survive and are found. If another solo magician is the unlucky recipient, the same scenario repeats. But now consider the master magician who has an apprentice. If the master were to die due to that same errant information, the apprentice would survive to destroy or correct it—and also seek revenge if appropriate. So you see, the system is self-correcting. The odds are extremely good—though not perfect—that we can rely upon the information."

He paused to ensure that he had my attention.

"You're the apprentice," he said.

"And so I should be prepared to exact revenge."

"Exactly." He laughed, easing the tension. "The master may get the glory, but being the apprentice is safer. And besides…you said yourself some time ago that I should be more trusting. Based upon our experiences with this gentleman from Boston, I'm starting to believe that he would not steer me wrong."

I found myself unable to disagree.

FIFTEEN

On Saturday, Andrew unexpectedly closed the store just after lunch. He said that he wanted extra time—both to relax, and to prepare for the upcoming invocation, in that order. We had different definitions of relaxation, though. For me, it meant sitting down with a book even though I spent my days studying. He wanted to do something more physical. Based on my past experiences with Elizabeth, I suggested rowing on the lake in the park, and he agreed.

The sky was overcast, and humidity had been building through the morning, threatening rain. Perhaps because of that, no one was using the boats. I was about to pay for one when Andrew stopped me.

"Look," he said, pointing at a pair of women not far off. "I like the tall one. Let's go over."

They were both attractive, I had to admit. When I made no move, he grabbed me by the arm and pulled me gently along.

"I don't want to diminish the love you had for Elizabeth," he whispered. "But you have a long life ahead. You're going to need to start interacting socially again. No commitments are necessary. Just talk with the pretty, young woman over there."

That got a smile out of me.

"Just relax and talk," he continued, "while I—oh, I know what to do. Just play along."

They took notice as we approached. Andrew dove right in.

"Ladies," he said, "my friend here has actually challenged me to a rowing race. We need some unbiased judges at the finish line. Do you think you can help us out with that?"

I could tell that he had directed his speech at the taller one because her own gaze never wavered from his. Right away, the other woman picked up on what was going on. If she had resigned herself to being my companion, she gave no indication that I had been forced on her. Her name was Donna, and the one who had caught Andrew's eye was Denise. His introduction had the intended effect, and before long, the four of us were talking and laughing as we all walked over to the rowboats.

We decided to row out at as easy pace, then turn around and race back. The ladies, waiting on the end of the pier, would see who passed the end of the pier first. On our way out, I could tell that Andrew was stronger, but my technique was more efficient, having been honed through practice. After we turned around and evened up the boats, I began to wonder about his plan.

"Are we really racing?" I asked him. "Or are we going to just try to make it interesting for them?"

"Oh, we're racing," he said with a grin. "After all, I need to prove my worthiness to Denise."

A race it was then.

It was a fair start, our oars hitting the water at the same time. I was ahead for a bit, then Andrew passed me with a furious effort. By the halfway mark, he had increased his lead to nearly a boat-length, but I began to close the distance as I sensed his pace slow. I heard the cheers of the women as we neared the dock. The view of his boat in my peripheral vision made me think that it would be close. And it was.

As we sat in the boats gasping for breath, our clothes soaked through with sweat, Denise declared Andrew the winner. Donna disagreed politely, and the exchange that followed swiftly became a heated argument. Andrew and I both found the situation hilarious. Our roars got the attention of the ladies, and they began to giggle when they realized what had happened. But even with the situation defused, neither would budge on their opinion. Another race would be needed. But because they had an appointment to keep, and Andrew and I were spent, we all decided to have the rematch in one week, with the women riding along in the boats to get a better perspective.

I wish we had been able to keep that date.

Because Andrew wanted extra time to ensure that he had everything memorized, I didn't arrive at the shop until ten o'clock. A few brief showers had wet the town during the afternoon, their evaporation adding even more moisture to the sticky atmosphere. Steady rain finally began on my way over, first as a light drizzle, but rapidly gaining momentum. I arrived, only slightly dampened, and pounded on the door. As I stood there waiting for him to answer, I had the most intense feeling of being watched. The hairs on my neck stood up, as I imagined the presence of someone right behind me. I whirled around quickly, but no one was there. With my back flat against the door, I scanned the darkness for any sign of life. There was nothing but rain.

The lock clicked and the door open behind me.

"Good heavens!" said Andrew, pulling me inside. "It's pouring. Were you caught in that?"

I shook my head.

"It only just started," I said.

When he had closed and locked the door, I peered out the windows to search the empty street one more time for a reason to justify my strange feeling. The trip to the bookstore in the darkness had been uneventful; it was only while standing outside the door that I had the sensation of being spied upon. My fears banished, Andrew led the way upstairs.

"I must admit," he said, "I can't wait to try this."

There was excitement in his voice, though his outward

appearance did not betray his feelings. To my eye, he was very re-strained, an almost palpable aura of self-confidence about him. The irritable tenseness that had preceded the previous ceremony was thankfully not in evidence.

"And thank you for helping me relax today," he added.

"No, I have to thank *you*. That was a good idea. I *will* beat you next weekend, though."

He chuckled.

"We'll see, won't we?"

The letter with the instructions was on the table, the top sheet showing the English and R'lyehian command translations. A dull roll of distant thunder penetrated the room. The curtains were drawn closed on all the windows, but I could still discern the light-ning flashes of the heart of the storm—still far off—through the white gauze.

"You can have a seat at the table," he said. "I'll be on the couch. I want to keep this simple: summon the creature, command it, dis-miss it. This time, the difference will be that we cannot contain it in a circle. When summoned, it will come, but will remain beyond our perception. Because we cannot contain it, we cannot protect our-selves. Regardless, you should be safe. I would be the focus of any…misunderstanding. We must trust that the sacrifice of my dreams will be accepted."

I swallowed the lump in my throat and nodded.

"My only request, as before," said Andrew, "is that you do not interrupt me."

I nodded again and sat down. Although this ceremony required more memorization than the one for summoning the salamander, no physical preparations were needed. He took a seat on the couch and began to cast the first spell. After speaking in Latin, he paused, then intoned a string of syllables which grated on the ears. He then got comfortable, laying so that he faced me, and murmured to himself for a few seconds. Sleep was upon him almost instantly. I alternated my attention between him and the lightning of the approaching tempest.

Within minutes, his breathing took on the slow, regular tempo of dreaming. The room was silent, the only sounds being the rain hitting the windows, and the airflow in and out of his nostrils. But then, he eerily began to speak while still fast asleep. In a hollow voice, he repeated aloud the terrible words he had commanded himself to utter not long before. When the final syllable was finished, silence returned, but in place of Andrew's peaceful sleep, his brow furrowed with worry, and his limbs twitched. He must have been conjuring the dream to be sacrificed to the Servitor. I wondered what kind of horror his sleeping mind had produced.

As I watched him struggle with the nightmare of his own devising, I became more and more alarmed. The unconscious thrashings of his limbs grew continually more violent, and his features contorted with fear. Would he awaken soon? Should I interfere? A flash of lightning from the coming storm stirred me from my seat. Judging by the delay before the thunderclap, the storm was closer, yet still a ways off. The thunder…there was a bizarre echo to it. I went over to Andrew, wanting to do something, but afraid to. His body wrenched violently, pulling him briefly up off the couch, before flopping back down like a dead fish. The force of his convulsions made my decision: I had to wake him. I hovered over him, gathering courage. But before I could even touch his shoulder, his eyes flew open, and he shot up to sitting.

"Alive!" he shouted. "Am I alive?"

"Yes! Alive and awake."

Shaken, but reassured, he laid back down on the couch. The continuing echo of thunder was disorienting, and I peered through the curtains to try to catch flashes of lightning. There were none at that moment, and yet the throbbing continued like the heartbeat of a titan. I looked at Andrew, filled with both fear and excitement.

He sighed and sat up on the couch.

181

"It is here," he confirmed, seemingly struggling to keep his voice calm.

"Then the sacrifice was a success," I said.

"Yes."

The emphasis he put on that one word conveyed so much. I heard a thrill of success, satisfaction of a job well done, and the confidence that comes with great power or secret knowledge.

"Do you remember what it was that you dreamed?" I asked him.

He closed his eyes tightly, and there was a visible shudder, as he grabbed his head with both hands. Seeing his anguish, I hoped that I would not regret hearing the answer. As I waited for him to answer, the muted sounds of the storm mounted as the center of it drew ever closer. Even more noticeable, though, was the unnatural throbbing that indicated the presence of the Servitor: That alien resonance chilled me to my soul.

After a few tense seconds, Andrew relaxed and opened his eyes.

"Unfortunately, I do remember pieces of it," he whispered in a ragged voice. "A string of images, only vaguely connected, all horrifying...perhaps not visually, but emotionally. Had you seen what I did, you may not have had the same reaction. It was as if the dream was keyed to my own personal fears. Or..."

I waited, but there was no further elaboration. Instead, he stood on shaky legs, walked over to the table and picked up the paper with the list of commands. A bolt of lightning illuminated the curtained windows; the lag of the matching thunderclap was much shorter.

"I must assume," I said, "that you are still committed to going Outside."

"Yes," he said, smiling grimly. "Based on the list of commands, there are few options."

"Are you absolutely certain?"

He cleared his throat.

"I am."

I had only one tack left to try.

"You succeeded in the summoning," I said. "You could just dismiss it without telling it to do anything, right?"

"I *could*, but please trust me here. You trusted my judgment when I handled the salamander. I have the confidence to handle this—and yes, I *do* remember my grandfather's warning. This will be a short trip. The summoning itself was the dangerous part. The creature is here. It obeys me. It would even obey you, in fact, if you would like to command it. Unless I explicitly tell it not to."

Another bright flash of lightning, and accompanying blast, made Andrew jump. He looked at me with a crooked smile.

"Though when it comes to storms like this, I must admit that I'm somewhat less confident."

I could not help but laugh.

"You fear the known, but not the unknown?"

"I fear what I cannot control. The storm is beyond my control. The Servitor is not."

"For both of our sakes, I hope so."

He moved toward the center of the room, about six feet away. With his back to me, he took a deep breath and gave the command. The blasphemous noise that poured from his throat was startling to hear. It was astonishing to think it actually had any meaning at all. But immediately after the final syllable was pronounced, it happened.

He disappeared.

There were no noises, no lights, nothing to smell or sense in any way. He simply disappeared. I hardly had time to react. Looking around, it was an indisputable fact that I was alone in that room. The storm continued to rage outside, but I hardly noticed the lightning flashes, the peals of thunder. There was only that throb—dull, aching, like the ticking of a clock—counting the seconds that I stood there, and with Andrew somewhere else entirely.

Then, he reappeared in the same spot. When he started to waver, I rushed over, and steadied him before he could fall. The moment I touched him, he seemed to snap to consciousness.

"Andrew! Are you all right?"

"Yes." He shook his head, and his stance became more solid. "How long? How long was I gone?"

"I…I'm not sure," I said, trying to think. "Certainly less than a minute."

"A minute?" He shook his head again as if to wake himself, then listened to the storm. "But it must be. The storm yet rages. The clock on the wall…"

His voice faded out, and he stared into the middle space. Mouth agape, his face was completely blank, though his eyes danced around and blinked rapidly. On anyone else, such an expression would have served as a mark of insanity. In light of the circumstances, however, it seemed as if his mind was trying to come to terms with what it had experienced. I was afraid of what he might say next, what he might do. It wasn't long before he emerged from his stupor—seemingly none the worse for wear—and began to speak.

"I can't even begin to describe everything that happened in that short span of time," he said, the words tumbling out. "It's astounding—while I was there, I could actually comprehend the extra-dimensional reality of the place. I could see you standing right there! And the Servitor! It's not…no, it's not the dream-eater your professor described. I saw those things, as well. The description of them as both angular and curved is probably most apt, given the words we have available in English. But regardless, the creatures that feed on dreams are akin to…mice. And the Servitor is a cat. I believe my nightmares were meant as a kind of bait to lure the dream-eaters, which the Servitor then preyed upon."

He paused and shook his head.

"Or I think so. I don't know. I'm still trying to digest it all."

He paused again, and listened. The ever-present thrumming was still about us.

"Wait," he said. "Let me dismiss this thing first."

"Are you ready to do that?"

"Oh, yes. I'm fine," he said. "This will just take a second."

I was still holding the sheet of commands. Andrew pointed out the last one on the list, read it over a few times, mouthing it silently. Then he stepped back, took a deep breath, and began to speak it aloud.

For everyone who experiences a catastrophe, their world becomes divided into two distinct parts: Before and After. The Before world is orderly; the After is chaos. The smooth unfolding of reality—something we often take for granted—is suddenly transformed to a choppy series of nightmarish images, forever burned into the memory. With Elizabeth's death, I had already experienced such an event. I was about to experience another.

At the precise instant at which Andrew began to enunciate the command, a spectacular bolt of lightning struck a tree outside, causing the building around us to shake. The flash, combined with the deafening blast, caused me to jump—and of the two of us, I was the one who was less fearful of the storm. He must have been truly terrified.

"My Lord, that was close!" I exclaimed, my heart thudding. Oddly, there was no reaction from Andrew. He stood unmoving, seemingly frozen in place.

"Andrew? Are you all right?"

As I took a step toward him, he started to fall backwards. I caught him, and lowered him to the floor, but quickly withdrew my hands in shock, as his jaws flew open, and dozens of thin, ropy tentacles shot forth in a stream. Within seconds, he was covered in a writhing, mass of snake-like things, each shiny black appendage terminated by a small mouth filled with teeth. They began to devour him, blood oozing from uncountable wounds. He undoubtedly would have screamed, had he been able.

He resisted for a while, writhing back and forth on the floor in front of me, but it was futile. There were far too many of the hungry appendages to fight with only two hands. Completely paralyzed with fright, I could not move. I did not help him. I simply watched in agonizing horror, as the tentacles, piranha-like, cleaned the flesh from his bones. But the peak of my nightmare was when the squirming appendages momentarily cleared a space to reveal his eyes. For a brief instant, those eyes—still clearly conscious and wracked with pain—met mine. Seeing that, I thought that I would truly go mad. I could only force my own shut, and pray for forgiveness, waiting for my own, similar fate, which was certainly inevitable. But the end never came. Despite the fact that I stood only a few feet away, the carnivorous appendages did not touch me. They did not even try.

After an indeterminate amount of time, the nauseating noises of the unholy feast finally ended. I forced myself to look at the scene. Before me lay, in a pool of blood, a skeleton stripped of muscle and flesh. The glistening bones, now devoid of connective tissue, rested on the floor in the vague outline of a man. The hair and teeth also remained, as well as remnants of clothing. The tentacles, however, were nowhere to be seen.

With a savage, heart-stopping attack of terror, the full impact of the tragedy hit me. The ghastly scene I had witnessed was tenfold more macabre than the worst nightmare of any sane man's mind. Somehow, I did not pass out. For uncounted minutes, I could only stand and stare at the bare, white skeleton upon the floor.

Slowly, intellect returned. Muted thunder from the storm outside reached me through my dazedness. The worst of it had passed. But as I became aware of the rain that continued to fall outside, another sound registered upon my consciousness.

The ominous throbbing of the Servitor. It was still there with me.

Fear threatened to paralyze me again, but the need to do something was too great. But what? I had been rooted in the same spot throughout Andrew's terrible ordeal, and still had not changed position, not even an inch. Was it only that spot that kept me safe? Dare I move at all? Becoming conscious of the need to be still, the effort to maintain it became very great. My limbs began to tremble. I knew that the shaking was too minuscule to be detected by humans, but an alien creature with indefinable senses? Shifting only my eyes, I looked as far as I dared. To either side, there was nothing to see. I could only assume that the tentacles had withdrawn to the extra-dimensional space from which they had come. The harder I tried to not move, the more my muscles quivered. I closed my eyes, and listened carefully to the hellish throbs of the Servitor, trying to pinpoint its location. The sound—if it was even something that could be heard with the ears—was of too low a frequency to sense its source. It was everywhere at once, surrounding me.

Great knots grew in my muscles, and I knew that I could not be still any longer. Holding my breath, I slowly relaxed my arms and hands. Nothing happened. I listened carefully for any noises, then turned my head to look left and right. Still nothing. I took one small step backwards, away from the remains of my friend, then two more. There was still no reaction; the Servitor apparently did not notice me.

It seemed as if I was safe, but for how long? I had no idea what to do. My first thought was of flight, but what of the consequences? Would I make it out of the building, or even out of the room, only to have that writhing death descend upon me? Assuming that I made it home safely, the Servitor would still be in this world. I did not know how long the spell would last, but it seemed safe to assume that it would not last forever. When the time elapsed, would the thing go back from whence it came, or would it be loosed upon this world, free to devour whomever it chose? Would it eventually come for me? Or would I be haunted by the unearthly heartbeat until I went mad?

Professor Josephson was right. He feared the path I had chosen would lead to madness. Or death. Of the two, I desired death. First Elizabeth, now Andrew—both had died before me. And I had been powerless to help either of them.

My hand yet clutched the sheet with the commands. Andrew had said it himself—I could command it, just as he could. This, I had the power to do—or die trying. I tore my eyes from the gleaming bones, focused on the paper in my hand. Gathering my courage, I forced myself to speak the alien command.

Once again, I waited for death, and again it did not come. As I stood and listened, the throbbing slowly faded, as if the Servitor was moving away from me through some invisible barrier. At last, only the sounds of the dying storm outside remained. Wind and rain. It was over. Overcome, I collapsed in a heap on the floor.

SIXTEEN

The dense fog of sleep was slow to dissipate. Through closed eyelids, I could tell that the sun had risen. For a while, I was oblivious to all but the shrill songs of nearby birds, and the hardness of the wooden floor beneath me. The question of how I came to be there nagged at my half-conscious brain. But it didn't take long for a memory of the previous evening to surface, that of an abominable sound, and the alien creature that had produced it. My heart pounded in my chest, as I listened nervously for the creature's throbbing. There was nothing to hear but the birds.

Still on the floor, I became aware of something else: a smell that was not at all pleasant. Trips to the butcher shop with my mother came to mind. On extremely hot days there had been a charnel odor of drying blood and bones. But that was long ago. Now…the remaining grogginess dissolved, as the most abhorrent details of the past evening flooded in. I found them difficult to accept. But as my father was fond of saying, *Seeing is believing*. Never was the aphorism truer. I finally opened my eyes and searched the room in the dim light, the curtains still drawn.

The insects had already begun to dine upon the tiny morsels of flesh left on Andrew's naked bones. The odor of death grew stronger in my nostrils. I inched hurriedly backward, until I could go no further. The guilt hit me like a blow to the gut: I was to blame for his death. He would never have been put at risk if not for me. I should never have involved him in my quest. At the very least, I should not have allowed him to perform the ceremony. With enough time to practice, I could have done it myself. If I had but taken the time…

As I tallied my mistakes, a sickening realization numbed me. I had already developed a reputation with the police after Elizabeth's death, and would assuredly be a suspect in this one as well. Though I had stayed out of view, there had never been an attempt to keep secret my presence at the bookstore. Numerous witnesses would likely be able to attest to that fact. There was no way to explain all of this in a believable manner. The circumstances would find me guilty. Could I be executed? There was no murder weapon to be found. A long jail sentence, then? If not jail, then surely an asylum—especially if I attempted to tell the truth. I could confide in Professor Josephson, but he had no power to protect me from the law…and he could certainly testify to my erratic behavior of late. Despite the fact of my innocence, I determined that I had no choice but to run.

On the floor before me was the paper that had saved my life. Despite that, the sight of the otherworldly jumble of letters brought a crawling chill to my skin. I flipped it over. On the other side were the instructions for the ceremony, written in a scrawling hand by Andrew's contact in Boston. *Victor Fenster*, read the heading of his stationary. It registered as an oddity that I had known both names from my youth: Victor my friend, and the Fensters the long-dead residents of that accursed house. There was some overlap in my mind between the two, of course, but they were still distinct subjects.

Regardless of the name, this man in Boston had to be my destination. He would likely know what had gone wrong. I hoped he could explain why the creature had killed Andrew, but had listened to me. And if Andrew's death had been deliberate to any degree, I would find it within me to play the part of a proper apprentice and take revenge. As for what to do after simply discovering as many answers as possible, I did not know.

As helpful as the notebooks had been, I felt that I had to leave them. Taking them along could be considered theft, and so getting caught with them could be another—admittedly small—piece of evidence against me with respect to the death. The only item I felt I needed to take was the letter from Mr. Fenster. Andrew had left the envelope with his address under the pages of the letter. My coat, the letter...the key. I would need to lock the door behind me when I left. I found it on his dresser.

There was just one thing left to do. There needed to be a final farewell, but 'Ashes to ashes, dust to dust' just did not seem appropriate for the situation. Those were normal words for normal deaths. I tried to picture Andrew as a vibrant, living person, but the white bones influenced the direction of my thoughts.

"And he said to me, 'Son of man, can these bones live?'," was all I could mutter before I was forced to turn away.

That would have to do. After whispering a closing "Amen," I went downstairs and crept close to the window. One man must have just passed by the storefront; he was moving further away. No one else was around. After going out, I locked the door, and left the key under the mat.

My exit from the store had gone undetected, and I made it two blocks before seeing another living soul. Trying to avoid all churches and their throngs of Sunday morning worshipers, my route back to the boarding house was much longer than normal. How the last few weeks had changed me. Before, I would have been one of them, another comfortable sheep moving with the herd, filing inside, looking forward to that feeling of companionship. Now, my guilt and paranoia made me shun all contact.

When I arrived at the boarding house it was obvious from the noises in the dining room that the majority of the tenants were eating breakfast. I was able to reach my room without an encounter, but realized that the odds of also exiting without being seen were small indeed. That being the case, I decided to wash up, stuff as much as I could into my lone suitcase, and have breakfast before leaving. It took some doing, but as I packed, I was able to banish those awful, lingering images into a corner of my mind, and induce an appetite. After also preparing a believable excuse for my trip, I grabbed my suitcase and went downstairs.

Most of the table had cleared by the time I got there. I took a seat near Mr. Pfenniger, who looked at me and smiled oddly. I was about to ask him what his reaction might mean, when Mrs. Bettings entered with a plate piled high with flapjacks. Instead of setting it near the center of the table, as per custom, she put the plate down next to me, but it clattered from none too gentle a placement.

"There you are, Robert," she greeted me. "Are you hungry? This morning?"

There was an edge to her voice, as she also looked at me oddly—troubled, perhaps. And the remaining men seemed to be waiting for my answer as well. Paranoia began to inspire fear, as my thoughts darted around, trying to determine what might be going on. I had washed and changed clothes, so there was no possibility of them knowing—that was it! My room was directly above Mr. Pfenniger's. He knew that I had never come home.

"I am," I said carefully. "Very much so."

I removed two flapjacks from the stack and pointed at the remainder.

"Plenty to go around, still," I offered, but each of the men declined.

"Fill up," said Mr. Pfenniger, and winked at me. "Young men need strength."

Relief and embarrassment both hit me at the same time, as I understood the assumption they had made. As my face turned red, the men drained their coffee cups, and took their dishes into the kitchen. In a minute, it was just Mrs. Bettings and me.

"I must admit, I have a hard time coming to terms with this, Robert," she said. "I am fully aware of the urges of young men, and I certainly know of the tragedy you endured. I *was* hoping you'd move on with your life, and I'm grateful that you did not try to sneak anyone into the house, but—"

"Mrs. Bettings, wait," I interrupted her. "Please."

She seemed to be relieved that I had spoken up.

"Yes," I said. "I did meet a young woman yesterday. In the park." I paused to remember which name belonged to which woman. "Donna. We talked for a little while, and agreed to meet again next Saturday."

That much was all perfectly true, at least.

"But last night was just work. Late in the evening, I had an inspiration that I thought would get me through a sticking point in my thesis. I went over to the university to get access to the resources I needed. Some naps at the desk got me through the night. Today, I am heading down to Providence for the week, so please let everyone know to not wait up for me."

I smiled, and she returned it.

"A retired colleague of Professor Josephson who could provide me with some special insights lives there, and the Brown University Library has some materials that ours does not."

It was her turn to be embarrassed.

"Oh, I'm sorry. Mr. Pfenniger said that he saw you at the lake with..." She raised her voice and looked at the kitchen door. "And he obviously jumped to the wrong conclusion."

I raised my right hand.

"I can honestly say that I was not with a woman last night."

And again, that was true.

She left me alone to eat my fill of flapjacks and bacon. When finished, I gave her a hug, wondering when I would see her next. Would I really be back in a week? I doubted it.

To my chagrin, I had to wait until nearly noon for the train. The delay was excruciating. At any moment, I expected to be arrested. I had to remind myself that Andrew's bookstore was never open on Sundays, and so the remains could not possibly be found until the following day at the earliest. I passed the time trying to remain calm and act normally. It worked for the first hour.

After that, the depot began to fill with others waiting for the same train south. A man sat down next to me, smelling of dead fish and old sweat. I myself had never been able to settle on any particular *eau de toilette*, not even considering the cost, but wished for anything of the sort to spray on either of us. Too late, I made the decision to push aside politeness and move to another seat. Looking around, it was plain that no others were available.

Adding to my irritation, the stranger began to hum. On and on, he repeated several stanzas with the same rhythm. Just as I thought I would need to ask him to stop, he did. There was only a short pause before he began again.

"What," I bit off my first word, "is that? What song are you humming?"

Seated on my right, he turned to me, and I to him. A scraggly brown beard, shot through with grey, covered a pockmarked face. His right eye was missing.

"An old sea ditty," he wheezed. Adding to his odorous emanations was the unpleasant smell of alcohol on his breath. "It tells of some messy work. I was warned by genteel folk to not sing the words in public."

He smiled, exposing teeth—the ones remaining, anyway—which were eroded in such a way as to match the rest of his features.

"Not loud, anyhows."

There was no time to protest before he started crooning to me, voice low. The first words froze me.

"No skin, no flesh, them bones shine through.

Hackin', scrapin', the best we do.

The best we can, though pretty rough.

Others though, they polishes off.

Beaks and teeth, they eat their fill.

All blood, all gore, a devil's meal.

So clean, so clean, that skel'ton gleams.

With flesh stripped clean, that skel'ton gleams.

It's white, so white. It's oh so—"

"Stop!" I finally shouted, an inner fury having grown large enough to burst out. "How dare you—"

I managed to hold my tongue, but not in time. My reaction had been far too strong. It was plain to all nearby that he had unnerved me. No one knew about Andrew but me! Why could I not remember that?

The man's eyes narrowed.

"Dare what?" he asked.

"Nothing."

It took a tremendous effort, but I sat back and looked straight ahead, knowing that I must not do anything to attract further attention. I could feel the gazes of the crowd upon both of us. He studied me for a while longer, then sat back.

"Oft' I hear guilty men say, 'Nothin',' " he offered.

My mind warned me to be silent. I should have listened to it, but emotion took control.

"Is that so?" I asked with as much disdain as I could muster. "And how would you know that?"

" 'Cause I says it meself!"

And he began roaring with laughter in a manner only suitable for a barroom.

That was enough. There was no need for me to feign politeness any longer when his true personality was on display for everyone. I grabbed my suitcase, and moved as far across the waiting area as I could. There were no seats, of course. I settled on a spot next to another man who was also standing, reading a book. My eyes were down as I approached him, and I labored to calm myself. From glances around, it seemed as if everyone had returned to their own business. It seemed so.

"He's not getting on the train," said the man quietly. "If that's any consolation."

"Oh?"

"Old Mac." He pointed at the repulsive man. "When he's not at sea, he sometimes comes down here. He takes delight in making people uncomfortable."

"He does it well. The stench alone is enough."

"Yes. He never acts up enough for us to run him in, though."

As the words echoed in my ears, a full-on panic threatened. My heart rate, which had begun to slow somewhat, tripled. My breath had disappeared, and I had to pretend a tickle in my throat to force a cough and inhale some air. He sensed my distress; I knew it. But distress of what? As a policeman, he surely had to wonder. I had to divert attention, and ease his suspicions. There was no blood on my hands, but yet they nervously gripped and rubbed each other. Becoming conscious of the movement, I forced them to be still.

"Going to Boston?" I asked as innocently as I could.

When he hesitated, I second-guessed my attempt at conversation. Surely it was appropriate. If not travel, then the weather. Maybe there was still too much nervousness evident. But he would probably chalk that up to my encounter with Old Mac. I held my breath, waiting for a response.

"No, just down to Salem," he finally said. "The department down there needs...well, that's business I shouldn't speak of. And yourself?"

I berated myself for not picking weather as a topic, and wondered how well I could lie to a policeman under the best of conditions. My state just then was clearly not the best.

196

"Boston," I said. "For a day. Then on to Providence."

"I see. Well, enjoy your trip."

"And you, as well."

And that was the end of the conversation.

I stood there next to the policeman, and waited for the train. In an impossible situation, I feared my head might burst. He left once for a short time, asking me to keep an eye on his suitcase. He moved in the general direction of the public toilets, but was he relieving himself, or did he continue out through the exit to find a patrolman? As the minutes passed, his continued absence ratcheted up the tension. But eventually he returned, and thanked me for watching his luggage.

The last hour ticked by at an unbearably slow pace, and was uncomfortable in more ways than one. I often shifted weight from foot to foot, and sometimes sat down on my suitcase for a while. The policeman remained focused on his book. Even if I had brought something to read, I was fairly sure that I would have just stared at the pages, seeing perhaps not even words, but only letters.

Old Mac would look at me occasionally, or tap his head with a finger then point at me. Yes, I had made the mistake of letting him get into my head. I pondered how he could have possibly found the exact words to disturb me. I decided that I was fretting needlessly— about that, anyway. If he had gone on long enough with that song, he would have disturbed anyone. After a time, he must have grown bored. No one else would speak to him or even look at him. He stood and began to shuffle away, but on his way out, he took the time to veer toward me. I refused to look at him. When he judged he was close enough, he said, "Nothin'!" and guffawed. My anger rose again, but I waited patiently for him to leave, and he did.

Eventually, I found myself on the train. The tenseness stayed with me, as I sat and waited for patrolmen to rush aboard and haul me off before it could pull away. None showed. Only when it departed the station did I begin to feel some relief. But only when the policeman departed at the Salem station did I truly relax. After that, there was only numbness, as I let myself be mesmerized by the lush greenery of the New England countryside passing by my window.

In Boston, I hired a taxi driver to take me to the address on the envelope. It was late afternoon when I arrived at the home of Mr. Fenster, a sprawling estate on the west side of the city. The grounds were immaculate, with many grand, ancient trees surrounding the mansion, and a variety of flowering shrubs decorating the yard. Although the architectural style of the building bespoke its age, it was in excellent repair. The gate at the entrance was open, so the driver delivered me right to the front door. After paying my fare and watching the motorcar depart, I nervously approached the door. It bore a large, ornate knocker in the shape of a lion. This was it. I had traveled all this way, fled my home in fear, perhaps never to return. I could only hope I would find answers. I could only pray it would be worth it. Hand shaking, I reached out, grasped the ornate handle, and knocked.

Before long, the door cracked open just enough to reveal a man with a markedly disturbing face. The skin was very rough and scabby, suggesting a disease of some sort. His scalp held only remnants of hair, a few tufts scattered about. I waited for a response, not looking away, but the man did not speak even a word of greeting. He only stared at me with large, unblinking eyes.

"My...my name is Robert Adderly," I said. "I have just arrived from Arkham. I would like to speak with Mr. Fenster. It is a matter of some importance."

His only reaction was to continue to stare, as if trying to make sense of what I had just said. Then, there was a sign of comprehension: He opened the door further, and looked behind me, both left and right. The door was opened wider. I entered. He scanned the area once again before slamming the large door shut. The *thoom* produced was deafening, and echoed strangely. Again wordlessly, he signaled for me to wait, and moved off with a bowlegged, shuffling gait.

I set down my suitcase, and looked around. The house's interior was in stark contrast to its exterior. Outside, all was well kept and perfectly in order. Inside, it was nearly empty. In the anteroom in which I stood, there were no furnishings or decorations of any kind—not even a coat rack. Through an archway, I could see a large foyer with a similar dearth of embellishment. The beautiful white marble floors were all bare. It was bewilderingly incongruous.

Before long, I heard a single pair of footsteps approaching. From the direction in which the servant had gone, a man was walking towards me, hands held behind his back. Somewhat slighter of build than even I, he seemed to be approximately my age, with the same sort of dark hair. Everything about him was neat and proper: His clothing was very clean, his shoes were shined, and the beard and mustache he wore were meticulously trimmed. Upon his arrival, I thought that I detected a faint odor of sulfur clinging to him.

"I am Vincent Fenster," he said, coming to a stop in front of me. "I am somewhat busy right now. What can I do for you?"

I stifled my nervousness.

"Mr. Fenster, my name is Robert Adderly. I have just arrived today from Arkham. You have been in contact with Andrew Cooke recently."

"A few letters have been exchanged," he said, eying me suspiciously.

There was no need to delay the news.

"He died last night," I said. In the event the servant might overhear, I lowered my voice. "He summoned a Servitor using the instructions included in your most recent correspondence. It was under his control. I witnessed it. But a storm was raging in Arkham last night. Just as he spoke the command for its dismissal, a titanic blast of lightning struck very close. Something went wrong. Suffice it to say that he was eaten by the creature. Only bones remain."

He was visibly shaken by the information.

"That is terrible! Were you there through that?"

"Yes."

"How did you survive?"

I shook my head.

"I have no idea," I said. "That is one of the questions I was hoping you would answer. Why did it not attack me? I was able to dismiss the creature by speaking the command specified in your letter, just as Andrew had tried. Why did it kill him, but listen to me?"

He gave me the impression of being as perplexed about the event as I was. There was a long pause before he spoke again.

"May I assume that Andrew Cooke did not command the creature to obey only his commands?"

"Yes. He told me so."

"Then that is precisely why it obeyed you."

He paused and thought again for quite a while, muttering wordlessly to himself at times.

"However," he continued, "I can't say why the Servitor killed him. Those creatures are certainly horrendous, but they are also servile. There is no reason for the man to have been killed if he conducted the ceremony properly, and if he spoke the commands correctly. One of those conditions must have been violated."

I nodded, again recalling the events of the previous evening. The actual invocation, as horrifying as the dream had been for Andrew, had gone off cleanly.

"It had to have been the command," I said. "I never heard what he said, though."

"Because of the thunder?"

"Could that have been it?"

"Possibly. Not the thunder or lightning itself, mind you. Such a thing occurring in our world would have no impact in the world Outside. But a stutter while speaking a command...yes, that could do it." He sighed. "I feel awful. I'm at least partly to blame. I supplied him with the instructions."

I shook my head.

"Andrew was fully aware of the risks involved," I said. "He admitted some anxiety with respect to the storm. There was no need for him to have gone through with the ceremony yesterday. He could have waited for another day with better weather. I could have spoken up when he exhibited less than full confidence. Several mistakes were made. I had only known him a short time, but had the impression that he was ordinarily a very competent magician. The circumstances last night were unique—one in a million, perhaps."

He nodded and relaxed his stance, arms swinging down to the sides of his body. His left hand was missing at the wrist. I tried to look away, but he read my glance immediately.

"I'm sorry," I said. "That was insensitive of me."

"Think nothing of it," he said. "It's been long enough. I must learn to get comfortable with…this."

He moved his left arm, flapping the material of his empty shirt sleeve.

"I had an unfortunate accident while traveling through Eastern Europe. There are many parts of the world that are yet savage. I wandered into one of them, alone. A wolf attacked me. I was lucky to stanch the flow of blood and save my life. It was memorable."

"Undoubtedly," I replied.

There followed a moment of silence, one of those moments that are meant to be taken as a social signal. I could tell we were done. He had already told me that I had interrupted him.

"Well, thank you for your time. I felt an obligation to tell you what had happened—"

"And get answers, you said. Do you have more questions?"

"I do, but…"

"No but. Your friend is dead. At the very least, I owe you information. Let's get a little more comfortable first, though."

My stomach chose that point in time to rumble.

"You haven't eaten?" he asked.

"No, not since breakfast."

"Join me for dinner, then."

"Thank you, Mr. Fenster," I said with a large grin. "I cannot refuse."

"It's Vincent. Please call me Vincent."

"Vincent. I am Robert."

We finally shook hands.

"Robert, please come with me," he said.

As he led me through the bare rooms, our footfalls made ugly, hollow noises. On the far side of the foyer was a small dining room, this one furnished. Indeed, the room was beautifully decorated, with paintings upon the wall and various bric-a-brac perched upon display tables and shelves. An oak dining table with six chairs occupied the center. He took my coat, and motioned for me to sit, then pulled on a rope. In a heartbeat, the same repulsive man appeared through another doorway at the opposite end of the room. My coat was handed off, along with a request for a bottle of wine. The servant left, and returned shortly with an open bottle and two glasses on a tray, which was placed on the table. Vincent filled the glasses after he left.

"To Andrew," he offered as a toast, raising his glass. "May he rest in peace."

"To Andrew."

We both took a sip of wine.

"Albert will have dinner ready before too long. But we should have plenty of time to talk. Where do you want to start?"

I began to think, going back farther and farther, until I finally laughed.

He smiled and looked at me curiously.

"I was just thinking how this is all so strange. As little as two months ago, I did not believe at all in neither magic nor extra-dimensional creatures. I would have rolled my eyes, turned away from any mention of such things. I was solidly grounded in the rational world of theoretical mathematics. But during the past few months, my world, my reality, has increased in size an order of magnitude. I learned much from Andrew. In fact, I recently cast my first spell— that simple fire manipulation spell which you supplied."

He blinked.

"Starting with nothing, you learned enough in a matter of months to be able to do that?"

"Yes."

"I'm impressed. You must have a natural inclination for it."

"Andrew also said as much."

"Please continue," he prompted me.

"Well, the reason I came here specifically was because of Andrew's death. And again, I must stress that you should not feel guilty. If anyone is to blame, it is I. He would never have met that gruesome fate if I had not involved him with my problem."

"Oh? What problem is that?"

"Trying to solve the mystery surrounding the death of my fiancée, Elizabeth Wentworth."

Vincent reacted as if shot.

"Elizabeth Wentworth?" he shouted.

"Yes," I said uneasily, alarmed by his extreme response.

"Good God! *You* were to wed Elizabeth?"

"You speak as if you knew her."

He paused, biting at his lip.

"Robert, you may find this difficult to believe—I am having a hard time believing all this myself. But Elizabeth Wentworth was my cousin."

I had no response for that, and looked at him incredulously. It simply was not possible, was it? Both of us were silent. My head was spinning; it was likely his was, too. When the turbulence in my own mind calmed, a memory surfaced.

"At the funeral, there was mention made of a cousin being overseas," I said. "That was you?"

"Yes," he mumbled.

He drained his wine in a large gulp. When he refilled his own glass, he topped off mine with more than I wanted or needed. On an empty stomach, the few sips I took were already having an effect, and I thought meaningful conversation might get be difficult if I were to have much more. A look in his eyes, though, revealed that there would be no need for either of us to speak. He was visibly saddened.

We drank quietly until dinner was served. It was delicious: a thick clam chowder, prepared and served by Albert. The heavy meal combined with the wine left me stuffed, and my eyelids grew heavy.

"I can see you're getting tired," said Vincent, voice heavy and words slightly slurred. "Please, stay the night. We didn't finish speaking, and I, for one, need to know more. Just...not now."

"Your offer is graciously accepted," I said, stifling a yawn.

"We can resume in the morning, over breakfast."

He stood up, but paused to ask one final question.

"But just out of curiosity," he began, "are you from Arkham?"

"I do live there now, and will at least until I finish my doctorate at the university. But I was born and raised in Mount Haverton."

"I see," he said, nodding his head slightly. "Well, good night."

And he walked off. It was a curious question with which to end the evening, but I thought nothing of it.

Shortly thereafter, Albert entered, grabbed my suitcase, and motioned for me to follow. He still repulsed me somehow, and so I gave him another look to try to determine why. A man of medium height and build, he walked with a slight stoop. His skin, aside from being very rough, also had a greyish cast, but that could have been attributable to his age, which I guessed to be anywhere between fifty and seventy. And he still had not spoken a word to me. I gave up trying to pin down a particular reason for my unease. It must have just been the combination of it all, or even the events of the previous evening still haunting me.

Upstairs, he showed me into a bedroom. Too tired to unpack, I collapsed on the bed and slept through the night.

I was up shortly after dawn, and followed my nose downstairs to the same dining room. A large platter was filled with breakfast potatoes and smoked salmon. Warm muffins and a variety of marmalades were also available. Albert helped me with my chair and poured me a cup of coffee, then waved his hand at the food.

"Thank you very much," I said, "but I would prefer to wait for the host before starting."

"Your mother did raise you right, didn't she?" said Vincent, entering the room just then. A grin was very evident, despite the full beard.

"My father, actually," I said. "He was more of a stickler when it came to etiquette."

"Oh, yes. William, was it?"

That left me slightly dazed.

"Was, and still is," I said slowly, staring at him.

"You still don't know who I am, do you?"

He obviously knew *me*, and I worked hard to mentally subtract the beard and mustache. It came to me then. It should have come

205

sooner.

"Vincent...Marsh?"

"The same," he said gleefully.

When Albert poured his coffee, he held it up and we clinked cups in a toast, both of us laughing.

I opened my mouth to ask any one of a thousand questions, but nothing came out. Faced with such a revelation, my mind whirled and nearly refused to accept the situation.

"How did you get here?" I was finally able to ask.

"Here? Robert, this is where I came after my parents died. I came to live with the *Wentworths*."

Again, the words were almost too incredible to comprehend.

"It's true!" he insisted. "I grew up in this very home with Elizabeth and the rest. This poor family...the twins, Mary and Catherine, succumbed to the influenza scourge soon after I arrived, so I hardly knew them. William was a casualty of the War. Soon after armistice was declared, I began my travels through Europe. Last year, my stepparents visited me while on a trip through Africa and Europe. A short time after meeting with me, they died of some sort of strange illness. And Elizabeth...of all of them, I favored her the most. She was so kind and so beautiful. Unfortunately, I was in a secluded part of Eastern Europe at the time of her death. That was when this happened."

He waggled his left forearm.

"The news took time to catch up with me. With both parents and all the children dead, I inherited this estate."

As difficult as it was to believe, it all began to sink in. Vincent's description of the family called to mind a conversation I had with Thomas Wentworth.

"The one thing that confuses me," I said, "is that Thomas Wentworth never mentioned you. And neither did Aunt Marie, for that matter."

"That doesn't surprise me," he said with a frown. "Uncle Thomas never liked me, and never made any effort to hide it. Aunt Marie is at least more polite, but she faithfully follows her husband's lead. Enough of that for now, though. Our breakfast is getting cold. Let's eat."

He was right. We took our time eating. It gave me a chance to ponder how Fate could have so intertwined our lives. Each of any pair of us knew the third, but was unaware of the third. It was a bizarre situation. I got nowhere near a solution and decided to chalk it up to coincidence. But what had Andrew said about that? There was no such thing. Eventually, I discovered that he had been right.

With coffees refilled, Vincent led me out a back door. We took seats on a porch overlooking a nicely manicured lawn. After a few minutes of bird watching, I decided to restart the conversation.

"When did you realize it was me? Your beard did an excellent job of disguising your identity from me."

"Toward the end of our conversation yesterday. Right before you told me of Elizabeth, I had an inkling. Some mannerism of yours gave me a clue. But when you mentioned your relationship with her, the desire to converse ended. I was hoping that we'd have a chance to continue in the morning, as we are now." He chuckled briefly. "You're actually the first of three men I've known with your name. There's a fellow here in Boston, and I once met someone else in England. After all this time since our childhood, I thought you were simply yet another Robert Adderly, not the original from Mount Haverton."

"And obviously, I knew both halves of your name, but not together. I did not associate Vincent with Fenster. Why did you choose that? Why not Vincent Wentworth?"

"Why? Through various means I discovered some long-hidden facts. I decided to adopt my true family name."

That baffled me completely.

"But in Mount Haverton the only Fensters were long dead

when you and I were born," I said. "That crumbling shell of a house on the other side of the river…that was all that was left of the Fensters."

"Not so," he said firmly. "The line is not yet dead. My father, Jonathon, was actually the illegitimate son of the last woman to bear the Fenster name, Konstanz Fenster. Shortly after my father was born, the entire Fenster household died. The Marsh family adopted and raised him."

"Did your father ever know that?"

"I don't think so. Forgive me for speaking ill of the dead, but he was a dull-witted ass. I know that sounds harsh, but you never had to weather the effects of his stormy and unpredictable moods. As the years went by, he grew more and more dependent upon the stupefying effects of cheap whiskey. My mother and I suffered severely at his hand. I do not miss him."

The bitterness in his voice was very evident at the end. Sitting next to him, so many years after the fact, I could still picture before me the young boy I'd known, battered and bruised at the hands of his father.

"I am sorry for dredging up painful memories," I said, feeling slightly embarrassed.

"It's quite all right." He paused briefly. "But while we're on the subject of painful memories…"

"Yes?"

"It's my turn to apologize, and I'll do it in advance, but I never did find out any details of Elizabeth's death. Can you tell me about it?"

I sighed, not wanting to speak of it. But he was entitled to know.

"There is not much to tell," I said. "I proposed to her one afternoon, after the final examination for her undergraduate degree. She accepted. That evening, I prepared dinner for the two of us. We ate in the dining room of the boarding house where I lived. After dinner, we sat in front of the hearth and talked. While I was returning the dishes to the kitchen, I heard her say, 'The fire is changing my shadow.' An instant later, she screamed. I rushed back to the dining room to find her completely covered in flames. In less than a minute, she was gone—completely consumed by the fire."

"That's not possible," he said defiantly. "A human body cannot—Ah! *That* was the reason for the initial inquiry which I received from Andrew."

I nodded.

"Yes. With an ordinary flame, it is certainly not possible. However, this was no ordinary flame. As Andrew and I later discovered, the fire was caused by an unearthly being known as Sothoth Pnath."

"The shadow of Yog Sothoth?"

His response stunned me.

"You know of it?"

Vincent shrugged and nodded. "I've come across vague references to it. What is the link between it and Elizabeth?"

"From what we were able to learn, the entity exists within shadows. Looking into a shadow that contains Sothoth Pnath provides a bridge for the creature to enter one's body. It is only a matter of seconds before the victim is *completely* incinerated, the *soul* as well as the body."

"I see."

"Yes," I said, rage taking root in me. "She is gone—even her soul, gone forever. That thing took her from me!"

He waited politely while I paused to calm myself.

"I still get upset at times. It was grief and anger that drove me to study as much as I did. And when Andrew suggested a form of revenge, I had to agree. But can you believe we were actually planning to banish Sothoth Pnath from the Earth?" I sniggered humorlessly. "What a ridiculous idea."

"Why do you say that?"

"Just consider the tragedy that drove me here. Granted, we established his death was accidental, but Andrew was just dealing with a Servitor, not an Ancient One. And calling and commanding that creature was only the first step along a path of unknown length… And with him dead, I cannot hope to continue on alone." I shook my head. "But with two deaths now, I would do anything to feel the satisfaction of revenge."

Hearing that, Vincent grinned.

"You can still have it," he said.

I knew immediately what he meant.

"No," I said.

"Please listen to me," he implored. "Elizabeth was my cousin. I have as much a stake in this as you. I am willing to take Andrew's place. I have years more experience than you, and can continue your tutoring. We can perform the necessary research together. And one day, it *will* be possible for us to banish Sothoth Pnath."

He spoke that final sentence with a confidence that gave me pause, but it did not change my mind.

"I cannot involve someone else in my personal vendetta. Andrew was of the opinion that we were being watched by someone who did not wish us to pursue this. He even encouraged paranoia and caution, but…I think the thrill of danger, the potential power, was too tempting for him. I think it overrode his normal caution. Going any further will be dangerous. In fact, I may have put you at risk just by coming here."

"But without my help, you may never achieve your goal. Those deaths may never be avenged."

I shook my head. I did not want to give in.

Vincent smiled in response.

"Ah, but you see—I have a card up my sleeve. I have a way of utterly convincing you to agree to my proposition."

He removed a flat, narrow stone from a vest pocket, held it up to show me, and then handed it over.

I examined it closely, but could detect nothing special about the rather unattractive, grey lump of rock. More than anything else, it looked like an Indian arrowhead, but the material was definitely not flint.

"What is so special about this?" I asked.

"You said you have some magical training," he said, smile growing larger. "Close your eyes and clear your mind, as if preparing to cast a spell."

I did so.

"Now, while keeping them closed, hold the stone with the tips of the fingers of your right hand. With the index finger of your left hand, trace along its length, starting with your fingertips, and finishing at the opposite end."

Again, I did as I was told. When the index finger of my right hand reached the end of the stone, I stopped.

"I feel the end. What now?"

"Look," said Vincent.

I was astounded by what I beheld. Although the object was only three inches long, my left index finger was six inches from the fingertips of my right hand. I could not see anything in that gap, but there was something to feel. I closed my eyes again and probed deeper. I became aware of a presence of some sort within the stone, an icy cold *intelligence* that transfixed me. There was also a sensation of movement, as if I was being pulled forward. A strange fluting or piping with an alien rhythm filled my mind, becoming louder, and so reinforcing that movement. Fear mounted within me. I wanted to scream, but was overcome with a paralysis of some sort. Helpless to do anything at all, I could only sense that I was nearing my destination.

"No!" shouted Vincent as he snatched the stone away from me.

211

I gasped and nearly fell out of my chair. The odd sounds and sensations ceased the very moment he snatched it from me.

"Are you all right?" he asked, his voice containing equal parts concern and anger.

I caught my breath and nodded.

"I should have warned you. If you had gone any further...in any case, you must realize that this stone is more than it appears to be. I have spent years *carefully* researching it." He tried to lower his voice, but could not contain his excitement. "It is an actual shard of the Crystal of Dha'al! That is, I believe it to be."

"I'm sorry, Vincent, but that name means nothing to me."

"No. I would be shocked if it did. Only a handful of people on this planet would recognize it. Allow me to enlighten you." The smile returned. "According to what I've been able to learn, the Crystal was created eons ago by the Elder Gods to somehow imprison or otherwise constrain the Ancient Ones. The legends are lacking any real details, but suffice it to say that the imprisonment was short-lived. The Crystal was destroyed, and the remaining pieces were scattered all over creation."

I nodded, but could not fathom where he was headed.

"That is interesting," I commented, "but how does it relate to the goal of banishing Sothoth Pnath?"

He gazed at the stone and was silent. It seemed as if he did not wish to say anything, as if revealing the information would diminish his position somehow. Finally, he looked up.

"As I said, the Crystal was used against *all* of the Ancient Ones. That implies that it was attuned to each of their...vibrations, for lack of a better word. Think of it as a tuning fork. Now, this dull-looking stone in my hand is no longer powerful enough to imprison any-thing, but without a doubt it could be used to *repel*. I feel certain that it would be an integral part of the banishment ceremony!"

I was dumbfounded. Fate had set up everything for me. Not

only did I find someone to work with, someone who could teach me, but a necessary piece of the puzzle had been supplied as well.

"This is too good to be true," I whispered, not sure how to react.

"It is both good and true," agreed Vincent, "but not *too* good. Consider what you've suffered through recently. Doesn't this goodness make up for that badness? Think of this convergence of people, place, and thing as a way to balance the scales."

Balance! Vincent could not have chosen a better word, feeling as I did. It swayed me in an instant.

"When can we start?" I asked greedily, thinking that victory was within our grasp.

He let out a sharp laugh.

"Excellent!" he said. "Tomorrow. We can start tomorrow. Right now, I need to temper your expectations. This won't be as simple, or go as quickly, as I may have led you to believe."

And then he told me the less exciting news: Two key pieces of information were still missing. The first concerned the dull grey stone in his possession. That shard of the Crystal was an extra-dimensional object, the three inches of which we perceived being merely a single facet. It needed to be rotated such that the facet attuned to Sothoth Pnath projected into our universe instead of the current one. Of course, it was possible that it was already attuned correctly, but that was likely not the case. Rotating the shard could only be done from Outside. The act could be accomplished, of course, by summoning and controlling a Servitor of Q'yoth. However, Vincent did not know the specifics of how much to turn it, or in which four-dimensional direction.

The second problem was simply the one which Andrew and I had been pursuing—that of discovering the exact ceremony for banishing the entity. Based upon his previous experiences, he suspected that it would be detailed somewhere within the many pages of the *Necronomicon* of Abdul Alhazred. He had had access to a copy of that ancient tome in the past, but could not recall coming across the specific ceremony we now desired.

As to the problem of finding any sort of volume that better described the Crystal, Vincent only said that he had been investigating fruitlessly for years. The legendary volume known as the *Pnakotic Manuscripts* was a possible source of information, but he had not been able to even discover where a copy of that document might reside. Because the *Necronomicon* was in the Miskatonic University library, I suggested that it was possible that the other might be there as well. Vincent agreed, saying that the university was the first place that he was planning to check. He frowned deeply when I told him of my encounter with Doctor Trautmann and the decree of a six-month ban on access to those books.

From there, the topic of conversation turned to our respective experiences in magic. We ended up talking through the afternoon, staying outside on the porch or walking around the yard. With much of my time over the past weeks having been spent in the bookstore, I enjoyed the time in the sun. Vincent, of course, proved to be much more knowledgeable than I, having spent the last several years dedicated to the research. He spent a lot of time quizzing me, as he needed to know what I had learned, and where I was lacking. Despite his superior magical background, he admitted that he was surprised by my disclosure that a mathematical formula existed which effectively predicted the behavior of each of the Ancient Ones given their source star.

After that, our conversation ranged all over. He spoke of his childhood spent with the Wentworths, and his travels in Europe. I told him of events in Mount Haverton after he had left. We compared opinions on current events, politics, and memories of Elizabeth, staying not long at all on the final topic, but still too long. Ultimately, his personality was revealed to be an adult version of the rebellious, mischievous child I had known in my youth, albeit with a well-developed intellect.

We ended up talking ourselves nearly hoarse. When he invited me to stay another night, I saw no need to decline, especially considering that I had left Arkham with little money in my pockets. I had another comfortable night, and looked forward to restarting my magical training the following day—and this time with a long-lost friend.

SEVENTEEN

After breakfast the following morning, Victor gave me a tour of the house. It was clearly not as empty as I had first imagined it to be. Aside from the anteroom and the foyer downstairs, the furnishings in the rest of the house were perfectly intact. As he led me from one floor to the next, he told me that the roof over one of the upper bedrooms had developed several leaks, which had gone unnoticed for weeks in the unoccupied room. All of the furniture within had been destroyed. Even worse, the workmen assigned to repair the roof had been careless, and instead of remedying the leaks, they had created new ones, resulting in damages all the way down to the foyer. Repairs and repainting were done, but no attempt had yet been made to redecorate. He had just returned to the States, and playing host to visitors had been the last thing on his mind.

To the right of the foyer on the first floor sat a large, impressive-looking den. Rows upon rows of shelves lined the walls, holding hundreds of thick volumes on a multitude of topics. The furniture was all leather and mahogany. Beautiful antique tapestries decorated the parts of the walls not covered with bookshelves. I looked around the room at random, searching for volumes on the esoteric arts, but could find nothing. I looked expectantly at my host. Vincent and I were apparently of the same mind. He motioned, and led me to the opposite end of the house. Through a door in the kitchen, we descended a narrow set of stairs, at the bottom of which lay a wine cellar. The unfinished ceiling was less than eight feet above the floor—I could touch it without standing on tiptoes. That cellar room was about half the size of the first floor of the house, but there seemed to be no other doorway or passage behind the wine racks or along the south or east wall. There was nothing to see.

Vincent led me to the far end of the room. He reached up toward the ceiling and pulled on a piece of wood that had appeared to be an integral part of the floor joist. It only moved about two inches, then a section of the wall shuddered almost imperceptibly, as if a pressure had been released. From the space near the hidden lever, he removed two candles and handed them to me. Retrieving a match from the same space, he lit both candles, took one for himself, and pushed on the section of wall that had moved. It swung open to the right, revealing a passage. The doorway was free of cobwebs, but still I cowered nervously as I followed Vincent into the darkness. We walked about fifteen feet before the corridor ended. On our left was a door. He set his candle within a nearby niche, turned the knob and swung the door open. The atmosphere in the room we entered was noticeably dank and musty, with a faint, almost familiar, sulfurous smell. A definite dripping was audible somewhere to my right, as were the faint noises of rats scampering away from the approaching light of our candles.

One by one, he lit three lamps already scattered about the room. The illumination from the ancient lanterns revealed a large, mostly empty space. The floor consisted of irregular stones mortared together. Because the unfinished ceiling was lined with floor joists, as in the wine cellar, I assumed we were still beneath the house—the foyer and the den, by my reckoning. An old stand near the door had been fitted with several shelves, each lined with books. I examined several of the spines and realized, to my satisfaction, that this was indeed the collection I had been looking for upstairs—Vincent's own magical library. One wall was lined with tables, which held various chemical apparatus, jars, and beakers of differing sizes. With the room now fully lit, I could see the source of the dripping: A section of the south wall bowed inward, and a few of the stones near the ceiling were pushed in several inches, hanging downward at a slight angle. Water seeped in along the stones, dripping to the floor. Aside from that one section of wall, and the deteriorated floor

217

beneath it, the rest of the room seemed to be dry and in good shape.

"I have not been able to discern its original purpose," explained Vincent, "but as you can see, the room makes an excellent laboratory. Being underground, it is well insulated from outside noise and influence. With the lights extinguished and the door closed, it is not unlike a tomb."

He walked around silently for a while, then continued.

"I found it just six months after coming to live here. I believe I was the first to set foot in it since the original owner. Every surface was covered in a layer of dust. As a child, it was a perfect place to hide when I didn't want to be found—though the other members of the household didn't seem to put much effort into finding me. For years, it was my secret, and mine alone. Eventually, I showed it to Elizabeth. She and I would come here occasionally to hide from everyone else, sit in the dark, and...talk. Just talk. She was the only one who understood me."

With the available light, I could not see his face very well, but his voice betrayed a definite sorrow. I walked around the perimeter of the room, pretending to examine its few contents, trying to distract myself from memories.

"Robert, I have an offer for you. I hope that you will think it over very carefully."

I ran my finger along the cracked leather spine of one book, then another, feeling their age beneath my touch.

"I would like for you to move into this house," he said. "Before you say anything: No, you would not be intruding. I am inviting you. We need each other, you see. If we are to pursue this goal— the expulsion of this monster—we have to do it together. You need my experience and guidance. In turn, I need your hands. I could, of course, go it alone, but I cannot believe that my handicap"—he pointed at his left arm—"would not get in the way. Needless to say, assuming that we learn all that we need to know, *you* will be the one performing the ceremony."

218

After his openness regarding the crystal in his possession and the detailed tour of the house, I suspected such a proposal might be forthcoming. If we were to work together, why not just stay under the same roof? But the idea did make me uncomfortable. I had no income, and no way of generating any. If I were to say yes, I would likely be dependent on Vincent's support for months, possibly years, and would probably never be able to repay him. The opportunity to be the one to perform the actual banishment, however, was too powerful an incentive to ignore. And besides, had Elizabeth not died, I would have come into this money about which I was so concerned.

"Once again, I accept."

"Excellent!"

"But where do we start?"

"I'm glad you asked," he said with a grin. "We can begin right now."

Though I asked him once more, Vincent refused to share any details. He led the way back upstairs, to the den on the first floor. After I took a seat at the writing desk, he began pacing back and forth and dictated a short, formal letter. It was for Doctor Trautmann, requesting access to the *Necronomicon*. Even as he spoke, I assured him that such communication was a useless effort, but he merely smiled.

"All will become evident in good time," he said.

I quickly grew to enjoy my stay in Boston, and the many benefits of such a luxurious home. Albert, for instance, was the perfect servant, handling all the duties of butler, cook, and gardener. Though he nearly always remained out of sight, it seemed as if he was never more than a few steps away. He performed his duties commendably, being especially skilled at preparing excellent, albeit heavily seafood-based cuisine. But Albert's service was not the only thing to which I was previously unaccustomed: The fine wines, antique furniture, the artwork, the space. My God, the space! My old room at the boarding house would have fit neatly into the anteroom, with a few feet to spare. The house was beautiful, extravagant. I could not help but love it.

But only a few days after beginning my wonderful new life, my problem-plagued old one caught up with me. One morning while I sat at the kitchen table, perusing the Boston newspaper, I came across a short article, detailing the inexplicable death of a man in Arkham. The story was hidden away in a corner of the newspaper, as if the publisher had been embarrassed to print it:

> (ARKHAM) After missing for several days, Mr. Andrew Cooke of Arkham was found dead by authorities yesterday in the apartment above his business. Local police have declined to give details about the condition of the body or speculate a motive. However, an eyewitness to the scene claimed that the victim had been butchered in such a way as to leave behind only bones. The witness, a neighbor identified as Mrs. Jean Blakewood, claimed it was the work of a madman.
>
> Mr. Cooke was the proprietor of Hunt's Fine Books, the small bookshop he inherited after the death of his grandfather, Mr. Bertram Hunt. Following two consecutive days of unexpected absences, during which time the store remained closed, Mr. Cooke's neighbors contacted the authorities. According to the victim's father, the business neither generated any great income, nor incurred any outstanding debts.
>
> "There was simply no reason for this," stated Mr. Arthur Cooke.
>
> Andrew Cooke, only twenty-seven years old at the time of his death, never married. He is

survived by his father, mother, and one sister, Ida.

No mention was made of a suspect, or a mysterious friend who may have recently disappeared. Ironically, the article was just the sort of thing that would have attracted the attention of Mr. Hunt. Had he been alive, it surely would have made its way into one of his scrapbooks.

From that morning on, Vincent kept me constantly busy. He had two short-term goals in mind: convert the hidden room into a proper laboratory; and continue my training in the magical arts. To that end, we spent several hours each day cleaning the room in the cellar, and moving in furniture and other necessary items. Additional gas lamps were set around the room, and traps for the rats. We attempted to repair the damaged, dripping south wall of the room, but neither of us were skilled in masonry, and our best efforts were for naught. The leak returned after only a single day.

At the end of three weeks of hard work, the transformation was remarkable.

Everything had been scrubbed clean, and the musty atmosphere of before was largely gone. A sizeable bucket caught the drips from the leaking wall. The center of the room was occupied by a circular table, which had just barely fit through the passage. I was amazed we had been able to move it into the room without damaging it. With a spacious desk for each of us, and a wide variety of chemical supplies that Vincent was able to obtain, we felt well prepared to take on the task that lay before us.

In the evenings, following dinner, I would take some time to meditate and review. After that, Vincent would teach me as Professor Josephson once had: Lecturing endlessly, quizzing occasionally, and always looking for perfection. In those weeks that followed, I found myself thriving under Vincent's tutelage. I had to admit, it was much more enjoyable than the tedious hours of self-study spent in the back room of Andrew's bookstore. The first week was dedicated purely to theory. But by the second, he already had me practicing simple spells and cantrips, and repeated successes drove my confidence skyward. Vincent seemed both surprised and pleased that I was making so much progress in such a short period of time. By the end of our third week together, he stated that I was ready to move on to something more difficult. The perfect opportunity was delivered to us the following day.

Just before noon, a letter arrived from Miskatonic University—specifically, from Doctor Trautmann. Vincent opened the letter, and read it to himself, a large grin plastered on his face. From his reaction, I could only assume that the unexpected had occurred, and we had actually been granted access to the hidden books. When he was finished, he handed the letter to me, which I read in earnest. My enthusiasm was replaced with confusion after just the first sentence.

"This is a rejection," I said.

"Indeed," he said, still smiling. "But..."

And he said no more.

"Then what else is it?" I asked, handing the paper back. "Besides being a letter from Doctor Trautmann?"

"That's all that it is, but it's enough. The content does not matter. What does matter is that it is written in his own hand. And having a sample of his writing allows us to use...certain spells to our advantage."

I recalled the parchment that I had stolen from Professor Josephson. Guilt over that episode rose up within me, but I pushed it back down.

"All we have to do is find a skeleton in his closet," he said. "And use it to blackmail him into allowing us access to the information that we want."

The suggestion did not sit well with me, and I paused to

consider alternatives. Vincent had told me that copies of the *Necronomicon* existed in London and Buenos Aires, but an ocean trip to either location seemed extraordinarily excessive considering that one was sitting a train ride away. And the thought of waiting for several more months, then begging Doctor Trautmann for access, did not sit well with me at all. In the end, he would simply wield the power that he held and deny us again. And again, ad infinitum. Jebediah Higgins had defeated my plans the first time, and I used him as a justification to ignore my gut reaction. If Higgins had not interfered, this underhanded scheme would not be necessary.

"All right," I said. "How do we do that?"

"Based on what you told me, you are familiar with the ceremony for speaking with the dead?"

An alarm went off in my head. Was he serious?

"I am...but would strongly prefer to not kill Doctor Trautmann."

"Hmmm? Who said anything about killing?" asked Vincent innocently. "Killing the good doctor will not get us anywhere. Besides, his death would draw too much attention."

"Then how will we...I mean, the spell is for speaking with the *dead.*"

He shook his head and smiled.

"It is, but few magicians realize—it can be used to speak with the living as well."

My expression must have been comical, because Vincent laughed aloud before continuing.

"It's true," he said. "While in deep sleep, a dreamer's mind is not unlike the dead. The spell is not as effective, of course, as when the body is dead. The dreaming mind retains a sense of self-preservation. It won't do anything it fears may bring itself harm. However, the spell can still be used to learn certain things."

He walked over to me, and put a hand on my shoulder. It was

an intimate gesture, one that reminded me of our time together as children.

"I believe," he said, "that the level of difficulty of that ceremony is appropriate for you. It will be a good learning experience."

"But you just said that Trautmann will not put himself at risk. How do we get him to tell us any sort of secret that we can use against him?"

"That's correct," he said. He seemed somewhat proud. "We will need to dig up a scandalous bit of information by other means. Go in with the gun already loaded, so to speak."

"How can we do that?"

"By scrying on him."

"Spying?" I asked, uncertain about the word I had just heard.

"In a way, yes. But, no: scrying. Clairvoyance—using a spell or device. We will spy on him remotely. When we have a piece of incriminating information, we will use the ceremony for speaking with the dead to contact his dreaming mind and confirm our suspicion as well as we are able."

"Then we visit him and challenge him with the evidence?"

"Yes. And sift through those volumes as quickly as possible. It's been my experience that blackmail is not a useful strategy in the long run. The initial shock usually forces compliance with one's demands, but never for long."

I wondered only briefly how much experience Vincent had with blackmail. I was impatient to proceed with his plan.

"When can we start this scrying?" I asked.

"Right now," he said eagerly.

I smiled to myself. Victor was such a conundrum. He had a strong tendency to be secretive to the point of annoyance, but still had child-like compulsions, where it seemed as if he wanted to share those secrets with a friend. And I felt honored by that. That combination of contradictions reminded me of Andrew, who had often espoused caution to me, but still allowed his ego to drive him onward—and at the end, too far. Elizabeth's death was never far from my consciousness, but Andrew's more recent demise overshadowed even hers at times. When those disturbing recollections of his final moments did come to mind, as they had right then, I had to work to suppress them.

Putting the letter in his pocket, Vincent led the way downstairs to our hidden laboratory. We walked over to a large, ornate mirror we had hung on the north wall between our desks. The thick oval glass was framed in dark, intricately carved cherry. I had initially wondered why Vincent insisted on including the mirror among our sparse decorations in the first place. It appeared it had not been for his vanity.

"Help me move this over there," he said, indicating the table in the center of the room. We lifted it off the hooks upon which it rested, and carefully laid it down flat on the table, mirror side up.

"This mirror is the most valuable object that I discovered on my travels through Europe," he said. "It actually has a variety of uses, some quite complex and obscure. But scrying is the simplest and most straightforward."

He retrieved a beaker of a pale, greenish solution from a shelf filled with chemicals, set it on the table next to the mirror and removed its stopper. The liquid sparkled somewhat, as if tiny diamonds were suspended in the solution.

"This oil," he explained, "will activate the mirror's scrying ability. It will last until it evaporates—approximately four to five hours. All that I truly need to do is pour it on; there is no real spell involved in activating the mirror. Controlling the view is simple, even for a novice such as yourself. One needs only the proper mindset. You will of course have to practice with the mirror so we may both observe Doctor Trautmann's comings and goings. But not today.

"Even when activated, the mirror only reflects its surroundings, as any mirror does. The oil allows us to move the view, but only at the speed a man can walk. In other words, in order to see Doctor Trautmann, we would have to essentially walk the reflection from Boston to Arkham at a pace of three to four miles an hour. But thankfully, we can focus directly on the good doctor, thanks to this."

He indicated the letter in his pocket.

"The other complicating factor is that, although we cannot be seen while using the mirror, we can still be detected. If you've ever had the feeling you were being watched—only to turn around and see no one there—you know roughly what I mean."

"Yes, I think I do," I said, a chill going up my spine. "In fact, I had that very feeling on the night of Andrew's death."

"Then it's quite possible you were being scryed upon," replied Vincent. "Even without a device like this, anyone with the proper knowledge can cast a clairvoyance spell with the same effects and limitations. Someone very well could have been tracking your actions."

"And what about right now?"

"There is nothing to worry about," said Vincent calmly. "At least, right here. I have proofed this room against scrying. No one can see into this underground lair. I have come to learn that you can never be too rich, or too paranoid,"

He flashed me a wry smile. In that way, he and Andrew were very much alike.

He placed the letter on the table beside the mirror. After a moment of silence, he spoke a few phrases in Latin, picked up the letter, and spoke a few more. He extended both arms above his head, and the sleeve of his jacket pulled back to fully reveal to me the stump of his left forearm. I could see that the hand, wrist, and an inch or two of arm were cut off cleanly, almost surgically. The very end of the stump was coal black. Additionally, a tattoo of some strange design snaked along his arm, terminating just before the stump.

When he finished speaking, he put down the letter, picked up the beaker of oil, and poured less than a teaspoon onto the center of the mirror. The oil spread itself in a thin layer over the entire surface, and in an instant, the scene shifted from the ceiling of our room to the office of the Director of the Miskatonic University Library. Doctor Trautmann was prominently in the foreground, sitting behind his desk. I hardly had time to adjust my eyes to it before the view retreated to the furthest corner of the room.

"That is the difficult part," Vincent sighed. "When that spell is used to shift the focus of the mirror to a distant location, the subject is shown, close-up and centered. It is at that point we are most susceptible to detection. Immediately after casting that spell, you must shift the focus at least twelve feet away. Understand?"

I nodded.

"As for manipulating the mirror," he said, "it is quite easy. Just concentrate."

He said nothing while he shifted the scene displayed by the mirror: up, down, left, right.

"You have been meditating nightly, and you were able to sense the true nature of the shard when you handled it, so I trust that you shall have no problems mastering the mirror."

That was all the explanation he felt was needed, and we watched our subject. It was fascinating—for all of five minutes. After another five, it had degenerated to boring. In that time, Doctor Trautmann had done nothing but sit at his desk and read some sort of memorandum. The process of scrying was far less exciting than I had imagined it to be. It was also silent. Though we could see the office plainly, there was no sound.

Vincent apparently had also had his fill.

"That's enough for today," he said, leaning back. "I only wanted show you how the process works. Now, only the person who pours the oil onto it can control it. You must learn to do what I have just done. Then we can set up a surveillance schedule."

He spoke a single word in Latin, and Doctor Trautmann's office vanished. The mirror once again reflected the ceiling.

"There is a very good method of practicing with the spell used to shift the focus of the mirror. Walk several blocks away and remove a small limb from a tree. It can be substituted for the letter from Doctor Trautmann. When you practice the spell using the twig, the tree from which it came will be displayed by the mirror."

"Amazing."

"No, not really," he replied, smiling. "It's magic, after all."

"Yes," I said, laughing. "I suppose it is."

We began the process of extinguishing our lamps and locking up the room. I briefly wondered whether or not I should broach the subject of the tattoo I had seen. In the end, my curiosity won out.

"Vincent, did I notice a tattoo on your left arm?" In the halflight, I thought I saw him clutch at the stump of his left forearm.

There was a pause before he cleared his throat.

"It's embarrassing, actually. When I was still young and foolish, I succumbed to a whim, but midway through the process changed my mind. Very childish, really."

He snickered nervously.

"Sometimes I wish that that wolf had taken off my arm at the elbow. Then I would have been rid of it forever. But I suppose that we must live with our mistakes."

"Yes," I replied. "As best as we can, anyway."

EIGHTEEN

Before long, it was evident that Vincent's teaching methods were indeed quite effective. I mastered the mirror within days, using his suggestion of scrying on trees in the surrounding area. I became adept at shifting the focus of the mirror by practicing on unsuspecting people who happened to wander into my field of vision. Once, instead of a tree limb, I substituted a scarf that Mrs. Bettings had knitted for me. For about ten minutes, I watched her go pottering about the boarding house, washing dishes, dusting—but I grew ashamed of my actions. Shifting the focus out into the neighborhoods of Arkham, I wandered those streets, searching for any changes that may have occurred in my absence. But it was just the same as I had left it. After only a short time, I began to notice an uncharacteristic anxiety growing within me. When I ended my session, however, my anxiety ceased. It was foolish, but I think I had been afraid of being seen in Arkham by someone who might recognize me—something plainly impossible through the mirror.

By the end of the week, Vincent and I had settled into a schedule for spying upon Doctor Trautmann. We alternated in four-hour shifts. I would stay at the mirror from six until ten in the morning, and from two until six in the afternoon. Vincent would relieve me at the end of those shifts, staying awake until Doctor Trautmann went to bed. Our subject lived only a few blocks from the university, so it was easy to follow him as he walked to the library in the morning, and then back home in the evening. Thankfully, he rarely rode in a motorcar, as it would speed away faster than we could follow. But except for those occasions, we observed him constantly.

On our side of the mirror, however, the atmosphere grew

strained. We held to the schedule for a week, then switched places: Vincent taking the first shift of the day, while I stayed awake until Doctor Trautmann went to bed. After the second week ended, we switched back. It was during the third week that my patience began to wear thin. It became obvious to me that our strategy was for naught. The man apparently had no vices, no secrets. He rarely drank alcohol, and then it would be precisely one glass of wine. He was even-tempered with his wife and three children. He didn't have a wandering eye for any woman. He didn't gamble. And when in his office, he worked constantly and reliably for the entire day. In short, there was nothing we could use. He may have had a skeleton or two hidden in his closet, but they were not the sorts of things revealed by our monitoring.

By that time, Vincent and I had both begun to show signs of frustration. We mostly saw each other only during shift changes, and when we did, we snapped at each other. I wondered more than once if he would simply announce our venture to be a failure, and throw me out on the street. After spending weeks in his home, I had not only come to enjoy his luxurious hospitality, but had grown dependent upon it. Bearing that in mind, whenever we started to argue, it was usually I who acquiesced.

At the end of that third week, we were nearly at our wits' end, when we had an unexpected breakthrough. Vincent had just shown up to begin his shift when Doctor Trautmann's secretary delivered his daily mail. Along with the usual assortment of letters and memorandums, there was a package. The doctor paid no attention to it in her presence. After she had left the room, however, we watched him grab it and eagerly rip away the wrapping to reveal a small, tin container. Within it was an envelope and an even smaller, ornate wooden box. As he opened the envelope and read the letter inside, I tried to maneuver the perspective to allow us to read it as well, but it was a very short note. He finished, folded it and put it back into the envelope before I got close enough.

Hands trembling, Doctor Trautmann carefully opened the

smaller box to reveal a palm-sized, five-pointed stone. Its deep green surface was irregularly peppered with small black spots. It reminded me of something Professor Josephson had described.

"Is that…"

"It's an Elder Sign," whispered Vincent. He let out a sigh heavy with defeat.

"What does it matter?" I asked, confused. "Will it interfere with the scrying?"

"No, but if he has an Elder Sign, that means he must feel himself to be in danger," he explained. "Have you been careful? I trusted you not to reveal us. Has he shown any signs of detecting us? Staring off into space? Listening for sounds that can't be heard?"

It was difficult for me to not react to his tone, but I merely bit my lip and shook my head. He stared at the image of the green stone in the mirror, seemingly unable to look away. But when he spoke next, his anger seemed to have morphed into pensive thought.

"I didn't consider that ours might not be the only request turned down," he said. "There may be several people who would like to have access to these books. Perhaps some more powerful than I, or more short-tempered, or both. Maybe the good doctor has received threats."

Still transfixed by the sight of the Elder Sign, he lapsed into silence. He remained unmoving for a minute. He did not even blink. After another minute, I reached out and touched his arm. He jerked visibly and looked at me.

"He may even have anticipated attempts at scrying and changed his habits accordingly," he said. Though a substantial pause had occurred, he spoke smoothly, completing his thought as if no time had passed. "It may become more difficult now, but our plan, however ill-conceived, must continue."

"Continue?"

"Yes," he replied simply, as if daring me to disagree.

Unfortunately, I couldn't contain my frustration longer.

"But we have nothing! In three weeks, we have gained nothing! Can you not see how ridiculous this has become? We watch him read, write, eat, brush his teeth. This is futile! There is nothing to see!"

Vincent closed his eyes, as if he viewed me as an impetuous child, one for whom a great deal of patience was needed.

"Robert…" Eyes still closed, he paused and licked his lips.

I waited for him to speak. The thought crossed my mind that my outburst may have been my final one. Had our relationship grown so strained that he had decided to dissolve it?

Whatever he had planned on saying remained unspoken, for when he opened his eyes, his gaze immediately shifted to the mirror.

"Look!" he said, pointing.

I glanced down in time to see Doctor Trautmann hurriedly open the top drawer of his desk, and sweep the contents of the package into it. The drawer was slammed shut as he forced a grin. Though I kept the mirror focused on the doctor, it was clear that someone else had arrived. His expression spoke volumes. Whoever approached was certainly unexpected, and someone to either be loathed or feared. It didn't take long for his unforeseen guest to wander into view of the mirror. For some reason I was not surprised in the least by who it was.

"Higgins," I said bitterly, trying and failing to control the irritation I felt.

"You know him?"

"All too well. He's the one who convinced Doctor Trautmann to restrict my access to the books in the first place."

We watched intently as the two men exchanged pleasantries, and then started talking business. Higgins seemed to be trying to persuade Doctor Trautmann to do something. The doctor resisted several attempts, becoming more and more adamant with his refusal each time. Higgins maintained the same pleasant attitude with each rejection, until suddenly, he snapped. He stood up, leaned over the front of the desk, and began a tirade. During our weeks of scrying, my lip-reading skills had not improved as much as I had hoped. I could not make out much of what either man said during this exchange—not until the end. Higgins concluded with "on your head." At this, it seemed as if the doctor had accepted defeat.

Higgins said something else at that point—a cheery "Good-day," perhaps—before he turned, and left. The doctor was left reeling as if he had just been beaten to a pulp. It was incredible to see the effect that Jebediah Higgins had on people. I had never known anyone who could induce so much misery with just an arrogant word or a condescending glance as he. A kernel of an idea formed in my mind as, once again alone in his office, Doctor Trautmann struggled to keep himself from weeping.

I spoke the word to stop the mirror's scrying, and my idea blossomed into a full plan.

"I believe that I have something," I said, a small amount of satisfaction in my voice.

Vincent smiled faintly.

"Oh? Out with it, then."

"I believe that your suggestion that the doctor has anticipated attempts at scrying and changed his habits is…wrong." I pushed straight on, not allowing time for Vincent to react. "I think we were unsuccessful discovering any of his vices because he truly has nothing to hide. He is an average man with a normal family. His job is his life. He is a bureaucrat. He gets pleasure from the fact that he wields some amount of power in his position as Director of the Library. For years, he has been living comfortably, not knowing any kind of fear. Now, possibly for the first time in his life, there is an obstacle: Jebediah Higgins."

He nodded.

"What we need to do is to confront him, and tell him that we know he is trying to keep something secret. We can threaten to inform Higgins of his plans. If he denies it, we can supply him with details, starting with the Elder Sign."

"And ending there, as well," he said, shaking his head. "We have no actual knowledge of his plans."

"No, we do not," I agreed. "We shall have to bluff if necessary."

"Can he be bluffed? Is the name of Higgins enough?"

"From the reaction we just witnessed, I would think so. But there's only one way to know for sure."

"There may be two," said Vincent. "We can try to get more information."

"From his dreaming mind?"

"Exactly so."

In order to perform the ceremony for communicating with Doctor Trautmann's dream self, we would have to sacrifice the letter we had been using for scrying. Because of that, we decided to spend one final day at the mirror to learn all that we possibly could. Vincent volunteered to watch our subject while I used the time to study, and prepare for the ceremony. The only useful bits of information he learned during his long day at the mirror were that the package came from London, and that Doctor Trautmann carried the Elder Sign home with him that evening. I asked him if the presence of that item would affect the spell I was preparing to cast. He replied that it should not.

When midnight at last arrived—and we were reasonably sure that the Doctor would be fast asleep—we returned to the laboratory. After we cleared the table and rehung the mirror on the wall, Vincent poured some of that familiar, near-invisible liquid into a glass container in the center of the table. Recalling that Andrew had conducted the ceremony from within a magical circle carved on the floor, I asked Vincent about needing some sort of similar protection.

234

He told me that the means he had used to protect the room from scrying also served to provide the appropriate amount of protection for the ceremony. Reassured, I twisted the letter from Doctor Trautmann into a wick and placed it into the container. After calming my nerves, I began.

The first two phases proceeded smoothly. Feeling confident, I struck a match and lit the letter. Almost instantly, a wind sprang up, and what I could only assume was the dream-self of Doctor Trautmann joined us at the table. But the gusts that blew around us were not cold, as they had been in the times Andrew had cast the spell. They were instead slightly warm.

When the air settled, Vincent remained silent while I led the way.

"Is Doctor Trautmann present with us in this room?" I asked.

Yes, came the response in my head. Soundless, I still imagined it to match the voice I had heard from my one brief meeting with the man.

"Did you receive a package from London today?"

Yes.

"Who, specifically, sent it to you?"

I cannot say, came the response after a pause.

"Did you request that the object be sent to you?"

Yes.

"Why?"

I cannot say.

"Did someone threaten you?"

For that question and all of the others on our list, the response was invariably, *I cannot say.* I grew tired of hearing it. With the paper yet burning, I looked at Vincent. He looked as disappointed as I felt, but pointed at the list and made a circle in the air with his finger. I nodded and ran through the list again, trying variations on the wording. Some small part of me hoped that we could learn *something*—some tiny fact, or a confirmation of any of our suspicions. But there was nothing.

With time running out, I tried in vain to think of a new approach. I shook my head and shrugged. Vincent finished writing something on a sheet of paper and handed it to me. Just before the burning letter was completely consumed by flame, I read aloud the words he had written.

"Doctor Trautmann, there is more to fear than you can possibly know."

It was not phrased as a question, so there was no answer. The flame extinguished itself, and the dream-spirit exited with the winds.

After concluding the ceremony, we sat for a moment in the silence of the laboratory.

"You've managed to flummox me," I said. "What did you hope to gain with that?" I pointed at the paper.

"Perhaps something, perhaps nothing," he said cryptically. "I'll know better once we get to Arkham."

Resigned to the fact that it was his nature to be secretive, I only nodded. However, one word of Vincent's reply—Arkham—reverberated through my mind. As deeply immersed as we were in our spying over the past weeks, I had given little thought to the past. Despite the fact that I was actually watching the town and the university in which I had spent the past years of my life, those places viewed through the mirror somehow seemed distant and illusory. Realizing that I would actually be going back, the town became much more concrete—with respect to both the living and the dead that I had left behind. There was also the matter of the police, and any possible investigation concerning Andrew's death. For the past month, I had felt secure staying with Vincent in Boston. Holed up in a house so large, all of my needs provided for, it was impossible not to feel safe. Arkham, though, was another matter. That small town had been transformed in my mind, the years of positive recollections overshadowed by death. I dreaded a return there. But the reward of eldritch knowledge was too great! I thought only of my mission: Revenge upon Sothoth Pnath. There could be nothing else.

"To Arkham, then," I said.

Nineteen

Though it was well after midnight when we concluded the ceremony, Vincent insisted that time was of the essence, and that we should depart for Arkham as soon as possible. Fatigued by the ceremony and the late hour, I convinced him to wait until morning. Due to my previous encounter with Doctor Trautmann, I told him that merely meeting with the man would be difficult in itself. It would serve no purpose to show up on his doorstep unannounced, as he would require us to have an appointment. Vincent, however, did not seem to be the least bit concerned with that trivial detail, as he called it. Too tired to debate with him, I dragged myself up the stairs, and collapsed onto the bed.

I slept soundly, but it was not nearly enough. I was awakened by Albert at dawn. Sill drowsy, I dressed myself, and ate a small breakfast. Vincent must have been just as tired, as I heard hardly a word from him the entire morning. Albert delivered us to the station in downtown Boston, and our train departed promptly at quarter to eight. We both napped sporadically on the journey. The rest seemed to refresh my partner, but not me. As we walked the half-mile or so from the Arkham train depot to the university, my mood grew steadily sour, and I prayed I would not meet anyone from my prior life, most especially Professor Josephson. It was the middle of summer, and with hardly any students and few classes in session, it seemed possible to complete our trip without any unexpected encounters. Head down, I avoided meeting anyone's eyes. Each passerby was a possible threat.

We arrived at the Miskatonic University Library just before noon, and without incident. Vincent had noticed a pattern in Doctor

Trautmann's daily lunch, which he had hoped to exploit. It could not have been better timed. We climbed the stairs and emerged onto the third floor just as Doctor Trautmann was leaving. He was still speaking with his secretary as we crossed the floor to her desk.

"...need to speak with him tomorrow morning. If anyone inquires after me, I will be at lunch."

"Yes, Doctor," replied the woman, glancing up at us.

The doctor, seemingly irritated by our presence, attempted to walk past us. But Vincent would not allow our quarry to escape that easily. He moved over to stand directly in front of him.

"Doctor Trautmann. Please forgive me for intruding, but it is vital that we speak with you."

"Now?" With a disdainful expression on his face he shook his head. "Gentlemen, you do not have an appointment. It is time for my lunch. Please, step aside."

"Doctor, please," said Vincent calmly. "It will only take a few minutes of your time."

"No." He puffed out his chest as if to dare us to argue. "You must make an appointment with my secretary. I'm afraid that I cannot help you now."

That was apparently the cue Vincent had been hoping for.

"You say you're afraid?" He inched closer and lowered his voice. "Doctor Trautmann, there is more to fear than you could possibly know."

The doctor's reaction to those words was astonishing. He seemed to have nearly stopped breathing. His eyes grew large as saucers as he stared at Vincent. No, not *at*. The doctor looked *through* him. As if he was not even there.

"Doctor Trautmann," said Vincent softly. The sound of his voice startled the man to attention.

"Yes," he said sharply, gasping for breath and focusing on Vincent. "Yes. I'm sorry. I..." He jerked his head around, as if trying

239

to orient himself. "We can talk in my office. Now. This way. Please follow me."

He walked off quickly toward the immense doors to his office.

"Thank you, Doctor," said Vincent graciously. As we followed our host, Vincent winked in my direction.

Doctor Trautmann held the doors open as we entered, then closed them and followed us over to his massive desk. As we all took a seat—we in front and he behind—I wondered briefly if he would remember me from our meeting weeks before.

"Gentlemen, I believe that you have me at a disadvantage," the doctor began. "Why don't you please tell me your names?"

Before I could say a word, Vincent spoke up.

"My name is Vincent Marsh, and this is my cousin, William Wentworth."

The doctor nodded to both of us in turn. No attempt was made to shake hands. Indeed, the distance between our seats made such an exercise impossible. He acted as if he did not recognize me.

"We're researchers," said Vincent. "We study certain fields of knowledge that have been largely forgotten or ignored by the human race. Unlike most people, you, as Director of the Library, must understand that a great deal can be learned from the past, and that every detail must be recorded and retained in the hope that someday, some use may come of it."

He paused, giving the man an opportunity to comment, but he was met with silence.

"Indeed," continued Vincent, "it's always possible that a seemingly trivial scrap can prove to be vital. It is one of those scraps that has come into our possession. We suspect that the secrets contained in our fragment will shed light on a question that has plagued the human race for millennia. But in order to corroborate our knowledge, we need to examine the *Necronomicon* of Abdul Alhazred and the *Pnakotic Manuscripts*. We are under the

240

impression that both volumes are currently in your possession. It is extremely important we be allowed a chance to study them."

The doctor looked first at one of us, then the other, perhaps expecting more. His manner, originally nervous and unsettled when we had entered his office, had changed over the course of Vincent's speech.

"And what should I fear, gentlemen?" he asked. Enthroned upon his large, leather chair, he displayed no anxiety of any sort. "You stated that there is more for me to fear than I could possibly know."

"Well, you see, there's a horror that has existed for—"

"This horror," he asked, interrupting Vincent. "Does it have a name?"

"Yes, but—"

"Gentlemen," he interrupted Vincent again. "First, the Library does not possess a copy of the mythical *Pnakotic Manuscripts*, as any reputable historian or archaeologist will tell you that such a document does not actually exist. Second, your request to view the *Necronomicon* does not merit special consideration. All such requests are currently given the same response: No. We are currently not allowing access to any of those volumes. Only requests with some bearing on a concrete or immediate threat will be honored. If this horror has truly been threatening humanity for millennia, then it can certainly wait a bit longer."

The doctor's attitude was smug and fearless. Allowing him to enter his office had been a mistake. In this place, his authority was supreme. He wielded the power of bureaucracy from behind his desk. I saw that there was no longer any possibility of asking or persuading him.

"Do you, personally, consider Jebediah Higgins to be a concrete or immediate threat?" I asked as nonchalantly as possible.

The doctor's transformation was a spectacular thing to see. His face turned ashen, as if he had just seen a ghost.

"What?" The word was barely audible.

I stood up, placed both of my hands upon his desk and leaned toward him.

"Jebediah Higgins," I repeated, clearly enunciating each syllable. "He does not *yet* know that you are working behind his back. He does not *yet* know of the package you received from London yesterday."

"Package? What package?" he asked nervously.

"Doctor, we know of the package." An overwhelming confidence surged through me as I played the bluff. "We know of the Elder Sign you now possess."

For a moment, his gaze went past us toward the door. As if he were measuring the distance between himself and his only exit.

"If you do not grant our simple request," I said, my voice still calm, "we will go straight to Higgins and tell him what you have been doing. Everything."

"You can't!"

"We can. And we will."

I stared at him, but he did not move. Vincent had only observed the exchange, saying nothing. I motioned for him to rise. Together, we turned and headed for the doors. My heart hammered in my chest as we walked away. The bluff was failing, it seemed, but any hesitation would have undermined the gambit. We were committed. As I reached for the handles, the doctor finally succumbed.

"Wait."

We stopped, and turned to face him. I struggled to disguise my relief.

"I'll do as you ask," he said bitterly.

"We truly appreciate your cooperation," said Vincent, taking control of the situation once again. "We shouldn't need more than a few hours."

Doctor Trautmann scowled at us. I could empathize with him. Vincent's faux politeness would have enraged me as well.

"Follow me," he said, gritting his teeth. "Speak to no one."

We followed him out of the office, across the floor, and down the stairs. On the first floor, he told us to wait on the landing, and he approached the main desk. We watched him confer briefly with a very young-looking man, who then accompanied the doctor back to the stairs. The four of us descended the flight to the basement.

Doctor Trautmann unlocked the door at the bottom of the steps and swung it open, revealing a long, straight corridor. He led the way, our collective footsteps echoing off the marble floor with a weirdly disturbing resonance. We walked for what felt like an impossible distance—much further than the length of the Library—before coming to a stop outside of an unmarked room. Trautmann removed a key from his vest and unlocked the stout, metal door.

When the doctor opened the door and turned on the overhead light, I was surprised by the stark simplicity of the tiny room. Against the wall to our left stood a single bookcase, partially filled with ancient texts; and to our right, a small desk with a blotter, pen and ink, and a single wooden chair. Doctor Trautmann went over to the bookcase, removed a massive volume, and carried it over to the desk. He set it down, then rubbed his hands together as if to remove some dust or grit. The book's cover was a nearly featureless dark brown, almost black. There seemed to be some red and black markings visible—a title, perhaps, or some sort of symbol—but they were faded to the point of illegibility.

"The *Necronomicon* of Abdul Alhazred," said Doctor Trautmann. "I trust that your Latin is up to the task, gentlemen."

"You need not worry, Doctor," replied Vincent. He eyed the tome hungrily.

"This young man"—he indicated the final member of our party—"shall attend you in my absence. He will not interfere with your studies. You, in turn, will remain in sight at all times. And will

243

not close this door."

"Agreed," said Vincent eagerly.

Without another word, Trautmann turned and left, his footsteps echoing down the hall.

Vincent swiftly took a seat at the desk. He studied the cover for a few seconds.

"Human flesh," he said with a faint smile. "The covering is made of human flesh. But in remarkably good condition for its age."

This did not go over well with our attendant. He gulped and moved out into the hall.

Vincent paused to whisper a few words—I could not hear what they were—and carefully opened the ancient tome. I watched over his shoulder, as he turned to a section about halfway through the book, and started reading the Latin script. At the pace at which he turned the pages, he seemed to be reading at least twice as fast as I could. It was obvious he knew what he was doing.

Our original plan had called for me to study the *Pnakotic Man-uscripts* as best I could while Vincent examined the *Necronomicon*. But with the good doctor's revelation that such a document did not exist, I had nothing to do but wait. I looked over the other volumes in the bookcase, but did not take any down. Our request had been specifically for access to the *Necronomicon*, and Trautmann had someone accompany us probably for the very reason of preventing such browsing. In fact, it seemed very likely that the doctor would return shortly, perhaps with a security guard, or the police, or—possibly worst of all—Jebediah Higgins himself.

An hour went by. Then two. All the while, Vincent moved through the pages at an amazing rate. Most he seemed to read, but some he skipped over completely, as if already familiar with them, aware that they did not contain the information he desired. Both the nameless young man and myself alternately sat on the floor, stood still, or paced. No words were exchanged at all.

It was getting close to three hours when Vincent's voice broke the silence.

"Found it."

I leapt to my feet, and rushed over to examine the contents of the page.

"Robert, please!" said Vincent. "You're blocking the light."

Without looking up from the text, Vincent removed a small notebook from his coat pocket, and began to copy the information that we would need.

He had been busy writing for about twenty minutes when the doctor returned—alone, to my relief. He dismissed the young man, then joined Vincent and myself in the small room.

"Doctor Trautmann," I greeted him. "We are nearly finished."

"No, Mr. Adderly," he said. The smug tone had returned to his voice. "You are finished right now."

Upon hearing my name, I froze. Vincent stopped his writing, stood up, and moved to the side of the desk.

"I thought I knew you," Doctor Trautmann said, studying me, "but I was not certain until now. Why were you trying to hide your identity? No, please don't bother to answer. I'm sure that it would just be a lie."

He reached into his right coat pocket and withdrew a small handgun. I took a step backwards. Vincent did not move an inch.

Still holding the gun in his right, Doctor Trautmann used his left to retrieve a crumpled white handkerchief from his coat pocket. Gripping a small bit of the material by only thumb and forefinger, he shook it lightly. As it unfurled, a greenish dust fell out and rained onto the floor.

"This is all that remains of that so-called package," he said, kicking at the dust. "You now have no proof of *anything*. As I said, you are finished. Get out! Now!"

He held the gun loosely, but it was pointed directly at me. I felt myself paralyzed by the unanticipated turn of events. When that young woman had arrived at the bookstore, brandishing her knife and threatening Andrew's life, I had been filled with dread. But this…this was something else entirely. Staring down the barrel of a loaded weapon was a novel experience. It occurred to me how much I had thrown away by stepping onto this path of vengeance—and now with death potentially a nervous finger twitch away, my very life was at risk. With the bizarre deaths of Elizabeth and Andrew, I had accepted the possibility of an equally horrific end, but never had I considered something so mundane as a bullet being the cause.

I likely only hesitated for a second, but it felt longer. As I made up my mind to move toward the door, I heard Vincent start to laugh. It began as a mild chuckle, but transformed into a hysterical roar. Doctor Trautmann was not amused.

"Stop it! Shut up!"

He pointed the gun directly at Vincent, who stepped forward slowly, still chuckling. The doctor did not yield any ground as his target advanced, but he pulled the gun back toward his body an inch at a time, until it had been drawn in as close as it could go. Vincent only stopped when the barrel of the gun was pressed directly against his ribs. His laughter also ceased then, the smile replaced with a scowl.

"You poor fool," said Vincent, shaking his head. "Destroying that artifact was probably the most ill-advised act you have ever committed in your entire worthless life."

The gun trembled visibly.

"Get out or I'll shoot."

The doctor's voice wavered unconvincingly, even to me. But the reality of the gun, and who controlled it, and in which direction it was pointed…it all added up to sway me. Again, I almost moved, but stopped as I observed Vincent. What really happened next is impossible to say. I can only say that the impression it left on my mind haunts me even now.

Vincent ignored the words completely, seemingly caught up in some sort of suicidal madness. He raised his left arm, exposing the stump, and pointed it toward the doctor, nearly touching him on the breastbone. Perhaps it was a trick of the light, but I thought I saw an odd shadow fall upon the doctor's chest. The older man twitched slightly, as if shocked. He clenched his teeth, and it appeared to me as if he had decided to pull the trigger. Both men were just out of my reach, too far away for me to grab either. I could do nothing but hold my breath, and wait tensely for the weapon's loud report.

But the sound never came. Instead, Doctor Trautmann's eyes suddenly went wide with pain. He let out an agonizing wail, and dropped the gun, clutching at his chest with both hands. He collapsed to his knees, then tilted over onto the floor. Vincent simply stood above his fallen form as I rushed to the man's side, but it was already too late. I could not feel a pulse. The end had come incredibly quickly.

"Poor fellow," said Vincent, looking down. "The stress of the circumstances must have gotten to him."

"The...the stress?" I asked uncertainly.

"What else? Just look at him. Not a mark upon him. He was old. It was plainly heart failure."

He walked out into the hall and looked down the length of it. Apparently satisfied that no one had heard the scream, he returned to the room.

"But why did you advance on him?" I asked. "How did you know he wouldn't shoot?"

Vincent looked at me blankly for a moment, then indicated the gun on the floor.

"He still had the safety engaged."

Kneeling down, he slid the pen that he yet held in his right hand through the trigger guard, and picked up the weapon with it. He walked over to the desk, and carefully placed the gun at the back edge.

"I was hoping to force his hand, force him to try and shoot us. Too late he would have realized his mistake. Between the two of us, we could have wrested the gun from him. Unfortunately"—he pointed at the dead man—"his heart gave out first."

After a final, dispassionate glance at the dead man, he returned to his seat at the desk, and resumed his writing.

"I only need fifteen more minutes, then we can go."

"Fifteen—but what about him?"

"What about him? He's dead. We can do nothing. And we certainly don't want to be questioned by the police, do we Mr. *Adderly*?"

The question was obviously rhetorical, but still it shut me up. I paced, waiting anxiously for Vincent to finish. Every minute, I checked the hallway, expecting to be discovered.

It seemed to take forever, but at last, Vincent signaled that he was done. After placing the notebook in his coat, he flipped forward about a hundred pages in the ancient tome. He skimmed through the text, turning a page or two at a time, sometimes murmuring to himself. It did not take long for him to find what he was searching for. He left the book open and knelt down next to the doctor.

"Help me lift him into the chair," he said.

I looked down at the body, not wanting to touch it.

"Robert, I can't do it alone."

This corpse at least had flesh on it. Unlike the last one. I convinced myself that he was merely sleeping, and reached down. He was still warm. Working together, we managed to seat the body in the chair, slumped over the desk. Vincent slid the gun along the desktop so that it was under the dead man's right hand.

"Why bother with the pretense?" I asked. "The gun never even discharged."

Vincent pointed to the book.

"That page describes a blackly terrible ceremony for killing an enemy while he sleeps. It calls forth a creature that is difficult to control. Only a lunatic would even consider using it. With any luck, the doctor may be blamed for his own untimely death."

I was still puzzled by the rationale, but Vincent seemed confident, enough so that he turned and walked out of the room. I hovered over the posed body, looking for anything amiss, then thought of one detail. The need to be holding a loaded weapon implied that the safety lock should be off. I bent down to examine the gun in his hand. Somehow, it was already off. I had no time to wonder about that before dashing out of the room to catch up with Vincent.

Exiting the library was relatively simple: We walked right out the front door.

Getting to the train station, however, proved to be more complicated. With Vincent following my lead, we took the shortest possible route to the depot, avoiding certain blocks I knew might have people who could recognize me. When we were only a few streets from our goal, a well-dressed man some twenty yards ahead caught my attention. After following him for about a block, it occurred to me that I knew his gait. I could not positively identify him—not at first, anyway. The muddled, anxious state of my mind prevented me from thinking clearly. But I was certain I sensed danger.

The man stopped abruptly, as if he had remembered some forgotten task. Even as he began to turn around, my heart nearly leapt into my throat.

"Higgins!" I whispered as loud as I dared, and pulled Vincent sideways into a doorway. I grabbed the knob, and prayed that it would be open. My prayers were answered. We entered hastily, composed ourselves, and looked around. We were surrounded by racks of dresses, purses, and shoes. The air was thick with the scent of roses.

We moved deeper into the store to escape the expansive and revealing front window. Those few seconds waiting for Higgins to move past the glass were torturous. Had he seen us? I sincerely doubted that he would have known me at that distance for such a brief instant, but we may have appeared suspicious to him by darting into the store so rapidly. Perhaps he would decide to follow us in to see what was so interesting. Or even worse, he might decide to wait outside until we emerged. I held my breath. With my attention trained on the door, the salesclerk was almost on top of us before I noticed her.

Just as she began to speak, I saw Higgins walk by outside. With a sigh of immense relief, I nodded to Vincent that we were safe.

"Gentlemen, how may I—"

But before she could finish her sentence, Vincent glared angrily at me, and began to berate me with a perfect German accent.

"Wir können Seitengewehre nicht hier kaufen, Wilhelm! Komm!"

And he stomped out angrily. At first, I was just as confused as the salesclerk. But when I caught on, I was once again grateful for his quick thinking. I played along, acting embarrassed in front of the silent woman, before following him to the door. We checked as unobtrusively as possible to make sure that the coast was clear, then exited the store, easily covering the final blocks to the train station.

TWENTY

At the depot, Vincent and I both received a shock when we checked the train schedule for the return trip. Neither of us had given it a thought beforehand. In the morning, we were half-asleep and preoccupied with reaching Doctor Trautmann before he left for lunch. Now, we wanted to escape Arkham as soon as possible, but the next train to Boston would not depart for over two hours. Rather than wait, we decided to take one that was leaving shortly. It was headed north, but that was of no concern to us.

We got off at the Ipswich station, satisfied that there was enough distance between us and the dead man. With a lengthy wait before being able to take a train south, we found a restaurant. I welcomed it as both a distraction, and a chance to fill my empty stomach. We ate in silence. Worried over too many things, I chewed mechanically, tasting nothing. Every now and then I looked up at Vincent, sitting across from me, slicing through his plate of eggs with a butter knife, and carefully scooping each bite into his mouth. I had been mulling over his explanation of events since we had departed Arkham. Clearly, I could not blame him for the sudden failure of an old man's heart, and yet the coincidence was astounding. It was only after Vincent got right up next to him that the doctor had collapsed.

But weighing more heavily on me was the fact that the young attendant could certainly identify us both. We had made no attempt to disguise ourselves. Also, the doctor may have informed someone—his secretary, perhaps—of my identity before revisiting us in the library basement. It was certainly only a matter of time before someone tracked my movements from Arkham to Boston, perhaps with the help of Mrs. Bettings innocently supplying some necessary bit of information? Then again, Doctor Trautmann's plans for the Elder Sign had remained unknown to us, and it seemed that whatever they were, he had hoped to keep them a secret from everyone. Perhaps his paranoia would turn out to be our saving grace.

What knotted my stomach most of all, though, was Doctor Trautmann's belief that we could never hope to find a copy of the *Pnakotic Manuscripts*. Assuming that Vincent transcribed all of the necessary information for the banishing ceremony from the *Necronomicon*, we were still missing that final piece of knowledge: How to manipulate the Crystal of Dha'al. We were so close! Hopefully Vincent had an idea of where to look for such forgotten knowledge. Since leaving the library, he had spoken very little. Yet despite his outward calm, his mannerisms had an uncharacteristic nervousness. I assumed that his mind was preoccupied with the same problems as mine.

After finishing our dinner, we boarded the train once again, and arrived in Boston after ten o'clock. Vincent telephoned Albert from the station, and he met us shortly afterward with a motorcar to take us home. I was more grateful than ever before in my life to be able to just fall into bed. Sleep came swiftly.

My dreams from that night, while not nightmarish, could also not be described as pleasant. The deadly confrontation with Doctor Trautmann echoed over and over in my head, changing slightly each time with the near-obsessive retelling. In one version, Vincent's insane laughter echoed louder and louder, until it transformed itself into the heartbeat-like thudding of a Servitor of Q'yoth. Distracted by the noise, I looked around the tiny room. When I turned my attention back to Vincent and the doctor, they were both gone. I was alone, a small pile of green dust at my feet, holding in my right hand that small knife which I continued to carry with me in my coat pocket. But in the next, Vincent was not present at all. It was Andrew who stood in his place, laughing. In another, a tall figure cloaked in shadows stood over the dead doctor. In yet another, I appeared twice—both in my usual role as observer, and also replacing Vincent as the one who faced the doctor. I took his life with just the touch of my palm.

I slept late. When finally I went downstairs, it was nearly noon. I discovered I had the dining room to myself, though I could hear Albert moving around in the kitchen. He was very good at his job, anticipating my needs before I even voiced them. Even after all those weeks, though, I had still not become comfortable with his appearance. I preferred to not make eye contact with him, and so rarely spoke to him.

While waiting for my breakfast, I skimmed through the newspaper looking for any mention of Doctor Trautmann. I was curious as to how his death would be interpreted, what kind of investigation would be conducted. There was nothing. It was too soon for the news to have traveled from Arkham.

A moment later, I heard the cellar door in the kitchen open, and Vincent stepped into the dining room holding a few loose sheets in his hand.

"Good morning," he greeted me. "I just finished translating the shorthand I copied yesterday into something more legible."

He gave no indication that anything abnormal had happened the day before. Somehow, this made it easier for me: As long as that fatal encounter went unacknowledged, I could delude myself into thinking that things could continue on the way they had been.

He sorted through the papers and handed me a sheet. As I began to read, I heard Alfred put a plate down on the table beside me, and I was grateful for an excuse this time to ignore him.

> *The Shadow of the Gate should also not be forgotten. Though only an echo of the infinite, the echo itself is infinite. Has an echo but one note? Can the All be divided into less than All? Knowing the answer, know then that the Shadow is distinct from the Gate. It has its own place in the*

Heavens. It has its own manifestations. Its own colors. Its own ceremonies. Its own sacrifices. Shall we live in fear of the Shadow? There is no need. Rejoice when thou art chosen. Know that the Gate and the Shadow have honored thee. Ia!

Perform not the ceremony when the stars are against thee. When the stars are neutral, a sacrifice is necessary. But when the stars are correct, the gift need not be offered, for it shall be taken! From where, from when, only the chosen shall know. Honored are those embraced by the darkness. Live not in fear of the Shadow! Rejoice! Thou art honored! Ia!

The Shadow stays with the darkness and is sent with the light.

If calling with darkness, the Shadow shall stay. Fear not! Embrace the Shadow! Commune with the starless dark! Revel in the oneness, the joining of self and shadow! But when the time arrives, dispel the darkness. Accept the fire. Thou shalt not be rejected. Thy soul shall be cleansed with the holiest of flames. There shall never be fear again! Thou art accepted! Rejoice! Ia!

Call with light, and the Shadow shall depart. Look as you will, but it shall not be there. It shall depart through thee. Where is it? Who can know? It can be anywhere in darkness; it can be nowhere in light. Without darkness, there can be no Shadow. By using the light, thou hast deprived thyself of the oneness! Despair not! It is not too late. Wait. When the stars are right, it can never be too late. Wait for the Shadow. Ia!

"The answer!" exclaimed Vincent. "This page is the answer!

Our answer!"

He seemed to be waiting for me to match my enthusiasm to his. I read it over again, more slowly this time, and tried to interpret the cryptic paragraphs. Try as I might, the meaning eluded me.

"Sorry. How are you interpreting this?"

He smiled and pointed at the last paragraph.

"Look at this first sentence," he said, leaning toward me. "'Call with light, and the Shadow shall depart.' That's it. A shadow disappears when confronted with light. If the ceremony is performed in light—and I mean literally a room full of light, with no shadows or blind spots—then the creature will disappear. It will be banished!"

I read the page a third time. It was true that through this new lens of Vincent's, the hodgepodge of phrases became much easier to understand.

"Which ceremony?" I asked with mounting excitement. "Where is it?"

He handed me three more sheets filled with complicated and lengthy instructions. Vincent watched me closely as I looked them over.

"You were right about one thing," I said when finished. "Two hands are definitely required."

"Do you think you can do it?" he asked.

Considered as a whole, the task was daunting. Broken into distinct pieces, however, it was definitely within my capabilities, even with my small amount of experience. Yet, I was hesitant. Magicians much more experienced than I had come to far greater harm attempting things simpler than this. Andrew, for instance. He had believed wholeheartedly in his abilities. He had thought himself capable of performing any spell laid out before him. His hubris had not only gotten him killed, but the flesh eaten from his bones.

"Yes. I can do it."

"Good," Vincent said, clapping me on the shoulder. "I'm glad to hear it. Confidence is ninety percent of magic. Memorization and physical ability make up the other ten percent. A successful magician needs one hundred percent."

He motioned toward his missing left hand.

"At this time, I can only manage ninety-nine."

I handed him back the pages, and pointed at the original sheet he showed me.

"Can you explain this?" I asked. "The paragraph that begins, 'If calling with darkness'."

"That stuck out to me as well. It seems to describe a form of ritual suicide. When the ceremony is conducted in complete darkness, Sothoth Pnath visits the magician and dwells with him. The magician becomes one with the entity, sharing thoughts. The text describes it as an exceptionally sacred moment, but I suspect it would not be as special as the author claims."

The chilling implications of his statement were not lost on me.

"In any case," he continued, "it seems that when the magician has had enough communing, he uses some light to create a shadow. This ends the ritual, as well as the life of the magician."

I shook my head, trying to imagine what sequence of events, what particular form of insanity, was required for someone to do such a thing.

We had only one remaining problem—that of the rotation of the shard. After finishing my breakfast, I went into the den and found Vincent at the telephone. He did not mind my presence. I stayed as he made one call after another, fluidly speaking German, French, and some sort of Slavic language, as well as English. But no matter what language he used, the result was the same.

"I find it hard to believe," he said with a sigh, "that the existence of the *Pnakotic Manuscripts* is taken as a fact, and yet no one in living memory has ever seen a copy, or known of anyone who has. But we still have a few places to check that a telephone won't reach. I have Albert copying some letters for me. He should be done before long, and we'll get them in the post right away. However, responses will likely be weeks away. Patience will be needed."

A heavy frown indicated his opinion on the matter.

"While I'm gone," said Vincent, standing up, "there is something you can do. It's worth having a second set of eyes search through these." He went a few steps over to a cabinet tucked between the bookcases. The upper portion had glass doors behind which were displayed various curios. The doors on the lower half were wooden, and he opened them and pointed inside.

"That box contains correspondence I received while I was in Europe. I haven't sorted it yet, and I'm very nearly sure that it won't contain anything that will help us, but there is a small chance it may. If I were to look through everything, I may read a sentence or two, recognize it, then incorrectly assume that I remember the contents. Your unfamiliarity may help find something that I could miss."

"What do you want me to do exactly?"

"For each one, note the date and the author. Then read through them as best you can. In particular, check for any reference to *Pnakotic Manuscripts*. You will at least be able to see the word *Pnakotic* or just a single letter *P* regardless of the language. A consolidated list like that may provide something we can use. Mainly, I'm interested to see the list of names. I may have forgotten a few."

I shrugged an agreement, went over to the cabinet and pulled out the box. It was made of a light-colored wood, unadorned, with simple brass hinges and clasp. Heavier than I expected, I saw the reason for it when I opened it up: four stacks of folded letters, each tied with string and jammed tightly together, filling every bit of available space.

"Good lord," I said, simply amused by the sheer quantity. "Did you spend all your time in Europe writing letters?"

"Oh, hardly." He chuckled. "Mine could have fit on a postcard.

'Comment allez-vous?' I might have written while enjoying a nice Chablis and watching the world go by. But the responses were novels detailing the area politics, finances, health issues, the latest exploits of the children—and, oh by the way, my oldest daughter is fourteen and still single. Feel free to drop by and marry her."

That got a laugh out of me.

"It wasn't worded precisely that way, but the sentiment was there." He smiled and shook his head. "I'll help you with these, but I want to send off this first batch of inquiries right away."

Vincent left then, and I sat down, and pulled the first stack out of the box. I knew it would take a while, but set my mind to it, and began the process of recording authors and dates, scanning through the text for anything noteworthy. As he had said, each letter was voluminous. About a third were from a pair of men in England, one in London and one in Birmingham, and so I spent the greater portion of my time going through those. They rambled over many subjects, and made only the barest reference to Vincent's "studies." Because my French was fair, I was also able to do an adequate job of wading through the monotonous expositions of a man in Paris who was preoccupied with a graveyard in the south of France. Language-wise, that was as far as I could go. My knowledge of German was minimal, and the one letter written in Cyrillic was just as alien as the language of the Servitor. Those ones I marked on the list in case Vincent wanted to look them over more closely.

I was halfway through the first stack before I even heard the motorcar pull away.

When I finished the first set and reached into the box for the second, my fingers touched a letter sitting at the bottom, unbound by the string. I had been going through them in order, top to bottom, as they had at least been organized chronologically, but decided to glance over the loose one first. It was written in English, and so that gave me an incentive to read it. The longhand, graceful and flowing, was eerily familiar.

It was Elizabeth's.

Dear Cousin:

I hope you are enjoying your travels through Europe, though I do look forward to seeing you again after you find the answers to your questions and return home. I am still at school, of course, and prefer to stay at the university. With you away, the house is much too quiet these days, and I almost dread the occasional trip home. Mother and Father will be leaving soon, and will meet up with you. I really don't understand why she decided upon a visit to Africa. It's very unlike her. Still, it's reassuring that she can be open-minded, and still have a desire to experience new things after all she has been through.

I've been thinking about what you've told me, but it doesn't seem to resonate within me as it does you. It's very hard to place a label on my feelings. I view the subject matter as neither evil nor good. I suppose the best word for me is ambivalence. I just do not see the lost knowledge of the Ancients as being very applicable to daily life. But have no fear—you can continue to use me as your sounding board on such matters. I do find it interesting to ponder the theories you present.

Doctor Gardiner did not have an answer to your inquiry, but he put me into contact with the New England Historical Society. A man there let me borrow an issue of the Arkham Gazetteer, dated November 1 of 1868, which has an article mentioning the event. Because I am well aware of your requirement for details, I am copying the text below <u>letter</u> <u>for</u> <u>letter</u>.

Please return home safely and soon.

Elizabeth.

(ARKHAM) A terrible and bloody scene was discovered early this morning in the small town of Mount Haverton. All members of the household of Johann and Konstanz Fenster (siblings) were found slaughtered, with one exception: the newly born child of Konstanz Fenster. Despite her advanced age, she had apparently carried the child to full term and had given birth during the night. The father is not known. The newborn, a healthy boy, has been sent to St. John's Orphanage in Innsmouth.

Aside from the brother and sister, other fatalities included the two servants, Jacques and Katrina Laurant, and the Reverend Caleb Pryce. Unlike the others, the Reverend was found in the bushes outside the house, his body unmarked. A witness to the scene, Mr. Theodore Yount, commented that it looked as though he had died of fright. That same man refused to describe the scene inside, however, except to say that he had totaled up more limbs than what could be accounted for by four bodies.

Constable Walter Benning was extremely tight-lipped on the matter. Aside from acknowledging the total of five dead, he would only say that Reverend Pryce was indisputably not a suspect—despite having been known as a vocal critic of the Fensters and, as he put it, their "unholy union," since their arrival in Mount Haverton a few years before.

Perhaps adding to the mystery is a claim by a local woman, Mrs. Margaret Evans, who insists that the small town was visited by Satan during the night. As proof of the event, she described a short period of time right at midnight where there was neither light nor sound of any sort in the village of Mount Haverton. She insists that the stars disappeared from the sky, and it became quieter than even a tomb. The fire in her hearth

continued to burn, emitting heat, but no light.
No one else in the town could be found who
was willing to corroborate her story.

I read it three times, staring at every curve of the writing. I even brought it up to my nose and inhaled deeply to try to detect some tiny, lingering amount of her. It was such a joy to find an unfiltered piece of Elizabeth, a glimpse into her life from before we had even met. But it was also an uncomfortable thing to read a private letter between her and Vincent. It felt as if I was an intruder. But setting that aside, the content spawned some questions. It implied that she and Vincent had spoken about magic to some degree, though her attitude made it seem as if they had not gone into specifics. And the mention of the Fensters again…knowing that there was such a stain upon the name, it seemed odd that he would later choose it willingly. Of course, given what I knew of his father, it was not an unreasonable decision to disassociate from the name of Marsh.

The sound of the motorcar grew loud enough to register on my consciousness. Still holding the letter, I needed to make a decision: simply ask Vincent about it, or hide it away, back underneath the letters…or steal it? I found justification for each, but in my soul, I knew what I had to do. Even as I heard the front door open, I refolded it, placed it back into the box, and covered it up with the second stack of letters. I would let Vincent find it, and he could make the decision of whether or not to tell me about it.

"How are you doing?" he asked as he entered the room.

"That first set of letters is done."

I stood up, and handed him the list I had compiled. He looked it over, nodding.

"Okay," he said, setting the list aside. "Nothing really…except that I forgot I had corresponded with Mr. Marley that early on."

"The man from Birmingham?"

"Yes. So, this exercise has already proven to be of some value."

As he reached for the box, I thought it would be best to remove

261

myself.

"Do you mind if I take a break and get some air?" I asked. "And stretch my legs for a few minutes."

"Please do. Enjoy your walk."

As his hand touched the stack I had just replaced, I turned and left.

Outside, the sky had clouded over, threatening rain. I walked around the backyard, watching the birds and squirrels, but thinking of Elizabeth. And her relationship with Vincent. Admittedly, it was a difficult thing for me to accept that he had known her better than I— which was perfectly natural, given that he had spent more than a decade with her. It was that extra time with her which I envied. No, more than that. I was jealous. During the past weeks, I had so much wanted to sit down and ask him about her, find out day-to-day details of her life, unexciting as they may have been. But each time the thought had occurred to me, I forced it aside. I sensed a reluctance on his part to speak of her. There were times he would visibly tense at the mention of her name. Maybe someday I would broach the subject with him, after all of this was over.

When I had judged that I had given him enough time to discover her letter, I went back inside. In the den, the wooden box was on the floor, empty. The three remaining tied stacks sat on the desk. Vincent was gone. As was the letter from Elizabeth.

TWENTY-ONE

The search through the entire box of correspondence was ultimately somewhat successful, as it yielded two more names for Vincent. But after those overseas inquiries were mailed off, the days that followed were joyless. He spent his time sitting by the telephone waiting for calls, and making lists of names as he searched his memory for friends of friends, then acquaintances of acquaintances. Albert made daily trips to send off a batch of telegrams, all with instruction to contact Vincent. On the rare occasions the telephone rang, the message was the same disappointing answer.

I spent much of my time over the next two weeks working slowly and methodically to memorize every alien syllable, every gesture required to complete the banishment ceremony. But regardless of my knowledge, actually performing the ceremony would prove to be another matter entirely. As far as I knew, any error, however minor, could be fatal. Under such stress, would I falter? Some of the movements required more than a modicum of physical coordination. At the climax of the ceremony, I would have to hold two items in a certain orientation between my hands above my head. Specifically, according to the instructions which Vincent copied from the *Necronomicon*:

> *Between ye hands hold ye Shard superior to ye*
> *Gateway. With ye hands above ye head, speak*
> *ye Words of Sending: Mbulg'r Sothoth Pnath*
> *d'nalbr urh'ctha rgho!*

What might happen if I dropped the Shard or the Gateway? Could I just pick them up and continue? Inevitably, when my anxiety began to mount, my final image of Andrew would come flooding into my mind. The flash of lightning. The flesh being peeled from his bones. I would have liked some answers, but Vincent was my only source of information, and I could not allow him to see any lack of confidence in me—asking him 'what if' this and 'what if' that. I just prayed that when the time came, I would be able to do what I needed. With something of this magnitude, there would be only one chance.

As the days went on, the strain of Vincent's fruitless searching became more and more evident. He grew continuously more fatigued, as if he was not sleeping at all. Everything irritated him, even deriding the telephone for not ringing. Instead of being a godsend providing the answer he desired, it was the scapegoat, and he distanced himself from it by removing himself to the basement laboratory for hours at a time. That, at least, helped me to avoid his negativity, and keep up my own spirits. I studied in the den on the main floor, wondering why he fretted so much, seeing no need for any urgency. It could take months to find the missing information, but I was confident that we would eventually finish what we had started.

It did not take months.

One fateful afternoon, I found my mind wandering. Unable to concentrate on what I was reading, I decided to take a break. The sun was blazing golden through the windows, a moment of beauty quite rare in that increasingly gloomy house. After walking a lap around the room, I closed my eyes, and took a few deep breaths. When I opened them again, I saw the answer. A few months previous to that, I would have praised God for striking me with such a bolt of inspiration. Now, I can only wish it had instead been one of lightning.

What I saw when I opened my eyes was simply the spine of a book. Perched upon a shelf, at the perfect height: *Stars of the Northern Hemisphere*. It reminded me strongly of the volume that Andrew had retrieved for me that one night, so long ago, after we had spoken with the dead author of the Portuguese parchment. On a whim, I grabbed it and began to page through. Much of it consisted of diagrams of constellations, with information about each of the component stars: histories, myths, vital statistics like brightness, and sky coordinates.

Coordinates.

Even as I began searching through the pages, I knew that I had the answer. I felt foolish and giddy at the same time. Everything we needed had been here all along! My years of study in mathematics, forsaken for months, would finally come in handy. I found the diagram of Leo. There was Regulus, clearly labeled. Below the drawing was a list of all of the star coordinates. Taking the book with me, I ran out of the den, through the house and down to the basement.

"Vincent!" I shouted as I opened the hidden door in the wine cellar. "I have the answer! I have it!"

He had already opened the door to the laboratory by the time I reached it.

"You have it?" he asked eagerly. "What?"

His eyes were red with fatigue, yet wide with excitement.

"We don't need the *Pnakotic Manuscripts* in order to rotate the shard. We already have all of the necessary information!"

"Where? What are you saying?"

"I brought it with me from Arkham! Look!"

I opened the astronomy book and showed him the diagram of Leo and the list of star coordinates.

"Remember what I told you when I first arrived?" I asked. "Every Ancient One has a corresponding star. The star for Sothoth Pnath is Regulus. From this book, we now know the coordinates for Regulus. We can use the equations developed by my former mentor!"

The thought of Professor Josephson gave me pause. He would undoubtedly be dismayed at the knowledge he had helped my ill-fated quest any further, no matter how accidental it may have been.

"Using those equations, I can perform a mathematical transformation upon the coordinates to convert them into the proper extra-dimensional equivalents."

"Which is precisely the information which we need!" finished Vincent, at that point understanding me perfectly. "We then simply need to take the shard Outside, and rotate it to the correct orientation."

Simply? The word rang in my ears. That had been our plan all along, but it suddenly did not sound like such a simple matter. My heart sank. I watched Vincent pace around the room as I tried to think of a way to break the news to him. From time to time he would smile and nod to himself.

"We will, of course, need an extra-dimensional reference point," he said, coming to a stop. "In order to be sure that the shard is aligned correctly."

"Oh, yes," I said somberly, certain that we were hardly any closer at all. The equations had the potential to help with the original problem, for sure—but leaving us with a new one.

"But no matter," he said, waving his hand dismissively. "Just perform your mathematical wizardry and tell me the results. I'll take care of the rest."

There was a condescending note in his voice, as well.

In the space of a minute, I had gone from triumph to misery, and then to essentially being insulted. Once again, I was a rat in a maze, bumping blindly into walls, and he the experimenter, laughing behind his hand at my every slip and falter. I knew this was no time for dissent, especially not now that we were so close to realizing our goal, but that cascade of emotions became too much for me to hold in.

"No, Vincent," I said. "I am sick to death of your secrets. Tell me what you know."

He was taken aback by my actions.

266

"Robert," he said with a stony voice. "Just do as you are told. We are too close to success—"

"That is exactly right! *We* are! You need me. We need each other." I closed the distance to stand directly in front of him. "If you do not fill me in on your plans, I will not cooperate. You can perform the transformation on the star coordinates yourself."

His face flushed, and for the first time in decades, I saw the little boy that I had known in Mount Haverton. Back then, any anger—most often due to something his father had done or said—had always lasted only a very short while. He seemed to swallow it, or disguise it, perhaps as a survival instinct in that household. Older now, and with no overarching authority, no need to hide it, he made no attempt. Jaw clenched tightly, Vincent lifted the stump of his left arm, and held it in the air. I thought he might strike me with it. Or perhaps not. Something about that act incited some alarm in me. There was a certain similarity with the events immediately before the death of Doctor Trautmann. His arm wavered toward me, then back.

"No," he said, closing his eyes and lowering his arm. "You must forgive me. I have been—*we* have both been—under some stress recently."

He took a few deep breaths.

"You are right," he said. "I have been too secretive. It is my nature."

He paused there, perhaps hoping that I would simply forgive him and let him pass. But I was resolute in the matter, so he was forced to continue.

"A Servitor of Q'yoth is an intelligent being, attuned to the extra-dimensional spaces we cannot sense. If you sufficiently describe the coordinates to me, I can explain that information to the Servitor, and it can rotate the shard to the correct orientation for us."

"But how will you convey such a complex mathematical concept to something so..."

267

I failed to find the word I wanted.

"The list of R'lyehian words I assembled in the letter to Andrew," he said, sighing, "was just a small set, one that I thought he might be able to use when practicing the spell. While in Europe, I met someone who taught me to speak the language. Through practice, I have become adept at it. Over the years."

Through practice. Those words, and the fact that he had threatened me only a minute before, should have set off an alarm in my head. It should have caused me to rethink my alliance with him. It *should* have. It did not. At the time, I only cared that I had just secured a small victory by finally prying some information from him. Now I know better. The clarity of hindsight has revealed to me just how single-minded I had become over the weeks preceding that confrontation. My goal of vengeance had become paramount, overshadowing important details, and squelching any desire to ask questions which may increase doubt or reduce trust. Doctor Trautmann's death, for instance, should have disturbed me a great deal. It did not. I did not investigate. I did not think. I merely accepted it, in much the same way that I accepted my childhood friend's shocking disclosure that he could fluently speak that infernal language.

An awkward silence persisted between us, and I felt as if I needed to say something. All that came to mind was an apology.

"Thank you for humoring me," I said. "There was no need for me to make demands. It was uncalled for."

He waved it off.

"Let us forget this madness for a while," he said. "This is something to celebrate! Let us drink to our forthcoming success."

And that is exactly what we did. Vincent was well mannered and warm—almost jovial—as we talked of the past and the future, and shared a bottle of one of the better vintages from his wine cellar. At one point, he even called Albert into the room, and the three of us made a toast. That was the only time I would ever see a smile upon the butler's sallow face.

Toward the end of the evening, the wine making me brave, I decided to test the depth of my friendship with Vincent.

"Can you do me a favor?" I asked.

"Certainly. What is it?"

"Elizabeth," I said, looking for any kind of reaction from him. This time, there was none. I sensed no discomfort on his part.

"What would you like to know?"

"Tell me anything about her, anything at all. Granted, it is difficult for me to speak of her, and likely you as well, but we never do. She is the reason for this...quest we are on. Every time I ask myself what I am doing, and why, the answer is Elizabeth, of course. I just need for the two of us to speak of her. It would lend some validation for this path I find myself on."

"Very well put," agreed Vincent. He closed his eyes for a bit, then looked at me again. "As you said, it is difficult to speak of her. I loved her in my own way, and miss her. We shared some rancorous debates as teenagers."

He thought for a moment, then smiled.

"You wanted me to tell you something about her? How about this as an example? She fully believed in the existence of the Devil. Satan. Mephistopheles. Choose whichever name you like, but she felt that he walked the Earth even to this day, spreading misery. For my own part, I have to admit that I shared that opinion. But I would never agree with her aloud. Instead, I would take an opposing viewpoint, or come nearly to agree with her, but then veer off. Sometimes, I would sway her with my own arguments. I could tell that she would change her position slightly. But what I enjoyed most was that she was so open-minded. I could speak to her about anything, and she would never retreat to hide behind the Bible, or science, or societal norms. She simply analyzed the facts as best she could, and spoke her mind."

The sincerity in his voice was evident. Finally, I had been given a glimpse, not only into Elizabeth, but also their relationship. I recognized in her some of what he had described, though she and I had never had discussions on that particular subject. Perhaps she had chosen to not challenge my beliefs at the time. Regardless, just being able to coax even more information out of Vincent qualified as another small victory.

The following morning, I immersed myself in the science of numbers for the first time in months. I searched my memories for those unused formulae and concepts, dredging them up from the bowels of my mind. More than an hour was required for me just to retrace the steps that Professor Josephson had taken. As I worked through the various equations, the clearer it became. I reflected again over the truth of what Professor Josephson and Andrew had both said: Magic is indeed as much a science as mathematics. It may use a different set of symbols and concepts, but experiments conducted in the same manner consistently produced the same result. Mr. Hunt had demonstrated that much to me by recording the results of his research in his journals. Of the two, magic was definitely the more exciting, but I was grateful as at no other time for the depth of my college education.

After verifying the results twice more through different analytical methods, I had the answer in hand. All told, it had only taken a few hours. I found Vincent in the laboratory with Albert. The two of them had carried down some cushions and blankets, which formed a comfortable bed to be used during the ceremony. After Albert left, Vincent became my attentive pupil, as I tried my best to describe the meaning behind the numbers I had calculated. After lecturing him in the rudiments of theoretical mathematics, I showed him Professor Josephson's equations, and walked him through each of the steps to the final result. To my surprise, he grasped the concepts readily. His intellect was truly phenomenal. It was barely more than an hour before I was convinced he understood what I had taught him. With that new knowledge in place, he sat down, and studied a notebook for a short while.

It was obvious to me when he was ready to begin. Weeks of study with Andrew and Vincent had allowed me to develop an extra sense. An invisible aura seemed to emanate from within him. It overlapped into my other senses as an odor of decay, but with an undertone of sweetness, as in fermentation. I steeled myself for the coming events, and took a seat at the table.

The ceremony unfolded much as it had on the night of Andrew's death. Vincent sat on the cushions, and cast the first spell, which would cause him to speak the summoning spell as he slept. Finished with the first portion, he stretched out on the cushions and cast the second spell, forcing him into a deep sleep. With Vincent now unconscious, I found myself effectively alone in the dim light of the laboratory. Having time to reflect, I recalled those early days with Andrew, the time I first assisted him in the magical arts—my pinning of the rat in the cage. That was my first intervention point, my first chance to walk away. This would be my last.

Soon afterwards—still sleeping soundly—Vincent repeated the words he had spoken previously. When he had finished, an eerie silence returned to our underground room. This was the point at which Andrew had begun to twitch, as he dreamt the special nightmare to be offered in sacrifice to the Servitor. But Vincent's reaction was remarkably different. Instead of worry and fear on his sleeping face, I saw contentment—in fact, almost a suppressed glee. The horror of Andrew's experience was nowhere to be seen in Vincent's features.

The dream-spell lasted for ten minutes. In all that time, Vincent lay still, with only the occasional twitch. As the time wore on, I found myself becoming increasingly nervous. Vincent had still not awakened when the hellish throbbing first began. The memories of my first encounter with the creature came rushing back. I relived Andrew's death as I waited for those tentacles to materialize.

"It is here," said Vincent, sitting up. Having been concentrating on the unearthly sound of the Servitor, just his voice was enough to nearly make me jump. Thankfully, I was able to control myself.

"I know," I said, swallowing hard. "I know that sound."

As before, my efforts to find it, or even guess its location, were futile. The Servitor was unseen, of course, wholly concealed in another dimension. The sound was everywhere at once.

"I'm ready," said Vincent, standing up. He removed the shard of the Crystal from his vest pocket, placed it on the table, and meditated for a short while. The aura he emitted seemed to grow stronger. Unsettled by the presence of the Servitor, I could think of no advice to offer. Even the simple words *Good Luck* refused to emerge from my lips.

After taking a deep breath, he spoke a string of alien syllables. I shuddered at the sounds. To say that he was fluent in that God-forsaken language was an understatement. If my eyes had been closed, I would have been forced to imagine a gibbering monstrosity from some alien dimension standing before me. But as they remained open, I watched as he vanished, without a noise, without a trace, just as Andrew had. A few seconds later, the shard also disappeared from the table. I tried my best to stay calm. At that point, I could do nothing but wait, and listen to the horrid throbbing of the Servitor.

I did not have to wait long. Perhaps only two minutes went by before the shard reappeared on the table, just as silently as it had gone. I walked closer, and blinked. Was it the same stone? Instead of oblong and grey, the object on the table was flat and round, about three inches in diameter, and glossy black. Initially, it appeared to be perfectly circular; in reality it was not. The edge was not smooth, but jagged—covered in tiny, triangular formations, not unlike the blade of a saw. The shape was actually difficult to make out. For some reason, my eyes would blur and water when I tried to focus on the edge. It was much easier to look at the center of it.

"I'm back," announced a voice from behind me.

I turned to see Vincent standing there, glowing with triumph. The strange aura of magical energy, if indeed it had ever been real, was gone. Also gone—confusing me utterly—was the alien heartbeat of the Servitor.

"Wait!" I whispered, as if it might hear us. "Where is it? The sound is gone."

"I commanded it to return me here, then depart from whence it came."

I listened again, but still heard nothing. At that point I was able to truly relax.

"You should have seen the true structure of the shard Outside," said Vincent excitedly. "It isn't large, but the facets must be nearly infinite. And the colors are indescribable. It looks like a…"

He started to move his hand and arm as if to draw a diagram in the air, then stopped as soon as he realized that—lacking a dimension—he couldn't.

"Well, never mind. I suppose that you'll just have to go out there and take a look for yourself."

"May I *never* be that curious," I said, laughing nervously. "If I am, you can consider it proof of my insanity, and you have my permission to shoot me."

"As you wish," he replied with a snicker. "I'll be sure to let Albert know."

"But is that the same stone?" I asked, pointing at the table. It appeared—at least to me—to be something entirely new.

"It is indeed," he said. "Merely a different facet."

Captivated by it, he walked over to the table. After studying it for a few seconds, he shook his head and rubbed his eyes.

"How strange," he muttered. Cautiously, he picked it up, but dropped it almost instantly. A look of utter surprise crossed his face.

"What happened?"

"Try to pick it up," he said. When I looked at him uncertainly, he giggled with an almost childlike glee. "Go on. It won't bite. I'm fairly certain, anyway."

I touched the glossy surface. It felt as smooth and polished as I thought it might. When I glanced at Vincent, he gave me a nod of reassurance. I tried to pick it up. It weighed an ounce or two, just as might be expected from an object that size. But just as before, it fell almost immediately back to the tabletop. There was no shock or sting. It simply felt as if it had been yanked from my hand. And oddly enough, despite having been dropped twice, the stone had somehow managed both times to land back in the original spot.

I grasped the shard solidly once again, and attempted to lift it straight up above the table. It worked. But when I tried to move it around, it again snapped back down to its home on the table. It seemed that the stone could only be moved vertically, and its orientation could not be changed in the least degree. I moved it up and down a few times, then set it down, and invited Vincent to try.

He lifted it up and moved it the same as I had.

"Amazing," he remarked. "And notice the gyroscopic effect? It can't be tilted in any direction. Lucky for us that we had already planned to perform the ceremony down here. We can't move this thing anywhere without help from our friend."

Despite my fear of the "friend" he referred to, I managed a light chuckle. Vincent's posture slumped right then, and I had to reach out with both hands to steady him.

"Sorry," he said. "That took more out of me than I expected."

I guided him into a chair.

"Have you calculated the next favorable alignment of the stars?" he asked.

"Not yet, but it shouldn't take long."

I sat down, and sorted through my papers. Vincent laid his head down on the table as I worked. The process of calculating the next favorable date was very easy. All I had to do was find the next date in the future when the final equation yielded an answer of zero. The best analogy for it would be a trigonometric *sine* function, except that it was not predictably periodic. Far from it, the equation had no detectable rhythm to it at all. In that respect, it more closely resembled a polynomial with an infinite number of terms.

The answer I received was shocking. Without saying anything, I checked again. The result was still the same.

"Tomorrow," I said.

Vincent lifted his head and looked at me.

"Tomorrow?" he asked, blinking.

"As unbelievable as it sounds, yes. The stars will be properly aligned for Sothoth Pnath tomorrow."

Speaking the words aloud, I was overcome with a wave of satisfaction. All of the accumulated knowledge from the months of study in these arcane fields of science would finally be put to use. All of the grief I suffered would at last be avenged.

"Can you be ready for your part by then?" The excitement energized him, erasing any exhaustion he felt.

I answered without hesitation.

"Yes."

"Just think," he said. "By this time tomorrow, the world shall be rid of Sothoth Pnath, once and for all. It shall be a memorable day!"

In retrospect, I cannot disagree.

It certainly was a memorable day.

Twenty-Two

I practiced the ceremony for the rest of that afternoon and through the evening, until I was certain that I could perform it flawlessly. At the last, I rehearsed in front of Vincent, as he checked every gesture and syllable against his notes. He was pleased with my hand movements, but coached me mercilessly on my pronunciation. By the end of the night, we were both satisfied with my efforts.

I awoke the next morning with a nervous energy, one I had known only a few times in my life. Most memorable of them was the day I had asked Elizabeth for her hand in marriage. As I dressed, I could not help but relive the events of that anxious morning, that joyous afternoon, that terrible evening. Only hours remained until the madness would finally end. At least, that is what I believed.

And cleansed of my obsession, would I be ready to return to a normal life? Possibly redirect my energies back to a more mundane goal, such as finishing my degree? The idea of regaining the trust and friendship of Professor Josephson was appealing, but returning to Arkham meant delivering myself into the hands of the police. Could I assume a new identity in a different city? Vincent had numerous contacts. Perhaps I could take advantage of them—or even Vincent himself. Could I stay in this house, and work with him? Magic was much more exciting than mathematics, after all…

There were too many thoughts, too many possibilities. I worked to push them all aside. There was no point in thinking about the future, when the needs of the present were so pressing.

It was still early when Vincent and I met downstairs in the dining room. I could tell he was as excited as I, but he kept the conversation to a minimum, avoiding the subject of the forthcoming ceremony almost completely. After we finished breakfast, he excused himself, saying he would be downstairs making necessary preparations. When I offered to help, he walked behind my chair, and placed his right hand on my shoulder.

"Don't worry," he said. "I'll take care of everything. You rest."

I acquiesced, and tried to relax, but it proved to be a difficult proposition. I needed a distraction. Making my way to the den, I chose a section of bookshelves at random, and began to browse. One book after the other attracted my attention, but I passed them by, and continued my search. My patience was rewarded, and minutes later, I pulled a volume of Poe off the shelf—the same one I had discovered in Andrew's bookstore only a few months before. I had always enjoyed The Cask of Amontillado. *The thousand injuries of Fortunato I had borne as best I could, but when he ventured upon insult I vowed revenge.* On that fateful day, the storyline rang with a certain relevance. As I write this, I admit that I was not incorrect. But not for the reasons I had hoped.

I had only read a few pages when a commotion reached my ears. Listening carefully, it sounded as if Albert was having some trouble at the front door. The angry voice grew louder as I crept toward the foyer—until all at once, I recognized it.

It was Thomas Wentworth, Elizabeth's uncle. He was demanding entrance to the house.

In the anteroom, Albert stood in front of the partially open door, blocking the way. I walked up behind him and motioned for him to let me through. He moved aside, and I opened the door completely.

"Good God, Higgins!" Wentworth exclaimed as I became wholly visible. "You were right."

Hearing that name had the same effect as a well-placed blow to my midsection. I wondered briefly if I had misheard him, but no.

He stood off to the left, just behind Wentworth's shoulder. Jebediah Higgins. He moved closer, standing shoulder to shoulder with the older man. For a moment there was complete silence, as the three of us just looked at each other. Then, he smiled, and my initial shock was replaced by the familiar hatred. I stared at him with contempt.

"Gentlemen," I said. "Is there something I can do for you today?"

I asked the question with as much politeness as I could muster, purely out of respect for Thomas Wentworth and the hospitality he had shown me.

"There are several questions I need answered, Mr. Adderly," said Wentworth. "But first—where is that scoundrel Vincent?"

He spoke to me more calmly than he had Albert, but his anger was only thinly disguised.

"Unfortunately, Vincent is unavailable," I said simply.

Wentworth accepted this without fuss.

"Then perhaps *you* can answer my questions," he said. "Who is that man? The one who answered the door? Where is Gregory, the man who has faithfully served this family for decades? And why is the anteroom devoid of decorations? Only a few months ago, there was a nearly priceless vase sitting upon an equally valuable table just inside the door, there."

He pointed behind me. I wished I had plausible answers to those questions. I remembered the explanation Vincent had given me regarding my similar query, and was trying to find the right words, but did not get a chance to voice any of them.

"Fine. A simpler question, then," he said to my silence. "Why are *you* here, Mr. Adderly?"

He looked at me expectantly. Indeed, all considered, we were a curious cast of characters: The uncle of my tragically deceased fiancée, flanked on one side by my former mentor's sinister colleague, while lurking below was my childhood best friend, the nephew of the man who stood before me, and cousin to my lost beloved. And I in the middle, mouth hanging slightly open, trying desperately to think.

"Research," I finally said. "For my doctoral thesis. I knew Vincent as a boy. He invited me to stay here with him."

That last sentence was absolutely true, and I spoke it with indisputable confidence.

"May I ask what the two of you are doing here today?" I continued, bolstered by the truth I had uttered. "Surely not to visit the butler, and take an accounting of the bric-a-brac?"

With my offhanded remark, Thomas Wentworth lost all vestiges of constraint.

"Mr. Higgins and I have figured out your little scheme, Adderly," he said, the volume of his voice increasing. "You and Vincent have conspired to attack my family, and steal our fortune! From the first, untimely deaths of the twins, I knew that something was up. Denial and disbelief made me too angry to see the truth. But Mr. Higgins has helped me put the pieces together. You are through, Adderly! And Vincent as well! At the very least, I shall drive both of you out of here! At best, I will see you behind bars!"

"Mr. Higgins is a fool," I said swiftly. "You have been misled by a fool, Mr. Wentworth. There is no conspiracy, only a set of very odd circumstances. Coincidence."

"There is no such thing as coincidence, Adderly—only fate," interjected Higgins, his voice neutral. "There is only fate."

I took a half step toward my adversary. I felt myself gripped once again by the unfamiliar passion that had been my guide through this ordeal. Before, I thought it might have been my studies in the magical arts that had borne it in me—this fire. But at that moment, standing mere feet from the man who had made himself my foil that night in Professor Josephson's study, I was finally able to understand. It was not the magic that had brought out my hatred. It was Higgins.

"Is it my fate that I must repeatedly encounter you, Higgins?" I looked him straight in the eyes, challenging him. This time, I would not allow him to walk away—I would provoke him and we would fight. And I would win. He inched closer to me.

"Yes," he said. "I am your Satan. And this is your own private Hades."

"You are not Satan." I smiled and readied myself for the melee. "You are merely a fly that is annoying me this morning."

His rage was growing more evident. Thomas Wentworth took a step backward. He realized that he could not stop us. Higgins raised his hands and formed them into fists.

"Adderly," he seethed, "I could kill you with my bare hands."

Before I could say or do anything, I heard from behind me the sound of a pistol being cocked.

"There will be no deaths this morning, Mr. Higgins!" announced Vincent, stepping into the anteroom. "Unless you would like to volunteer."

As he came to stand to my left, he smiled, and pointed the weapon at Higgins' chest. I felt both disappointment and relief with Vincent's intrusion—and then a split-second later, terror, as it seemed that Vincent actually meant to fire. A silence borne of the anticipation of thunder hung over us all. Higgins stood still, seeming to consider his options. I could see the anger begin to dissipate. The seconds ticked by, too slowly. He lowered his arms, relaxed his fists, and backed up a few steps. Vincent continued to hold the gun, still smiling, seemingly debating the issue of whether or not to shoot. Although I hated the man fiercely, I did not want him shot down in cold blood. I was on the verge of asking Vincent to lower the weapon when, finally, he did so himself.

"Albert."

The servant entered, and accepted the proffered gun.

"Please put that away," said Vincent, not taking his eyes off the still-fuming Higgins. "We are all grown men. We can settle our affairs with words. There is no need to use violence, is there Mr. Higgins?"

Higgins made no response, verbal or otherwise. Seemingly satisfied, Vincent turned his full attention to Thomas Wentworth.

"Good morning, Uncle Thomas," he said pleasantly. "Do you wish to speak with me?"

At that point, Vincent seemed to stop paying any mind to Higgins. Not trusting that man to remain peaceful, I continued to keep an eye on him while the other two spoke.

"Vincent, you devil," said Wentworth vehemently. "You are through!"

"Whatever do you mean, Uncle?"

"You know damn well what I mean! We know what you and Adderly have been doing. Although it has taken years, you—along with whatever agents you may have used—have eliminated everyone that stood between you and the family fortune. Even if there is no evidence as far as the law is concerned, I shall have you thrown out of this house and disowned. I shall see you destroyed!"

Vincent's pleasant demeanor turned dark, and he made no attempt to restrain himself.

"Uncle, you know as well as I that my inheritance is incontestable. I am the rightful owner. I grew up in this house. It is mine! Mary and Catherine died of the influenza, not an uncommon event that year. William died in the War, also not unexpected. My stepparents died of some strange disease, nurtured in the steaming jungles of decadent Africa. And Elizabeth died of an inexplicable phenomenon! At least, it is inexplicable for a buffoon such as you."

"An agent of the Ancient Ones," said Wentworth, "could make anything appear accidental."

I was so stunned to hear those words from that gentleman that I missed Vincent's reaction. When I did look over at him, there was indignation upon his face.

281

"I am not quite so much of a buffoon as you believed, am I Vincent?" asked Wentworth.

"How *dare* you make such a preposterous accusation!"

I noticed Vincent's hand clench into a fist.

"When one is willing to accept the insanity of the forces of evil which lie just beyond the boundaries of our world, a great many things suddenly make sense. Mr. Higgins has opened my eyes. We are allied against you, Vincent. We will strip you of everything you own, everything that you hold dear. You shall be exposed for the monster you truly are."

As Vincent listened to his uncle, I saw him relax with astounding rapidity. His hand uncurled, and the anger in his face melted away.

"Uncle Thomas," he said calmly, "you are proceeding under a delusion induced by this madman. As I'm sure my compatriot has already told you."

I could sense Higgins begin to get upset again. I placed my hand in my coat pocket and grabbed the knife within.

"I invite you to take whatever steps you feel are necessary at the present time," Vincent continued. "When all of this is over, and you finally realize that you have been led astray by this man, I shall forgive you. Then we can take our revenge upon Mr. Higgins together. In the meantime, feel free to bring the police in on these matters."

At that point Higgins spoke up.

"Yes, perhaps you are right. We do not have any legally binding proof to implicate you in the misfortune of this family."

He paused, then looked directly at me with a bitter smile.

"But the trail of bodies you have left in your wake is not very well disguised, Mr. Adderly."

I tried to not react at all to the accusation, but I'm not sure I was able to control myself completely. Did I flinch slightly? Did my eyes shift or widen? I do not know.

"It is a fact," he continued, "that the police have not yet connected the recent unexplained deaths in Arkham. Not yet. But I have. The stench of primordial evil hovers over them all."

He balled his right hand into a fist and raised his thumb.

"First, I must admit that I was wrong to dismiss your claim regarding Elizabeth Wentworth's death."

He extended the index finger of his right hand.

"Second, Andrew Cooke could not possibly have been killed by an earthly assailant. No human madman could leave behind such a corpse. Only a few extra-dimensional nightmares are capable of such a gruesome feat."

He extended the middle finger.

"And lastly, there is Doctor Jakob Trautmann, who died of heart failure while perusing the *Necronomicon*, gun in hand, with the broken bits and pieces of an Elder Sign nearby. It is a most perplexing set of circumstances, until one considers that the description of the last two people to see him alive matches the two of you. And that the autopsy report revealed that his heart was crushed! Without a mark upon his skin, his heart was crushed within his chest."

Higgins lowered his hand and waited. My initial reaction to his revelation about Doctor Trautmann's death was one of shock, but I quickly recovered my sensibilities. Higgins was my enemy. How could I trust him to tell me the truth?

"To implicate us in any of those deaths is quite a stretch of the imagination, Mr. Higgins," responded Vincent with a smile. "I believe that you shall have just as much difficulty convincing the police of our guilt as you are having with us. But please—do not let us get in the way of your attempt to publicly humiliate yourself."

"Do not be so sure of yourself, Vincent Fenster," said Higgins, inching closer to us. "You may have taken steps to clean up after yourself and keep suspicion away, but what of the young and naïve Robert Adderly? He is not so clever as you. When the police decide to bring him in for questioning, they will be very curious about his presence here, so many miles from Arkham. And if a murderer is found hiding in your house, what does that make you in the eyes of the law?"

We all stood frozen in the wake of his pronouncement. It seemed as if no one wanted to be the first to move. Then, Higgins stepped back and looked at Thomas Wentworth, who only nodded in reply.

"We shall return, gentlemen," said Higgins, as the two men turned to leave.

"Mr. Higgins," said Vincent. Both men stopped and looked back. "I must request that you to return in the daylight, and only to this door. Any other time or place, and I shall be forced to exercise my legal right as a property owner to shoot you dead on sight."

There was no response from either man. They walked away. We watched them go in silence, until they had moved beyond the gate, and disappeared.

"How interesting," said Vincent. I would not have chosen "interesting" to describe that encounter. At the very least, they were vexing. The threat of police intervention had definitely made me anxious.

"Why do you say that?" I asked.

"On the eve of our great triumph, Mr. Higgins tries this act of desperation. I believe he has revealed where his allegiance truly lies. He must know that we are close. He probably hoped that the presence of my uncle would sway you."

He paused and searched my face for a reaction.

"Has he?"

I stared at the gate through which the men had exited, an iron veil between this world and the next.

"Not a bit," I replied without hesitation. "Not a bit."

TWENTY-THREE

With the departure of our unexpected visitors, Vincent decided there was no time for further delay. And indeed, there was no need. I was ready.

He instructed Albert to guard the front door, and we descended the stairs, making our way to the laboratory. He had pushed all the furniture against the walls, and hung thick curtains and sheets over everything. A twelve-foot circle of unlit candles sat in the center of the floor. His covering of the walls was largely effective, but I could tell that it would not eliminate all shadows from the room.

"The sheets were a good idea," I said, "but there will still be some shadows."

"Yes, but they won't matter."

"Are you sure?"

"I am."

To his credit, he realized that my confidence was more important than his natural inclination toward secretiveness.

"It is impossible to completely eliminate all shadows from the room," he explained. "The real goal is only to eliminate any shadows from the magical circle which you will trace upon the floor. In particular, the final step of the ceremony is really the only time that the issue of light or darkness comes into play."

Along the base of the far wall, Vincent had lined up the items we would need: A silver censer with a removable lid; incense and matches; a glass of wine; a small brass hoop about six inches in diameter; a piece of white chalk; and a short, thin wand, like the baton used by a symphony conductor. I began to examine the items carefully. As the magician, it was my prerogative to accept or reject the material components laid out before me. I had to be convinced they were of good quality, and appropriate for the ceremony. It was my confidence, my mind that was crucial for the success of the spell. It cannot be stressed enough that my life was at stake.

The scent of the incense stopped me for a moment: the subtle but unmistakable scent of lilac, Elizabeth's favorite flower. I took a long pause, and a deep breath, filling my lungs with it. Revenge had forced my full attention to the study of magic for the past weeks. More pleasant memories had been pushed aside, relegated to remote, unused corners of my mind. That would soon change, I swore to myself. Once this business was concluded, I vowed that I would spend more of my days recalling our time together.

After placing all of the components at appropriate locations within the circle of candles, I stepped inside. The shard sat in the center. Standing over it, I silently rehearsed the ceremony once, twice, going through the motions of picking up the brass hoop, then the shard. Satisfied that there would be plenty of room within the circle for me to conduct the ritual, I returned the items to their proper places on the floor, and nodded to Vincent. He struck a match and lit the first candle. He then lit a stick of wood using the first candle and transferred the flame to the others. Within two minutes, the room was ablaze with light. I removed my coat, and handed it to Vincent, who stepped back against the wall. I looked all around me: No shadows intruded into the circle.

"Are you ready?" he asked.

Until that point, I'd had no doubts, no fear. But as I tried to clear my mind to begin, something bizarre happened. I thought at first it was just the warmth from the candle flames distracting me. It seemed as if a presence, another mind, was pressing against my own, probing. The stress spread instantly across my nerves, as a crack through a sheet of glass. Suddenly, I could not concentrate. My thoughts darted everywhere—a confusing mass of incoherent ideas.

I could not understand how I had become so unsettled. The first signs of panic set in. It was no use. I shook my head violently and looked at Vincent.

"What's the matter?" he asked.

He smiled, but it was skeletal and false. His eyes remained cloaked in shadow despite the intense light in the room. I sensed something there—something dark and old. It is said that the eyes mirror the soul. Seeing those two pits of blackness, I wondered what could possibly lie behind them. His image began to swim in my vision. The panic causing my imagination to run wild, I believed that I saw my death in those dark orbs. I saw a devil hiding within them. No, worse than a devil: It was chaos incarnate. His face morphed, no longer the Vincent I knew, had known since childhood. He had become something else. The more I looked, the more I felt my intellect slipping away, barely staying afloat in a sea of animal urges. I thought that only seconds had elapsed, but all sense of time was gone. I closed my eyes, thinking that I might be going mad.

In desperation, I bit down hard on my lower lip. Pain, and a taste of blood, brought back a sense of normality, of sanity. But if I opened my eyes again, what would I see? Gasping for breath, I counted—one, two, three—and fearfully cracked them.

Vincent stood there, just as he had been before my...episode, except that the smile was gone, replaced by an expression of concern. He took a few steps forward and looked at me closely.

"What happened?" he asked. "Are you bleeding?"

I touched my lip and examined a reddened fingertip. Did I hallucinate? I swallowed the salty bit of blood in my mouth.

"I saw..." I said. "I *thought*...a demon."

"Demon?" he asked, startled by my statement. I could only point at him with a shaking finger. He examined all parts of himself, poking and prodding here and there.

"There is no demon here," he said, "that I can detect."

He tried to smile, but the look of concern returned.

"Are you sure that you're ready for this? We can postpone the ceremony."

"No." I shook my head. "I've waited too long for this. I knew it would be difficult. I need to do this now."

"Very well."

Vincent stepped back against the wall.

I readied myself again, breathing deeply, and relaxing my mind. With each breath, I eliminated one more distraction. Inhale. The bite in my lip had begun to clot. Exhale. There was nothing to taste. Inhale. The pain was slight enough to ignore. Exhale. There was nothing to feel.

Inhale.

Vincent stood before me, as he did before.

Exhale.

There was nothing to fear.

Inhale.

I closed my eyes.

Exhale.

There was nothing to see.

Inhale.

Exhale.

Inhale.

Exhale.

I was focused.

I was ready.

The ritual began with the creation of the magical circle. After speaking a few phrases in Latin, I drew it on the floor with chalk—a pair of concentric circles with a gap of about six inches between them. In the gap, at each of the four points of the compass, I etched several ancient symbols. Facing first north, then south, east, and west, I uttered a short invocation to the gods of each. Immediately upon completion of the fourth invocation, there was an indefinable shift in the atmosphere. It felt as if the area within the circle had become in some way disassociated from the rest of the laboratory. The sensation was unlike my experiences with the ceremony used to communicate with the dead. In that case, there had been definite sensory effects at the boundary, where we were temporarily transported to another plane. In this instance, the area within the circle felt wholly disconnected from reality, but still in place, as perhaps an iceberg in the ocean right after it calves from a glacier.

With the preparations out of the way, the ceremony proper began. I placed the incense into the censer and lit it, then closed the lid. A rose-scented smoke wafted through the holes in the lid and spread out, but only as far as the edge of the inner circle I had drawn on the floor. I next recited a lengthy invocation while tracing a series of swirling designs in the air with the wand. As I proceeded, the tip of the wand glowed red, and the air became charged. After several minutes of continuous chanting, I put down the wand, and picked up the small hoop. Holding it in both hands, I spoke a single short phrase. The charge in the air was channeled into the hoop, which began glowing with a reddish hue. It was no longer a simple piece of metal, but a gateway, one through which Sothoth Pnath would return to the hellish outer spaces from whence it had come.

The next phase of the ceremony tested the limit of my vocal cords. I was required to speak into the glowing hoop a dozen larynx-twisting commands in the R'lyehian tongue. Though I had practiced the string of syllables many times in the last twenty-four hours—I was sure I could have said it in my sleep—there was something about looking into that glowing hoop that caused my throat to tighten. But regardless, I managed to get them out. Something happened after I spoke the very first phrase: I actually imagined that I heard a response. A faint rumble, more felt than heard, seemed to reverberate in the air. *I hear* it said from beyond the gateway, if anything so alien could be translated into words. But whatever it was, the responses seemed to be positive.

Next, I knelt down and inhaled deeply of the smoke issuing from the censer. I brought the hoop near my mouth and emptied the contents of my lungs through the opening. The smoke did not exit the other side. I spoke another magical phrase, and once again felt the faint, rumbling reply. I repeated the procedure with the glass of wine, with similar results.

After speaking that phrase, however, there was no subtle, half-imagined reply. Instead, a wind began to blow. Rather, I heard a wind blow, but could not feel it. Neither the smoke from the censer nor the flames of the candles showed the least sign of a breeze. Nevertheless, the sound quickly rose in intensity. Within seconds, it had escalated from a light wind to a furious gale.

I then picked up the shard, careful to move it only vertically from its spot on the floor. I held it firmly out before me, and recited a lengthy incantation. The sound of the wind around me had continued to rise, threatening to drown out my words even before I said them. Increasing the volume of my voice to its physical limit, I shouted out the required phrases. With each syllable of that guttural, alien language, I could feel myself growing hoarse. I spoke continuously for more than a minute, then paused and swallowed, trying—and only barely succeeding—to generate some moisture.

A conscious realization that I was nearly finished with the ceremony almost distracted me. Kneeling down carefully so that I would not drop the shard, I held onto it with my right hand, and picked up the hoop with my left. Taking advantage of the unique, nearly gravity-defying characteristics of the thing, I managed to place both it and the hoop between my hands so that I touched only their outer edges. The hoop was centered in my palms; the shard was above the hoop, held between my fingertips.

I stood up slowly and raised my hands up over my head.

Involved with the mechanics of this maneuver, I did not notice until then that a great charge seemed to have built up. It was not like the static charge that energized the hoop. Rather, it was more of a *knowing*, a definite realization, that something specific was about to happen, something as incontrovertible as the sun rising in the east. Even above the din of the constantly blowing but unfelt wind, I could sense a profound silence, as if the universe itself was holding its breath, waiting for my action. As loud as I dared, I bellowed the final words.

"Mbulg'r Sothoth Pnath d'nalbr urh'ctha rgho!"

The sensations I experienced at that juncture can hardly be put into words.

First, it was evident to me that I had succeeded. What was not as certain, however, was whether or not I would survive to enjoy my triumph.

There was a momentary paralysis that then gripped my entire body, as some reverberation passed from the hoop to the shard, which I still held in my fingertips, before bouncing back to the hoop again. The immense power it unleashed rattled me. If I had not been frozen in place, I believe that I would have been shaken to pieces. Without the protection of the magical circle, I imagined the city of Boston may have suffered an earthquake of titanic proportions.

After the tremor dissipated, the sound of the blowing wind increased in pitch, becoming a piercing whistle. Still holding the shard and the hoop above my head, I tried to use my arms to block my ears. But it was no use. The noise was not a physical effect. Somehow, my mind was interpreting an unknown magical or extra-dimensional event as a shrill whine. It continued at a nearly unbearable volume and intensity for a few more seconds—until, all at once, it stopped.

I knew it wasn't over, but nothing happened for so long that I became confused. I was nearly ready to relax my arms. Unexpectedly, with that sound still echoing through my mind, a liquid darkness poured from the hoop above me, enveloping me completely. A deep, instinctual fear took hold, and a shriek formed in the recesses of my brain.

The blackness was total, and I could feel nothing. But I heard...something. Or maybe there was no sound. Maybe, it was a certainty that the darkness was not just a shadow. Maybe I could tell that something else was there in my mind, with me. However, just as soon as the sensation of that otherness registered on my consciousness, it was gone. The reappearance of light blinded me temporarily, and the shock almost forced a scream out of me. But I fought the urge, and contained it.

I glanced around. All was silent; all was still. Vincent had a look of awe upon his face, which slowly turned into a huge smile. I nodded in acknowledgment, and smiled back. Yet the horrific realization that I had just been touched by Sothoth Pnath momentarily overshadowed the success of our achievement. I lowered my arms, and carefully put down the hoop and the shard. The hoop was, once again, merely a brass hoop. Its red glow was gone, the magic depleted. I whispered the few simple phrases to dispel the magical barrier delimited by the circle on the floor.

"We did it," I said, too enthusiastically, and regretted it almost instantly. My throat was nearly raw. When I started to cough, Vincent ran over, and handed me an open bottle of wine, from which he had presumably drawn the glassful for the ceremony. I greedily drank straight from the bottle. It did not soothe my burning throat, but it was wet.

"We did it," I repeated with both joy and relief. "We did it."

It was over, I thought. It was all over.

TWENTY-FOUR

Not long after, fatigue set in. As I had expected after seeing both Andrew and Vincent affected, the physical effects of casting such a powerful spell were great. The vitality had been drawn out of me, leaving me weak. Merely standing was difficult; walking unaided was nearly impossible. Mentally, rather than feeling tired, it was an inability to concentrate, like the exhaustion one felt after staying awake far too long, with unending thoughts and anxieties unmercifully prodding at one's consciousness.

Vincent helped me into the wine cellar and up the stairs. Once in the kitchen, Albert and Vincent together dragged me the length of the main floor, and into the den. Along the east wall, a loveseat sat beneath the window that looked out into the gardens behind the house. After situating me upon it so that I was comfortable, Vincent placed my jacket over me, then moved off to confer quietly with Albert.

Through the window, I saw that the formerly clear sky had clouded up, and the wind was starting to blow. There was no doubt that a storm was on its way. As I watched the trees behind the house sway rhythmically in the gusts, the excitement of the ceremony ebbed away. I began to relax, and allowed my mind to wander. Despite not feeling tired enough to fall asleep, I soon felt my consciousness slipping away. I remember seeing Albert leave the room, and Vincent sit down in a chair facing me.

Then, I slept.

I awoke to a world where the sun was shining, and a great weight had been lifted from my heart. Vincent was so pleased over the outcome that he offered me a job as his assistant, with room and board included. Though the offer was tempting, I needed to stop hiding behind the doors of this home, and rejoin the world I had left behind. With a firm handshake and a hug, I promised—at the very least—to correspond with him on a regular basis, and continue the friendship we had restored.

Gathering my courage, I then returned to Arkham to face the consequences of my actions. My first stop was the boarding house. I held my breath as I searched for Mrs. Bettings, wondering what her reaction would be upon seeing me again after so many weeks. She was delighted, of course, greeting me with tears of joy, and a warm hug that lasted forever. As was wonderfully typical, the woman smelled more of the kitchen than anything else, an aura of cinnamon and apples clinging to her. She had saved my room, and I was welcome to move back in.

Professor Josephson was next. This was a more difficult confrontation, but after his initial shock over my arrival wore off, he also welcomed me. I explained the deaths of Andrew Cooke and Doctor Trautmann to him in great detail. Though I had witnessed them both, it was a fact that I had participated in neither. He listened closely and believed my words. He also believed me when I told him that my need for vengeance was spent, and that I was ready to return to work. My time off had thoroughly derailed my original timetable for the completion of my thesis, but I would commit to whatever was necessary to live up to his expectations. At least, I would do that if possible, because my next visit would be to the police. I would make myself available for whatever questions they had, and submit to whatever punishment was required. That pronouncement, specifically, pleased the professor. He announced that, not only would he vouch for my character, but he knew an excellent lawyer who would represent me.

That was the best news I could hope for, and my remaining worries began to dissipate. The next day, accompanied by the lawyer, we went to the police. The detective I had encountered at the train station was there, and seeing that slightly familiar face helped me feel a little more at ease. I admitted to him—

A tremendous blast of thunder startled me awake. When my eyes flew open, I was surprised by the darkness of the room. My first thought was that I had slept through the afternoon and evening, but the clock on the wall showed only a few minutes past three. I had barely slept an hour. Outside, a storm was raging, the sky nearly black from the ominous clouds. Very little light penetrated into the study, even with the curtains wide open. The last time I experienced a storm of this magnitude was the night of Andrew's death.

"Awake already?"

I nearly jumped at the sound of Vincent's voice. Looking in the direction from which it had come, his shape was indeed still in the same chair. In the low light, his unmoving form had blended into the shadowy background. He seemed to have not shifted position at all. Had he merely sat there and looked at me the entire time?

"Yes," I replied, speaking carefully, my throat still sore from the ceremony. "I feel rested."

Aside from my throat, however, I felt much better overall. The general weakness was still there, but that overwhelming fatigue was gone. A ravenous hunger made my stomach growl.

"Good."

We both sat silently for a little while, watching the rain and the wind and the lightning. The fury outside increased; evidently, the edge of it had just arrived. My hunger was coaxing me to get out of the seat and eat something, but I ignored it, choosing instead to sit still, and stare at the storm.

"Tell me, Robert," Vincent said, after a time. "You were a religious man? In your former life?"

"I was," I said. It seemed so far away then, the Christianity of my upbringing, and up through a few months ago. Those formerly comforting beliefs called to me, but I held them at arm's length.

"Can you define evil for me?"

"What?"

I was fully awake, but unprepared to answer such a question.

"Evil. Can you define it?" he repeated.

I thought for a moment.

"Evil is the tendency to act without the consideration of others."

"Many decisions are made without the consideration of others," offered Vincent.

"No," I countered, sitting upright. "It can seem that way. But there is an inherent sense of good within man. An unconscious consideration of others. A morality."

"The voice of God?"

"Some might say."

"A conscious or unconscious consideration of others, then—by your definition—is good?"

"Yes."

"Can an unconscious decision be evil?" he asked.

"No," I replied. "Evil is a conscious choice."

"Even if done for a good reason? Love, say?"

For this, I had no answer, and was growing weary of his semantic game. The storm continued to spout its rage, wind lashing rain against the windows.

"What if," started Vincent. "What if one unintentionally—but consciously—makes the wrong choice? What if the information to make the right decision—the *good* decision—is lacking?"

"I suppose," I said after some consideration, "that responsibility is a factor. It is one's responsibility to gather the necessary information to make fully informed decisions. Irresponsibility is plainly evil, because the impact of one's actions upon others must always be considered."

"Yes, responsibility."

He seemed to like that answer, judging by the tone of his voice. There was a pause, then he asked another question in a similar vein.

"If man has an inherent sense of good—this voice of God, say— then evil must be external, yes? Do you consider evil to be a learned behavior?"

"Yes."

"Well, then—from where does humanity learn it?"

"Vincent, why are you asking all of these pointless questions? Where are you headed?"

"From where does humanity learn to be evil?" he asked again, patiently.

"According to the Bible, it was the serpent," I answered nonchalantly.

"But it wasn't just a serpent. Not just a snake."

"No. It was Satan in the guise of one."

"That is one of His names, yes. Although, He is much older than the Bible." There was a pause before he added, "A difficult and unforgiving master."

"What are you trying to say?"

He answered me by asking another question, apparently deciding to try a different tack.

"Isn't evil just another word for freedom?"

"Are you serious?" I asked, my annoyance turning to worry.

"The consideration of others limits one's options," he said. "Fewer options means less freedom. By thinking less of others, one gains more freedom. Imagine a hypothetical society where absolute freedom of action is considered to be the primary right of every member. In such a society, the constraints imposed by being 'good' would be tantamount to slavery."

"But you cannot have freedom without responsibility," I insisted. "Society cannot exist without constraints. All would be reduced to chaos."

"Not necessarily," he said calmly. "You assume that all members of such a society would take full advantage of the enlightened approach—which would not be the case. The few who did would find themselves in a position of power. They would be the strong among the weak, shepherds among the sheep."

"More like wolves," I interjected.

"And what if they are? It would be their right."

I responded with silence. Outside, the storm continued. The delay between the lightning flashes and the accompanying blasts of thunder were noticeably shorter.

"Do you know how you came to be here, Robert? I don't mean by train—but how you, originally a religious man on his way to a successful career in mathematics, came to be sitting on a couch in Boston, on the run from the law, your beliefs having been replaced by a system to which you gave no credence only months ago?"

It was then that a chance flash of lightning cast some illumination upon the chair in which he sat, glinting off an object in his hand, though what it was, I could not say. Then just as quickly, it was dark again. But the impression it left on my mind cast a chill down my spine.

"To do what I set out to do," I said at last. "The banishment of the entity Sothoth Pnath from—"

"Yes, but why?" he asked. "Why, Robert?"

"What do you want to hear? Elizabeth was…"

"Yes!" The violence of his reply was disquieting. "Precisely. Your love of Elizabeth. It is because of her that you set yourself on this path. Because of her that you sought me in Boston, rushing headlong into things you could not begin to understand. It is because of her—and only her—that you find yourself here, now. You have been led like a sheep. You could be more."

"Vincent, what are you saying?"

He sighed.

"I am offering you a chance to join me, Robert." I heard him slide forward in his chair. "You have already taken the first step. Accept Him completely. We can work together to create this society. We can be the wolves, with the whole world our sheep."

His eyes. In the low light they glistened with the unblinking fervor of a zealot. He was serious. Where was this coming from? During the previous weeks, he had never spoken to me of such matters. Had he broached these ideas with Elizabeth? Perhaps some of them, but not all. Theoretical discussions are one thing, but his current attitude indicated an inclination toward action. Why? Had the ceremony somehow changed him? Lost in thought for a time, the sounds of the storm dragged me back to reality. He was waiting for an answer.

"No, Vincent. I do not perfectly epitomize the best of human virtues, but I do try. And I continue to believe in goodness. Yes, it is because of Elizabeth that I am here. But that does not make me a sheep. Even the shepherd looks out for his flock. His power is not just for rule."

Once again, he sighed.

"If you do not stand with me, then you are against me. I'm sorry, Robert."

It was then that another flash of lightning illuminated the room, and in its harsh light, I was finally able to see what it was he held. The metallic click of the hammer was loud as thunder in my ears.

There was nothing that I could do to defend myself. Although not as weak as I had been, I was still in no shape to attack him. Besides, the distance between us—while not great—was enough to allow him plenty of time to react. My only strategy for survival was to keep still, and try to keep him talking. Confuse him, perhaps? I pulled a memory out of the depths.

"You killed the rabbit," I said, recalling the image of a small boy grasping a ball of fur in his arms.

If he hesitated at all, I was unable to detect it. He knew exactly to what I referred.

"I did," he admitted. "That was the very first step along *my* path. Somehow, I caught the rabbit. I believe He granted me that ability. In return, I did as He asked, and squeezed the life out of it. You came upon me in the field just as the body had stopped trembling. I learned right then just how easy it was to kill."

"And now? Are you ready to kill again?"

There was a flash, then a blast of thunder boomed loudly, shaking the house.

"It is a shame, but I am." He continued to point the gun at me, but seemed to be distracted by an itch in his left arm. He rubbed the stump of it against the chair. "I need to dispose of an enemy."

"I am not an enemy," I said calmly. "We have known each other all of our lives. In Mount Haverton, you were my best friend."

Another thunderbolt struck nearby, its flash brightening the room. At the same time, the intensity of Vincent's itch seemed to increase, and he rubbed his arm more deliberately.

"Yes," he said, with a grin I no longer interpreted as friendly. "That is why I extended the offer to you in the first place. A formality, really. I had a feeling that you would reject it. But human weakness forced me to ask you anyway. It does get lonely, at times. I was hoping to find an equal who could appreciate my point of view—a compatriot. Elizabeth wouldn't have been an equal, but I was willing to spare her in the hope that, in time, I could have swayed her. Time and fate removed that choice, though."

He barked out a laugh that was strangely out of place.

"You. Then you came along, and I had hope again, for a short while."

"So, if I do not agree with you, that automatically makes me your enemy?"

The sky let loose with another ferocious bolt. The windows rattled with the force of the blast. No longer able to quell the itching in his arm merely by rubbing it, he held the gun loosely, and used his fingernails to scratch at what was apparently becoming a maddening sensation.

"Damn this—" I heard him mutter under his breath. Then he stopped scratching altogether, and looked up at the ceiling, around the room, searching for something, perhaps listening as well. All of a sudden, he stood up. Dropping the gun onto the chair, he grabbed at the stump of his arm, and doubled over.

"He is coming!" he cried, the fear in his voice palpable.

Before I could pose any question or react at all, there was another immense flash. The titanic explosion of sound that followed seemed to shake the very air. Vincent let loose a howl, the likes of which I had never heard before in my life. It was soul-wrenching, overflowing with both despair and rage. He fell to his knees, repeating *no no no* endlessly.

With him looking at the floor, I took the opportunity to stand up and start inching toward him. I had only taken two or three small steps when he noticed me.

"Stop right there!"

He shot up from the floor, and snatched the gun from the chair. Face still twisted in pain, he held his left arm straight out and away from his body, a diseased thing he wanted no part of. He motioned with the gun.

"Sit down!"

I backed up, and complied.

"Are you going to shoot me in cold blood, Vincent? That's a cowardly act, indeed."

"I am going to…"

We both heard, then saw, the doors swing inward. Yet there was no one there. The only other living soul in the house, Albert, was nowhere to be seen. The doors simply opened by themselves.

"He is here," Vincent whispered with a deadly finality.

I cannot say for certain from where the tall, dark man came. I did not see him approach. But in the blink of an eye, he was standing there, in the opening between the doors. He may have stepped out of the shadows from either side of the doorway; he may also have appeared out of thin air. He stood silently, robed in darkness, an aura of menace surrounding him. He took a few steps into the room.

And all at once, I knew Him.

I knew this was whom Vincent feared, to whom he referred when he spoke of Satan. This was no man, but an entity in the guise of a man. Most incredible of all, however, I knew that I had seen him before. Three times in fact: Once as a boy in the ruins of the Fenster mansion; once in the dark streets of Arkham; and last, just a few hours previous, in the basement laboratory, peering out through Vincent's eyes. As I looked at Him more fully, I sensed chaos lying just beneath the surface. Madness seemed to radiate from him so intensely that I grew dizzy. When I forced myself to look away, the unsteadiness lessened.

For a few seconds, there was complete silence. Even the thunder had stopped. Then Vincent knelt down, and uttered a stream of nonsensical R'lyehian syllables. Despite the alien nature of the language, I felt a sense of adoration in his outburst. A supplication. But the tall man did not respond. Again, Vincent tried, and this time, he received a reply.

"Ngalth'rh!"

It was otherworldly, the sound of a thousand tortured souls. No human being was ever meant to hear such a thing. Its effect upon me was an instant, crushing despair that hit me as a hammer blow. If I had been standing, I surely would have collapsed.

Vincent was defiant. Enraged, he let loose with another burst of indecipherable words. I tensed myself for another alien reply and waited. Thankfully, none came. Instead, the dark man acted, pointing at Vincent with his right hand. Vincent responded with a scream, his entire body shaking. As he continued to hold his left arm out from his body, I saw the arm of his coat begin to slowly collapse, as if the limb was no longer within, or was being somehow drawn inside.

"No!" shouted Vincent. "It's not yet time!"

There was no response from the dark man, which seemed to enrage Vincent even further. Out of what was left of his soul came a cry of pure frustration.

Then, before my horrified eyes, I watched as he placed the gun in his mouth and pulled the trigger.

The report was deafening. The top of his skull exploded outward in a spray of blood and gore. He crumpled like a doll. Unable to look away, I saw him strike the floor, landing on his back.

Death came swiftly. Only a heartbeat before, he had been kneeling on the floor, anguished, but alive. And the next—nothing. It may have been my imagination, but to this day, I believe that I sensed his soul slip away, off to whatever fate awaited it.

As his body ceased its horrible shuddering, the nameless man began to move my way. I had been preparing myself for death since Vincent first pointed his gun at me, but my stomach knotted up even more tightly. There was simply no possibility of escape. My route to the doors was blocked. The window glass, I could tell, was too thick to easily burst through. The gun was my only other option, but as I wondered if I had the determination to follow Vincent's example, I knew that the hesitation had cost me. He had come near, too near. My only hope was that death would be quick. I sat there, closed my eyes, and waited for the end.

But it did not come.

I looked. It seemed that he had not been coming for me, but

for Vincent's now-still form. Being careful to not look directly at him, I watched as he bent down, and grabbed at the air in front of the stump of Vincent's left arm. I was perplexed, until I noticed that, even though he grabbed at empty space, Vincent's left arm moved as if the man had actually got hold of some part of him. With the dim lighting only occasionally enhanced by flashes of lightning from the retreating storm, I must state here that I am not absolutely certain of what I next witnessed. Nevertheless, I truly believe that when the being again stood erect, it held in its hand a shadow shaped like a glove. More astounding, however, was the sight I witnessed on the floor at his feet, where the body of my childhood friend lay. Vincent's left hand was no longer missing! It was a pale, thin, sickly thing that extended from the left arm of his jacket, but it was undoubtedly there.

A glance back at the dark man proved to be a mistake. I tried to look away, but could not. My gaze was locked onto him, magnet-like. Once again, his overpowering presence caused a hurricane of chaos to tear through my mind. Even recalling those moments now is difficult, as if my mind has been permanently scarred. Memories of my entire life swept through in no particular order at all. Images of my time at Miskatonic University were interleaved with the earliest ones of my parents. Andrew and Elizabeth occupied my thoughts simultaneously, even though the two had never met. Professor Josephson and Mrs. Bettings were thrown together, as well. The malodorous Old Mac and the reviled Higgins also made appearances, though I intensely disliked thinking of either. The roaring whirlpool churned and mixed them all together.

Then it stopped.

I was again in control of my mind, but with one particular picture set squarely in the foreground of my consciousness. It was the fateful day that young Vincent and I had explored the ruins of the Fenster mansion. On that occasion, the dark man had looked directly at me and smiled. As I continued to stare at him this time, still unable to look away, he repeated that awful grin. A flash of lightning lit the room, allowing me to see the ghastly remnants of past meals still lodged within his teeth. I wondered what a creature such as that would feast upon—men? Or the nightmares of men? Or their sins?

A shriek had been building within me, and I was unable to restrain it any longer. As it burst out, the being simply disappeared. Panting and shaking, I looked around the room and tried to calm myself. There was nothing to see. Nothing to hear.

I located the switch for the overhead light, and turned it on. Another look around reassured me. Aside from myself, the room held only the body of Vincent Fenster. Blood had poured out of the broken remains of his head, pooled all around, and flowed into the cracks between the floorboards. Averting my eyes from that mess, I walked over and examined the body. It was not yet cool. But his pale, shriveled, left hand was ice cold. It was noticeably smaller than his right, and covered with hundreds—perhaps thousands—of tiny welts. I once saw a fisherman whose face had been latched onto by the suckers of an octopus. The effect was not altogether different.

An unfamiliar, guttural voice startled me.

"You are not permitted to live," said someone from behind me.

I turned around, and was shocked to see Albert standing perhaps ten feet away. In his hand was a knife. In all of the time I had been in that house, I had never heard him utter a single word, and had simply assumed that he could not speak. That was clearly not the case. His voice was thick and phlegmy, but understandable. The knife he held in his right hand was more than just a little familiar looking. It had a short blade, and a dark handle, appearing more like a surgical blade than a knife or dagger.

Terrified, my first thought was of the gun. Vincent's right hand still cradled it, the index finger inserted through the trigger guard. I judged there would be no chance to dislodge it before Albert was upon me. But one other weapon, though small, was near. With it, we would at least be evenly matched. I stood and slowly backed up. Albert advanced, holding his knife before him. From the loveseat, I grabbed my coat and kept retreating. Soon, I had backed myself into a corner.

"Very good," growled Albert, apparently pleased with the situation. "Now, submit."

"Come and get me."

Carefully reaching into the pocket of my jacket, I gripped the handle of my own knife without removing it. Using both hands, I held my coat out in front of me, hoping to make him think I would just be defending myself. My advantage would not last long.

Albert made the first move, lunging forward and stabbing at my left arm. My reaction was fast enough, and I blocked his blow with my coat. But as I prepared to attack him, I discovered that my own knife was lodged in the pocket. Narrowly dodging another thrust from the nimble old man, I pushed the knife partially through the jacket material, exposing the blade. For that brief span, I relaxed my vigilance, and it cost me. He caught me with a knee to the midsection. The air was knocked from my lungs, and I fell to the floor. My only thought at that point was to at least wound him in order to have some time to recover. I managed to grab his ankle with my left hand, then stab at his leg with my right as hard as I could, catching him just above the knee.

His scream seemed to be more of surprise than pain. He jumped backward, and though I had been gripping the knife tightly, I lost hold of it when he moved. Somehow, my knife was embedded in his leg, the jacket still entangled around it. Weaponless and defenseless, I rolled away, fearing another attack.

But, instead of advancing on me and finishing me off, Albert instead wailed and collapsed. As I knelt on the floor, still trying to catch my breath, I saw him try—and fail—to remove the knife from his leg. At last, he tore my jacket away, and I was astonished to see it sunk very deeply into the flesh. Only two inches of the handle remained exposed! I knew I had not struck him nearly that hard. Before my incredulous eyes, however, it sank further and further into his thigh, until it was completely gone. I could watch no longer, and turned away, plugging my ears to mute his cries.

His anguish went on for minutes until, finally, there was silence. I uncovered my ears, stood up, and surveyed the nightmarish scene. Two men lay dead at my feet. Spotting the knife with which Albert had attacked me, I picked it up. The thing was identical to the one I had used. Aside from a bloodstained hole in his dark pants, there was no sign of it in his leg, though.

On the floor, Albert's hands were clutched over his heart. I moved his hands apart. There was a stain of blood on his chest, and a lump beneath the wetness of his shirt. Slowly, I forced my trembling fingers to undo the buttons. There, in his chest, outlined in his sallow flesh, was the knife. Like a broken bone, it pressed against the inside of his skin. I looked at the thing in my own hand and shuddered, dropping it to the floor. All those months, I had been carrying around a cursed object in my coat pocket. If I had so much as nicked myself with it...would I have suffered the same fate?

The horrors of that room were too much to bear. I fled it, and ran the length of the house, through the kitchen, down the stairs, stopping in the wine cellar. Grabbing a couple of bottles at random, I retreated to a corner. The first shattered completely when I tried to open it by breaking the neck off, but my second attempt worked well enough to leave most of the bottle intact. The alcohol helped to ease my pangs of hunger as I gulped it. On an empty stomach, it hit hard. I passed out cold.

I awoke in the dark, my stomach making loud demands. Stumbling upstairs to the kitchen, the alcohol still affecting my brain, I filled my belly with whatever I could find. Bread and butter were an easy meal, but even buttering the bread slowed me down too much, so I left it plain as I stuffed it in my mouth. And the caviar. How many hundreds of dollars of caviar did I practically inhale, barely tasting the bursts of salt? When I started into a supply of smoked salmon, the gnawing hunger that gripped me began to ease. I forced myself to pause, and wait for the feeling of satiety that I knew would come. And it did.

Back in the den, all was the same as I had left it. The events swirled, incomprehensible, in my mind. For some of my questions, I knew the answers; for others, I had only guesses. There was a way to be certain, though. There was a way to fill in all of the holes.

I went down to the laboratory. The furniture was still moved against the walls, everything yet covered with sheets. After setting the furniture aright and restoring some order, I located a beaker with the strange liquid I would need. Next, I searched through Vincent's notebooks, and found the instructions for the ceremony. From that same notebook, I tore out several unneeded pages. Twisted together, the papers became a wick, which would last quite a while. At the table, I took some time to study and concentrate, then began. I knew I had succeeded when the frigid wind of his spirit visited me.

"Vincent Fenster," I spoke, my voice shaking. "It is I, Robert Adderly. I require answers."

Twenty-Five

Our conversation began with silence.

For some reason, I expected Vincent to simply start speaking. But as I watched the flame burn, I came to realize that my opening statement was too ambiguous to warrant a response.

"Vincent, when did you first get involved in all of this?" I asked, but knew right away that I needed to phrase it even more clearly. "When did you first learn of magic and the Ancient Ones?"

The day we made that hole in the ground on the Fenster property, when your father stopped us. Something called to me. I didn't know where it was, but felt that it was nearby.

"It was that stone—the shard—calling to you?"

Yes.

"The morning after the storm, when you saw the secret room and took me along. You found it then?"

I did, while you were looking at the books above the desk.

"And you hid it from me?"

Yes.

"Why?"

As I held it in my hand, it told me to. He told me to.

I knew to whom *he* referred, but needed confirmation of the name.

"What is his name, Vincent?"

Nyarlathotep.

I nodded to myself and swallowed. That had been my guess.

"That same night, you were the one who killed your parents?"

Yes.

"Why?"

He told me to. I did not want to kill my mother, but it was necessary. For her, it was quick. For my father, it was not. I paralyzed him deliberately, then watched him slowly bleed to death. It was the first time I enjoyed murder.

The first time I enjoyed murder, said my childhood friend. Did I ever know him at all?

"Did you kill Elizabeth's sisters?"

There was a pause before he replied.

Not explicitly. The illness was natural. I was also sick with it. I only took steps to prevent them from recovering.

I sighed inwardly, not wishing to know those details. I pressed on.

"Did you kill Elizabeth's brother, William?"

Yes.

"You did? While he was in Europe? How?"

After Elizabeth wrote him a letter, I placed a curse on it.

"And you obviously killed her parents."

There was no response. It needed to be a question.

"Did you also kill her parents?"

I did.

"But why? They took you in after…after you left Mount Haverton."

I grew to like the comfort of wealth, and wanted to ensure that I would always have it. The requirements of employment would have taken away from my magical studies. I thought their deaths would give me the estate because I was older than Elizabeth, but the will had not been updated after William's death, and so she was left in control.

"You had nothing to do with the death of Elizabeth?"

That is correct. I was not responsible for her death.

This method of communication was strange, I had to admit. After speaking aloud my questions, the answer would appear in my mind, always in a monotone. It seemed as if nuances and emotions were difficult for the dead to convey. But that reply seemed to be different from the others: a stress upon the *I*. Ignoring the aberration as my own imagination, I continued.

"You were surprised by her death?"

I was. I did not wish her to die.

That time, there was no detectable stress.

"Did you kill Andrew?"

I was not responsible for his death.

"But you used the mirror to spy on us?"

I observed the two of you a few times after he wrote the first letter. I also questioned his dream-self. His inflated self-confidence led him to reveal more secrets than most people would.

"And you truly did not know it was I whom you watched?"

As I told you before, I thought you were merely another Robert Adderly.

My mind gathered in the answers, began to fit them together.

"The girl with the knife and flowers. She mentioned a crippled street vendor. Was that you?"

It was. I was instructed by my master to take advantage of Andrew Cooke's personality, and push him along the desired path. The knife was not meant to kill him. And if it did, you would still have likely followed the path to my door.

The path, yes. Andrew led, I followed. With Andrew's death, Vincent led, and I still followed, with never a question on my part.

I had originally wanted to ask about Doctor Trautmann as well, but in light of recent events, the answer seemed to be glaringly obvious. No, all thoughts of Trautmann went out of my head when Vincent repeated the word *path*. My path, my goal, had been the banishment of Sothoth Pnath from the Earth. Up until then, it had been Vincent's as well. Or had it? I began to grow anxious as a new theory formed in my mind. Pieces clicked together. Anxiety became pure fear, then denial.

Ignorance is bliss, I reminded myself. The wick burned lower and lower, and the spirit of Vincent waited patiently for me to say something.

Finally, I forced my mouth to function. It asked a question that was nearly inconceivable.

I was only semi-conscious of the wick burning out, and the accompanying departure of Vincent's spirit. Somehow, I managed to properly conclude the ceremony. Afterward, I put my head down on the table. Sleep came, my dreams haunted by an unbearable guilt.

I do not know for how long I slept. When awake, still weary, I stumbled my way to the wine cellar. The desire to benumb myself was my only thought. I glanced at bottles, searching for the dustiest—and, I assumed, oldest—wine available. An eighty-four Bordeaux seemed to be extra dusty. I grabbed it, and started up the stairs to the kitchen.

I was only halfway up when a faint sound impressed itself upon my consciousness. There was someone moving around upstairs! I paused, and listened more closely. As I froze there, doing my best to quiet my breathing, a faint voice penetrated the layers of wood and plaster.

"Has anyone searched downstairs yet?"

Without waiting to hear a response, I slunk down the stairs and crossed to the hidden door. The footsteps were now in the kitchen, right above. Whoever it was had surely seen the carnage in the den. Keeping the door propped open with my body, I gripped onto the release mechanism in the rafters. It seemed to be possible to break off the wooden lever without much noise. I had little time, and decided to chance it.

A hard yank straight down caused the handle to snap off fairly silently. I ran my fingers along the broken end in the rafters. There were splinters, but nothing obvious sticking out. I grabbed the matches and candles that were hidden there, then stepped back through the door, and closed it just in time. With my ear flat against the wood, I listened as well as I was able. There was only the sound of footsteps descending the stairs, then a few minutes later, those same footsteps returning to the kitchen. I breathed a sigh of relief: Cornered, but not yet caught.

It seemed I had slept through the night. Jebediah Higgins and Thomas Wentworth had returned, and even if they had initially arrived without police, the authorities would have been summoned after the bodies were found. If I were discovered in the vicinity of two more corpses, there would be no explanations possible to which any jury would listen. My fingerprints were on both of the knives, so at the very least, I would be convicted for the death of Albert. I would have to run, but that posed even more problems. There were no windows in any part of the cellar, so I would be forced to sneak upstairs into the kitchen and out one of the windows there. However, even if I managed to elude capture, how could I undo what I had done? I would somehow have to gain access to all of the forbidden knowledge Vincent had accumulated. It would take decades of study, all the while in hiding, always on the run. It simply was not possible. In order to properly make things right, I needed both time and freedom—luxuries I knew I would never have again.

Hours passed. I fought against despair, discarding ideas as fast as I found them. All but one. One idea seemed to be workable. When the calculations indicated that the stars were not against me, I resigned myself to it. Most definitely not the best possible solution, it depended upon one unknowable assumption. But the more I

313

thought about it, the more I convinced myself it would work. In the event that it failed…I tried to not think about that. In either case—success or failure—the punishment would be appropriate. Harsh, but appropriate. I did not need a trial and a jury of my peers to judge me. I was plainly guilty. And I had enough honor within me to carry out my own sentence.

One of the final acts of my human life was to barricade the hidden door in the wine cellar with some of the laboratory furniture. I disposed of the ring of candles, save one, which I placed on the floor near the bizarrely shaped shard. This time, there would be no need to use that particular item. All else was close by. I lit the single candle on the floor, then extinguished all other sources of light. There were no other preparations necessary. Without any hesitation, I began the process of my redemption: I began to perform the ceremony once again.

The ritual proceeded the same as before: The retracing of the circle of protection; the creation of the gateway; the shouted R'lyehian commands. My throat wasn't completely recovered from the first time, and thus, the process was torturous. But regardless, step-by-step, the same effects occurred. The circle became charged. The hoop glowed. That hellish wind blew. There was one important difference, however, between this performance and the previous. Near the finale, I extinguished the one candle, leaving me in absolute darkness. My eyes attempted to find some speck of light, but there was nothing. Surrounded by complete blackness, I completed the ceremony. With an aching throat, I spoke the words to call Sothoth Pnath to me.

"Mbulg'r Sothoth Pnath d'nalbr urh'ctha rgho!"

This time, there was no shock wave from the gateway. The wind did not become that ear-splitting whistle. Instead, there was an immediate and profound silence. I was so startled by the lack of sound, that I did not realize at first what had happened. Eventually, though, I felt it—the infinite darkness of Sothoth Pnath covering me completely. But unlike last time, the darkness did not lift away. The sensation of being covered by the creature made it feel as if I was suffocating. It was just illusion, though. In reality, I had no trouble at all breathing.

I sensed a presence, but one without mind, without thought. The raw simplicity of it was akin to animal impulse. When I concentrated, trying to communicate with it, the reply was always the same: *I hear.* Perhaps a different mind, an insane mind, would interpret the reply differently. And yes—even now, I generously classify myself as sane.

There was nothing left to do but seal my fate.

I struck a match, and bent down to light the candle. As the single flame cast its light, I held my breath. Slowly I turned, then opened my eyes and gazed deeply into my own shadow.

The air roared from my lungs in a scream of agony. I knew then exactly what Elizabeth had felt. With most varieties of human suffering, it is easy to point to a cut or a bruise and say, "It hurts there." With this, there was no *there.* The pain was everywhere at once, every single nerve ending on my body afire. Sothoth Pnath began to melt and twist me, devour my soul. With all of the willpower I could muster, I fell backwards onto the lone candle and extinguished its flame, praying that my assumption would be correct.

It was. All pain stopped instantly.

Without a source of light to cast a shadow, Sothoth Pnath had been forced to cease its consumption of my body. I had guessed correctly. I was alive…though no longer human. Only minutes before, I had felt my empty stomach crying out to be fed. But the knot was gone, as was the burning ache in my throat. There was no more suffering at all, no requirement for any sort of sustenance. I held my breath, counted off a hundred seconds easily, and still felt no need to breathe.

Although my death had been forestalled, my plan was not without consequences. My left hand was gone entirely. Using my good right hand, I explored my body, taking stock of just how badly I had been ravaged by the flames. Yes, I was permanently crippled, disfigured. My utter demise—indisputable, but indefinite—would forever be just moments away, should a stray beam of light penetrate this hidden room. But I yet...existed.

What of Sothoth Pnath? That was the key. Was it still with me? I quieted myself once more, probing inward to try to sense that other presence.

I hear.

It was still with me.

I had won.

Yes, I know it sounds absurd, to consider this a victory: Sitting here in the dark, trapped with the entity known as Sothoth Pnath, the shadow of Yog Sothoth. Why, then, do I feel, even now, a smile pull across what is left of my face?

Because I know—

No, I need to correct that. I *know* nothing. There is no certainty involved. It is a guess, my best guess, plain and simple. My imagination and mathematical expertise were pushed to their limits when I tried to calculate how a god-like entity might perceive time. The only thing I know for sure is that the past cannot be changed. Those who have already died will remain dead. But the future—has it been written yet? Can those in the future be saved, those unlucky ones who accidentally look upon their own shadows at the wrong moment? I think so. I hope so. As long as I remain here, it remains with me, trapped. I believe that, as long as I can maintain this existence, I will prevent anyone else in the future from suffering that fate of incineration. Perhaps, this final act of mine—one of evil, but with good intentions—can serve a purpose after all. I will have atoned—at least partially—for my sin.

Sin.

I hate the word, but is there one more apt? Transgression, perhaps? No, I say. Adding more syllables only softens the concept, makes it more palatable. The brutal abruptness of *sin* is the word needed here. It adds an emphasis devoid of the least bit of linguistic pleasantry. I would like to blame Vincent for that *sin*, for he was the one who had guided me. But it was I who had trusted him. I was the one who believed that the Shadow of the Ancient Ones could not darken my life. It was my responsibility, as I had told Vincent not long ago. It was my responsibility to know, and to not do the evil.

And Vincent? In all, he had hardly done anything. In fact, the totality of his malicious deception had amounted to no more than one word—one missing word in the translation of the pages that he had copied from the *Necronomicon* and shown to me. "The ways of calling and sending," he had written. In reality, the translation would have been more accurately rendered as, "The ways of calling and sending *forth*."

Sending forth *into the world*.

The ceremony he had transcribed was not one of banishment at all; it was one of summoning. Performed in darkness, the ceremony is intended to be a form of ritual suicide. Performed in light, it was a way of calling Sothoth Pnath to our world and sending it forth.

I was the one who had summoned it.

How is that even possible? It had consumed the souls of innocent victims long before I was even born. But just as Yog Sothoth is not limited by time, neither is its shadow. It was less than a day between the two ceremonies. Can it have moved backward through all the long centuries before Anno Domini 1925 in less than a day? A day, a minute. To a god, is there a difference? The human comprehension of time does not apply. Just as the salamander had slipped through the narrowest of cracks to kill the rats in Andrew's bookstore, even a fraction of a second would have been enough for Sothoth Pnath to terrorize all of human history to that point.

I am responsible for all those deaths. More than that, I am the one responsible for the death of my beloved Elizabeth! As the words transcribed by Vincent had noted, *when the stars are correct, the gift need not be offered, for it shall be taken.*

And she was taken.

My only remaining hope is that I can hold it here with me until the end of time itself, in order to prevent anyone else from suffering her fate.

If I succeed, no one will ever know.

If I fail…I'm sorry.

ACKNOWLEDGEMENTS

I would like to thank my wife Karen, she who is blessed with patience; my brother Steve, my biggest fan; my friend Adam, who helped me polish the rough cut into a gem; the gang at Carnegie Mellon and Chatham, who provided early encouragement; and ole H.P.L. himself, whose darkly entertaining visions provided me with a universe to explore.

About the Author

Born and raised in Pittsburgh, PA, Daniel Reiner was formed not of clay, but of peanut butter. And it wasn't the Holy Spirit that gave him life, but an unhealthy does of Warner Brothers cartoons. Spending his formative years at Carnegie Mellon University, it was there he discovered the world of H.P. Lovecraft in the old Del Rey paperbacks. Later, with a burst of creativity, he eventually became comfortable enough in that world to carve out his own niche, and populate it with memorable characters.

A lover of dogs of all shapes and sizes, his readers can be assured that any dog appearing in his writings will never be killed by a monster, human, or otherwise.